Parris Mitchell
of
Kings Row

By HENRY AND KATHERINE BELLAMANN

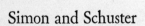

Simon and Schuster · New York · 1948

❧ To Edith ☙

"... what we call destiny comes out of people, not into them from the outside."

Letter of R. M. Rilke

Commentary on *Duino Elegies*

FOREWORD

THE STORY OF Kings Row *was originally planned as a trilogy, depicting the life of a small town from the turn of the century through to the present time. The first volume was published in 1940 and was to have been followed in 1945 by the second volume,* Parris Mitchell of Kings Row. *However, my husband's failing health made it impossible for us to complete the work, and the task long planned has fallen to me alone.*

After his death, Simon and Schuster, knowing how closely my husband and I had collaborated, suggested that I complete the story, following the outline which had been submitted and approved. I undertook the exacting task fully conscious of the magnitude of effort required to sustain the writing at the level of the first volume. But by following conscientiously the outline on which my husband and I had worked, and with the use of copious notes which we made together during the years that elapsed between the publication of the first volume and the death of my husband, I am able to offer this story of Parris Mitchell. There has been no effort to copy my husband's style as evidenced in Kings Row. *There has been only a sincere effort to tell the story as I knew it from the many hours of our discussion of the proposed incidents and our development of the characters involved.*

Recognizing the fate that so often befalls "sequels," I hasten to say that this is not *a sequel, but a continuation of the story of the town, introducing many new characters and situations.*

Henry Bellamann's method of work was an unusual one. We talked stories out in minutest detail, and he rarely wrote a line unless I was in the room with him. He never, at any time, wrote a scene that had not been clearly rehearsed, and after it was written, he never revised a passage. Any revision or cutting or editing fell to my lot. For that reason the characters created were my constant companions as well as his. They did not always act as we expected. They often went their own

[ix]

way—sometimes to our dismay. But by the time a story was written, we both knew the characters intimately.

I have often wondered how it was possible for two writers of totally different background and training to collaborate successfully on a story, yet it has been done often. However, I wish to explain that my husband and I were married young and most of our training was obtained together. For nearly forty years we read the same books, studied the same music, saw the same pictures, knew the same people, and had the same hobbies. During all that time we were seldom separated for a week at a time. When he taught piano, I taught singing in a studio not more than twenty feet away from his own. When he worked on the translation of the Brahms song texts for a French publisher, I sat across the table and wrote a novel, My Husband's Friends. *When he reviewed books for a literary page, which he did for many years, I looked over each week's accumulation of volumes, eliminated those of less importance, and read with him those he needed to review. It is not strange that our tastes and ideas should have followed parallel lines.*

The present volume departs somewhat from the original purpose; it was to have been the psychoanalysis of the town as viewed and understood by Dr. Mitchell. It so happens that it has turned out to be more of a personal history of the young doctor and his frequently frustrated efforts to help the unwilling people about him.

The reader will recognize many characters carried over from Kings Row: *Parris, Randy, Miles Jackson, Fulmer Green, Jamie Wakefield, Mrs. Skeffington, and others. Paul Nolan, Laurel, and David Kettring were taken from* Floods of Spring. *I have tried to develop these characters logically and naturally.*

Wherever possible, I have incorporated actual pages from suggestions made by my husband during his illness. Any diversity of style must be attributed to the fact that I wished to preserve every particle of any actual writing that he had done. A good memory has enabled me to record more accurately than one would suppose the precise phraseology of his comments. To mention some of the work that is set down precisely as he dictated, I call attention to the Davis Pomeroy compulsion—the scene at the hilltop in the moonlight—the death of Pick Foley and the near tragedy of Drew Roddy. The Punch Rayne story had been fully planned and partly written.

[x]

On the whole, I have followed as closely as was logically possible our plan for the book on which we worked together before and during his illness.

Katherine Bellamann

August 22, 1947
Jackson, Mississippi

Parris Mitchell of Kings Row

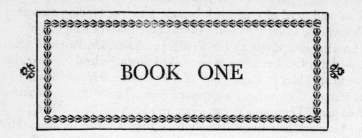

BOOK ONE

I

THE COURTHOUSE, nobly porticoed and domed, dominated the business section of the town of Kings Row. It had been built before the Civil War, and was a handsome building for a town of four thousand. The floor of the west portico jutted out to make a stand which had been the auction block when the region had sold large numbers of slaves down the river. The huge four-faced clock in the tower kept time with surprising accuracy, and the great bell tolled the hours in a deep and drowsy tone.

The deep shade cast by the elms and maples on the lawn surrounding the building was inviting on this morning of late July in 1916, for the little Midwest town was experiencing an extraordinarily hot day as noon approached. The tall trees seemed to be waiting for some wave of wind to give them voice and gesture, but the air was as still as if the last wind had gone home forever. The humming spell of a summer day was heavy about the place.

Groups of shirt-sleeved men idled about in chairs or on benches underneath the trees. Across the street on the south side of the square was another group at the door of Matt Fuller's feed store. The popularity of this particular spot was partly due to the fact that it was next door to McKeown's saloon.

In Kings Row, as everywhere else in the world, these groups of men observed and talked. Year after year, in the casual way of the frontier, they watched and estimated, weighed and decided, praised and condemned. Talk, like the everyday life, was ingrained. Gossip was crossed with gossip; hearsay was grafted on certainty; warp of suspicion and woof of guesswork became a web of binding assurance. This was the tissue of life—the tissue of the town of Kings Row.

Looking deceptively cool in a palm beach suit, Dr. Parris Mitchell viewed this familiar scene as he walked down Federal Street on his way to see Miles Jackson, editor of *The Gazette*. He caught sight of the men on the benches and returned their salutes with a smile and a lifted hand. The young doctor's face was browned by wind and sun, and his black hair swept damply back from a broad forehead. His mouth with its full upper lip was sensitive—a little sensuous. It was large enough to denote a generous nature, but there were no lax lines about it. The discipline, the eternal watchfulness of a man whose business was the healing of sick minds, had left firmness in his mouth and chin. And there was no mistaking the strength of purpose and confidence bred of achievement in the carriage of his head and shoulders, though his walk and his general look suggested an age ten years younger than his thirty-five. His hazel eyes, set rather wide apart, were shadowed and thoughtful.

Young Dr. Mitchell, now so well established at the big State Hospital for the Insane there at the end of Federal Street, was a rather lonely man. The very nature of his work isolated him somewhat. The practice of doctors among the insane was mysterious to the layman, and Dr. Mitchell's work was especially so. People spoke of it in vague terms—even the town doctors. Psychiatry was a new word. Gradually, in the popular imagination, Dr. Mitchell was set apart from other doctors, and to a greater degree from other men. No one quite understood why he had studied all those years in Vienna, just to end up right here in Kings Row—out at the asylum. None of the other doctors had thought it necessary to go to Europe.

True, there was a shortage of practicing physicians in Kings Row just now, and there were times when Dr. Waring, desperately overworked, called on Dr. Mitchell for help. Mitchell's medical training was superior, and while he was necessarily devoting more and more time to his psychiatric work at the hospital, he never failed to respond to these calls. He was particularly prompt when the calls came from Jinktown, the little settlement of poorer people under Aberdeen Hill.

His was a well-known and highly respected figure on the streets down there. His poignant sympathy for those who endured untoward fates and the bitterness of defeat informed his nature with unusual warmth and insight.

Yes, Parris Mitchell was respected in Kings Row, but he had few close friends. An habitual absent-mindedness gave him a detached air, a seeming aloofness that the town vaguely resented. It was perhaps fortunate for him that those few who liked him wholeheartedly were not only intensely loyal but influential as well. Dr. Paul Nolan, his chief at the asylum, was the most intimate of these.

Three old Germans, familiar figures in Kings Row, sat on a bench in the shade. Parris was crossing the square to say hello to them when he met Davis Pomeroy leaving the courthouse grounds. His interest had recently been quickened by rumors concerning Pomeroy Hill, and Parris studied the owner more closely than usual. It was common knowledge that certain Negroes in the neighborhood refused to pass the Pomeroy place after dark, even if it meant walking half a mile out of the way. Parris had laughed when he first heard it and still considered it a wild tale concocted out of nothing—a matter of ghosts, probably. But in spite of his skepticism he was conscious of a certain nagging curiosity about the central figure of the story.

Parris judged Pomeroy to be about fifty—a vigorous fifty, for he walked with the long yet agile stride of a much younger man. His walk, like everything else about him, attested to his years of outdoor living. He looked what he was: a country gentleman. He was a fine physical specimen, well over six feet, broad-shouldered, with a look of muscular hardness that extended even to the capable, big-boned hands. His carriage was erect and proud, his light gray business suit was well cut, and he wore a panama hat set squarely and firmly on his head. He swung along easily, a picture of calm self-confidence. He looked—Parris fumbled briefly for the right adjective—*substantial*. The last man in the world to associate with small-town mystery.

It was only on closer observation that Parris was aware that Pomeroy's expression was at variance with the rest of him. The deep furrows in his sun-browned skin reflected strain and—could it be—fear? Was there something almost furtive in the way he peered eagerly into his face, to look hastily away again? A flicker of doubt touched Parris' mind. There might be more to the rumors than he had conceded.

Pomeroy's response to Parris' greeting was curiously eager, confirming his idea that the man was ill at ease. "Dr. Mitchell! Well, well, well! It's been a long time—several weeks—you stay pretty close at the hospital, it seems. How is your charming wife?" He talked fast and disconnectedly as a man does, Parris noted, who wishes to forestall an unwelcome question or comment. "I walked over to the old von Eln place the other day," Pomeroy said, not waiting for an answer. "Beautiful place. Beautiful. I wondered if you ever paid it a visit. Run down, of course—not like it was when your grandmother lived—"

"I haven't been out in a long time. Not since the state closed the Experimental Station there. I guess I'm a bit sentimental about the old place. I was born there, you know."

Davis Pomeroy did not reply, and Parris, determined to put the man at ease, went on. "I've been hearing a lot about your new herd of prize cattle. The finest collection in the state, they say. I'd like to stop by at Pomeroy Hill one day soon, if I may."

At mention of his hobby Pomeroy's tension visibly relaxed. "Do come. Any time at all," he said cordially, the tight lines around his mouth giving way to a half smile. "I *am* proud of my stock," he said. "Like a kid with a new wagon, I like to show it off!"

"Pomeroy Hill is very beautiful, I think. Your trees are magnificent."

"Yes, and there's nothing Hart Sansome, our honorable Mayor, can do about cutting them down."

Parris laughed, and Pomeroy's eyes twinkled as he added, "Sansome thinks we must destroy beauty in the name of progress."

Parris looked at Davis Pomeroy with growing respect. "I'm glad you feel the same way I do about such things. I think you and I should know each other better."

Pomeroy's smile froze. He suddenly averted his eyes. "Yes—well, it's been nice meeting you, Dr. Mitchell." He shook hands rather stiffly and hurried off.

Parris stared after him, surprised but thoughtful. Now what had suddenly got into the man? he thought. He seems to be a likable fellow—but he's a queer duck at that.

As Parris approached his three German friends, he felt a surge of

[6]

sympathy for them. He had already become aware of a growing hostility in the town to these gentle old men because of their nationality. The war in Europe was doing this. Knowing how deeply they would be hurt, he hoped they had not sensed it. They had helped to build Kings Row—Lenz and Kelner and Eger, and others like them. He remembered how his grandmother had liked and respected them as honest workmen.

"Are you taking a holiday?" he asked in his easy German as he joined them.

Louis Kelner shook his head, disclaiming any such frivolity. "Not much of a holiday for me, Doctor. I got too many coffeepots to mend, and Herman, here, a row of shoes he's got would reach from here to Camperville and back."

Jacob Lenz lifted his blind face and spoke eagerly. "Won't you sit here with us and tell us what you think about this war? Will we be brought into it, too?"

"Yes, Doctor, tell us what you think," Herman, the hunchbacked shoemaker, urged. He moved nearer to Lenz to make room on the slatted bench.

Parris sat down, fanning himself with the brim of his panama hat. "It's hard to say, but it looks bad, very bad. Germany seems to have set out to conquer the world."

"I'd like to tell that Kaiser a thing or two," Louis grumbled.

"I'm afraid it's not simply the Kaiser, Louis. Many of your people—"

"My people are American people—Kings Row people—like yours and Herman's and Jacob's."

The other two nodded in agreement, and Parris spoke hurriedly. "Of course, of course. I meant people still living in Germany. They go about saying, 'The seas must be free' or 'We demand a place in the sun.' I heard it many times spoken by Germans in Vienna."

Jacob leaned toward Dr. Mitchell and spoke earnestly. His voice shook a little. "I was born in Vienna. I was thirty when I came away. I do not remember that there was talk like that. Men sat in cafés and ate their sausages and drank their beer and talked of—*music*. I remember well."

"But that was before the day of German domination. Your Vienna is not the same."

[7]

"Yes, maybe now is different," Jacob agreed sadly.

"But there was talk of music when I was there, too, good talk. And, by the way, my wife has learned some new things to play for you. She's never satisfied about them until she has had a lesson from you. When could you come?"

The blind musician flushed with pleasure. "Any time you say, *Herr Doktor,* any time at all."

"On Sunday at four, perhaps?"

"On Sunday at four, and thank you. The little Frau Elise, she will play Mozart, *hein?*"

"Probably. She is happy when you come to help her."

"Maybe you will play Beethoven for me? That is too big for her small hands."

"Maybe—but I have too little time for any real practice. I'm neglecting my piano these days."

"Now, that is wrong. Music, it is necessary for a man like you—a man who works always with sick minds. Music will rest you."

Parris nodded in agreement. "Music has definite curative value. I've introduced a special department of musical therapy out at the hospital. It's hard to get the equipment we need for—well, for anything new. But we're making a start."

"That is good," Jacob said. "Could we help? I have a little money saved up."

"Oh, no. Thank you for the offer, but it is the state's business to finance it."

"Doctor," Herman Eger said rather timidly, "there will soon be a litter of dachshund puppies at my place. Do you think your wife might like one?"

"Why, I'm sure she would. Thank you very much. She will be pleased that you thought of her."

Parris rose to go, his heart warmed by the simple kindliness of these old friends. As he walked toward *The Gazette* office the three old men looked after him.

"That young doctor," Herman said, "he speaks languages very good—very good."

"*Vorzueglich!*"

"*Ausgezeichnet!*"

Matt Fuller, owner of the feed store, looked across the courthouse lawn and watched young Dr. Mitchell talking with the three Germans.

"That's a funny thing," he said to the group ranged along the walk in splint-bottomed chairs they had brought across from Burkhalter's hardware store. "What the hell do you reckon them Heinies find to talk about? Jim B. says he passes 'em sometimes an' they're talkin' Dutch."

"'Tain't Dutch, it's German." Ricks Darden prided himself on his accuracy. "I see Parris Mitchell over there talkin' to 'em. Bet he's tryin' to show off. He talks German to 'em. He can talk French, too, maybe Italian, fur as I know."

"Aw, he don't have to show off to that gang. He's already got 'em buffaloed."

"He's got a lot of folks eatin' out o' his hand. I can't understand it at all."

"Beats me how he does it. He's awful hard to talk to."

"You don't have to talk to Parris Mitchell—unless you plannin' to go out to the asylum to live." This sally brought a guffaw from the crowd.

"That asylum ain't no laughin' matter," Ricks said. "Long's I been passin' that place out the end of Federal Street, it makes me feel creepy ever' time I look up at them barred windows."

"Go on! That's one of the biggest an' best hospitals in the country. We got to have a place for crazy folks. An' what's more, we got to have doctors for 'em."

"Say, how come Mitchell to marry a foreigner, you reckon?"

"Well, he was sort of half foreigner hisself. His gran'ma von Eln come from France an' she had them German servants an' all. Guess he just got used to foreigners."

Matt Fuller brought his chair down from its tilted position with a bang. "You all knowed Parris Mitchell all his life. He growed up here, went to school an' the Presbyterian church an' to Aberdeen College, where his pa used to teach. You talk like he was a stranger or somethin'."

"He acts like a stranger—sort of foreign—like his wife."

"He ain't *purty* as she is," Ricks said with a grin.

"Ain't but one woman in Kings Row can hold a candle to her, that's the truth—an' that's Randy McHugh."

"Randy's a well-to-do widder now, Ricks. Looks like all you bachelors around here would be settin' yore caps for her."

"Shucks! She ain't studyin' marryin' again. She was mighty fond of Drake, seems like. Since he died she's made a right smart pile sellin' real estate. Got as much sense as a man."

"She's got the nicest house in Kings Row, if that's any sign. She don't put on no airs, though, fur as I can see. Her an' Doc Mitchell's wife is mighty thick."

"Yeah. She's thick with Fulmer Green's wife, too."

"Fulmer Green an' Parris ain't chummy so's you'd notice it."

"That's the truth. Looks like somethin's always croppin' out between 'em. They got no use for each other."

"The Doc jest seems to get Fulmer's goat, somehow. Even that kid brother of Fulmer's, that Donny, he's always puttin' in his oar about Parris Mitchell."

"Oh, he'd say anything Fulmer put him up to."

"That's the God's truth. Danged if I ever seen anything like the way Fulmer puts up with Donny's shenanigans. That kid's a tough 'un, an' looks like Fulmer ain't ever got on to him."

"Fulmer shore has spoilt Donny. He'd give him the shirt off his back, seems like. Funny, too. Fulmer's a skinflint fur as other folks is concerned."

"I reckon Fulmer's doin' a pretty good job over to the capital. They tell me he's a big shot 'mongst them politicians."

"Oh, he's got sense all right. Sharp as a razor. We need folks like that in politics."

"You reckon he's got his eye on the governor's mansion?"

"Who?"

"Fulmer."

"Wouldn't surprise me none if that ain't what he's got on his mind. He ain't satisfied with bein' big boss in Kings Row. He 'lows to git holt of the whole state. Art Swenson's gonna git elected in November. Fulmer's electioneerin' for him."

"Fulmer's got a right smart followin'. Whoever he backs is more'n apt to git elected."

"But I bet Fulmer'll run next time."

"If he does come out for Governor, Miles Jackson will just about skin him alive. He's got no use for Fulmer, judgin' by the things he prints in his paper ever' now and then."

Momentarily having finished with gossip and politics, some of the men drifted away and gradually the group dissolved.

2

Just after one o'clock Judge James Holloway emerged from his columned house on Cedar Street. He was dressed in a much crumpled linen suit. The suit had been fresh that morning, but the Judge had spent the forenoon in a hammock under his favorite shade tree, as the crisscross of wrinkles testified.

He put on a wide-brimmed panama hat and slowly opened a huge black cotton umbrella. He glanced once, rather ruefully, at the condition of his linens. "Looks like a terrapin's hide," he muttered. No matter. He made his way majestically toward the square.

The Judge's costume was a concession to progress. Less than five years ago he had worn black broadcloth and a high beaver hat at all seasons. Under his overhanging eyebrows his glance shone irascibly. Everyone knew Judge Holloway. His cronies liked him. Many people were a little in awe of him. "The best criminal lawyer in the state, by God." Witnesses feared him as the devil, and juries wept when he played the varied registers of his eloquence.

The tall figure was as well known as the courthouse itself. He stopped from time to time to exchange greetings with friends or to call out some impudence to ladies sitting on front porches. A great ladies' man, the Judge. He loved the world and all the good things in it. He laughed at it and with it. He drank its beauty and its charm and found the draught refreshing. The earth was his home. He saturated his mind with the rich flavors of a pagan literature, and valued a gracious gesture above a pious deed.

Judge Holloway was giving himself a treat today. He intended spending the afternoon with his friend Miles Jackson, editor and publisher of *The Gazette*. Jackson was a man of brains. Damned fine man, the Judge thought as he crossed the square. He's got sense and tells a good story. The latter was a prime qualification in Holloway's estimation. He chuckled as some choice obscenity crossed his memory. I mustn't forget to tell that to Jackson. . . . Hot as hell today. The old man's eyes blinked in the glare.

Miles Jackson's office was a dingy room, a mad clutter of papers, books, and pamphlets. The room was hot and reeked of the various and ancient smells peculiar to print shops.

Jackson himself was standing behind the heaped-up table turning the pages of a bound newspaper file. The Judge nodded and sat down, fanning himself with his floppy panama. Jackson continued turning the pages, and Judge Holloway lighted a long, misshapen stogie. No need for conventional amenities between these two. Holloway's ribald story retreated to some far corner of his mind for future reference. The moment was not favorable. He was as quick to feel the mood of an individual as he was to sense the temper of a jury.

Miles Jackson's figure was heavy and bulgy from years of slumping in a swivel chair. His massive head was majestically modeled. Large gray eyes moved under the most luxurious eyebrows in Kings Row. People often wondered how he could see at all through the thicket of bristles that hung over his eyeglasses and seemed to reach out in all directions like angry tentacles. When he spoke his voice was surprisingly low and mellow—the voice of a man who has meditated much and who expresses his meditations in appropriate richness. When he indulged in some flight of sarcasm his voice rose in pitch and sharpened perceptibly.

The editor flicked a page and made a sound which his friend recognized as an invitation. The Judge, adjusting his gold-rimmed spectacles, peered at the column, then quickly glanced at the dated line topping the sheet.

"Hm, that Tower suicide. Didn't realize how long ago that happened."

He read slowly through the half column, then leaned back in the rickety chair, removed his spectacles, and tapped them thoughtfully against his thumbnail. "I wonder now what the truth of it was?"

Jackson pulled himself up on the table, took out his corncob pipe, filled it, and gave it the careful attention of an habitual pipe smoker.

"There you go, like all the rest of them, Jim. Everybody wants to know what the real truth of a story is."

[12]

The Judge nodded and endeavored to repair a seemingly hopeless fissure in the side of his stogie.

"That's what your real business is, and mine—trying to answer that old question."

Jackson drew at his pipe before answering.

"Yes, I always had an idea that the truth was the prime concern of a newspaperman. Can't say that I'd ever thought the profession of law was similarly concerned."

Judge Holloway ignored this. Jackson leaned back against a stack of books and locked his fingers about an uplifted knee. The Judge settled himself more comfortably and put his feet on the table. This was what he had come out for.

"Jim," Miles began, "I've asked the same question a good many times myself, and I've never answered it. Most people believe an editor knows more about the truth than anyone, but that he won't print it, or doesn't dare, or that out of pure cussedness he likes to keep the public fuddled. Now, that's half a truth—and half a truth is just about in the neighborhood of what we know about the simplest thing that happens out there on Poplar Street, isn't it?"

"Maybe truth is just relative?"

"That's something to think about. Puts a lot more juice in dried-out facts and opens up a general argument. I like that. It adds an element of mystery to the commonplace."

The Judge nodded and turned to the file again. Jackson refilled his pipe and laid it carefully on the table beside him.

"I like to look through those files. They run back sixty years. *The Gazette* was a weekly then. I often read up on the old stories and compare them with the way they've worked out or changed in thirty or forty years. It's quite a study in human nature—and human error."

"I was just thinking, Jackson. Take these columns of Personal Mention. All the comings and goings, the hints of courtships, the marriages and births—it's a biography of Kings Row, that's what it is, a biography of the town." The Judge knocked the loose flakes from his disintegrating stogie and continued. "And I suppose you'd say that deep down under all that somewhere is a final aspect that we're hunting for."

"I doubt it, Jim, I doubt it. I've never found a tale yet to have any more truth in it just because it's old."

Holloway grunted. "There's a popular notion that truth will come to light. That's poppycock. Truth won't out."

"What makes you so sure?"

"I've been a lawyer for fifty years and I've seen men come and go in that old office of mine in mortal fear of that same truth they talk about. It's strange how much they claim for truth—the power it has to work for good—and how afraid they are some little bit of it may leak out!"

"Or that I might print a few stray paragraphs of it."

"Exactly. I lay there in my hammock this morning trying to take a nap, though I've never been able to sleep in the daytime. I lay there thinking about some old tales that went the rounds of Kings Row years and years ago and how little any of us ever knew about what was really behind them. I suppose if you could get at the truth of some things we might know something more about the way the world is planned, if it has any plan at all."

"Are you talking about the plan we hear about in church?"

"No, I'm not. I'm afraid the church is getting to be just so much sand for ostriches to bury their scared heads in, or for sly old birds like Fulmer Green to hide behind—"

"Watch your metaphors, Jim."

"Damn the metaphors. Look at that stogie, Jackson. What in the hell do you suppose it's made of?"

"Smells like Jimson weed."

"Tastes like Jimson weed."

"Why don't you smoke a pipe, Jim?"

"Smells worse and tastes worse."

Jackson opened a desk drawer and proffered a box of very long, very black cigars. "Here, switch to one of these."

"Customer's treat?"

"No. Gift from your friend, Fulmer Green. He wants an editoral lead on the waterworks. Think I'd better give it to him?"

Judge Holloway did not answer immediately. He shook the ash from his cigar and twisted it slowly around to assure himself that it was burning evenly. "Let him have it," he grunted. His brows drew down in a reminiscent effort and he made absent-minded attempts to smooth the "terrapin hide" across his knee.

The courthouse clock struck two. It was as if the drowsy town itself had waked for a moment to take note of passing time. The bell vibrated strongly, and then the waves of sound lessened as they spread out across houses and treetops to lose themselves in the warm haze of the countryside. Kings Row settled itself for another hour's doze.

The Judge set his heavy gold watch ahead two minutes. The town clock kept better time than his watch did.

Jackson straightened up and extricated a thick silver turnip from his waistband pocket. It was seven minutes slow, but that was near enough. He returned the watch to its tight fit and folded himself up again.

"That Tower tragedy, now. How did you figure that business, Jim?"

Judge Holloway gnawed his lower lip for a moment, then restored his cigar to its rightful place before he mumbled, "My theory's no more likely to be right than yours."

"I never could figure out why Dr. Tower left all his property to Parris Mitchell."

"Just liked the boy, I guess. Thought he had brains enough to make use of it the right way."

"Parris is pretty well off, I take it?"

"Plenty to keep him from worrying. The Tower money set him up —that and the sale of the von Eln place to the state, to say nothing of the money Drake McHugh piled up for him."

"Remember *that* was made by using the Tower estate for capital."

"Well, the Tower suicide wasn't caused by money worries, that's certain. I wonder what happens to make a smart man like Tower murder his pretty daughter and blow his own brains out?"

"Lord knows! The fellow was always queer—an unfriendly cuss. Don't believe he ever liked anybody but Parris Mitchell—or let anybody else come to his house. I never understood why Marie von Eln ever sent Parris to read medicine with Tower in the first place."

"He was an able man, no doubt about it."

"I reckon so." Jackson turned his massive head toward the window. "I reckon—look, isn't that Parris headed this way now?"

"Looks like it. Think I'll wait and speak to him. Long as I've been handling his business, I never feel I know anything about him. He never talks about himself."

"Other folks do the talking."

"Mysterious chap, I'd say."

"Mysterious? No such thing. Don't forget, Jim, that boy was brought up by his grandmother, Marie von Eln, one of the finest women in the world. He gets his foreign manners from her. Why, he spoke French and German, I reckon, before he ever learned English. But there's nothing mysterious about him."

"Well, he's different from the other young men hereabouts. Seems a cool customer to me. Acts as though he held himself still inside by some tremendous control—kind of quiet and watchful. But I like him. I like him. He's got good manners."

"Fine folks he comes from. His mother and father died before he was a year old, and his grandmother raised him. She didn't stand for any interference in the rearing of her grandchild from those Virginia swells—his pa's people."

At that moment Parris Mitchell walked in through the open door.

"Well, Mitchell, don't tell me you're taking a holiday!" Judge Holloway said.

"Don't make me feel guiltier than I do, sir. But occasionally I have to break away to keep my own sanity."

"Don't blame you," the Judge said. "After talking all day to people who don't know your language, you need it."

"It doesn't work that way, Judge. They are mentally unbalanced, but they understand what I say to them. And I understand what they are trying to say, too. I learn something from them every day."

"Stuff and nonsense, Mitchell! Don't tell me you take their ravings seriously."

"But I do, sir." Parris' voice was grave. "A psychiatrist learns a lot from the patient. And everything he learns helps him to become a better doctor. It's a magic circle, you see."

"You can't kid me. I think it's poppycock." Judge Holloway dismissed the topic with a toss of his head.

"About that new wing at the hospital, Mitchell—" Jackson puffed at his corncob pipe before finishing his sentence. "Ran into Paul Nolan down at Hyde's last night and got the dope. He was mighty proud of getting that appropriation last spring."

"Wonder what kind of rabbit foot he used on that skinflint legislature?" Holloway said. "They've been cutting down on everything in the state—getting ready for the next election."

"Playing up to the taxpayers, in other words. They don't give a damn what happens to our eleemosynary institutions. Glad Nolan got his new building, though. Smart fellow, Paul."

"Paul's smart all right and one of the finest men I know, and in this case he had the backing of Kings Row," Parris said.

"Yeah? You're forgetting that bastard Green." The Judge's voice was edged. "Made a special trip over to the capital to try to block it. Damned pup. I can't savvy what Fulmer Green's got against the State Hospital. My money says he's got it in for Nolan."

Miles Jackson shot a quick glance at Parris. "And it's my bet that Nolan isn't the only one. How about it, Parris?"

Parris shrugged. "I wonder," he said, "if he's really such small potatoes as to take out an old grudge by trying to block our plans out there?"

"He's got the memory of an elephant. He never forgets a slight or a defeat."

"If I remember rightly," Parris sounded a bit rueful, "he always won out."

"All the same, my lad, you managed to show him up a time or two. Remember the time you made him back down—in *print*—about that St. George sale?"

"Oh, that."

"Yes—that. And several other times you showed him up as a bad actor. He won't forget those things. He could be dangerous," Miles warned. "If he keeps meddling in your affairs, Parris, why don't you lace into him? Hold him up to ridicule. That would get him quicker than anything else."

"I shan't need to do anything about Fulmer," Parris said confidently.

"Why not—if he acts up?"

"Look, Miles, I deal with people's minds. I know how minds work. Fulmer will defeat himself—if he runs true to form."

"What makes you think so? He gets by with an awful lot of dirt."

"Give him time. Psychologically, men of his type destroy themselves. I'm no fighter. I deal with ideas. I'm no two-fisted guy to get out and lick the stuffing out of somebody just because I don't like the color of his eyes or the cut of his hair."

[17]

"That sounds all right—but what do we do when he's 'destroyed himself,' as you so optimistically predict?" Miles scoffed.

"We preen ourselves and mutter something that sounds remarkably like 'I told you so.'"

Miles grunted. "That's not enough. Nothing but gore would satisfy me when I think of that young whippersnapper pushing folks around like chessmen."

"Trouble with him is that he's scared stiff," said the Judge. "Nobody in his position would drink so much if he wasn't scared out of his boots about something or other."

"Scared he'll get found out—that's all," Miles jeered.

"Come to think of it," Parris said, "I don't believe I've seen him for several months."

"That's because you don't take proper cognizance of our public affairs, my friend. *He's* always on hand at our band concerts, our home-coming days, and even the opening game of the baseball season."

Holloway chuckled appreciatively. "Trust Fulmer to be in the limelight."

"Parris," Miles asked, "how do you explain the unholy affection Fulmer has for that wastrel brother of his?"

"You're full of questions I can't answer this afternoon, Miles. I'd never thought about it."

"It might be worth thinking about. Maybe you psychiatrist birds have some sort of a three-syllable name for it, but a plain man like me just takes it for granted that Fulmer is fooled by the young scamp."

"Does it work both ways—the affection, I mean?" Parris was interested.

"Got your curiosity roused, eh? Maybe you can figure out just what kind of a complex it is."

"Not necessarily a complex at all," Parris said. "Could be a carry-over from some childhood sense of responsibility."

"By golly, you could be right," the Judge agreed. "When Rod Green died, Fulmer took over the care of the kid. That sanctimonious mother of theirs was too wrapped up in church work to bother with the boys."

"Hear, hear!" Parris laughed. "Judge Holloway's getting to be a psychologist, too."

"Psychologist or not," the Judge said, "I think there's something kind of unwholesome about Fulmer's attachment to that good-looking scamp. It looks—shall I say *unhealthy?*"

Miles Jackson's eyebrows twitched. "You might," he said, "if you're afraid to put it in plainer language."

The Judge rose from the rickety chair with caution. "Well, if you get anything figured out—anything interesting—let me know. Seems to me there's a statute on our books that takes care of unusual behavior. I shouldn't mind trying it out. Guess the time has come for me to make a pretense of opening my alleged office. Going my way, Mitchell?"

"Not today, sir. I'm going to wander over to the old place across the creek. I don't get there often. It looks rather forlorn, I'm told, after four years of neglect."

"Should think it would. This country goes back to wilderness in a hurry. Never saw such fecundity except in the tropics. Drop in at the office any time you can. You'll keep an eye on your lawyer, young man, if you're sharp. And how's your wife? Mrs. Holloway sees her occasionally at Sarah Skeffington's."

"Elise is not standing the heat too well, I'm afraid. Good old Sarah," he added, "she's been almost a second grandmother to me."

"As fine a woman as ever lived—but getting old. You young folks ought to drop in to see her more often than you do. Well, s'long, son —stop by with your wife next time you're in the neighborhood."

As Judge Holloway's umbrella, substituting for a cane, beat a rhythmic tattoo on the paved walk of Federal Street, Parris felt almost as though he might turn and find his grandmother at his side, for, of all the people in Kings Row, these three, Sarah Skeffington, the Judge, and Miles Jackson, had been closest to her.

Miles Jackson stood idly looking after the two men who had just left his office. Leaning against the door facing, his hands thrust into his pockets, he gave himself over to reviewing the feud that had existed for so many years between Fulmer Green and Parris Mitchell.

It wasn't exactly that Kings Row had taken sides in the matter, but the town was reminded of it from time to time by some overt act on the part of Fulmer and the seemingly unimpassioned but often effective reaction on the part of the young doctor. By George, people *ought* to take sides, and to stick by their choices, good or bad; otherwise, the town would never get anything settled.

"Trouble is," he muttered angrily, "the mass of people is inert. It only moves under calamity or catastrophe."

Miles shrugged aside his annoyance. The extreme materialism of these people, he thought reasonably, makes them unaware—incapable of perceiving spiritual values. But it was the same everywhere, he supposed. Everything that is good or bad about this country is good or bad about Kings Row. For every Parris Mitchell here there are a hundred thousand Parris Mitchells—and that is impressive. For every Fulmer Green there are a hundred thousand Fulmer Greens—and that, too, is impressive.

That Benny Singer affair had been the first adult clash between Mitchell and Green. Benny was undoubtedly the town half-wit, and as such he should have been protected from the outrageous persecution of hoodlum boys. When a crowd of them one day threw rocks at the Singer house, breaking the windows and hurting his dog, Benny fired a gun into the crowd and killed two of the gang. Parris, called in as an alienist, had done his best to have the boy committed to the asylum, but Fulmer, as the new Prosecuting Attorney, had pushed the case with malign persistence and had succeeded in sending Benny to the gallows. Miles grunted disdainfully, remembering that Fulmer had acted only to further his policitical aspirations.

And then there had been that scurrilous article in *The Evening Chronicle* accusing Parris of a crooked deal in the sale of the St. George tract of land to the State Hospital. Parris had forced Fulmer to retract, Miles recalled gleefully, and, in fact, had forced Fulmer to give up the publication of *The Chronicle,* which was nothing more than an organ for boosting Fulmer as a rising force in state politics. Kings Row had applauded. It had been vastly entertaining to see Fulmer eat crow.

There had been other run-ins, too, Miles remembered with wry amusement. In a town like Kings Row there were always opposing forces. Well, Parris didn't seem to be worried. Nice guy, Parris Mitchell.

Kings Row was a little fearful of new ideas, Miles reminded himself. And certainly Parris was an exponent of the new. Modern society, he mused, has a way of guarding itself against the impact of the novel. It has in mind the retention of its individuality—and there was undoubtedly a lot of "we-sentiment" in this town. Too much.

There must be a good deal of tension, too, underneath the seeming placidity, Miles reflected. He grinned wickedly as he added, "Man has dwelt too long in the murky shadow of the knowledge tree."

Turning back to his desk, he closed the file he and the Judge had been discussing earlier. "The biography of Kings Row," the Judge had called it. By Jove, he wished he knew more about that Tower business. There must have been more to that than ever came out. Somehow, he felt Parris could enlighten him if the boy would talk. But Parris had a way of keeping his mouth shut. You never heard Parris sounding off about other people's affairs. He didn't sound off about his own, for that matter. But for some reason the recollection of that strange, tragic death of Dr. Tower and his lovely young daughter clung like a faint shadow to the progress of Parris Mitchell. Conversations about the young doctor—and there were many—were likely to take a turn beginning with "Yes, but—"

Miles settled down in his old swivel chair and went to work on an editorial on the waterworks. He'd not say what he suspected about Fulmer Green's connection with the contract. It would come out soon enough. Fulmer could not resist boasting when he had put over a sharp deal. He'd be sure to let it out. Maybe Parris was right when he said Fulmer would destroy himself.

Miles shrugged a kink out of his right shoulder. "Doggone," he said aloud, "I'm getting old. I need a vacation. Maybe I could get Drew Roddy to come down and take over while I got in a good fishing trip. Do Drew good to come out of his shell for a while."

As Parris walked, his thoughts moved away from the two men with whom he had been talking, away from the town to the old place across the creek where he had spent his childhood, down the years to the boy's mind and its first meetings with the realities of Kings Row and the dim world beyond.

He was brought back sharply as he passed Pomeroy Lane. Again he speculated on the mystery of Davis Pomeroy. Was there indeed a mystery, or was it another of those Kings Row fancies that were still so hard to separate from the truth? But as he looked up the hill at the imposing length of white stables, the big house, the magnificent trees, he scoffed at the idea of its being a sinister place, full of frightening things.

With teasing insistence his thoughts returned to the von Eln place; his grandmother's dominating presence; his childhood sweetheart, little Renée Gyllinson, whom he could not remember without that familiar stab of pain; Elise, his wife, that first time he saw her standing in the orchard against a backdrop of apple blossoms, her silvery blond hair glinting in the sun. How strange it had seemed to him, returning for the first time to that familiar scene after five years in Vienna, that he should find there a grown-up Renée smiling at him. He had even called her Renée, so strong had been the resemblance. She had laughed and said, "My name is Elise, and I live here with my father."

Even after she spoke with that charming foreign accent, it was hard to believe that she was not at least a *projection* of Renée. He had felt a sudden rush of protectiveness, a feeling that had grown stronger as the days passed. Gradually his memory of Renée had been dimmed and Elise remained. But all this was in the past. Now, Elise, gentle, frail little Elise, was his wife. She still appealed to the protective instinct she had awakened in him at that first meeting. Sometimes a passing wish that she would "grow up" had to be forcibly banished from his mind. But he often felt he had married a memory—a dear, sweet image from his youth.

For a time after his marriage he had been able to shut out that other memory—the painful memory of Cassandra Tower. Cassandra, whose strange and urgent passion had left its mark on him, had left him emotionally shy, physically averse to demonstrative outbursts. Perhaps that was why Elise, with her timid childish affection, had brought him such contentment—such escape.

He smiled as the word "escape" formed in his mind. His thorough training in the field of psychiatry had taught him much about his own motivations, and while he refused to dwell on them, his recognition was quick and sure.

3

The creek bent like a silver crescent around the von Eln place. As Parris followed it for a little way, he realized that his expeditions down the creek had always taken on the color and flavor of real adventure. The sparse young rose leaves of early spring had become dense masses of deepest green. On the low hills rising from the opposite bank there was already a touch of yellow and red that presaged autumn. But here along the creek the intense green of summer persisted. The shadows resting on the shallow waters were inky, but in the sun-splashed stretches the small rocks, washed by years of running water, made a pink and yellow mosaic that took his breath.

Summer at high tide. A curious blend of opulent fulfillment and adumbrated decay. There was still something of spring—if no more than the remembrance of April anticipations and seeing them in full realization; there was the very peak of summer; and there was in the look of surfeit that rested on all vegetation enough of autumnal melancholy without the despair of the actuality when the end is at immediate hand.

At this time there were always mysterious things going on, he thought. Little dry bushes beside the rutted roads would rattle suddenly when all too evidently the day was windless. Curious.

Retracing his steps to the entrance of the avenue, he heard the song of a hidden bird in the branches above him. He paused and listened as the thin music laced the air. In a moment like this he could believe himself to be an acolyte, wonderingly lighting the seven tapers in the ecstasy of communion.

From the top of the old familiar stile he looked up the long avenue leading to the house. The scene was more ragged and neglected than he had expected. It had been so well kept when his grandmother owned it; and even when he had revisited it after his five years of absence in Europe, it had been in beautiful condition—kept so by the state, which had bought it for an experimental station. But since it had been closed for lack of space for expansion, it had been neglected. The house was boarded up and weeds were taking the gardens.

Parris thought soberly that it was here he had felt the first faint thunders of conflict—a conflict that began when the opposed strains of his ancestry merged in the making of his troubled flesh and bone. Now it seemed to be sharpened by the tangle of silent, growing things.

Bees zoomed by him. Grasshoppers shot here and there with minute creaking sounds. A butterfly wavered on a thistle bloom. He

[23]

turned aside to avoid stepping on a small green lizard that was basking in the afternoon sunshine, and began to walk rapidly down the slope toward the pond which had been his "secret lake." There had been a time when that place was his untroubled Eden, but that world had receded, had turned infinitely strange, and had come to rest in a profound unknown. He had a strange compulsion to recover it— that world of Renée—that familiar and lovely world that was lost to him.

The secret lake lay at his feet—the little stretch of water, clear and serene under the light that was already slanting a little, already shifting from hard silver to softer gold, in a way that to his eyes marked the real turn of the day. There it was, hemmed in by the encircling wiry grass and the overhanging willow trees, familiar yet unreal, with that peculiar quality of something untouchable that invests leaves and flowers seen through the glass walls of a hothouse.

He sat down on the flat rock he remembered so well, clasping his hands about his knees as he used to do when he came here to think. He summoned a clear vision of his grandmother as she walked about the place, making suggestions about the plantings or laughing at the small mishaps that would have annoyed a less gay personality. He remembered once when a gardener had complained of the encroaching poppies that seemed to spread with such incredible greediness, how she had laughingly said, "But poppies are so much handsomer than cabbages!" Dear, dear *gran'mère*. How sweet and how good she had been. Her going, when he was eighteen, had left him entirely bereft, entirely without anchor, facing with frightened misgivings a future barren of home ties.

He thought gratefully of his dearest friend, Drake McHugh, who had taken him into his home and had stood between him and utter despair during those bad days. Drake—what a generous, unselfish, loyal friend Drake had proved to be! Poor, ill-fated Drake, who had turned to him in his last days of pain and illness with a pathetic faith that he would help him. No other friend could ever take the place of Drake McHugh in his heart.

And there beside Drake stood Randy. She had fought so against the fate that was overtaking Drake. Together she and Parris had created a life of usefulness for his poor, maimed body. By her devotion she had staved off death itself for a long time.

What a wonderful woman Randy really is, Parris thought. There was a heart-stirring warmth in her low-pitched voice—a warmth that always stayed with him after he had left her. He felt a faint stir in his blood, like the ripples made by a wind whose casual passing troubles the shy silver of a stream. For a moment he sat very still, scarcely breathing, listening to the quiet hush of the woods. The windless air seemed to be waiting—and *afraid*.

Insistently his thoughts returned to the past. He tried to summon a clear vision of Renée, the blond child-sweetheart, as she was on that last tragic day. He shuddered, recalling the sound of her pitiful crying under the brutal beating she had suffered as punishment for their innocent love-making. He remembered his own helplessness to protect her from her father's rage. He had lost her through the blind stupidity of older people who could not understand the importance of that lyric episode, but she had become to him the very *imago* of youth.

Thinking of his whole life up to now, there had been, he decided, more tragedy than should have shadowed the life of so young a man. He felt as though he had stood alone on a hilltop while the elements raged about him. He knew that all his past had gone into the building of his character and behavior, and he was conscious of the depth of the imprint it had made on his spirit.

I am about to feel sorry for myself, he thought, and rose determinedly. He shook himself free of the images. No matter how deeply he yearned for the old companionship of his familiar haunt and the comfort it had brought him in his youth, its response was gone and he knew himself to be no longer a harmonious integer of the sum of existing things.

He walked slowly toward the old stone house, recalling details of the place as he had known it in his childhood. It was foreign in style, the grounds more elaborate than was customary in this part of the country; there were bricked terraces, a long avenue of cedars, and the many walks were bordered with hollyhocks and other old-fashioned flowers. Between were small beds of vegetables. It was a combination of frivolity and usefulness that elicited sniffs of disapproval, he had been told, from many in Kings Row who scorned a strawberry patch surrounded with ruffles of flowers as a "foreign affectation."

He caught his breath as he came in sight of the walls warmed by the afternoon sun. The mossy flagging was touched with a curious green gold. Vines against the house dragged at the wooden shutters. Box hedges, grown fat and old, edged the walks where ancient red bricks sank into the soil under a thin velvet of green moss. There was a bitter odor from the box, hot in the sun, and the crushing sweetness of tuberoses seemed to come to him from many years away.

The long avenue stretched straight from the house, a green tunnel with a deceptive look of coolness. But here, he thought, here in this garden, he had long ago begun to ask questions of destiny. Here he had faced the enigma of existence, had pondered beginnings and ends, had even demanded reason of the present. Again he was trying to gain a foothold, to establish geography and say, "Here am I—here, and here, and here." He was casting out feelers like the vines that snaked through the hedges and fought to take hold of the unresponsive sand.

An old willow tree looked secretly busy, acutely intent, he thought, like a top that sleeps when it spins. Busy being green and holding on deep in the ground with its fingered roots, reaching deeper and deeper and holding tighter and tighter each day in that desperate seriousness of hidden purpose which expressed itself in every leaf that hung without a quiver in the thin air.

Suddenly Parris knew what he must do. If he hoped to recapture any of that past which was so dear and yet so painful to him, he knew that he must come back here to live. The impulse was so strong that he was almost choked with excitement. Many times in his life decisions had been reached in this incredibly swift urgency—an urgency too compelling to be resisted or delayed.

Randy was the best real-estate agent in Kings Row and she would be able to buy it for him. Randy would help him—Randy could always be depended upon—no matter what was needed.

4

The living room was hot, although the windows faced east and a light breeze had just sprung up to stir the curtains. Randy McHugh straightened up from the desk over which she had been working for the last hour on a pile of rent receipts. She ran one hand through the mass of her disordered, short, red curls.

Every time I do these sums, she thought, I remember the fun Drake and I had because neither of us was very good at figures. They had to be checked and rechecked—but it *was* fun.

She was assailed by a familiar pang of loneliness. Oh, she kept busy, there were a thousand things to do. She had the new playground down in Jinktown which Parris Mitchell had suggested last summer, and which she had provided almost singlehanded. But what a reward she had, just seeing those poor kids enjoying their vacations and their after-school hours!

Of course, she admitted, the responsibility was no longer all hers. She thought gratefully of the enthusiasm with which Hazel Green and Bethany Laneer and Caroline Thill had entered into the work down there. There were others too; it seemed everybody was willing to help in one way or another.

From upstairs came sounds of laughter, and she remembered that Dyanna Slater was helping old Tempy, the colored maid-of-all-work, with the hanging of fresh curtains.

Randy was glad to have pretty little Dyanna about the place. Father Donovan, always watchful of the needs of the members of his parish, had asked for the job of "helper" for the fifteen-year-old girl from Jinktown.

"She needs to help out. Her Aunt Carrie is not able to do as much as she used to do and Dyanna is a willing little worker. You will be good for the child, Randy," he had said.

And Randy had found the child a shy, amiable little thing, pretty and appealing. She had been less lonely since Dyanna came every day and moved happily about the house. Randy would miss her when school opened again and Dyanna could come only on Saturdays.

She leaned back in her chair and closed her eyes. The long, curled lashes, leaf brown, brushing her flushed cheek gave her a look of childish sweetness, but the soft, sensuous line of her cheek, the full red lips, and the firm chin proclaimed the maturity of her womanly appeal.

Something in the bright quality of the day had made her think of Drake. A shadow of pain crossed her face. She was remembering how he had gone, how brief the period of their marriage.

Why, she thought, did it have to happen to Drake—the gay, generous-hearted boy—Drake, who never could bear seeing anything suffer? Randy knew beyond question that Drake's legs had been amputated unnecessarily—deliberately—by an evil, conscienceless surgeon who held a personal grudge against him. Her hands clenched on the arms of her chair. When she heard footsteps on the brick walk, Randy opened her eyes and started up.

In spite of all she could do to calm it, her heart beat faster as she watched Parris Mitchell coming toward her door. Feeling as guilty as if she had been caught eavesdropping, she brought to bear all her powers of self-discipline to regain her calm. She gave a hurried glance into the mirror and wished that in spite of the heat she had worn a more becoming dress.

Even before he greeted her she saw the excitement in his face. As always she was caught up into his mood—lifted to the plane of his emotion without knowing its reason. It was only a moment, however, before she realized that his mind was focused beyond her on some excitement in which she played no part.

"Randy—"

"What is it this time, Parris? God didn't give you a poker face, you know."

"I warn you," Parris said, "I've come to beg a favor. I've been out to the old place."

"Your grandmother's?"

"Yes. Randy, I'll never be happy until I go back there to live. I want it. I want that place back, and I want you to get it for me."

His desire reached out and touched her; the warmth of it surrounded her. She was drawn again into the midst of his wanting and felt her share in its fulfillment. But she said only:

"Of course. I've wondered when you'd get around to something like this—to making a real home, the sort you ought to have. The sort," she added gravely, "that Elise, especially, needs."

Parris realized with a quick sense of shame that his decision had been a selfish one, that he had thought mainly of his own happiness and very little of Elise's.

"Randy," he asked, "is Elise unhappy at the hospital? Has she ever said anything—"

"She's said nothing, the darling—but I know institutional life can't be good for her. I couldn't bear it myself," she said frankly. "Parris, haven't you noticed that Elise doesn't look well? She's too much alone, too concentrated upon herself, and of course she must worry a lot about her father. Can't you persuade her to go down to the Ozarks with me for a little vacation? It's dreadfully hot."

"Have you asked her?"

"I've *insisted.*"

"She won't agree to go?"

Randy shook her head. "For one so—so quiet and gentle, Parris, your wife has a surprisingly strong will. She has an idea you need her and she doesn't want to leave you. I wonder," she said slowly, "if Elise is ever lonely."

Parris looked bewildered—and Randy felt such a surge of unaccountable tenderness for him that it frightened her. "Parris," she added impulsively, "I've no right to ask—but why don't you and Elise have children?"

Parris answered soberly. "We want children, but Dr. Waring says it would be unsafe for Elise."

"It was impertinent of me to ask, Parris, but I have so often hoped you would have children. What a fine heritage for them! And Elise— I know how much it would mean to her. With all my rushing about, never a day passes that I don't wish that Drake and I had had children. Elise probably feels the same way. I think that's why she pours out so much affection on little Kam Nolan."

"Perhaps," he said absently.

"Parris, Elise said something this morning that I've been wondering about. She said that you called her 'Renée' the first time you saw her. Why did you do that?"

Parris smiled. "It's funny I should have been thinking of that this very afternoon. I suppose I never told you about a little sweetheart I had, Renée Gyllinson. You wouldn't remember her. When I came back from Vienna and saw Elise for the first time, there at the old place where I had loved Renée—and lost her—I thought she was my childhood sweetheart grown up, and I called her name."

"So that was the reason you fell so quickly in love with Elise and married her?"

"That—and other reasons." Parris thought for a moment and then said slowly, "You know, Randy, I was very lonely after Drake died. He seemed my last tie to the old life and—I wanted to build for myself a home of some kind. It seemed to me Elise would create the same sort of half-European atmosphere that my grandmother had done. I suppose Dr. Freud would have said I was really marrying my grandmother."

Randy laughed. "Oh, you and your Dr. Freud! I can't imagine anyone less like a grandmother than Elise."

"He's a wise man. In a way he might be on the right track. Maybe I was just being selfish. I'm not sure it was as good for Elise as it was for me."

"You haven't given Elise a chance to make a real home, Parris, living out there at the hospital all this time. Let's get down to business on the von Eln place." She became determinedly brisk. "It's state property, isn't it? That means it can be sold only by direct act of the legislature."

"How long will it take?"

"The next session will be in January. In the meantime we'll need to do some groundwork. If any dealers find out you want it, they'll try to get an option on it in order to hold you up for a stiff price. I'll handle it myself, Parris. I'm not a bad lobbyist when I find it necessary."

He leaned forward and covered her hand with his own. "Randy, what would I do without you? I often wonder how such a lovely—such a *feminine* person can at the same time be so downright competent. You amaze me more every day."

Randy's face colored. Then she realized that he had not spoken seriously—that he was no longer thinking about her. He was thinking of his old home.

After a moment's silence he spoke again. "Sorry, I'm being distrait. Maybe I'm a little tired—but not too tired to know how much I owe you for all you do for me."

"You exaggerate my competence. I was just going to ask your advice about something I don't know how to handle."

"Is there really such a thing?"

"Don't joke. It's about Donny Green."

"What's he been doing now?"

"He's been annoying the girls at the playground."

Parris' look of surprise changed to one of concern. "Is it—serious?"

"I don't really know. This morning I went down to watch a basketball match. Donny was leaning over the fence of the girls' court. When he saw me drive up he hurried off down the creek path."

"Did you speak to him?"

"He didn't give me time. I asked little Clare Whittaker what he had said to her. She told me he called to her, 'How about a walk down by the creek?' Clare's answer was to pick up a rock and throw it at him. Then, according to her story, he said something nasty. She asked if I couldn't stop him from hanging around there. I promised to see what could be done."

"Then what?"

"I went to see Hazel and asked her to speak to Donny—tell him we had made certain rules about the playgrounds, and that boys were not welcome at the girls' field."

"Maybe that will settle it."

"I'm afraid not. Hazel's awfully worried about Donny. She says Fulmer's spoiled him so dreadfully that it's hard to do anything with him."

"People like that—like Donny, I mean—need to have preventive measures taken to forestall serious trouble later."

"It's my private opinion that it would take some doing to make an acceptable citizen out of Donny Green. That lad's a menace."

"Afraid I haven't been much help, Randy. But keep me informed. If you need me, just call."

"Thanks, Parris. I'll write David Kettring tonight about the von Eln property. He knows about those things and he can engineer most anything over at the capital. Anyway, it's Thursday—and I don't like to start any project on Friday."

"Superstitious?"

"Irish."

"Sweet."

Her heart contracted as he took his hat and rose to go, but try as she would she could not read into the word a meaning she knew it didn't have.

She stood in the doorway and watched him until he had gone down the walk and through the gate, until he finally disappeared among the trees and tall hedges that lined the street.

She turned and started resolutely toward the desk. I'll get the house for him, she thought. It won't be easy, but I'll handle those politicians—Randy stopped as her eyes caught her reflection in the mirror over the mantel. "Darn," she said petulantly, "why did Parris have to find me in this ugly old dress?"

Parris' steps lagged as he walked out Federal Street. His conscience was hurting him badly. Had he really been so concentrated upon his own problems, so absorbed in his work, as to have become indifferent to his wife's needs and moods?

He knew how close she had been to her father and that she had grieved for him ever since he went back to Austria. While she seldom spoke of him, it was only natural that in these troubled times, separated as they were, Elise should have him much on her mind. I haven't taken his place as completely as I should, Parris thought regretfully.

It simply had not occurred to him that Elise might be unhappy about her surroundings. All of the staff members had suites in the big central building of the asylum. She liked Laurel Nolan and the other physicians' wives—even Mrs. Carruthers compared all the latest recipes with her. How could she be lonely, he asked himself. Possibly—just possibly the cries of the patients sometimes disturbed her. In any case, it would be a good thing for Elise to move out to the old place. He hoped Randy would expedite the deal.

Randy's confidence had set his mind at rest on that score, but she had filled him with unease by the way she had spoken of Elise. He wondered what it was that had alarmed her. Surely, if anything were seriously wrong he would have known it, close as he and Elise were. Still, Randy seldom made mistakes. Parris felt that she lived with an amazing honesty. She was not afraid of anything in the world, and coupled with her fearlessness was a tenacity and strength seldom attained. At the thought his mind touched on Elise and her timidity— her withdrawn quality, and he wished—well, that she had some of the wide-open forthrightness Randy possessed.

He liked Randy's way of making instant decisions for herself. Elise never decided anything. There was something sweet and appealing about her way of waiting for him to express his wishes on every small detail of their lives—but it could be exhausting at times. He resolutely brushed away the irritating thought and quickened his step as he neared the hospital.

Great columns marked the entrance to the hospital grounds. As Parris walked between them he looked up at the windows already alight, and on beyond to a spent strip of yellow in the west above a-dove-gray horizon. He had not realized it was so late. He contrasted the glow from the setting sun with the inviting amber light of the steady window lamps. But—could he ever feel that this was home? Or could Elise?

No, he decided. Home was in the house where he had been born—the house that had sheltered his grandmother. After all, it was the same house where Elise had lived with her father during those few years when the state had run the Experimental Station there. It would bring back to Elise the warmth and security which was her birthright. The unease born of what Randy had suggested, however, still pervaded him. Maybe Elise needed more than just a change of residence. What was it?

This massive gray building looming before him seemed to him a thing of dignity, a refuge for tormented and unhappy minds, but appraising it through Elise's eyes, he saw the barred windows, the sterile aspect of the place, the buildings seeming to crouch threateningly. Was this the way it looked to his sensitive little wife?

At that moment a high, terrified cry came from the East Wing and was echoed by several voices from another ward across an areaway.

He hurried toward the central building and his own apartment. As he opened the door of their suite he saw Elise busying herself with supper preparations. He could detect nothing unusual in her appearance. Her small, white-clad figure moved quickly from table to china closet and back again. Little loose silvery blond curls, escaping from the long braids wound about her head, framed her heart-shaped face, giving her a look of innocent youth. She was humming a theme from a piano suite he had heard her practicing this morning. He whistled the closing phrase of the melody and she looked up, startled.

"Oh, there you are! I've a surprise—*Parris!*" She ran quickly to him. "Is anything wrong? You look—troubled. What is it?" But when he grinned at her and tweaked her ear, she was instantly gay again.

"I've a surprise for you, Dr. Mitchell, my dear," she said. "A chafing-dish supper. There's peach cocktail, creamed chicken with peas, lettuce salad, Camembert and crackers—and coffee. How's that?"

"Absolutely right and proper—and I hope it's soon."

[33]

"Better than that, it's now."

She was full of talk about the happenings of the day. She had visited with Laurel and Randy and she had done a little shopping. She had several stories to tell of Kam Nolan, who had spent a large part of the afternoon with her.

"Really, Parris, he's the most adorable child in the world. He's so original. He never says an obvious thing and never does what other children do. He's wonderful."

"I'm going to be jealous if this keeps up."

"Oh, Parris, you simpleton! But I shouldn't want *you* to be too fond of him. You belong to *me*."

"Honey, when you are through with supper I have a surprise for you. I have something very important to talk about."

"Wonderful! I love large, grave discourses, when you act as though I were really growing up."

An hour later they were in the little living room, Parris with his pipe and Elise with her sewing cabinet beside her chair. There was a protected, shut-in quality about the room, and between them a sense of joyous conspiracy.

Sitting there near the open windows, they came closer together than they had been for a long time. Elise reached out through her strange, enveloping obscurity toward him. Perhaps, she thought wistfully, if they could stay like this long enough, they would have moved sufficiently in that rhythm of thought and feeling to make it permanent.

But the essential Parris, too, was elusive. His complexity—the complexity of a highly civilized man—presented so many facets she was unable to reconcile and harmonize.

"Elise," Parris began almost formally, "are you happy living here at the hospital?"

"I can be happy anywhere you are, Parris. Have I seemed to you unhappy?" She did not raise her eyes as she spoke.

"No, sweet," he said quickly, "you have not *seemed* to be unhappy but perhaps you would like better to live in a place of our own?"

"Oh, yes, yes, *yes*! *Could* we, Parris? This great cold place—and *madness*, Parris. So ver-ry much madness, and just here, in these walls. It is as strange and terrible as some old Gothic story to wake at night and to realize where I am."

Parris was dismayed at her intensity. "Why haven't you told me this before? Surely you aren't *afraid*?"

"Some nights," she said hesitantly, "when I hear them. Do you think, Parris, we could really live someplace away from these dreadful walls?"

Parris felt vaguely hurt by her words. "Elise, you mustn't *think* the word 'madness.' It's a violent old word with all sorts of storybook connotations—old wives' stuff all mixed up with your notions. They are just people. Not many of them are violent. They are ill, that's all—off balance."

"They look to me—terrible. Even those who walk about the grounds."

"Please, darling, try to correct that idea. They are childlike, so many. Sick, yes, and that isn't pleasant. I remember that I once said that insanity actually appears a little silly more often than it appears tragic. I was blamed for that remark. I guess it wasn't a fortunate remark, at that." Parris smiled a bit ruefully.

"But I can't like living here, no matter how hard I try."

"Then, how would you like it if we buy my grandmother's place and go there to live?"

Elise's expression was one of astonishment and almost disbelief. "Parris, my ver-ry dear, do you mean it? Perhaps I could not bear that much happiness. Oh, Parris, you aren't teasing?"

"Why didn't you tell me, you poor baby, that you felt like this? Don't you know that I would have managed anything that would make you happy?"

"I didn't wish to complain."

"But that's what I'm here for. That's my job, honey, to make you happy."

Elise moved over into his lap. "Maybe you don't know it, Parris, but you, too, would be different there. You were always so—so *young* there, and less the ver-ry serious doctor."

Yes, he thought, he would feel younger there. Perhaps that was one reason he wanted to go back. He would recover a lost content. He did not admit to himself that he was retreating to something, but he knew that his thoughts dwelt frequently on the place, and with a passion and a yearning whose intensity he did not even try to analyze.

"But, Parris, can you afford to buy it? It would cost a great deal of money. Maybe it would be hard for you?"

"We can buy it—if the state will sell. Randy can get it for us and we can have it restored. Would that be fun?"

"*Such* fun!" Elise was radiant. "A big garden like that—and flowers and—"

"And my Elise making an Eden for her tiresome old husband."

She stopped him with a kiss and looked up at him like a small child waiting to be told another, better fairy tale. She began suggesting small plans for the house, the terraces, the gardens. Her quick excitement troubled Parris, who cautioned her that it might be months before they could get possession of the property.

"Just the same, Parris, I want us to decide on a name for it right now—this minute! It can't go on being the von Eln place. But—oh, Parris, why not call it just von Eln?" she asked, sitting up suddenly.

"Just von Eln? I'd like that—if it's your choice."

"After all, Parris, your grandmother created the place, and I think we should call it by her name."

"Most of all, Elise, I want what will make *you* happy—from giving it a name all the way through."

And then, to the astonishment of both of them, she burst into tears. Parris drew her close.

"Here, here, cry-baby, this will never do! At least wait until I've a chance to deliver all the messages I brought you. First, I promised Judge Holloway I'd bring you over to see them; second, Mr. Lenz will come at four Sunday to hear you play and, I *hope,* to give you some criticism; third, and most important of all, Herman Eger is going to give you a dachshund puppy."

"So much good news all at once, Parris! People are ver-ry good to me. When shall I have the little dog?"

"Not until we get moved. You can't keep it here. Regulations, you know."

"That horrid word again! Regulations! Maybe Kam and I could keep it hidden away."

" 'Fraid not, darling. You'll have to wait. Maybe it won't be so long. Still crying? You've been doing too many things today—or maybe you don't really want to live in the country? Is that it?"

Her wet eyes flashed at him and then she buried her face against his shoulder. He stroked the soft curls back from her brow. Why, he wondered, with all her appeal and beauty had his feeling for her none of the ecstasy that his boyhood love for Renée had possessed, none of the madness—the fury—he stopped and mentally stumbled at the word—of his affair with Cassandra?

Much of this Elise sensed. Perhaps, she mused, she was only a ghost of something which he sought and had not yet found. Perhaps, she thought with a curious weight at her heart, perhaps that was her role in his life, just to remain always a ghost of some sort of happiness that he had lost or had never found.

Sitting there with her head against his shoulder, listening to the steady beat of his heart, she felt a new hope springing up in her own mind. She knew that the old place was an escape for him. She, too, she realized, was an escape. But at von Eln, maybe she and the place together might supply something that would satisfy his restless search. And maybe, out there, she wouldn't feel so tired all the time. She could meet his moods with more response and more understanding. Yes, things would be better at von Eln. He would seem close to her there.

5

Later that night Hazel Green had telephoned and asked for a morning appointment with Parris. The interview was a short one. She came to the point without preliminaries and asked Parris to take Donny Green as a patient, admitting that she had come without Fulmer's knowledge.

Parris reluctantly agreed to have a talk with Donny but did not promise definitely to take the case. He felt sure from what Hazel told him of Donny's behavior that the boy could profit by treatment, but he was equally sure that Donny would never agree to the long, slow, and often tiresome treatment necessary if a cure was to be effected.

After Hazel had gone, Parris sat at his desk wondering about the Greens. He had met Hazel a number of times, but this was the first time he had talked seriously with her. Hazel was really beautiful. Hers was an overemotional face, he thought, but there was something so balanced, so assured in the carriage of her head, that his first thought had been that here was a woman of extreme sensitivity yet of complete self-control. If she had felt any discomfort about the interview there was no indication of it in the direct gaze of her long, gray eyes, or in the steady, well-bred voice, but he sensed a tenseness beneath the seeming poise. She is not a happy woman, he suddenly decided, and was immediately assailed by a suspicion of his own ability to judge of the happiness or unhappiness of Fulmer Green's wife.

He smiled at his own prejudice, but continued to wonder how a woman like Hazel ever came to marry Fulmer Green. Perhaps, he thought, trying to be fair, perhaps she was in love with him—but it must be difficult to stay in love with a man so—so lacking in integrity.

Parris' lifelong habit of making an effort to be just took over. Perhaps, he admitted, Fulmer had not taken the time to decide what to do about questions of obligation, responsibility, pity, compassion, sacrifice, and their opposites. What to do about them, what to reject, ignore, accept, and what to incorporate. Maybe Fulmer was not so much to blame. A man could be knocked prostrate by some blow of fate and not be able to struggle to his feet. God knows, he thought, I have no right to assume a "holier than thou" attitude—when I am so uncertain about my own obligations. It's not easy to distinguish always between right and wrong.

Feeling all at once depressed, Parris straightened the papers on his desk and was rising to leave, when there was a tap at his door. Miss Stolberg, the nurse in charge of the newly inaugurated musical therapy work, was there.

"Come in, Miss Stolberg. In trouble?"

"Not at all—quite the contrary. Can you give me a few minutes?"

"Certainly. Sit down."

"I want to talk to you about Vera Lichinsky."

"I've been wanting to ask how she's responding."

"It's unbelievable, Doctor. She's so much improved that I want to ask if I may take her to stay in my apartment. I have an extra room where she can practice without disturbing anyone."

"I see no reason why you should not take charge of her if you wish."

"I know so little of her past history, Doctor, but she is so unusual that I'd like to know more."

"Vera was a classmate of mine in public school. She was gifted and worked like a slave at her music. She was driven by a father who concentrated all his own frustrated love of music in the child. He determined to make a great violinist of her—and he succeeded. She had no childhood—as such. She went early to Berlin, studied, made a sensational success as a concert artist, and after a short career—found suddenly that she could no longer play. That is the history of the case."

"Did no one diagnose her trouble?"

"Seiss of Vienna tried, and later I talked with her here. The truth is, she diagnosed her own trouble with surprising accuracy, but she couldn't rid herself of *fear*. Strangely enough, she was afraid of being shut up here in this hospital—and finally she *committed herself*."

"Well, I'm happy to report that she is practicing for hours at a time, and with growing enthusiasm. She wants to talk with you. May I send her in—now?"

"Yes, of course."

Vera Lichinsky stood quite still with her violin hanging at her side. She held it with seeming carelessness as violinists do after long years of acquaintance with their instruments. She was pale, and her lusterless hair was carelessly pinned back from her thin face, but her eyes were clear and she looked frankly at Dr. Mitchell, waiting for him to speak.

"Sit down, Vera. I want to know how you are getting along with your practice."

"Parris, you are a friend as well as a physician to me. What you have done for me since I have been here is really incredible. This—" she swept her violin to her shoulder dramatically—"this is the treatment I needed. I had been starved—had starved myself. God knows why. But now I am beginning to play—*really* play."

"I felt sure you would, Vera, given time to rest and think things out. You've been a remarkable patient."

"I have a suggestion to make, Parris. Could you get some instruments for us? I'd like to organize a small orchestra among the patients here. There are a few really good musicians in the hospital. What the pianos and—and my fiddle have done should prove the value of music as a curative agent. Can't we do that?"

"It's a fine idea, Vera. Would you direct such a group?"

"Miss Stolberg would direct it. I could be concertmaster." Vera's eyes were sparkling.

"I'll see what can be done, Vera. Miss Stolberg tells me you are going to share her apartment. You'll have more time to practice there."

"Parris, I'm going to be ready before long for concerts again, just as you promised me. How did you have the patience to work with me so long?"

"You must have been bored a great deal of the time by the endless repetitions of certain routines."

"No," she protested, "I think I'm too much of an egocentric to be bored as long as we talked about Vera Lichinsky. Maybe that's why I wanted to be a concert artist anyhow—just sheer exhibitionism."

"I think not. You simply gave your heart to music. You are still young, Vera. An interrupted career is not fatal. When you feel that you are ready, you'll go east and place yourself in the hands of a reliable manager and you'll make a new success for yourself."

"I want to make money," she said unexpectedly.

"Money? Why?"

"For the first time in my life, Parris, I'm thinking of someone other than myself. I've been thinking of my brother Amos."

"What about Amos?"

"He always wanted to paint—to be an artist. His head was always full of pictures—but he had to keep the shop. After Father's death Amos had to make a living for—for me as well as himself. He never had a chance to do what he wanted to do."

"He doesn't complain. I've talked with him often. His only concern has been about you."

"I know—but Amos can *still* have a chance to do what he wants—if I can make some money. Do you really think I can?"

"I'm convinced of it."

"Money's another thing I never thought about. There was always enough for my needs. What is money, anyhow?"

"My grandmother used to say that there were two kinds of money —the kind that was flat and could be stacked and the round kind that rolled. I'm afraid mine has been of the latter variety."

Vera laughed aloud. At the sound, a look of astonishment spread across her face. "Do you realize, Parris, that this is the first time I've laughed in—in ten years?"

"Enjoy it?"

"Loved it. I'm a happy woman, Parris Mitchell, and I have you to thank—you and Miss Stolberg."

"And your own good sense. I have a favor to ask of you, Vera."

"Ask it."

"Will you come to our apartment on Sunday afternoon and play for my wife and Mr. Lenz? I'll play your accompaniments."

Vera was silent for a moment, examining her own mind. All at once she made her decision. "I'll be glad to, Parris."

He drew a breath of relief—of satisfaction. This was more than he had hoped for.

"This is a good beginning—almost an end in itself, isn't it, Parris?" Vera asked soberly.

"You've won a victory—a real one."

Donny Green looked nervously at his watch and slowed his step. He was a little early for his appointment. The truth was he didn't want to see Dr. Mitchell at all, but Hazel had put it squarely up to him. Either he had to go see Parris Mitchell or she would tell Fulmer he'd been hanging around the girls' playground. He wondered uneasily just how much Hazel had found out. Why did she want to drag Parris Mitchell into this, anyhow, he thought resentfully. He was just nervous—just jumpy here lately. He didn't see the connection. But anything was better than having to face Fulmer. Fulmer could be mean as the devil when he was mad. Well, there was nothing he could do about it. Hazel said he had to go—or *else*!

He looked warily up and down the street and turned into Dr. Mitchell's office.

Parris' trained eye recognized the uncertainty that lay behind the brazen air that Donny affected. A quick glance revealed the shaking hands and the unnaturally expanded pupils of his beautifully set blue eyes. A handsome boy, he thought, but lacking the ingratiating manner of his brother.

After a few preliminary questions, Parris offered the boy a cigarette. The act of lighting it seemed to restore Donny's poise. He leaned back in his chair and looked for the first time straight into Parris' eyes.

[41]

"I don't know what I'm doing here, Dr. Mitchell. You work with crazy people and I'm not crazy. Hazel sent me because I'm—I'm all shot to pieces."

"I can see that. What's wrong?"

The boy hesitated, then said, "I've got to get some advice. I think you're a doctor who wouldn't gab."

"Why, of course, Donny. It's unthinkable that any physician would betray a confidence."

"That's what *you* think. I wouldn't trust 'em—most of 'em. But—" Again he hesitated.

"Donny, you've come for help or you wouldn't be here. What's the trouble?"

"Didn't Hazel tell you?"

"She only asked me to see you.

Donny lifted his head and asked defiantly, "Well, what do you want to know?"

"Only what you wish to tell me."

"I don't know what makes me so nervous—unless it's—Fulmer.

"Fulmer?"

"Everybody thinks how good he is to me."

"And isn't he?"

Donny laughed mirthlessly. "Listen, Doctor, I'm fed up with—with belonging to Fulmer. I want a little freedom."

"That's a natural wish. No one wants to be *possessed.*"

Donny looked sharply at Parris, a quick flush spreading over his face. "I like *girls,* Doctor, and—Fulmer watches me like a hawk. He's treated me like a—like a *sweetheart* ever since I was a kid." He hesitated, then in sudden desperation, "Jesus Christ, Doctor, I've got to get free of this sickening business and I don't know how."

"The solution is simple. Live somewhere else."

"On what?"

"Go to work. You're old enough to get a job."

"I don't know how to do anything. I don't want to work."

"Have you told Fulmer how you feel?"

"Christ, no! He'd—he'd probably kill me. Even Hazel can't talk to Fulmer. He flies off the handle too easy. Nobody can tell Fulmer anything. He's so God-damned sure he's right about everything."

"You should probably talk more with Hazel. She wants to help you."

"Hazel thinks I was born bad."

"You're mistaken about that. She knows people aren't born bad—that conditioned responses have been learned. They aren't biological."

"Do you mean that when I do something wrong it's because somebody taught me to do it?"

"Not exactly, Donny, but a casual remark may result in an emotional conditioning that persists all through your life—and may result in disaster."

"Gee, that's an idea. You know, Doctor, I'd like to know more about this stuff."

"Donny, there's very little any outsider can do about your problem. You'll have to solve it yourself, but you must break off this unfortunate relationship. That is an absolute necessity—for the sake of your mental health. You've got to live a normal life—free of the kind of dependence on your brother you feel now."

"I don't see how it's goin' to work out. I've thought about it until I'm nearly crazy."

"Get Fulmer to send you to the university."

Donny narrowed his eyes with dawning suspicion. "That's what Fulmer wants me to do—but I'm not going."

"Why not?"

"I hate school—but at least I can get by here at Aberdeen. Fulmer pays a coach to help me keep up, but I couldn't have one at the university."

"You're trumping up alibis."

Donny flushed angrily. "If that's all the help I get from you, I'm wasting my time."

"I'm offering you practical advice—trying to make the break easy for you."

"Sure, but the things you want me to do are—well, out of the question."

Parris was touched, looking at the distraught young face. A weak face, but not really vicious, he thought. "Donny, you are allowing anxieties and hostilities to pile up until your mind is completely baffled. If it finds no way to get through the barriers set up, you'll hide from yourself—escape through secret doors and lose yourself in the dark."

"Those are just words. They don't mean a darned thing to me."

"Would you be willing to come to talk with me at least once a week for a while, and let me explain what I'm trying to tell you?"

"No, I guess I'd better not. Fulmer would have a double-action fit if he knew I came here."

"I'm afraid in that case there's not much I can do to help you. A psychiatrist—"

"Good Lord, Doctor, I didn't come for that kind of fancy stuff. Hazel thought I ought to get advice from some doctor about—about my nervousness and I wanted to talk to *somebody*—just to get some things out of my system."

"I see. You were looking for a *'father confessor,'* as it were."

Donny laughed then and his tension lessened. "Something like that. But," with sudden suspicion, "I'll probably do nothing about it. Old Fulmer's been good to me. How do I know you and Hazel haven't cooked up this scheme just to turn Fulmer against me?"

Parris rose and stood waiting for his visitor to leave. He felt himself growing cold inside, a certain precursor of an uncontrollable rage. He was able to check it, reminding himself of what he had been told so often—that no good analyst ever permitted himself to resent anything a patient said or did.

"I didn't really mean that, Dr. Mitchell. I've got so I'm suspicious of everybody." Donny was abjectly apologetic. "But honest to goodness, I'm as much in the dark as ever. I don't know what I'm going to do." He waited a moment, but Parris said nothing. "Give me time to think things over, Doctor. Maybe we can work something out."

"You'll have to be less hostile if you want help from me. Suppose we forget all about this interview?"

"I made you mad, didn't I?"

"No."

Donny glanced apprehensively at Parris and got himself awkwardly out of the office. Parris turned to the telephone.

Reporting the interview to Hazel, he carefully omitted any mention of Donny's admission of his relation with his brother. At the moment Parris' resentment at Donny's crude behavior extended to Hazel. She had thrust this interview upon him and now he found

[44]

himself the unwilling possessor of damaging information about the Greens.

Donny, on his part, was in a state of acute embarrassment. Why had he told that stuff to Parris Mitchell—of all people? Hazel got him into this, damn her. One thing was certain. He'd not go near that place again. Funny, though, Dr. Mitchell had said some things that sounded interesting—all that about not being born bad. He'd like to know about that. Oh, what the hell!

One spring day Punch Rayne and Dyanna Slater had discovered the old von Eln orchard and the willow-bordered pond, and they had begun to think of the place as their own.

They lived in Jinktown, that small group of houses at the foot of Aberdeen Hill, and as children they had played in its narrow streets. But now it was different, for they were deeply in love.

Walker Rayne, nicknamed "Punch," was an orphan and seemed older than his seventeen years. Life for the underprivileged in Kings Row was hard enough at best, but in his case a sense of being unwanted had contributed to a kind of timid repression and deprived him of the free look of youth. He was stocky, muscular, and exceptionally shy. His eyes were brown and long-lashed and serious. A lock of dark hair dropped across a wide brow. He had a way of thrusting it back with an angry gesture that utterly belied the simple and patient nature that was his.

Just now he was concerned with one thing only—Dyanna. He must get a better job so he could take care of her. He must do so well that her Aunt Carrie would let them get married. Of course, Dyanna was only fifteen, but they were willing to wait until her sixteenth birthday. That was a long way off, it seemed to him.

Walking along the avenue of cedars, his arm around Dyanna's waist, he realized how thin and frail she was. The color in her pretty face reminded him of the pink hyacinths they had seen blooming here in the spring, but maybe the color meant she was happy just walking with him. A swift stab of apprehension ran along his nerves. What if Dyanna should get sick? What if she should die? He drew the little figure closer and their steps slowed.

"Let's go sit by the pond, honey. Ain't you tired?"

"Not a bit, Punch. It's a wonderful day. But it's nice in the shade down there. Let's run!"

"Maybe it's too hot for you to run, Dyanna. You're so little an' all."

Dyanna laughed and ran down the slope with a lightness that was like dancing. She wore her happiness like an aura. Punch followed more slowly. He felt a curious tightness in his throat. Surely nothing in the world had ever been so beautiful as that slip of a girl running across the tangled grass. Her shabby clothes could not spoil the picture for him. He did not know they were ill-fitting and unbecoming. To him she was lovely.

Maybe, he thought shamefacedly, he would not be able to wait until she was sixteen, until he had a better job. Maybe Aunt Carrie would understand how he felt if he could only talk—only say what he felt for Dyanna. But, he knew despairingly, he'd never be able to think up the right words. Aunt Carrie would be hard to convince.

When he caught up with Dyanna he was hunting frantically for something to say that would show her what he was feeling. They sat down on the ledge of rock just above the spring that fed the pond.

"Dyanna, you love your Aunt Carrie a lot, don't you?"

"Why, yes, I guess I do. We don't never talk about it none, her an' me. I'm all she's got, though I guess I don't rightly belong to her. She took me in when I was too little to know anything, an' she's been awful good to me. She does for me like I was her own child. I'm awful beholden to her. She was all I had, too"—Dyanna looked timidly away—"till you an' me—"

"Found out we loved each other?" Punch spoke boldly enough now that he saw Dyanna floundering in embarrassment.

"I guess Aunt Carrie'd just about die if anything happened to me. Like I said, I'm all she's got."

"And believe me, honey, she's lucky to have anything as sweet as you around."

"You're just talkin' to hear yourself talk! I bet you don't mean it."

"I got half a mind to show you how much I mean it, but I reckon I hadn't better."

"Dare you, mister!"

"You just wait! Dyanna, what you reckon your Aunt Carrie will do when we get married?"

Dyanna pulled up a blade of grass and chewed it speculatively before she answered. "She'll want us to live with her. I got a room of my own an' you could live there with us."

"I wasn't exactly figurin' on that," Punch said. "I figure I can take care of you an' get us a house to live in. I'm gonna get me a new job."

"Well, we don't need to talk about that for a long time, yet. I ain't but fifteen an' I know she won't let me get married till I'm real grown up."

"When folks are grown up enough to be in love, they're grown up enough to get married, an' I don't see no sense in waitin'. Dyanna, I'm lovin' you so much that I'm hurtin'. Maybe if we don't get married pretty soon somebody might take you away from me. I couldn't stand that. I believe I'd *kill* anybody that tried to take you away from me."

"Nobody's ever goin' to try, Punch. I'd tell anybody in the world that I'm your girl an' I've got no time for other folks."

"Aw, Dyanna, you're awful sweet. I can't hardly keep my hands off you, but I reckon I got to."

"I ain't skeered."

"*I* am. But I'm gonna ask Aunt Carrie soon's I get my job."

"You can't surprise her. She caught me tellin' my fortune with apple seeds an' she said, 'You thinkin' about that Punch Rayne?' an' I said maybe I was."

Punch had been lying back, resting on his elbow, but he sat up quickly and asked excitedly, "Was she mad, honey, do you think?"

"Of course she wasn't mad. Just sort of teasin' me about my fortune an' all."

"Maybe she'll let us!"

"Let us what, silly?"

"Let us get married."

"Well, I don't know," Dyanna said doubtfully.

"Gee, Dyanna, seems as if I can't stand it any longer not havin' you. It ain't right. Honest, it ain't. You got no idea how a feller feels when he loves a girl like I do you."

"I do, too, know how you feel. I got feelings my own self. If we can't get married for a long time I aim to be with you just the same."

"What you mean, Dyanna?" Punch asked breathlessly.

[47]

"Just what I said. I aim to be happy while I can. You might go away or—or somethin', an' I wouldn't ever know what it was like to—to—be right close up to you like we was married."

"Honey, I'm gonna talk to Aunt Carrie tomorrow an' she's just got to do what we want. Listen, Dyanna, how about meetin' me Sunday night an' comin' out here for a little while? We got to talk about our plans. I got to go in town now to see Mr. Dyer. He promised me a job at the butcher shop an' I want to see him before he goes home."

"Aunt Carrie might not like me to come out here at night."

"It's all right to come with me. I don't mean you no harm, but I just got to be with you, honey. I'll die if we can't fix it so's we can get married."

"All right, Punch. I got to tell Aunt Carrie, though. I ain't ever been anywhere at night by myself."

"I better come by an' get you at home. Aunt Carrie won't care if you come walkin' with me."

For a week after his talk with Dr. Mitchell, Donny Green went about sullen and morose. His hostility to Parris Mitchell was mounting with his unease. Suppose Fulmer should find out that he had told Parris—had told him the truth? What would Fulmer do? Probably kick him out. No use talking, he'd have to do something to get in solid with Fulmer so if he *did* find out about the visit, it wouldn't make so much difference. Somehow he felt sure the doctor wouldn't tell, but there was Hazel. She might let it out sometime when she and Fulmer were having a run-in. Pity there wasn't some way to set Fulmer against *both* of them and then—to hell with the two of them!

Donny had started out this Friday afternoon with the intention of walking down to the Jinktown playground. He'd show Hazel she couldn't boss him around. But when he reached the foot of the hill he saw Hazel's car and he turned off and followed the road to the von Eln place.

As he approached the big front gates he saw Dr. Mitchell and his wife and Randy McHugh leaving the place in Dr. Mitchell's car. Donny's blue eyes narrowed to calculating slits and then opened with interest as he thought, I bet he's planning to buy this place back. Fulmer might like to know that. Gee, this was a break. This would get him on the good side of Fulmer.

Just then Donny saw the little Jinktown couple turn into the gates. He decided to trail them and see what they were doing.

Taking a short cut through the willow thicket, he had just reached the seclusion of an overgrown ditch when he heard Punch and Dyanna coming down the slope. He hoped they wouldn't see him but if they did he would tell them he was looking over the place for Fulmer. Everybody knew Fulmer was in the legislature and had a perfect right to know what was happening on state lands. But Punch and Dyanna evidently weren't up to anything they wanted to hide. They sat at the edge of the spring where anybody passing could see. Oh, a few kisses and a little hand-holding, but nothing really interesting. Donny wished they would hurry up and leave. He wasn't too comfortable crouched down like that. All at once, he lifted his head to listen more closely. They were planning to meet here Sunday night. Now that was something like!

As soon as Punch and Dyanna had gone, Donny hurried away to find his crony Elwee Neal. He'd get Elwee to come back here with him Sunday night and they'd have some fun. Punch Rayne had no business running around with that pretty little Slater kid, anyhow, he thought. Donny had seen her several times when he had been down in Jinktown on errands for Fulmer, or on shadier business of his own. They would give Punch a good scare. Who'd he think he was, anyway?

On his way to the hardware store where Elwee Neal had a summer job, Donny decided to drop in at Fulmer's office first and tell him about seeing Parris Mitchell at the von Eln place.

Fulmer Green sat at his desk, frowning over a list of figures that evidently displeased him. His close-set blue eyes stared unbelievingly at the page and a wave of red spread from his thick neck up into his heavy, handsome face. He reached for a cigarette without lifting his eyes, found a match, and lighted it, still without looking, then with a muttered "Damn!" he leaned back in his chair and sighed heavily.

His expression warmed into an affectionate grin when he saw that it was his young brother whose shadow fell across the desk. There were exactly two people in the world Fulmer really loved, his brother Donny and his own young son, Prentiss.

"Hello, Don, what's on your mind?"

"Plenty."

"Spill it."

"I was out on the von Eln place today projecting around, and I saw Parris Mitchell there."

"So what? His old home, isn't it?"

"Bet you a nickel he's figuring on buying it back from the state. Randy McHugh was with him."

Fulmer's head came up with a jerk. "Randy McHugh? Wonder what his wife would think of that?"

"Oh, shucks, Fulmer, Mrs. Mitchell was with 'em. That ain't what I'm talkin' about. Couldn't you get an option on the place and sort of hold him up? He's got the money and you might pick up a tidy little sum. If I know Dr. Mitchell he wouldn't stand back on a little difference in price."

"You don't know Parris Mitchell if you think it's easy to put anything over on him. He's got plenty of sense if he does seem to have his head in the clouds. And there's Randy McHugh to reckon with."

Donny knew the way Fulmer's mind worked and it always irritated him. It was Fulmer's habit to combat suggestions until he had seen for himself all the weaknesses of a scheme.

"No—lookit here," he persisted. "I'm bringing you a hot tip, Fulmer, and you haven't sense enough to realize it."

"No use to go off half-cocked. You have to think these things out. He can't buy it anyhow without a special act of the legislature. State lands are hard to transfer."

"How would he go about it?"

"Send in his bid and wait for the next session of the legislature before getting any action on it."

"That ought to make it a cinch for you. Get it fixed so you'll have first chance."

"You talk like a damn fool, Don."

"Looks easy as fallin' off a log to me."

"I'll be up there, but so will several hundred lobbyists. Nolan's got influence, and if Parris Mitchell wants to buy state land it will take some doing to keep him from getting it. I don't know why it is, but Paul Nolan's got a lot of people behind him," he added irritably.

"You got influence, yourself. All you need do is to get a move on."

"Maybe. Dave Kettring's the man to watch. He and Nolan are

thick as thieves, and he's really smart, that Kettring. I remember that time we had the run-in about the university—say, there, I knew there was something I wanted to talk to you about!"

"Oh, gosh, Fulmer, don't get going on that school stuff again. I've definitely made up my mind I'm not going to the university. Elwee Neal's not going, either."

"I don't give a damn what that bum does, but you're different, Don. You're a good-looking chap—"

"Aw, Fulmer," Donny's voice took on a whining note, "you know how I feel about you. I—I can't stand the idea of being away from you like that."

A slow flush spread over Fulmer's face and the lines about his mouth slackened, but he did not look at Donny, whose half-closed eyes were watching his brother sharply.

"Fulmer, you mean everything to me. What do I care about an education—or anything that keeps me away from you?"

Fulmer spoke with an evident effort. "Don, you've got plenty of brains and I want to see you make something of yourself."

"What do you mean, make something of myself?"

"You ought to be ready to take over here when I give out. That's why I want you to go to the university and get an education."

"Why can't I stay here and learn the business from you? I'll bet you learned more from experience than you ever did at law school."

"Don, you don't even know what I'm talking about. I want to see you take your rightful place in the community. There's not a boy in Kings Row who has a better chance than I'm giving you right now. Not even the Pomeroy boys."

"Oh, those nuts."

"I wouldn't exactly call them nuts. There's Ross doing graduate work at Harvard, and McKay in the junior class at the university. You're the same age as McKay and you aren't anywhere yet."

"I sure wouldn't want to grub like those boys. Their old man's got plenty of dough to leave 'em well fixed, anyhow. I don't see why they don't stop and have a little fun."

"They have fun enough. They don't need to run around with a lot of hoodlums to have their kind of fun. That's exactly what I'm talking about. You'd be a lot better off if you'd run with their crowd."

[51]

"Too damned stuffy for my taste. Those boys are stand-offish anyhow. They think they're better than the rest of us."

Fulmer's face purpled slowly and he leaned across his desk, pounding softly with his fist to accent his words. "Never let me hear you say a thing like that again, Don. Nobody's better than we are, do you hear? *Nobody!*"

That got under his skin—does it every time, Donny thought. "It don't get me fussed up none," he said airily. "I just say to myself I'm Fulmer Green's brother and that's something in this town—in this state, too." With that he placed his hat on his crisply curling blond head at a particularly jaunty angle, adjusted his green striped tie, and with an airy "So long" walked out of the office.

Out of Fulmer's sight Donny drew a breath of relief. He looked at the courthouse clock and quickened his gait. It was time for Ned Porter's store to be closed and Elwee Neal would be waiting.

Ned Porter had gone home, leaving Elwee Neal to sweep out and lock up the store. The boy set about this last job of the day with a reluctance of movement that showed boredom rather than fatigue. He was still sprinkling the oiled sawdust on the floor, tossing it out with wide, careless sweeps of his right arm, when Donny came in.

Elwee grunted an acknowledgment of his friend's presence.

Donny took a seat on the wooden counter, his legs swinging. "Hurry up, kid. I want to talk to you—private."

Elwee tossed the sawdust sack aside and took a broom from its resting place against the wall. "Talk," he invited. He had a high-pitched, childish voice. "Old squint-eye Porter's gone."

Donny followed him to the front door and moved with him slowly, talking all the way, as Elwee swept toward the back of the store. "And there they were, Elwee, two smart-aleck Jinktowners—sitting out there horsing around just like it was their own front yard. On state property!"

Elwee paused in his sweeping. "Horsing around?" Elwee had no interest in state property or what was done on it, but he had a great deal of enthusiasm for titillating gossip. "What were they doing, exactly?"

"Well, old Punch had his arm around Dyanna's waist—"

"Was he kissing her? I mean did she let him?"

"Well, not exactly—not while I was looking, that is. But like I say, they are meeting there Sunday night." He winked. "And, boy, you know what that means. When a girl will' sneak off to meet a boy at night—"

"Gee, wouldn't you love to be right there an' see 'em get hot? I bet Punch is a humdinger."

"Bet anybody'd be with that pretty kid."

"Boy, I wish I was in his shoes. She's a good-looker, ain't she?"

"Too pretty to be wastin' herself on Punch Rayne."

"Say, maybe we could take her away from him. I'd like to get me a piece."

"Me, too. This might be a good chance."

"How you mean?"

"We could do it, maybe."

Elwee resumed his sweeping, thoughtfully. "Awright," he said, "I'll go with you."

Donny had been glancing furtively, as they talked, toward a glass case in which were displayed a pair of pistols and a shotgun. Now he walked over to the case and leaned against it. "We could have some fun," he suggested, "if you had nerve enough to borrow one of these guns to take with us. We could scare the living daylights out of old Punch."

Elwee shook his head. "Mr. Porter might find out."

"Aw, come on, Elwee, don't be a sissy." Donny slid back the glass door and lifted out one of the pistols. "Stick 'em up," he commanded, pointing the pistol at a water tank near by. He lowered his naturally gruff voice, coarsened it until it had a guttural sound. "You're on state property, boy. Start runnin' or I'll drill you so full of holes you'll look like Swiss cheese!"

Elwee laughed and added his bit. "Make tracks, boy, or eat lead!" He was beginning to see dramatic possibilities in Donny's plan. He took the gun into his hands and gripped it experimentally. "Do you think, he asked slowly, we could maybe borrow a couple of these— and nobody would find out?"

Donny's voice was casual and assured. "Sure, boy. Sure. You open up Monday mornin' don't you? All you got to do would be to put 'em back before old man Porter comes in."

Elwee leaned on his broom and chewed his lip, considering. It did seem simple enough. Maybe they'd scare old Punch away, and then Dyanna would be left there. Pretty kid, that Dyanna Slater. He'd walk home with her and maybe he could get her off in the woods with him. After all, a girl who goes out alone—at night—

He grinned. "It's a deal. Come by my house about eight-thirty. I'll have the guns."

Donny nodded. "Bullets, too?"

"Bullets? Hell, no! What do you think this is? It's risky enough just takin' the guns!"

Donny laughed. "Awright, awright. Take it easy, boy. The guns'll be enough to handle a Jinktowner."

6

The willow branches stirred in the night breeze that swept the von Eln place, making a slow-moving pattern of shadows on the moonlit water of the pond. Punch, his arm about Dyanna's shoulders as they sat silently together on a rock, looked at the shadows, then slowly, turning his head, at the trees and shrubs and wide grassy fields that stretched out behind him.

"This place—" he struggled for words with which to describe his feeling, a feeling all the more intense because he could not express it. "This place, Dyanna—it's like you, sort of."

She let her head come to rest, gently, on his shoulder. "What you mean, Punch?"

"Well—it's sort of peaceful, and—well, *nice*. It's clean, and cool. It smells clean, out here. Like your hair smells when I'm standing close to you."

At her quick laugh he spoke in a rush of words, defensively. "Well —aw—you know what I mean. It's *nice*. Not hot and dirty and smoky like it is in town."

Dyanna turned her head lazily and gave him a quick kiss on the cheek. "I know, Punch. I know what you're tryin' to say."

He sighed, relieved and happy, and rubbed his cheek against the top of her head.

"Punch." Her voice was drowsy, lush with content.

"Yeah?"

"Let's get us a farm, Punch, after we're married. If we work hard and save our money, maybe we can buy us a little chicken farm."

He caught her mood, answering, "And then we would build us a house—a big log house, maybe, with a fireplace tall enough to stand in. I could do it myself, with a little help. We'd have a farm and a house—"

"And Aunt Carrie could live with us."

"And we'd raise eatin' chickens and sell 'em to those truck men that buy for the St. Louis hotels."

"And make lots of money, Punch!"

"And raise our kids in the fresh air and sunshine, with plenty of milk to drink."

They laughed, giddily, happily. His arm tightened about her shoulder.

Dyanna broke a short silence with a chuckle. "I hinted somethin' to Aunt Carrie at supper tonight, about me maybe wanting to get married one of these days, and you know what she said?"

"What?"

"She looked at me in that calculatin' way she has, an' she said, 'Well, Dynnie'—she calls me that sometimes—'I reckon I couldn't ask for no better thing than to see you married to a good honest boy like Punch Rayne.'"

"Did she say that, honest?"

"Honest. Looks like it won't be so long now. Just you get yourself a good job and—" She sat up quickly. "What time you reckon it is? I told Aunt Carrie I'd be home by ten."

"It's early yet," Punch said, looking up at the moon.

The movement of a bush close behind him in the darkness made him turn his head. "What was that?"

Dyanna stood up. "Who's there?" she called.

The voice that answered was gruff, unfamiliar. "We're guards on this place. This is state property."

Another voice added, "Don't you know you're trespassin', breakin' the law? You got no business up here at night."

Punch, vaguely suspicious of "guards" who hid themselves behind bushes while they talked, rose and moved around the rock, peering into the darkness. "Where are you?" he demanded. "We ain't hurtin' anything."

Suddenly a pistol thrust forward out of the concealing brush, its

[55]

barrel glinting in the moonlight. It was followed a moment later by another. "Halt!"

The sight of the pistols was enough to convince Punch of the authenticity of the guards. No one in Kings Row carried a gun unless he was an officer of the law. Frightened, he stepped back and caught Dyanna's arm, ready to retreat. "We ain't doin' nothing," he explained earnestly. "We was about to go, anyhow."

"Well, you better get on out of here—and quick. We'll see that this girl gets home safe to her folks."

Punch's grip on Dyanna's arm tightened. "I'll take her on home myself."

"No you won't. She ain't safe with you, and you'd better be glad we ain't tellin'. Now you get on out of here or we'll fill you full of holes."

Dyanna, wide-eyed with terror, urged, "Go on, Punch. I'll run along home by myself."

Punch stood his ground. "I'm goin'," he told the invisible men, "and I'm goin' peaceable. But I'm takin' my girl *with* me."

"All right, boy—" A masked figure, taller than Punch, broke through the branches of the shrub. Dyanna screamed.

Too late, Punched ducked. The butt end of the upraised pistol came down on the back of his bent head. He sagged unconscious to the ground.

Sobbing, hysterical, Dyanna stumbled forward toward the attacker. "You yellow dog!" she gasped. A Jinktown phrase sprang welcome to her lips. "You dirty bastard!" She clawed wildly at his face, trying to tear away the handkerchief that masked it.

The man retreated, grunting unintelligibly, throwing up his arms in self-defense. Dyanna kicked at his legs, she threw her whole weight against him, blindly, in a headlong lunge, not knowing or caring what she did.

Suddenly her arms were seized from behind and she felt herself jerked upright and pinned against the attacker from the rear. Strong arms encased her, clasped themselves over her breasts, pinning her own arms tightly against her sides.

She twisted, sobbing, and kicked backward. Her heel struck into the man's shin. He cursed.

"You little hellcat," he panted.

Struggling, they fell and rolled on the ground.

Donny Green, brave enough now that Elwee had come to his rescue, came close and stood over them, gun in hand. He wiped his hand across his forehead. "She scratched the hell out of my face," he whined. "Damned little she-devil! I oughta wring her neck, girl or no girl."

Elwee Neal, the struggling girl pinned beneath him, laughed excitedly. "Wring her neck, hell," he panted. "Just gimme a little help with this wildcat—I got a better idea!"

Punch woke—slowly, foggily—to a world so filled with pain that it blinded him. Twice he forced his eyes open and tried to focus them on what seemed to be a swaying tree limb above his head. They closed of their own accord. Through the pain, which shot through his head like incessant small electric shocks, one after the other, he tried to remember what it was he had to do. There was something urgent, something that required action—quick action—on his part. But he couldn't think, not with the pounding in his head. Not with the surging nausea that gripped him whenever he opened his eyes. He turned over on his side, weakly, and gave himself up to the sickness.

After a while he was able to sit up. Awareness came back. He knew where he was and what had happened. He wondered, dully and with a bitter sense of defeat, where Dyanna had gone, whether she had reached home safely. He rose and stumbled to the spring, where he lay flat on the ground and sloshed the cold water into his face. He rinsed his mouth, then drank deeply.

Immediately he felt better. He would be able to get up, he thought thankfully, in just a few minutes. Get up and go home. Find Dyanna. It must be awful late. Nearly midnight, to judge by the moon.

A small complaining sound, like the whimpering of a puppy, reached his ears. It came from the willow grove, from the other side of the big rock where he and Dyanna had sat—

Dyanna! He jumped to his feet, the throbbing in his head forgotten, and ran toward the sound.

She lay crumpled on her side, like a fallen bird. One arm was flung back, awkwardly, across the ground, hunching her shoulder. Stunned, he looked blankly at the torn clothing, the bared shoulders and breast, the twisted skirt—and for a long moment could not take in their significance.

[57]

He dropped to his knees beside her, mechanically rearranging her clothes while he tried to fight off the hideous knowledge that began to beat in on him. She had fallen, that was it. She had fainted. She had struck her head against the rock when she fell. Somehow, she had torn her clothes.

Desperately, he turned his face away, his dark eyes narrowed to shining slits, and looked out into the darkness. He spat, and spat again. She hadn't fallen. He faced it: the two "guards" had done this.

He jumped up and ran wildly, insanely, through the willow grove, looking behind trees, peering into bushes, striking out blindly with clenched fists at everything in his path, searching for two masked men he knew he would not find. Panting, he ran through an open field to the gate and looked up and down the road. He turned back, still running, and stumbled through the trees to the rock.

Gently he lifted the almost unconscious girl and carried her in his arms toward the road. She stirred feebly. "Punch," she whispered. "Punch, I'm hurt. Bad."

He felt the hot angry tears, held back until now, welling out of his eyes and rolling down his cheeks. He bent and kissed her gently.

"It's awright, Dyanna. We're goin' home."

Aunt Carrie Slater, when she opened the door of her cottage to Punch's urgent kick, was already in a state of agitation. She had her bonnet in her hand, ready to start on a hunt for her charge. She held the lamp high, studying the boy's face with a narrow-eyed, probing keenness. "What's the matter? Where you two been all this time?"

Her glance dropped to the girl in his arms and she gave a horrified gasp. "What's the matter with Dyanna?"

Punch strode past her and laid the girl gently on the bed. He threw a shawl over her. "She's bleeding bad," he said. "You better help her." His voice was dull, lifeless—and the words came slowly, haltingly, as if they had to be forced out one at a time from his throat. "Do what you can while I go for a doctor."

He turned away and started for the door.

The girl was awake, now, and crying softly.

Aunt Carrie caught his arm and shook it. "Did you do this, boy? If you did I'm goin' to kill you."

Punch looked at her, started to speak, then changed his mind.

He moved toward the door. "Dr. Waring?" he asked, tonelessly.

Carrie Slater's deep-lined face in the lamplight was like something carved out of stone, but she spoke softly, as if in apology. "He ain't in town, son. Git Dr. Mitchell, out to the asylum."

Punch turned back briefly. "I'm awful young," he said. "I know that, but I want to marry Dyanna. Right away. I can work."

He walked out into the night, turning at the gate toward the hospital at the end of Federal Street. He tilted his head a little to one side, in a listening attitude. The voices. "We're guards on this place. This is state property." That was the big voice. The gruff, heavy one. It belonged to the man who had hit him on the head.

His eyes narrowed, his whole face became alert as he strained to recapture the sound of the other—the lighter, higher voice. "You got no business up here at night." Yes, that one, too, he would remember. He must never forget it.

"We'll see this little girl gets home safe to her folks." Yes. Yes! He felt a strange excitement growing in him. He broke into a run. Now he had that one, the heavy one, for sure. Forever.

Parris Mitchell looked up at the ormolu clock on the mantel and closed the heavy volume he had been reading. He should have been in bed before midnight, he thought, since he was to be up earlier than usual in the morning. He had accepted an invitation to have breakfast with Father Donovan at the little rectory on Walnut Street.

As he was about to turn off the light, he was startled by an abrupt pounding on his door. A second, more insistent knock came before he could reach the door to open it. He was aware of some frantic urgency when he saw the disheveled boy standing there.

"Yes? Rayne, isn't it?"

"You got to come, Doctor."

"Where—"

"Come on." Punch half turned to go, impatient. "It's bad, Doctor."

Parris asked no questions. There was more than urgency in the boy's voice; there was desperation.

"I'll get my bag."

Parris stepped into the bedroom. Elise had not awakened. He hurriedly wrote a line saying he had been called to Jinktown, laid it on his pillow, and went out with Punch.

"We'll go in my car, Punch. It will be quicker that way."

At the cottage in Jinktown, Parris Mitchell worked swiftly and efficiently. He asked no questions; his physician's eyes, seeing Dyanna's ravaged body, read the essential facts of what had happened. After he had snapped shut his bag, he turned to Aunt Carrie.

"She'll sleep now. I'll be back tomorrow."

"Will she—" Aunt Carrie's hands fluttered nervously. "Doctor, will she—will she be all right?"

Parris nodded slowly. "Yes," he said, "she's suffering from shock now. But she'll be quite all right—very soon."

"Oh, thank the Lord, Dr. Mitchell. You think we can—can keep this quiet, Doctor?" The old lady's voice broke pitifully.

"Yes—unless there's some way to find out who—"

"Punch didn't do it, Doctor."

"I know."

"They don't know who it was. The men was masked."

Parris was silent for a moment. "For the present, I think you should say nothing. Later, we can decide."

"Dyanna might want to tell Miss Randy. I don't know."

"Wait until Dyanna is well again and then decide about it. Where is the boy?"

"Punch?"

"Yes. I just want to see if he's all right."

"Why—" the old woman looked puzzled. "Punch wasn't hurt so bad, was he?"

"Never mind."

Wearily, Parris left the cottage. Young bodies were hard; they healed readily, quickly. But, he reflected with bitterness, what of their minds? In a few weeks the girl would be perfectly sound—physically. Punch Rayne hadn't been "hurt so bad," either, but Parris knew that the events of this night could injure Punch far more than the girl.

Punch returned to the cottage after Dr. Mitchell had left. He sat on an upended soapbox near the bed and held the sleeping girl's hand. The sedative had done its work; her breathing was slow and even. The small hand in his was limp.

"She's restin' now," he told Aunt Carrie. Having spoken, he be-

[60]

came very still, tilting his head to one side and looking upward toward the ceiling of the low room.

Aunt Carrie, busy at the stove across the room, turned and looked at him curiously. That was the fourth time Punch had made that same remark in the last ten minutes. He acted like a boy gone out of his head. "I know, son. She's all right."

She crossed the room to lay a hand on his shoulder. "Drink some coffee, Punch. Might do you good."

He shook his head.

The old woman sighed and walked across the room to the oil lamp that burned in the window. She leaned down to lower the wick and blow out the flame. Without turning to face him, she said, "Daylight's comin'." She straightened her shoulders. "You don't know who it was?"

The boy's voice sounded old, old and tired. "No, ma'am. It was dark where they was hidin', an' we couldn't see their faces."

There was a long silence, while Aunt Carrie came to the bed and laid a brown, calloused hand across the sleeping girl's forehead.

Punch looked up at her and Aunt Carrie drew back, startled and vaguely uneasy at the change that came, all in a moment, over his face. Even as she watched, the dark, heavy-lidded eyes, usually so childlike and trusting behind their thick lashes, grew hard and crafty. One corner of his wide mouth lifted into a hideous grin—a cruel, triumphant grin.

"I didn't see their faces," he whispered. He spoke carefully, as if to a conspirator—as if it were vitally important that she understand. "But I'll remember their voices. Yes," he promised her hoarsely, "I'll remember."

He rose suddenly and ran out of the house into the gray dawn.

At the sagging gate he stopped short. He looked up and down the street. "I'll find 'em." He spoke aloud, and laughed mirthlessly. "I'll find 'em, if it takes all my life. And then—" he pounded one fist against the gatepost, "I'll kill 'em—I'll kill 'em both. I'll chop 'em up into little pieces. Nice an' slow. Inch by inch."

Fulmer Green had been unable to sleep. Now, at two in the morning, he was still restless, still tossing in his bed. He raised himself on one elbow, listened intently as he heard Donny's furtive entrance into the house—the tiptoeing up the stairs, the stealthy crossing of the upstairs hall to the door of the back bedroom. Angrily, yet somehow relieved and oddly pleased that he had found an object on which to vent some of his pent-up anger, Fulmer threw back the sheet that covered him and got out of bed. Wearily he ran his stubby fingers through his stiff blond hair, then tugged fretfully at the wrinkled, sweat-dampened pajama coat that clung to his stocky body.

He padded barefoot down the hall, glancing uneasily at Hazel's door as he passed, and threw open the door to Donny's room. "Donny!" He blinked a little against the light that stung his eyes. "Fine time of night for you to be getting in, I must say—where the hell've you been?"

Then he noticed what Donny was doing. The anger he had been nursing turned into a chill of apprehension. Donny's face was bleeding and the boy was trying to bandage it. His eyes, turned hastily on Fulmer, were terror-filled. Donny actually shrank back against the wall under his brother's amazed stare.

Fulmer advanced across the room and looked closely into the boy's face. "How'd you get cut up like that? Who—"

Donny's voice was weak, his face chalk-white. "Aw—it's just a couple o' scratches."

Fulmer watched him narrowly. There was more to this, he could see, than Donny was willing to tell. He had never seen Donny so agitated before—why, the boy's hands shook as though he had a chill.

"Tell me—and be quick," he ordered. He gripped Donny's shoulder. "You in trouble?"

Donny hesitated, obviously torn between caution and the desire for help. Then his face broke up like a child's about to cry. "Gosh, Fulmer—I'm in a mess, I reckon." His voice took on a whining note. "I didn't mean to get into trouble—it wasn't my fault any more'n Elwee's—" He began to cry, weakly, holding the loose bandage against his badly scratched cheek. Slowly, through his agonized gulpings, he got out the story of the night's events. It was an interesting, a terrifying story, but inaccurate. Donny's version was intended to lead Fulmer to believe that the whole plan had been Elwee's idea, and that he, Donny, had done nothing except in self-defense.

Fulmer was not a fool. He filled in the blank spots in the story, he salted down the protests of innocence, until he had the whole affair, and Donny's part in it, pretty well figured out. His first impulse was to draw back his fist and knock the boy flat. He was enraged at the foolhardiness of the act. Only the knowledge that a beating would not help matters, that the damage was already done, made him un-curl his fist. "Don't hand me that malarky," he said menacingly, "about you not touching the girl. You had to get close enough to her to get your damn' face scratched."

Donny avoided his brother's eyes.

They sat until daylight, arguing and planning, deciding what must be done for Donny's protection.

"You've got to get out of town—that's settled," Fulmer insisted at last. "If this thing gets out—" His anger returned again, briefly. "What the hell did you do it for, anyway?"

By this time Donny had lost his fear and he answered impudently, "What the hell did you get married for?"

Fulmer reached out and drew Donny's face down against his shoul-der. "I don't know, Don—honest to God. Maybe if I hadn't—"

Donny, without lifting his face, said meekly, "Look, Fulmer, if you still want me to go to school—well—" It was with obvious effort that he made the concession. "Well, I'll go on to the University."

For the first time Fulmer lost some of his look of strain. Well, he thought, this night, with all its ugliness and its danger to the Greens, had at least solved one important family problem. Donny would get a decent education after all—and school life would keep him out of trouble. "Now you're talking sense. The university's the answer." He rose stiffly and yawned. "Get some sleep, Don—and put this thing tonight clear out of your mind. That's history now—ancient history." He tried to sound more carefree than he actually felt. "Forget it."

He walked slowly back to his own room, a worried frown on his face. For the first time in years he felt defeated; the clear logic of his mind told him that he, as well as Donny, was guilty. He had taken charge of Donny and—he had to face it—he had done a bad job.

"My God," he thought, "I hope Ned Porter won't find out about those guns!"

7

A bright dream glimmered in the borderland of sleep as Parris waked the next morning, leaving only a single silver thread like a profile against the dark. As it faded there came the warming thought of the breakfast visit he would have with Father Donovan. The old priest had come to be a trusted friend and counselor.

Parris recalled the many times people had questioned him about that friendship. The Catholic element in the town was small and belonged largely to that unconsidered part of the population living in the south end of Kings Row—foreigners, for the most part. Parris had found Father Donovan, the parish priest, to be a wise and cultured man and a most congenial companion, sharing as he did Parris' love of music and literature, where these things were more than apt to be ignored, or looked upon with scorn in the little Midwest community.

Suddenly Parris, wide awake, remembered the thing that had kept him up most of the night—his trip down to Jinktown at midnight, his reluctance to leave the troubled pair of watchers, and his own quandary as to what he should do about the case.

Elise was still asleep. As she lay there, her cheek softly flushed, her bright hair loose against the pillow, she seemed a little girl, and he was puzzled by the troubled expression that came and went across her face.

How gentle she was! But there was about her a curious resignation that was no part of youth. His sense of protectiveness, his tenderness toward her, had become so much a part of him that Parris believed himself deeply in love with her. But what Randy had said worried him. He was not now so sure of Elise's happiness and content.

The sun was not yet up when he turned toward the south gate of the hospital grounds. The dew was heavy and silvery on the grass, still lushly green, although this was almost the beginning of August. The air was very still but one felt the stir and murmur behind the walls as the huge buildings awoke to another day.

The thought of the place and his work always sent a slight tremor of excitement along his nerves. Every day of his life the realization that he was a part of it had the impact of a fresh experience. Living and working among the monstrous phantoms, the distortions, the violent tensions and grotesque exhibitions of sick minds could never be a happy experience, but it could be immeasurably exciting. So, although the place did not weigh on his nerves, he anticipated with relief an occasional day of freedom.

As he left the hospital gates, he could see straight to the end of Federal Street, where the gray stone buildings of Aberdeen College for Men reared themselves solidly across the street. They looked like a heavy bank of clouds against the lightening sky. He passed the entrance of the School for the Deaf, an ugly, unprepossessing red brick structure, and looked out toward the end of Poplar Street where the grove of trees cut off the view of the State Penitentiary crouching behind high walls of masonry and brick.

Except for an occasional Negro cook on her way to work, the streets were almost deserted. He could hear in the distance the clop-clop of the milkman's horse.

This was a good hour to be walking through the town, and because it was still too early for his breakfast appointment, he was glad of the time for a leisurely stroll. Kings Row looked unfamiliar in the dim gray light. The tremulous, shy quality of the dawn was just about to give way to the sharper look of day.

The brief season of lilacs and roses was over, and only verbenas and geraniums smoldered in occasional flower beds. In more pretentious yards a pair of trellises, diamond- or heart-shaped, lifted purple clusters of clematis.

The yards were all fenced. White pickets or palings set these front yards apart from each other and from the street. Fences kept out children and dogs, but they were also symbols of the privacy of the family—symbols of those social barriers which preserved caste. Only very poor people neglected their yard fences.

Just now, in the quiet of the early morning, a quality of peace, as wide as the pleasant farm country stretching out from the town, and as deep as the clear azure overhead, seemed to brood over the town and bless it. A bed of brilliant red geraniums on Ned Porter's lawn gave forth a secret excitement.

A geranium, Parris thought, draws its red from a *conviction*. It *believes* in red.

He carefully avoided stepping on the bright silver trail of a snail that had set out upon its painful odyssey. As Parris crossed Union Street, he could see Randy McHugh's house.

The thought of her was like a cool finger laid on a fevered pulse. Parris had been amazed at the way Randy had been able to stand alone. She had lost Drake and her father, and her brother Tod in quick succession, and yet she had assumed a quality of command that no one had dreamed she possessed. She was a remakable person, rounded, complete, self-contained, and possessed of formidable strength and control. A beautiful woman! Something regal in the way she carried her red-gold head, something staunch and steadying in the direct gaze of her gray-blue eyes.

Thinking of Randy, he felt warm and comforted.

Mariah Shane, thin and gaunt and incredibly energetic, was serving breakfast to Father Donovan and Parris on the little brick terrace that connected the modest rectory with the Catholic church. Father Donovan always had breakfast out there when the weather permitted. The vine-covered lattice that cut off the view of Walnut Street gave it complete seclusion, and it was open to the flower garden that was the pride of Mariah's heart.

Mariah had been caretaker and cook at the little rectory even before Father Donovan came to Kings Row. She was surprisingly active for her age, but she complained bitterly that she could not get as much work done in her garden as she would like.

The two men were talking of the varied aspects of the country about Kings Row, speaking particularly of the von Eln place and its possibilities.

"I quite understand, my son," Father Donovan said, "your wish to reorient yourself in that place. Its natural environment has had much to do with building your character. But there is danger, too, for you there. You must recognize it, and in that way destroy its power to harm."

"Danger?" Parris was startled. "What possible danger could there be?"

"It is this: that landscape is in some mystical sense your real home. It was traversed, studied, and reconsidered countless times during your childhood and during that more disturbing period, your adolescence. As each day changes the total of experience, a new light is cast backward over the familiar ways and places, changing their aspect and illuminating their importance. Now this is where the danger lies. It would be very easy for you to begin valuing the present not so much for its living actuality as for its effect upon the past. The past, my son, is a dangerous anodyne unless you can see it for what it actually is."

Mariah placed a fresh pot of coffee before Father Donovan. Parris waited until Mariah had gone before he spoke.

"Probably you are right. I can think of events that have become bearable only when they have been divested of the harshness of proximity."

Father Donovan leaned toward his young friend. "There's a touch of bitterness in that remark, Parris. Do you wish to tell me what is troubling you?"

"Many things, Father. A cruel and unjust thing has just happened to a poor child in this town. It is so devastating that I wonder how she can face a present which must seem monstrous to her, and a future which is uncertain for herself and for two people who love her. She has had so little in the past to help her—and I pity her. She has nothing to draw on."

"And you think a richer past would help her now in her need? Is that your honest belief?"

"Frankly, Father, I don't know what I believe. But my own past has always stood behind my chair, touching me in every waking moment, pointing the way and propelling my steps."

"Have you stopped to think," Father Donovan's voice had taken on a note of severity, "that perhaps this partakes of the nature of phantasy?"

"Not as I think of the phantasy of dreams. My past has entered deeply and completely into every fiber of nerve and muscle. I would not be divorced from it if I could."

"That is why I warn you, Parris, about immuring your mind in that estate too often or too deeply. You may be relying on it as a protection against the too violent impact of present reality."

"Might not that be a good thing?"

"Not in your case. You belong in the front ranks of men of service. Too much concern with the past could hamper your progress. Your problems, whatever they may be, must be faced in the light of today, not in the faint, remembered glow of yesterday."

Parris' eyes sparkled with interest. "I live the present with a certain amount of gusto, I think, and I welcome the future with a certain eagerness—"

"But," Father Donovan interrupted, "are you sure you do not accept them because they will so soon be one with the timeless past?"

Parris smiled. "I give up, Father, I do try to go forward without reluctance, but I admit that I look backward with something like ecstasy."

"There! You see? Already you have lost your way. I know one person who can hold you on your path. Your wife. My son, I am going to ask you something very personal. If you resent it, I shall be sorry, but I must ask it in any case."

"Ask anything you wish. I always come to you when the going gets difficult."

"I've no right to ask you this question, but you are too young a man to be retreating from life. Are you happy with your wife?"

"Happy? Yes—" Parris answered frankly, "but troubled, too. Elise is peace and sanity to me. She is my refuge from all the madness and unrest in the world. Of what I am to her I am not so certain."

"It is your business to know. You understand other people—your patients. Why not your wife?"

"I can't explain—quite. There's an obscurity there I can't reach through. She is like—like the shadow on a sundial. But," he added hurriedly, "I'm sure she loves me."

The voice of the old priest softened. "Perhaps she senses this backward-looking tendency of yours and feels she is not completely a part of your life."

"But, Father, she *is* my life. I could not conceive of a world without her." His voice was almost defiant, a fact that the wise old man noted.

"Yet you admit you prefer living in the past." As he spoke, his patient fingers moved back and forth across the satiny damask.

Parris moved restlessly in his chair. "In a way, I think she represents that past to me. I am confused—I don't know how to answer you, Father. I don't even know what she would think of this discussion of the past we are having."

Father Donovan poured fresh coffee in both cups before he replied. "Parris, you know how to cure others. You are singularly slow in recognizing symptoms in yourself. Again let me remind you that you are very young. It may sound platitudinous, but there are many experiences still in store for you."

"Life is entirely too short," Parris said, "for me to crowd into it all I wish to experience."

"Perhaps it is the tragedy of consciousness that we desire to encompass the whole in our little flick of existence."

"I'm afraid I confuse thinking with feeling and I get hopelessly lost."

"Sometimes, my son, when thinking and feeling slide into each other and become one, some secret mathematic of the soul measures that segment which consciousness provides, and a leaping intuition spans the whole. In that instant the ceaseless trends of seeking are quieted for a moment and infinity is identified with peace."

Parris leaned back in his chair, a puzzled frown puckering his brow. "I'm not sure that I follow you entirely."

"Never mind, son. All of this is a cloudy kind of thinking and you will no doubt loose pragmatic destruction on my airy structures."

"Not at all, Father. I believe you have taught me how to walk around every thought and to view it from every angle."

"If you do that you can't get very far off the track. I wish I could do as well."

"But you do! In spite of your being a confirmed mystic, you—"

" 'Tis my Irish blood, no doubt. Mystics we are, but we've our practical side as well." Father Donovan's smile was deprecatory.

"Maybe you are born mystics and become practical through environment?"

Father Donovan rested his chin on his clasped hands and gave the matter a moment's thought. Then he shook his head.

"Maybe. More like, it's our education. I was brought up in County Cork. My grandfather's house was full of children. There were always lots of dogs and horses, and there were many people going in and out of doors and a great talk and laughter all the time. We didn't learn anything very well, but we heard about everything."

"But that sounds marvelous! What more could you want by way of an education? You were very lucky."

"Yes," Father Donovan nodded in agreement. "I was lucky. But it does not make me happy when I remember the many things I failed to do in those years." He reached out with his strong, bony hand and touched the trellis near his chair. "Let's sit here and look at these leaves that trouble not at all about their imperfections."

Parris looked closely at the old man. The long-lashed lids of Father Donovan's fine eyes showed a tired line that slanted to the net of close wrinkles about them. Eyes that seemed, above all else, wise—wise but keeping still the odd shyness that had always been so appealing.

"My son, we are so enmeshed with the earth that we seem somewhat born again with leaves and somewhat die with them. There is something that comes—a cargo from the infinite—when their green signals fly, and something goes when the bright, myriad, eager sails are set." Father Donovan looked across the lawn to the thinning maples, and his voice was almost inaudible. He seemed to have forgotten his companion.

After a little he went on. "They will come and go so many times for you—but I have seen them go so often that all the past seems dark with falling leaves—falling and always falling, until soon they will cease as though there were no more dark leaves to fly or fall."

"It's curious, isn't it," Parris began hesitantly, moving his chair out of the sun, "how human relationships are clarified by a day such as this—by consideration of leaves and grass and water and clouds?"

"For those who can see and read them, yes." Father Donovan ran his fingers through his thinning hair. "Yesterday, Parris, Randy Mc-Hugh said much the same thing, but in different words. She has her problems but she has a remarkable philosophy."

"Oh, Randy solves her problems by using her common sense. Even inanimate objects obey her. She lays friendly and healing hands on everything. I don't believe mystery exists for Randy."

"Have you seen her lately?"

"Just yesterday. Elise sees her often. Randy's very busy. She's been drawn into every activity in the town, it seems."

"It's that same common sense you were talking about. Randy Mc-Hugh is a fine citizen. Kings Row has need of others like her."

"I agree with you completely. There's something very gallant about her. She *marches*. The last we shall see of Randy will be a flag flying over the crest of a hill."

Father Donovan nodded appreciatively. "Your own behavior is not unlike hers—in spite of your apparent withdrawals from conflict. I see you bringing those same forces to bear on diseased minds and disturbed personalities that Randy directs against injustices and inequalities where *she* finds them."

"You are too kind, Father. I admit I need just such a boost as you are giving me, but I haven't Randy's complete and ready concentration. Where do you suppose she gets its? There's nothing in her training and education that has even pointed in that direction."

"You are mistaken about that." Father Donovan smiled—a frank, engaging smile.

"But what—" he left his query suspended.

"Randy's experiences have been unusual, to say the least. She's had a fine education of the *heart,* my son."

"Education of the heart," Parris said musingly. "She turns to *people* for instruction, I suppose you mean, where you and I turn to books and to nature to identify our values. Is that it?"

"Not altogether. Preoccupation with the phases of nature helps us to know human values. And you, Parris, your zest for the manifestations of the workings of the human mind seems endless. I am not surprised that you are so comprehending of natural phenomena."

"I'm not sure that I do comprehend them. It's stupefying, really, this wilderness of leaves and stems and things that shoot from the ground with such formidable energy and in such confusion. All of this is raw material."

"But it gives you pleasure," Father Donovan suggested.

"It gives me pleasure, yes," Parris answered a bit uncertainly. "I can contemplate a leaf, a single blossom, with a certain simple enjoyment, but for the whole of it—there's something savage and terrifying about it. I feel it should be ordered, *arranged.* It should be made into meaning."

Father Donovan shook his head slowly. "You always speak of 'design,' 'order,' but you are apt to ignore the basic significance of the thing itself. This leaf may be symbolic of birth, of life, of death. In the study of one little leaf you can encompass the lore of the universe. Wordsworth said it, more poetically."

"Now you are being mystical again, Father. Someday I hope to be able to follow you on your imaginative flights, but not yet. I'm still trying to be a scientist."

"Never mind. We understand each other. But you spoke earlier of some child who had received an injury—the child who had no past to

[71]

draw on. Could you tell me more about what happened to her? You say she is poor. I wonder if I could help."

"I think you could—but this is a matter of professional secrecy, Father. I can't give you names. I suspect they are members of your church and you will probably learn it from them. The circumstances are these: a young girl was brutally assaulted last night by two unidentified men who first took the precaution to beat her escort into unconsciousness. In view of what would probably be the effect on the girl's future state of mind, the family asked me to keep it a secret. I think they are right. There's not much hope of discovering the criminals in any case."

"That's a tragic thing, Parris. Psychologically what is likely to happen to the child?"

"Any one of a number of things might result. Fortunately, a lad who is in love with her wants to marry her right away. That may serve to wipe out the horror from her own mind, but she will probably carry some deep soul-scars for the rest of her life."

"To have been bodily assaulted was terrible enough," Father Donovan said sorrowfully, "but to have suffered such an indignity to her soul—that could be incurable."

"That is why I said I pitied her because she has no past to draw on. She probably has already a sense of inferiority, brought about by her lack of security in early childhood. I am afraid she may feel it more than ever now. She will feel that she has been defiled, contaminated, and always there will be the haunting fear of exposure. I can only hope that it won't destroy her future happiness with the boy she will marry. They are deeply in love. I could see that."

"Parris, you and I as well as all society can be blamed for this crime."

Parris looked up, startled. "You and I?"

"Yes. As long as evil walks the land we should be doing something about the prevention of outrages such as this."

Parris' shoulders seemed suddenly to sag, a strange thing to see in so young a man, Father Donovan thought.

"What can we hope to do—other than to relieve pain? And that in itself is a puzzling thing."

"Pain, my son, comes to everyone—sometimes it comes too early, as in this particular case. It is a concomitant of Creation's travail. A man who ravishes a child is a brute, but much that passes as legalized love is brutish also. That is common knowledge."

"I am a biologist, Father, but even a biologist doesn't know how passion can be raised above the level of lust."

"Now you are speaking bitterly because of this unhappy case which is weighing on your heart. Passion can be lifted above lust if it is sifted through the heart."

"You really have faith in humanity, haven't you?"

"I have faith in God, and faith can work miracles. It may even do something for this poor child."

"Father, I feel unsure of my own stand in this matter. I've spent an uncomfortable night wondering if I'm doing the right thing in concealing this crime from the authorities. I want your advice."

"Has the girl no clue as to who her assailants might be?"

"None. And it is not likely that any clues could be picked up. I must admit that I took my stand in an effort to protect the child and give her some chance to recover her mental health. Publicity would destroy that slender chance."

"I think," the old man said slowly, "you have done the wise thing, my son. Have you talked with your wife about it? Her reaction might help you to decide."

"N-no," Parris admitted, realizing that he had not considered telling Elise, that he had known intuitively that she could not understand the problem at all. It would only frighten her.

The wise old man was conscious of the momentary confusion in Parris' mind, and went on in his level voice. "Try to dismiss the question, but try to help the child in her struggle to forget."

"You take a load off my mind, Father. It was troubling me. The child will marry the boy she loves soon, I hope, and that will help her to forget."

"If the affair is romantic enough to appeal to her imagination."

Parris looked inquiringly at the old priest. He had not expected the conversation to take this turn.

"I wonder," he said, "if romantic love isn't, after all, more of a shadow than the real thing? Like walking in the dusk and never in the full blaze of sunlight."

Something in the quality of Parris' voice caught at the old man's attention. He scrutinized the thoughtful face curiously.

[73]

"Pleasure, my son, is not happiness. Glory and heartbreak add up to the union. That's God's purpose."

Parris rose to go. "It's been good of you, Father, to give me so much time."

"Your visits are the bright spots in my rather drab existence, my son. You must come as often as you can spare the time. I see Mariah looking a little troubled about her flowers. Shall we find what is wrong before you go?"

The dahlias Mariah had planted along the paling fence had not done so well this year. She was shaking her head mournfully over their skimpy appearance.

"What's the matter with them, Father? Last year they was that pretty you could hardly bear to look at them, and this year we ain't even had a bouquet of them for the church."

"Never mind, Mariah," Parris said sympathetically, "the season's not right. They'll likely be fine again next year."

"The season's got nothin' to do with it," she said with conviction. "Must be somethin' I done or ain't done. Maybe that peat moss was too hot for them, I wish I knew."

"Don't worry about it, Mariah," Father Donovan begged. "Your marigolds and zinnias make up for the defaulting dahlias."

"Yes, sir. I don't rightly know what that word means, but I'm sure you're right. I want to give Miss Elise a bunch when she comes by next time."

"Thank you, Mariah. I'll tell her. She will be very pleased. Thank you for the delicious breakfast you gave me."

"It was a pleasure, Doctor. The Father likes to have company. I hope Miss Elise comes to see the garden soon. I like to look at her. I like the way she carries her head. Some people *poke* their heads up there, and some heads just naturally *grow* up there. You can tell the difference."

"Why, thank you, Mariah. It's a fine compliment you are paying her."

"Well, I do think yourself should be rolling in gold, what with all the good wishes that do be following you this day."

The old woman stood, hands on hips, looking after Parris as he walked down Walnut Street. "I do think, Father, that when the doctor passes it's like a regiment was marching down the street."

[74]

Father Donovan nodded, understanding the Irish compliment, and turned back toward his study.

8

Bethany Laneer's heels struck hard at the mossy bricks as she turned into the walk at the Holloways'. She was hatless and the wind had blown her black hair into a tangle.

Judge Holloway laid aside his paper as his young great-niece burst into the Victorian living room.

"Don't get up, Uncle Jim," Bethany urged. "I just—just knew I'd explode if I didn't get to tell my troubles to somebody. Where's Aunt Beth?"

"She'll be down presently. What's all the excitement about?" asked the Judge, noting the angry color in the girl's face. Black Capers eyes, he thought, as always when he noted the way Bethany's slanted upward a little at the corners.

"Just about everything's wrong—and you've got to help me out."

"Tell all!" the old man invited.

"Uncle Jim, it's—it's *Mother.*"

"What's she done this time?" he asked with mock gravity.

"Why does Mother have to keep up such a front—make all this silly pretense about being so exclusive, when there's nothing to be exclusive about? Everybody knows we're poor as church mice."

"Your mother's just fighting for a little decent privacy of mind. There's precious little of it allowed in Kings Row. She's doing her best to shut out prying outsiders."

"Outsiders! I'm surprised to hear that word from *you*. What about your vaunted democracy? The times I've listened while you talked on and on about—"

"I can be democratic and still be a little choosy, can't I?"

"You can be whatever you like, darling. But you listen to what I have to say. Mother objects to everybody who doesn't conform to her ideas of—"

"And you like nonconformists. Is that it?"

"Not always. I'm a conformist myself. I find it convenient to conform. I'm too lazy to rebel."

Her uncle solemnly assumed his judicial air and tapped his eyeglasses thoughtfully against his thumbnail. "Well, you musn't forget that nonconformists are the ones who ordinarily make history."

Bethany's nose crinkled up like a rabbit's. "There you go again, arguing on both sides of the question!" She moved over to sit on the arm of his chair.

"You lay yourself open to suspicion, my dear, when you do this," the Judge growled. "Next thing, you'll have an arm around my neck, and that's your last and most effective argument."

"How's this?" she asked, giving him a quick hug.

"Pretty good as far as it goes. Now, 'shoot the works,' as you young folks say."

"I'm tired of being told I'm going against custom!"

"You're not the first to suffer, chickabiddy. I think Plutarch said we are more sensible of what is done against custom than against nature."

"Well, I, for one, am determined not to go against *nature,* and heaven only knows where that will lead me! Mother ought to know better than to try to stop me when I get started! She was young once, wasn't she?"

"Well, what's it all about?"

"This morning she's in a dither about my running around with boys and girls nobody ever heard of. How does she expect to hear of anybody, sitting stuffily at home day in and day out like she does?"

The Judge looked quizzical. "So that's it!" he said. "Come on, now, tell me what particular nobody you are referring to."

Bethany answered soberly, but instantly. "Ross Pomeroy."

"You don't mean your mother thinks *he's* a nobody?" The old man was obviously astounded.

"Well, Mother doesn't want me to go around with Ross. In fact, she has positively forbidden it—forbids it several times a day!"

"But, Bethany, I can't understand her objections. I should have said he is probably the pick of all the young chaps in Kings Row."

"Don't I know it! Every girl in town is after him."

"Rather to be expected. He's well behaved, well mannered, *and* he's going to be a well-fixed young fellow when he gets through school and settles down to business. That's enough 'wells' to suit even your particular mother. What in God's name does she want?"

"I don't give a darn what she wants. It's my life and I'm going to live it my way. I intend to see Ross as often as he asks me, and if he doesn't ask me often enough, I'll go after him myself."

Mrs. Holloway came in just in time to hear Bethany's threat. "Bethany, my dear child," she deprecated, "you don't mean what you are saying!"

"Oh, yes, I do. I'm determined to see Ross, Aunt Beth—and I'd like it to be here—at your house."

"Can't say I blame you, honey. I know I can trust you not to do anything rash," the Judge said sympathetically. "Would you like me to talk to your mother about it? I confess I'm curious to know what she actually has against young Pomeroy."

Bethany gave him a grateful kiss. "You're an angel, Uncle Jim, but it wouldn't do a particle of good."

"Maybe, Bethany," Mrs. Holloway ventured, "she is thinking of the talk there's always been about the Pomeroys being rather—well, *mysterious.*"

"Nonsense, Beth," the Judge answered his wife's conjecture impatiently. "Angie has too much sense to pay any attention to all that whispering gossip. It's got no foundation and you know it."

"Of course I know it," his wife answered spiritedly, "but *Angie* might have it in the back of her head."

"There's nothing to that stuff. Davis Pomeroy's a straight shooter if there ever was one. They've lived in Kings Row for twenty years and not a breath of scandal has touched them in all that time."

"But you haven't told me," Bethany said, "how I can get Ross to talk about marrying me, Uncle Jim."

"Just let things rock along, and be your own sweet self. I fancy things will work out all right. How old are you, Bethany?"

"Nineteen."

"A mere baby. Ross is not through school yet and *you* shouldn't be. How about the university?"

"Nothing doing! I don't want anything or anybody but Ross."

The Judge rose from his chair slowly and with obvious reluctance. "Well, my dear, I've got to be plodding along. We'll be thinking this over, won't we? Can't have you breaking your heart over any young whippersnapper like Ross Pomeroy."

Mrs. Holloway laid a hand on Bethany's arm. "You stay and have lunch with me, my dear. Let your mother and Maud worry a little about where you are; it will do them good."

"You're a darling! Aunt Beth, if it weren't for you and Uncle Jim, I'd do something desperate—jump in the creek, maybe."

"The creek's pretty deep and pretty wet, and I think jumping in would be an exceptionally poor idea. You wouldn't like it. I think I'll call Randy to come over and have lunch with us. Like that?"

"But, of course! I haven't seen her for days."

"Suppose you call her, my dear, and I'll see what we can find to eat."

"I warn you, Aunt Beth, I'll be 'eating my bread in sorrow,' but there'd better be plenty of it. My appetite is disgustingly good."

There was a good deal of talk during lunch about Ross Pomeroy, for Randy McHugh liked him and she was fond of Bethany. She had no suggestions, however, as to how Bethany might iron out her troubles. "I think the Judge was right, honey," she said comfortingly. "Just let things ride, and they'll probably turn out all right."

Bethany paused, her fork in mid-air, and turned upon Randy a look that scorned even as it begged for understanding. So Randy didn't understand, either. Nobody understood.

Bethany indulged in a moment of self-pity, which fanned out slowly into anger—at Randy, at her mother, at the Judge. At Ross, even. He claims to be in love with me, she thought scornfully, but he always hedges when I want to discuss future plans.

The luncheon, she decided afterward, was anything but a success. She had gone for help and she was returning empty-handed. A pat on the back was what she had been given, and a "run-along-little-girl." As she walked down Union Street she worked herself into a state of active resentment against the whole world. "They don't care," she thought, and blinked her eyes to keep back tears. "What's it to them— to *anybody* in the whole cockeyed world—if I lose Ross?—if he goes back to Harvard without our having settled anything?"

The thought of the nearness of September—it was only two weeks away—struck into her sharply as she turned into Capers Court.

She stood still for a moment, looking with distaste at the tall ginger-bread house that dominated the short, dead-end street. "Hideous," she decided. "Hideous—inside and out." She wondered, looking at the jumble of gables, towers, and chimneys, what manner of man had built it, what sort of beauty-blindness must have possessed her grandfather Capers in his youth. But perhaps the house had not been so ugly then. She half closed her eyes as she walked forward, trying to visualize the place as she knew it had been many years ago. Perhaps, in the days before the lots had had to be sold off, and the street was cut along what had been the fine avenue of elms leading to the door, the big house with its turrets and gingerbread had had a sort of majesty.

Bethany turned aside at the foot of the front steps and walked around to the side door that opened into the sunroom. Still thinking about the house, still unreasonably hating it, she ignored her mother and her sister Maud, and glanced with loathing around the big, many-windowed room. She looked with particular distaste at the platform rocker that Maud was just leaving as she started out of the room. When Bethany spoke her voice carried defiance. "Mother, why don't we get rid of a lot of this junk and get some comfortable pieces that we can *live* with?"

"Bethany." The name was softly spoken but it carried with it a sharp quality that was like the sound of a whip cutting through the air. "Bethany," Mrs. Laneer said again, her eyes fixed on the girl's shoulders, "you're slouching again. Is that any posture for a lady?"

"Probably not," Bethany responded indifferently, "but it's good enough for a brat like me."

"Where you pick up such language is beyond me."

"Wake up, Mother. You've been sound asleep for a long time. Manners are changing."

Mrs. Laneer carefully folded the camisole she had mended, picked up another garment, and gave it a minute inspection before she spoke. "Yours, at least, are unpardonably bad. Bethany, it's extremely annoying to have to repeat something I have spoken about so often, but I repeat you are not to see that Pomeroy boy again. Maud tells me—"

"Oh, Maud." Bethany's shrug showed plainly she was not interested in what Maud had said. "You haven't made it clear to me, Mother, what your objections to Ross really are."

"Is that necessary? I am your mother and naturally I have your interests at heart—to say nothing of your good name—"

[79]

"Careful, Mother! You are about to say something you'll be sorry for."

"Bethany!" Mrs. Laneer's pale face flushed darkly. "You forget yourself. I repeat, you are not to speak to that boy again. This comes of your running around with all sorts of people."

Bethany laughed. "I'd hate for Ross to go poking around in *our* family archives. Uncle Jim has told me certain lurid tales of our own—"

"Bethany Laneer," her mother's voice rose in pitch, "how dare you? What do you expect me to think of such behavior?"

Bethany whirled defiantly on her mother. "Think anything you like; say anything you like; *do* anything you like, but I tell you once and for all, I will see Ross Pomeroy as often as I can. I'm pretty sure he doesn't want to marry me, and I know his family thinks I'm not good enough for him, but I want to marry him and I'm going to do everything in my power to change his mind. Neither his family nor mine can stop it." Her voice broke on the last words.

Mrs. Laneer closed the sewing box at her side with hands that were shaking and left the room without looking at her daughter.

Bethany dropped into the hated platform rocker and ran her fingers distractedly through her hair. She began to cry, the thin sounds threading the silence of the big room.

9

It was a cool evening, for August. Parris sat near the living room window in his favorite armchair, his feet propped comfortably on an ottoman, debating what he should do with the three or four hours of leisure that stretched before him. There was a new book on the shelf— a compilation of case histories recently written by a rising young psychiatrist in New York. It tempted him. But through the open window he could see the hospital grounds, fast darkening and breeze-swept, the treetops silhouetted against a beribboned sunset; the outdoors beckoned him, too. There would be a full moon—a nice evening for a leisurely walk through the grounds.

He was about to call Elise, who was just finishing up her after-dinner chores in the tiny kitchen, when he thought he heard a knock at the door. The knock came again, timidly, the two short raps sounding like those a child might make. Little Kam Nolan, he thought, for Kam frequently slipped away from his parents after dinner to pay a good-night visit to Elise. Parris tiptoed softly to the door and swung it wide, ready to appear obligingly startled should he be greeted by Kam's usual "Boo!"

It was the visitors, however, who were startled as the door burst open. Ross Pomeroy took a quick step back, bumping into his brother McKay, who stood behind and a little to one side of him.

"I thought it was Kam Nolan," Parris explained, "the little Nolan boy. Come in Ross—McKay."

The Pomeroys accepted his invitation, but with obvious reluctance. The attitude of unease on the part of both boys was puzzling to Parris. He had seen and nodded to them on the streets a number of times, but he had never had occasion to talk with them.

Ross, he had noticed, was extraordinarily good-looking. He was big and blond like his father, with that same intensely masculine, virile look. His prominent chin had a slight cleft in it—which, Parris decided with a certain wry amusement, probably endeared him to the ladies. Parris could hardly restrain a smile as he recalled something Sarah Skeffington had said once. "I always feel as if that Pomeroy boy was looking that way on purpose. It seems immodest to be that good-looking—almost indecent, I'd say, if he affects young women the way I imagine he does!"

The younger boy, McKay, was tall and thin and dark. He seemed especially shy.

"Sit down"—Parris indicated chairs—"and tell me what's on your mind."

He wondered what had brought them. Girl trouble? The "girl in trouble"—usually one of the poorer, less sheltered youngsters from Jinktown—was almost an institution in Kings Row. Doctors were periodically visited by worried young men wanting to know if there was "anything she could take—you know." They never seemed to learn that there wasn't.

"I know you are wondering, Dr. Mitchell," Ross blurted suddenly, "why we have come to see you."

It sounded to Parris like the desperate beginning of a carefully rehearsed speech. He waited.

"You see," Ross went on, avoiding Parris' gaze, "you see, well, I'm in—I've been in love for a long time—"

"With Bethany Laneer," McKay put in hurriedly, as if trying to help his brother over a rough conversational spot.

"Yes, I think that's common knowledge, Ross," Parris said as quietly and casually as he could.

McKay, who seemed now less disturbed than his brother, said earnestly, "This is pretty embarrassing, Doctor. You see—"

Parris kept his voice calm. "Doctors are used to that, McKay. What's the trouble?"

Ross straightened his shoulders and sat upright. "It's like this, Dr. Mitchell. I want to marry Bethany. But I can't—that is, not until I find out something I think you can tell me. We want you to come with us, right now—tonight—and see for yourself what's worrying us."

Then there *was* something going on up at Pomeroy Hill—something strange. He felt a little thrill of excitement along his nerves.

"Come with you?" he asked, as though he had not understood.

"Out to our place—to Pomeroy Hill," explained McKay. "We want you to see something and tell us what you make of it."

"Sure, I'll go with you," Parris said. "All this secrecy—how could I resist?" He called to Elise to say he was going out but would be back shortly.

There was a small isolated hill to one side of the big house, about a quarter of a mile distant. The top of the hill was clear but the sides were heavily wooded. Under the full moon that had risen, the place had a beautiful, unearthly aspect.

Pomeroy Hill in the moonlight, Parris thought, should be put on canvas; it has a mood.

"Ross," he asked, "what's this all about?"

"We'll show you." Ross' voice was grim as he led Parris along a narrow path that led upward toward the crest of the hill. "Please wait, Doctor, just a little while—"

Parris concealed his amusement at what he felt to be the exaggerated caution of the boys. McKay's dark eyes were tragic. "Keep quiet," he urged in a stage whisper as he led the way to an improvised bench in the shadows.

They sat in silence for several minutes. There wasn't a sound anywhere on the hill.

Presently there was a rustle among the shrubbery as of a wary and cautious progress.

Parris became suddenly alert. He felt his scalp prickle.

Then from the hilltop came a long-drawn sound, a terrifying, agonized howl that rose and held and broke into tatters of hideous clamor. Again and again.

Both boys sat rigid, their eyes fixed straight ahead. Suddenly McKay covered his face with his hands.

"Ross, what is that sound?" Parris' voice was harsher than he had intended because he was himself more unnerved than he cared to admit.

Apparently neither boy could bring himself to speak.

"You know what it is?"

They both nodded.

Parris rose. "What, then?"

"Sit down," said Ross dully. "Sit down and wait."

Again that fearful sound. It must be a dog, Parris thought, baying at the moon—but was it? There was something strange, uncanny in the sound.

The unearthly clamor came again from the hilltop. It *was* like the bay of a deep-voiced hound, almost human in its burden of agony. It was as if some superhuman—or human-consciousness was added to an uncontrollable animal terror. *Human* consciousness? He turned suddenly toward the boys.

"Ross!" He spoke roughly. "Do you know *who* it is?"

Ross turned terrified eyes first toward Parris, then toward his brother, but he did not speak.

Parris waited now. He thought he understood. The long, wavering howls died down, whimpered, and ceased. Presently he heard someone coming down the hill. It sounded like a headlong descent. Someone was staggering through the bushes and leaves in the thicket.

In a moment Davis Pomeroy passed within a few feet of them, blindly plunging in the direction of home. His face was ghastly white and drawn, his collar torn away from his throat, and even in the moonlight Parris could see that the man was drenched with sweat.

Parris spoke softly. "So that's it?"

Ross answered miserably, "Yes, sir. And we don't know what to do. We thought maybe you could help us."

"How long have you known?"

"A long time—since we were children." Ross' voice carried a sort of resignation.

"Have you spoken of it with your mother?"

Ross shook his head. "Never. But I'm sure she knows. I've *seen* it—in her face. More than once."

McKay asked quietly, "Dr. Mitchell, what kind—of—insanity—" he stumbled a little at the word—"is it?"

Pity held Parris silent for a moment. "Perhaps it isn't *insanity* at all," he said finally. "If you've been fearful that this is some frightful form of madness that threatens you and the whole family—your own security—I don't believe you have any cause for worry."

"Then what is it, Doctor?"

"Oh, I can't say at once." He paused. "Some compulsion, based probably on something that happened in your father's childhood."

Ross looked skeptical. McKay clutched hopefully at the suggestion. "How could we ever find out about it? We couldn't possibly talk to *him*."

"And if we knew," Ross said miserably, "we'd only know the cause, that's all."

McKay asked, "Do you think you could help us, Dr. Mitchell? We *had* to talk to somebody. There's Ross—he wants to marry Bethany. And there's Mother—think what she's had all these years." His voice shook.

Parris offered what comfort he could. "There's probably no danger—to you or Ross. We'll just have to go to work on this thing together. Find out everything you can about your father's childhood—gather all the family history you can, any facts that might bear on your father's life. Are there older people with whom you might talk?"

"Only one really old," said Ross. "Our family has about died out. Maybe there's a reason for that—"

"Who is the—"

"Aunt Dixie. She's pretty old. She's Father's great-aunt."

"*Great*-aunt? Where is she?"

"She lives down in the river hills. That's where the family came from."

"Yes, I know. Do you know Mrs.—what's her name?"

"Pomeroy. Miss Dixie. She never married. I guess she's about ninety."

"Are you friends with her?"

"We don't see her often, but we like her. She won't budge from where she lives. It's just a sort of cabin."

"Go down there and camp; stay near her. Get her to talk about her childhood. Start her on stories of your father. Write it down, all of it, no matter how unimportant it seems. Will you do that?"

"Certainly, Dr. Mitchell. Maybe you'll go with us? I want to get this thing cleared up, or understand at least that—that it's not congenital insanity. I can't—I *won't* marry Bethany until I know," Ross insisted.

Parris, remembering the tales of "mysterious goings on" with which Pomeroy Hill was credited, asked, "Do you suppose anyone outside your family knows about this thing?"

"I think not, sir." Ross rose from the log and looked toward the big white house. "You know Father always lived out on a big place like this, at the edge of town, even at Coleman—that was before he came here. I was just a kid and McKay wasn't born yet. I—I guess that's why he fixed up a big place like this—so he wouldn't be too near anyone. So it could be mistaken for one of the dogs. We've always had dogs."

"I see." Parris nodded thoughtfully. "But don't worry too much about it. It's a terrible burden, of course, for you to carry, but don't feel that your lives are ruined because of it."

"Gee, Dr. Mitchell—do you suppose he could be *cured* of whatever is the matter?" McKay asked.

"I can't give you a definite promise—your father himself would have to become a willing patient, I would have to know him much longer and better before I could even make a diagnosis. But—you get all the information possible from the old aunt, and I'll have something, a beginning, anyway, to work with."

The drive back to the hospital was a silent one. Ross and McKay were busy with their own thoughts and speculations, and Parris was wondering whether he had been too optimistic. Certainly, he thought, he had spoken unprofessionally when he half promised them safety. He was far less sure than he had sounded. There are factors of character, too, which pick the locks of security and sanity. He knew little about the Pomeroy boys.

They sat in the car for a long time after they reached the hospital grounds, talking. Parris was trying to learn as much as he could about the Pomeroy family and about the boys themselves. He asked, among other things, how they knew they would witness this scene on this particular night, and learned that their father was always in a strangely nervous state preceding one of his seizures.

It was late when Parris went up to his apartment. Elise had already retired. Parris felt a sudden desire to make love to her. He stood quite still for a moment in the living room; his eyes, fixed on the open bedroom door, became thoughtful.

Abruptly, he turned to his bookshelves. The names of great men in his field of science stood out in small letters under the dozens of titles.

He hesitated, looked again at the dim outline of the big double bed in the bedroom, then reached out a hand to one thick, black-bound tome, *Compulsions*. He sat down, adjusted the light and began to read.

IO

This was not the first time Ross Pomeroy had gone to Judge Holloway's house to see Bethany Laneer, but he had never gone with such a dismal sense of defeat. He and McKay had just returned from a camping trip in the river hills, where they had hoped to get some information which might help Dr. Mitchell clear up their father's strange and awful affliction. But Aunt Dixie, old and shrewd, suspicious and watchful as a squirrel, was close-mouthed and reticent about family affairs. Ross had been too despondent to report his failure to Dr. Mitchell, but he would have to go to see him tomorrow.

His step lagged as he turned in at the Holloway gate, a fact that was noted by Bethany as she watched from the vine-covered porch. Not much like the step of a man in love, she thought, with a curious constriction of her heart. Her voice was a little cool as she greeted him.

They sat together in the porch swing talking politely, like strangers, of the camping trip he had taken, of his preparations for the trip to Harvard, of McKay's youthful poetry.

"Does he actually let you read it?" Bethany tried to sound genuinely interested in McKay.

"Sometimes," Ross answered seriously. "When he thinks he's got something good."

Bethany's mouth tightened at the corners with a sudden impatience.

"Oh, Ross—I don't give a tinker's damn about McKay or the old camping trip. Let's talk about *us*."

For the first time Ross laughed. He put his arms around her quickly and drew her close. "Let's don't *talk*," he suggested airily. But Bethany sensed that his gaiety was forced, that he was using it as a shield to hide his real feelings.

When he leaned forward and tried to kiss her she turned her face away.

He caught her chin in his hand and pulled her face around. "Bethany," he whispered, "you're *crying*!"

"Look, darling," he said after a moment. "Now listen. I know you think I'm crazy, or don't love you or something—because I haven't asked you to marry me. But believe me, Bethany, it's not because I don't *want* to. Lord, if you only knew!"

Bethany felt the first vague stirrings of hope. "Go on," she suggested softly. She knew she was being shameless, but she had long ago forsaken pride where Ross was concerned.

"There are reasons," he explained slowly, "that you don't know about. And that I can't explain. Not yet. Don't ask me, Bethany," he said hurriedly.

"But, Ross, I *have* to know. Please. Is it anything about my family—my mother's attitude?"

Ross had to turn his eyes away from the hurt and bewilderment in her face. "No, darling. It has nothing to do with you."

"There's no other girl mixed up in this?"

"You know better than that. It's been just you since grammar school."

"All I know," she said dully, "is that I can't stand this much longer—this not knowing whether you love me or not. Ross, I can't see why—"

"If it's hard for you, what do you think it is for me? I can't work, I can't sleep, I can't even *think* any more." He set the swing into gentle motion with a push of his foot against the floor. "Listen, Bethany, I'm afraid of only one thing in the world—doing something that might botch up your life. I promise you we'll get married just as soon as possible. Is that enough for now? I'll do my level best to clear up this thing—" He paused. "It has to do with *my* family, Beth, not yours. And I'm going tomorrow to see somebody who might be able to help us."

"Oh." She said it again, more softly. "Oh."

She asked nothing more, for fear of embarrassing him. But she considered carefully what the trouble might be. It might have some connection, she thought uneasily, with the vague but disturbing rumors about the "screaming ghost" of Pomeroy Hill. Had someone been—murdered—out there? Had a Pomeroy done something that might plunge the whole family into scandal and disgrace?

That was it. Ross was afraid—that was all—that he might involve her in what he thought could happen to the family. He *did* love her. Bethany stopped the swing. She caught his face between her hands and kissed him fiercely. "I'm sorry, darling. I love you, love you, love you—and I don't give one of the Judge's 'damns' what the trouble is!"

When he left her eyes were too full of tears to follow the vanishing figure down the walk. Her world—her limited little world—fell in on itself, and out of the wreckage one wish stood clear, commanding and stark. She wanted Ross, nothing else—no matter what happened to the family.

She had no chance to see him again. But even when he called just before leaving for Boston, and told her that he must go away without having settled their difficulties, she was not too downcast. He loved her. For the moment it was enough.

Bethany resigned herself to waiting.

II

It was not difficult for Randy McHugh to reach the attention of David Kettring, the most promising young figure in state politics. Kettring's newspaper had already become the mouthpiece of his party, and his editorials were read with respect and quoted liberally throughout the Middle West. He had more influence than any other man in the state.

As Randy sat in his office facing him she felt the power of his dominant personality. His very height was impressive. His somber eyes were shaded by heavy dark brows. She noted his sensitive lips and his strong, stubborn chin.

Randy went directly to the point without wasting time in preliminaries. Since she already knew the purpose of her visit, she meant to be brief. It was not so much a manifestation of taste as a simple trait of character. She was a person of transparent honesty.

"This is the situation," she told him. "The von Eln place is too small to be of use to the state. I understand the Experimental Station was closed because the location did not offer room for expansion. It is lying idle and the house is already in need of repairs."

"Does Dr. Mitchell wish to buy it for a home?"

"Yes. It belonged to his grandmother, and he lived there until he was grown. He has a sentimental attachment to the place and he is willing to pay a fair price for it. He wishes to move into it at the earliest possible moment."

"I see no reason why the property should not be sold to Dr. Mitchell. I feel a personal interest in that young man. My son, Jan, is a medical student and hopes that he may eventually work with Mitchell in his particular field. We hear great things about him from the Nolans."

"He's a very fine doctor and a fine person. I wish to make it clear, Mr. Kettring, that there will be an effort to block this transfer."

"From what source?"

Randy hesitated, then spoke frankly. "It is probable that Fulmer Green, a legislator living in Kings Row, may try to buy the place— as an investment, purely—with the idea of holding Dr. Mitchell up for an exorbitant price. There's a matter of personal spite involved."

"So Fulmer Green's interested?"

"I feel sure he *will* be when he finds out Dr. Mitchell wishes to buy."

"I know Green's reputation in the realty business. But I don't think he could muster enough support to block this sale."

"Nevertheless, I hope to keep our plans quiet as long as possible. He's capable of some sharp manipulations. I've had dealings with him before."

All at once David Kettring felt himself allied with this young woman's cause. He did not need to know any further details. It was an attitude he often assumed when he came in contact with a fundamentally honest nature. Instinctively he trusted her. He leaned forward confidentially and his voice was warm and friendly.

"Do you know, Mrs. McHugh, a fight with Fulmer Green is rather to my liking. I've found myself on several occasions supporting the opposition in some matter being sponsored by Green."

"He's smart, and he's tricky. You need to keep *two* eyes on him."

Kettring laughed. "I'm inclined to agree with you. Perhaps it's not too politic to say so, but you aren't the first to warn me about him. My good friends the Nolans have mentioned him, and Senator Sandifer grows highly vocal at mention of his name."

"I felt, Mr. Kettring, that with your help we could put the deal through, no matter what Fulmer tries."

"I'm sure it can be done and I shall be glad to speak with certain men before it comes up in the house."

"Then I consider it as good as done! If at any time I can help *you*, sir, I hope you will call on me. I'm interested in state affairs, for all I'm barred from taking active part in them."

"We men are waking up to the shameful waste of woman-power in this country. How soon will you make a strong enough demand to get the vote?"

"We're trying—and President Wilson is at heart sympathetic. I think he's simply afraid to push it at the moment. There are such weighty things on his mind right now. But, perhaps by the time you want to be elected Governor, we shall be able to cast our ballots for you."

The corners of his mouth twitched, but he spoke with exaggerated gravity. "In any case, I'm in favor of suffrage for women like yourself and Laurel Nolan."

"And by all means add the name of your wife, Mr. Kettring. I've been told that she understands the temper of the Middle West better than any other woman in the state—better than most men, as far as that goes."

"You must come to know each other, Mrs. McHugh. You are much alike."

"Thank you, sir. Nothing would please me more than to meet your wife. Laurel Nolan speaks of her often."

She rose, thanked him for the promised aid, and went away confident.

Kettring looked after her admiringly. Now, that was the kind of woman he liked. Intelligent, forthright—and with an exciting femininity as well. A beautiful young woman, he said to himself—and certainly one who knows how to go after what she wants. And, he added justly, one whom it is a pleasure to help.

David Kettring pushed the sale of the von Eln property through early in the session. He had been surprised to find how many supporters Fulmer Green had been able to muster. It did not promise too well for future legislation.

He dismissed the matter from his mind for the time being, but, as he was in the habit of doing with unfinished business, he merely laid aside the name of Fulmer Green for later consideration.

Randy was jubilant. It was good to feel that she had been of real service to Parris.

The affair was discussed by every group in Kings Row. Most of the comment was of a jocular nature.

"Tell you what, it takes more'n Fulmer's got to get ahead of Randy McHugh. She's smart as a whip." Matt Fuller took a fresh chew of tobacco and chuckled.

Ricks Darden nodded in agreement. "Hard to git ahead of them Irish Catholics. Never seen anything like it. Don't stand to reason that they got more sense than other folks, but somehow they always come out on top."

"Fulmer's got plenty of sense, too. He jest gits a little *too* smart sometimes, an' he gits his ears pinned back."

"Needs it, too. He gits too big for his britches. Did you hear how he closed out old Thad Williams down on Timmon's Creek?"

"Yeah, I heard about that. Low-down trick, I call it. But that's the way he's made most of his money."

Matt tilted his chair back against the gallery wall of his feed store, and Ricks leaned against one of the square supporting columns. This was going to be a good session.

"Say, didn't Fulmer's wife have some money when they got married?"

"Wouldn't be surprised. Them Allinghams was always pretty well fixed, I hear. She's a good-looker all right."

Ricks winked. "Told you Fulmer was smart. When a good-looking woman's got money to boot, she ain't likely to have no trouble findin' a husband."

"I'm kind o' glad the Doc got his old home back," Matt said, returning to the original subject of their gossip.

"Yep. I'd sure hate to live out there at the asylum with them crazy folks all the time. Must be pretty hard on the doctors' families. Don't blame him for movin' out."

"They say him an' his wife is fixin' it up mighty nice out there, an' gettin' ready to move in."

"Yeah, she drives out there near ever' day to watch the work goin' on—her an' Randy McHugh. Seems like Randy's as much excited about it as Miz Mitchell."

12

The election in the fall of 1916 of Arthur Swenson as Governor and David Kettring as Lieutenant Governor met the general approval of Kings Row. Even Fulmer Green had made campaign speeches in Swenson's behalf. Miles Jackson, surprised to find himself on the same side of any question with Fulmer, editorialized at length and forcefully on the wisdom of electing to office two such outstanding personalities. It had been a little strange to find the two associated on the same ticket, for they were known to have serious differences of viewpoint on many issues.

However, political discussions had given place to uneasy talk of what we were to do about Germany. Our ships were being torpedoed without warning, and eventually we would be forced to do something drastic. Even some of the town meetings, called merely for the discussion of school or sanitation or fire-protection matters, developed somehow into general talk of possible war.

At one such gathering, however, Fulmer Green launched unexpectedly into a tirade against Parris Mitchell's connection with the State Asylum.

"We'd better be keeping an eye on everybody in Kings Row that we *know* to have German connections and German sympathies. Do you realize that we've got a man right now on the staff of the State Asylum that got his education over there in Germany—or Austria, and that's just the same thing. He's even got an Austrian wife and nobody can tell me that his sympathies are not with those folks that are engaged right now in sinking our ships and murdering good Americans.

"And do you know what we're spending the state's money for, and that's your money, brother, and mine—that hard-earned tax money? Why, let me tell you. Parris Mitchell, excuse me, I ought to have said Dr. Mitchell, I guess—well, sir, they tell me he gets those poor crazy people to tell him what they dreamed about, then he writes it down—sure, I mean what I'm saying! And then he just sits there and asks them thousands of questions. Poor things, they don't know what they're saying. Upon my word, I don't know who's crazy, the patients out there, or the doctors, or the board that lets this kind of thing go on, or *us* for letting it go on. I think it's a shame and a disgrace and I'm going to do something about it.

"He learned all that stuff from those very people we're going to have to fight pretty soon. It's come to a pretty pass if we can't have good Americans holding the state jobs and getting state money.

"Furthermore, that same Dr. Mitchell has just recently beat the state out of a good piece of property right here in Kings Row. Don't ask me how he did it! He paid for it, sure, but he paid a mighty pitiful little price for it. The state practically gave it to him. If you don't believe it, just go down to the Capitol and make a few inquiries."

That was only one of the many attacks launched by Fulmer, always in the absence of Parris or any of his friends. The matter, however, was reported to Dr. Nolan, who promptly called David Kettring by phone and told him that trouble was brewing.

"I tell you, Dave, that fellow Green will stop at nothing. If he gets at Swenson in just the right way he might force Mitchell's resignation. We can't afford to lose him. He's the most important man on the staff, barring none."

"So I've heard, Paul. Green's not so dangerous out in the open like that as he could be if he were working under cover. At least we know what he's doing. I'll see what I can do."

"Well, Dave, I'm depending on you to look out for our interests. If Parris Mitchell has to go, I'm resigning, too. Just when things are going so well here, everything being reorganized and the new wing completed, it would be a tragic mistake on the part of Swenson to upset the applecart."

"Swenson means to do the right thing."

"Maybe, but Fulmer Green did a lot of campaigning for him and Swenson may feel under some political obligation there. And, believe me, Fulmer will not fail to press his advantage."

"What has he got against Mitchell, anyhow?"

"Oh, any number of things. Trivia, really. But they add up to something pretty big in the mind of a little man like Green."

"What is Mitchell's attitude?"

"So far as I know, Mitchell never gives him a thought. Parris could no more play politics than I could—and you know what a babe in the woods I am at that game."

"I'll do my best, Paul. I'll have to find out Green's approach. Swenson will be naming the new Board of Managers for the asylum soon. That's his prerogative—the Board appointments—and I'm not sure he won't put Green's men there. But I'll try to see that safe men are appointed."

"Thanks, Dave. Let me know of any developments in the matter, and watch out."

13

The winter had dragged interminably for many people in Kings Row. But in early March it broke suddenly and running water began to fringe the ice-locked creek. For days a south wind had been blowing and the freeze was over. But it was chill and there was as yet no feeling of spring in the air.

The landscape was brown. Thin brown switches rattled empty brown pods, and the bassoon notes of wild geese sounded high. Brown leaves, dry as beggars' crust, clung with desperation to the stems from which neither the weight of snow and ice nor the torment of winds had been able to sever them.

The threat of war hovered closer over the country, casting its own pall of unease upon an unwilling people. The Middle West was self-contained and the Middle Westerner felt less the pressures that were beginning to gall the coastal regions. But just as an engineer knows instantly when anything is wrong by the complex noises of his machine, so did this same Middle Westerner become aware of something hampering the smooth-running government he trusted—trusted because he had helped to create it.

He had, back in 1914, expected Austria to draw back, Austria had refused to temporize. She had relied on the help of Germany, and even of Italy, her traditional enemy. Germany had preached for many years the necessity for a clash between the Slav and the Teuton. But what possessed Germany, anyhow, to brave the ill will of the United States, whose sympathies had definitely swung around to the Allies? The severance of diplomatic relations should have been enough, he thought, to show Germany that we had stood all that we could, yet our ships were still being torpedoed. Why?

This the Middle Westerner was asking himself, but his own answer that "it is not our war" was coming to be less and less assured, and he looked anxiously at his stalwart son, who might in the end be called upon to help settle the question.

The boys themselves were wondering, and some of them were making secret plans. Already young Dr. Jan Kettring, son of David Kettring, had joined a Canadian unit and had gone overseas with a major's commission. He was well known in Kings Row and had many friends among the young people of the town. Other young men were becoming restive. McKay Pomeroy, too young to get into the Canadian service, had gone to the Citadel, a military school of excellent standing, at Charleston, South Carolina. He meant to be ready for Officers' Training School in case we should be drawn into the war. His older brother, Ross, was at Harvard hoping to complete his engineering course before we became involved.

There was discussion, too, among other-minded groups. Elwee Neal expressed himself to the courthouse crowd in no uncertain terms.

"They sure got to *ketch* me before they get me into a uniform. I got no intention of goin' over there to fight for the frogs an' the limeys. No, *sir*!

"That's what *you* say. Uncle Sam ain't gonna ask you what you want to do, boy. You'll be learnin' to click your heels before you know what's happened."

"You wait an' see. I'll figure out some way. Between you an' me I think Jan Kettring's a fool. I'd a thought his father wouldn't let him go off that way."

"Looks like bein' Lieutenant Governor, Kettring could o' got his son outer the war even if we git in."

"Yep. When Swenson an' Kettring was elected last fall we all thought things was goin' to be hunky-dory. Even Miles Jackson had a piece in the paper about how electin' men like that would stabilize the country. But looks like we gonna git in the war anyhow."

Ricks Darden hitched his chair a little to get out of the wind and said jocularly, "Wouldn't s'prise me none if young Jan didn't want to get out of workin' in the hospital down at St. Louis. You know them young doctors has to get some experience before they can begin lawful practice."

"That's right, Ricks," Matt Fuller agreed. "An' fur as I'm concerned they might as well experiment on them furriners first. Might be a good thing."

"You know what I think? I believe I'd ruther have one of these young doctors than the old ones. There's a lot of new medicine an' cures that the old fellers haven't learned about yet."

"I'll git me a old-fashioned country doctor ever' time. Did you hear what happened to old Bill McChesney last fall? One of these new fellers took him to the hospital over at Camperville an' he died right there on the operatin' table. Like as not there wasn't nothin' more wrong with him than a stomach-ache."

"Well, any of 'em's liable to make mistakes. You just got to take your chance these days. But the longer you keep outer their hands the better off you are."

"If we do git in the war I reckon most all the young fellers will have to go in the army."

"Plenty of 'em won't be no good when they git 'em. It takes guts to be a good soldier."

"Oh, I don't know. There's plenty of soft jobs in the army."

"Tell you one young feller Uncle Sam oughta git holt of if we *do* go to fightin'. It's that Punch Rayne. He's a danged good shot, they tell me."

"Yep. I seen him once when we went rabbit huntin'. He could hit 'em ever' time. He's the best shot around Kings Row."

"I wouldn't want that boy to have it in for me. He's got sort of a killer look in his eye. But come to think of it, I don't believe I ever heard tell of his bein' in a fight."

"Nossuh, Punch ain't a fightin' kid fur as I know. But you can't never tell about them quiet kind."

No one noticed the unease in Elwee's eyes, but when he spoke his voice had a strangely subdued quality.

"Aw, Punch is a good kid, I reckon. He goes about his own business. I don't know as I ever spoke to him in my life. He ain't what you might call clubby."

"Dyer says he's the best butcher he ever had in his shop, an' that ol' man is shore hard to please."

"Well, if we *do* get in the war," Elwee said, anxious to change the subject, "I aim to let somebody else do the fightin'. I'm stayin' right here in Kings Row."

"Seems to me, Elwee, you'd be the first one wantin' to git over to Paris. They tell me them French gals is hot stuff! Anybody that goes around liftin' as many petticoats as you do might have some fun in Paris."

Elwee grinned but shook his head. "Plenty petticoats in this part of the world without huntin' 'em up that far away."

"I'll be doggone if I wouldn't like to be young again. I'd go quick as a wink. Soldierin' ain't so bad. Me an' Teddy Roosevelt done pretty good in the last war. My pension ain't so bad neither."

"I seen Davis Pomeroy's youngest boy here at Christmastime in some sort of a uniform. They tell me he goes to a military school down south somewhere. He'll git hisself chock full of fightin' notions if he stays down there long enough."

"Golly, yes. Them Southerners are sure hot-blooded. They'd turn right around and fight the Civil War all over again at the drop of a hat."

"They always been good fighters, though. You got to hand 'em that."

"Shucks! I don't believe in sendin' boys off that far to school. What's wrong with our schools out here? Some folks just like to put on airs. I reckon Davis Pomeroy thinks his boys are better'n anybody else."

"Well, now, they're pretty nice boys when you come to know 'em. They behave themselves. You never hear of either one of 'em raisin' any hell around town, an' they are always pleasant when you meet 'em. I think they're all right."

"I hear that pretty little Laneer girl thinks Ross is all right. They say she's crazy about him and don't care who knows it. He's lucky if it's so. They don't make 'em no prettier than her."

"Mmm, mmm," Elwee drawled. "She sure is a good-looker."

"Your taste ain't bad, Elwee, but you're shore barkin' up the wrong tree if you got any ideas about the Laneer gal. I wouldn't wait around for her if I was you."

"You never can tell what might happen," Elwee boasted. "I ain't been so unsuccessful in my time. There was one little number—"

So the idle talk went on, insinuation, speculation, and curiosity finding vent.

14

Suddenly and disturbingly the peace and security Parris had al-always felt at home gave way to a restless unease. Gradually he recognized that it had its source in Elise. Her mercurial moods were more pronounced and she was agitated over every smallest detail that had to do with the proposed move to von Eln. She was easily irritated and resentful of any delay in completing their plans.

One day in early March Parris brought in a letter. "It's from Anna Hauser," he said.

She reached for the letter avidly. "What does she say, Parris? Can she come? Will she be here soon? Oh, Parris, I'm afraid to look at it. What if she—"

He smiled. "She can come. I don't mind saying that it takes a great load off my mind."

Elise hurriedly opened the letter;

Dear Parris [she read]:
Your letter has made me very happy. My relatives here in St. Louis no longer need me and I am not happy when there is no one to care for. Madame (God rest her soul!) would have wished me to look after you

and your wife. I have never been happy since I left your service. To make my home there once more and to be allowed to serve you as long as I am able is all I ask of life.

I can come at once and get the place in order. If it suits you I shall arrive on Monday, and you should be able to move into the place by the end of the week. I am glad you call it 'von Eln.'

I hope you will wish me to take charge of the house just as I did during Madame's lifetime. If your wife wishes I can relieve her of much care.

With affectionate greetings,

Anna Hauser

Elise waved the letter over her head like a flag. "Darling, this makes everything perfect. I am ver-ry, ver-ry happy. Now I shall see if all the wonderful things you tell of old Anna are really true."

"Elise, Anna is more than a housekeeper. She was my grand-mother's trusted friend, and she means a great deal to me. She will do much toward making a home at von Eln for both of us, and I am sure you will love her as I do. She was never treated as a servant—and she will be as much a part of the household as you or I. I want to explain that before she comes so that there will be no awkwardness in our adjustments."

"But I understand, perfectly, Parris, and I shall *love* Anna. Don't be uneasy. I know how much she did for you all those years. What does she look like, Parris?"

"Plain and substantial and kind."

"We'll be friends. You shall see."

"It might be lonely out there without someone like Anna to keep you company."

"I am happy for you, Parris, but I am selfishly *most* happy for myself. I'm not clever about managing—and I'm afraid I'm a lazybones."

"Maybe Anna's *pastete* will put some flesh on your 'lazybones.' You're too thin. Know it?"

"Would you like me to be round, like—like Mrs. Neal?"

"Not quite that round, chicken," he answered absently, "but you should get a few more pounds before you blow away from me."

"*Can* we be moved by the middle of March?"

"Undoubtedly. You see what Anna has to say and Anna is always right. That's one thing you need to learn right now, young lady. Anna rules with an iron hand. There'll be no foolishness around Anna."

"I'll be ver-ry, ver-ry good," Elise promised solemnly with her hand on her heart. "Randy is going out to von Eln with me this afternoon. I want to measure the windows for curtains and—"

"No, Elise—not until that place is heated. You'd catch your death of cold. Tell you what I'll do. I'll have Nathan start the furnace tonight and you can go out tomorrow. How's that?"

"Well, I suppose I shall have to wait."

Anna Hauser came, as she had promised, and in less than a week after her arrival Parris and Elise were comfortably settled at von Eln and things were running as smoothly as though they had never been away. This was largely due to the quiet efficiency of the strong German woman who took hold of the place and of its occupants with the firmness characteristic of her.

To Parris she seemed not to have grown a day older since he had parted with her after his grandmother's death. Her smoothly braided hair showed no trace of gray, and her carriage was as erect and her movements as quick as he remembered them to have been.

For several days after they came to von Eln, Parris lived in a state of quasi-suspension. He expected a reaction, a surge of feeling, but if those remote forces stirred, the avenues of approach to his consciousness had been effectually blocked. However, he found himself following Elise about from room to room, dreading to be left alone. The echoes of old words whispered in the corners against the encroaching silence.

Elise was unaware of his discomfort. She was engaged in creating about them an atmosphere of cheerful and restful peace. She discarded many small objects that made what she felt were discordant notes in the furnishings of the rooms. Parris felt a faint twinge, not quite pain, as he saw some familiar bit go into the discard, but he was able to recall the unimpassioned fatalism of his grandmother, who often had quoted airily the phrase *"Tout lasse, tout casse, tout passe!"* She said it when she broke a vase, when a favorite frock wore out, and when black-bordered envelopes came in the mail. Sometimes her repetitions of the words seemed as heartless as the tinkling of the little clock on her dressing table.

Gradually Parris began to feel that he was really at home again. The weather was too bad for him to walk about the grounds, but he stood at the windows and planned plantings here and there, a broader terrace on the south side of the house, and a fountain which Elise insisted must be an *old* one. Just how that was to be managed was not quite clear to Parris, but Elise was sure it could be done. Everything was possible here at von Eln.

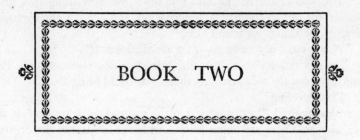

BOOK TWO

I

Kings Row thought well of the twentieth century. So many things had ceased to be merely dreams and were now realities. The horseless carriage, so long the butt of yokel jokes, was a joke no longer. Culbertson's livery stable had been converted into a garage and filling station. Not that a livery stable wasn't still necessary, but Ben, with what the courthouse crowd called "right smart foresight," decided that Wes Collins could take care of all that out at the end of Cherry Street. He had a pretty good-sized stable out there.

Farm wagons stood on stock sales days behind the feed store, but a man named Ford had cannily sensed the needs of farmer folk and was already supplying low-priced automobiles. There was talk, too, of auto-tractors and farm machinery that was exciting news to the hard-working, thrifty Middle Westerners who made up the backbone of Kings Row's business.

Even the less prosperous homes were equipped with bathrooms and new-type iceboxes. The Middle West did not lag behind other sections of the country in adopting the new. In fact, it prided itself on being in the van. Rich and poor alike were clamoring for every improvement in living conditions that the changing times were bringing.

Miles Jackson had seen all this come to pass and never ceased to speculate on what the results were likely to be. He looked about him at the changes that had taken place and with characteristic pessimism talked of them with Parris Mitchell. Parris, Miles thought, leaned too heavily upon what he would *like* to see happen in Kings Row.

"You know, Parris," he said one day, "the very thing that men looked for in this country is disappearing, and a war right now will destroy the things we found here."

"War would not reach us—in a physical sense."

"I'm not talking about material things—cities, roads, schools. I'm talking about the social changes that a war could bring about."

"Class leveling?"

Miles laughed. "In this section of the country there are scarcely social *classes*. There are upper levels and lower levels, but the degrees between them are not clearly stepwise. The social top and bottom are connected by gradients of imperceptible angle."

"Well, at least that has the advantage of facilitating movement in either direction."

"Maybe, but is that desirable?"

"I think so, Miles. My grandmother used to say she liked the Middle West because there was elbowroom."

"Just what I was talking about. The men who came here in the nineteenth century wanted just that. They wanted to stretch out—to be completely and superbly themselves. They found what they wanted."

"And you think they are going to lose it?"

"Look at yourself—at all your generation. Already you are beginning to succumb to the demands of a closer knit society. If you don't conform, God help you! The pack is after you in full cry. What's become of the breathing space we had here fifty years ago?"

"Don't tell me you are grieving for the 'good old days' the Judge refers to from time to time!"

"Not exactly, my lad, but we gathered here from all parts of the country. We have become a fairly amalgamated body. We look with some suspicion, not unmixed with disdain, upon the East; we treat the South with an easy tolerance, almost contempt; and we look on the Far West with another kind of tolerance, tempered with amusement. All our smug satisfactions will be disrupted if we are plunged into war. War is a great leveler, you know. Our young men will find out that those other sections have some things to recommend them—and then where will we be? Our balloons of vanity will be suddenly deflated."

"If that were the only thing we should suffer from a war, I'd say the sooner the better. But there are such frightful things—" Parris' face clouded and he broke off abruptly.

"Parris," Miles asked with quick understanding, "what do you hear from your wife's father in Austria?"

"Very little. He has been trying to get out of Austria to come here to us but it has been impossible. The last word we had from him he was going by invitation to Switzerland for an indefinite stay. I hope he makes it."

"It must be trying for Elise."

"Aside from her father she has no real ties over there, but the anxiety about him is making her ill. If we are actually forced to declare war on Austria I am afraid of the effect on her health."

"She had better be prepared for it. It will surely happen—and soon. How does it look to you?"

"I'm afraid you are right, Miles. There seems nothing else for it. Much as I hate the idea of war, as a nation we can't take much more, I'm convinced."

"And just when life was becoming easier, too. Elegance has lapsed in its observations and dignity has put on looser clothes. Personally, I was just settling down to a soft old age, and now—"

"Settling down? Why, you couldn't do that—not *you!*"

"Oh, yes I could. Tell you what I have in mind. I'd like to get Drew Roddy to come in with me down here. *The Gazette* could use a man like Roddy. I'd like to be able to turn things over to him gradually—just keep a finger in the pie—but get out of the drudgery."

"Kings Row wouldn't hear of your leaving *The Gazette*. You're an institution. I wonder if you know how much you've had to do with forming what I might call 'the Midwest temper'? Not just locally—here in Kings Row. *The Gazette* has done a lot toward the development out here of a group mind, a community sense of *like* and *common*. You've helped to congeal this part of the country."

"Nonsense! My role has been that of the gadfly."

"But gadflies can make people move."

"Their sting wears out after a while. I'm mellowing in my old age. I can't feel the reformer's zeal any more."

Parris laughed, but he went away thinking seriously of what Miles had said. Yes, he thought, the Middle West was an entity. It had found itself and it liked what it found. This world was wide open. One might go here as far as his strength or his funds or his quest for adventure might carry him.

And then, on the sixth of April, two days after his talk with Miles Jackson, Parris heard what he had so long dreaded.

On that day the Middle West suffered what many felt was a decisive defeat. For there was no question that they were still holding out against the idea of war. The anti-British sentiment was stronger than the anti-German feeling throughout this section.

But now, war against Germany had ceased being a threat—it was a grim reality.

The dignity of the United States had been attacked and these good Americans could not endure that. They were ill-informed as to the issues involved. Those of their leaders and newspapermen who could have enlightened them had held back because at their first outraged protests they had been attacked as "warmongers" and "Anglophiles." And for lack of that information many were unwilling to go to the extreme of declaring war on a country they had always admired.

People were suddenly inarticulate—overwhelmed by the conjunction of the two great movements—the Russian Revolution and the entry of the United States into the war for freedom.

An emotional reaction was in the offing. It only needed a growing conviction that their way of life was threatened. Someone was trying to "put something over" on them and that they could not endure. No, sir!

Kings Row was quick to feel this reaction. Its young men were volunteering, few waiting for the inevitable draft. Donny Green and Elwee Neal were among those who chose to wait. The tempo of the town quickened. Women hurried through their household tasks and rushed to Red Cross headquarters or War Relief meetings. There was a feeling of dynamic urgency in the very atmosphere of Kings Row.

2

Mrs. Fanny Porter was surprised at the early afternoon visit from Mrs. Fulmer Green. Surprised, but pleased.

She decided that Hazel Green was the most beautiful woman she had ever seen. She was tall, slight, and everything about her was in perfect proportion. Her brown hair was drawn smoothly back, and her green linen dress with its immaculate white embroidered collar and cuffs was well tailored and becoming. Even the small pearl ear-rings belonged. She had a trick of slowly lifting the lashes of her long gray eyes and giving her undivided and concentrated attention to any slight thing you said.

I wish, Fanny thought, I could be on really friendly terms with Hazel Green. I'd learn so much of what I want to know about gracious living. But I'd never have the courage to return a social visit. Never!

Mrs. Green touched upon a dozen topics, lightly, gracefully, as a fine pianist might improvise. Then she revealed the purpose of her visit, which was in the interest of the Y.W.C.A. campaign. But Mrs. Green talked so well and so easily about the work the Y.W. was doing for the young businesswomen and what she was modest enough to call her own small part in it that Fanny was captivated anew in imagining details of her caller's busy life.

When Mrs. Green left it was with a liberal subscription from Fanny to the Y.W.C.A. fund.

Fanny's donation was much larger than a few moments later she felt had been necessary; and to her acute dismay she heard an echo in her mind of the hateful long ago—"We can't stand that." During her childhood there had been constant talk of what things cost and whether or not they could afford this or that. If a thing seemed too expensive her mother would exclaim, "Good gracious, we can't stand that!" as though someone had threatened them with the rack.

She felt a terror rising within her—a terror wholly incommensurate with the happening. But the ease with which that sentence had un-coiled from some shadowy place in her brain frightened her. Because she practiced the necessary economies of her circumstances, was she growing to think them? Was she caught in the wheels of this ma-chinery she had helped to build?

Throughout the rest of the afternoon she fought a depression that threatened to suffocate her. She rearranged an already orderly linen closet. She even improvised some further meetings with Hazel Green in which she bore her share in airy conversations of the greatest elegance. She nearly forgot to order meat for supper.

Rushing to the telephone, she called Mr. Dyer, the butcher. "For porterhouse? That's too much! I can't stand—" she said. "Send me some round steak, then. No, that's all." Her eyes had a curious, strained look as she hung up the receiver and turned from the telephone.

She recalled a phrase she had read somewhere long ago, "living with a beautiful gesture." It had blossomed in her imagination in pictures vaguely outlined but alluringly colored. She was not sure what it meant, but she was sure that it should mean many of the things she was reaching out for in her effort to escape.

Escape from what? She certainly did not wish to escape from Ned. She was fond of Ned. She was pleased with the neat, almost commodious house on Cedar Street, with its furnace, its garden, and its garage.

She did not mind cooking and cleaning. She had rather some pride in her housekeeping. Now suppose she nagged Ned about the many things wives do nag their husbands about? Suppose she wanted servants or a big house on Union Street or something like that?

Half an hour later Fanny moved the pieces of frying steak in the pan and stood back from the splutter of the popping fat. She glanced at the white clock above the kitchen cabinet and hastily shook up the potatoes in their stewpan. Her movements were efficient but decidedly impatient, for she was behind in her schedule.

It was a pleasant kitchen, light and clean. But the late August sun was pitiless. Dying vines on a stretched lattice of wire and cord across the west window rattled in the hot wind and emphasized the general feel of prickly heat and stinging perspiration. Mrs. Porter's blond hair was loosening with the vigor of her steps, the short strands at the temples and at the back of her neck hanging outward like limp grass. Her pretty face was extremely flushed with the heat as well as from the irritated, headlong thinking that now kept pace with, and now outstripped her hurried exertions.

There were so many things in the world and so many people failing to play just the parts they should play, or to make of themselves just the background they should, to make living the graceful, almost lyric thing she so surely knew it could be.

She placed the platter of steak in the warming closet and poured milk on the rapidly browning flour for the gravy that was an essential part of Ned's supper. "Give me plenty of good cream gravy and potatoes," he said whenever the word "gravy" was mentioned, "and I can do without a lot of little fancy things." Fanny knew this speech of her husband's so well that it no longer registered in her consciousness. He had, every time he pronounced it, the air of stating a profound dietetic discovery. The milk hissed loudly in a quick cloud of steam and Fanny's little mental maelstrom hissed and steamed in concert.

Relentlessly pursuing the shadow of her discontent, she found herself remembering things of her childhood—a childhood lived constantly within the sound of the sordid mechanism of living, close to questions that were vital enough but which she wished, even then, to keep out of sight like some shameful secret.

Her mother's plaint, "We can't stand that"—that saying, and all the attendant talk of money in those scrimped days she half recognized as a sort of ground base of much of her unrest. Not that she wished for more, but she didn't want to *talk* about it. And Ned was as bad about discussing costs as her mother had been.

When Ned came in she was rearranging some nasturtiums in a flat glass dish.

"Lord, but today's been a scorcher!" he said loudly, dumping his packages on the sideboard. "Why didn't you have a cold supper tonight? What you say we go out to Langley's Lake after supper? It'd cool us off." He went whistling upstairs and the sound of noisy ablutions followed. Fanny carried the packages to the kitchen and hung up his hat and coat.

"Think I'll just leave off my coat," he said coming into the kitchen. "Gee, didn't you nearly roast getting supper ready?" She noticed with a fresh distaste the bright blue elastic sleeve holders on his arms.

"What's old man Dyer charging you for steak now?" he asked as he helped himself. "You have to watch him. If he sees you go across the street to the Crystal Market every once in a while it'll keep him down a little."

Fanny looked despairingly about the attractive room. The light curtains moved now in the stir of the oscillating fan buzzing on the mantel. It was a wholly satisfactory picture to her eye—a satisfactory setting. Ned, in his shirt sleeves with those abominable holders, was a false note, but even that could be overlooked if it were not for this everlasting talk of the cost of things.

"By the way, honeybunch," Ned's voice was saying, "did the Colony Coal folks put in coal today? You know I got it for eight-seventy by ordering in July. Saved eighty cents per! What do you know about that?"

She caught her breath with a swift, hysterical giggle and throughout supper her color was high. She watched her husband with a nervous fascination as though in some sort of eager anticipation of his next remark.

On the way out to the lake Fanny settled back to something like a genuine enjoyment. Ned looked well in his fresh palm beach suit. He was too heavy but his clean-shaven face was healthily pink and his brown eyes had a direct look.

"Running sweet," he chuckled, as they came in sight of the line of cars parked outside the enclosure. "I bet we came out on fifteen cents. Hey, Charlie," he called banteringly to the ticket seller at the turnstile, "any reduction to folks that come as often as we do?"

It was only a week or two later that Dr. Waring stopped Parris Mitchell on the street and asked if he'd drop by at Fanny Porter's and have a look at his patient. His shoulders had a discouraged droop and his face was lined with fatigue.

"Frankly, Mitchell, I don't know what to make of her. I am convinced she's on the verge of a crack-up, and if you can do anything it will be a blessing. Poor Ned is almost frantic. He doesn't know what to do."

"Why, of course I'll go. When?"

"Today, if you can."

Parris found Fanny Porter indeed on the verge of a nervous crack-up. She was in a state verging on hysteria.

"Dr. Mitchell, you can help me, I know. Dr. Waring has been our physician for years and he says you're the only person who can. And now that you're here, I hardly know where to begin. You see—"

"But you have already begun. There's plenty of time for you to say everything you wish. You don't need to hurry."

"It's Ned," she almost whispered.

"What about Ned?"

She touched his arm timidly. "Dr. Mitchell, it seems like I can't *bear* to have him around. It's a terrible thing to say—a terrible thing to *feel*!"

Parris nodded. "That's interesting but not terrible," he said. "What does he do that disturbs you?"

She clasped her hands tightly in her lap and waited a moment before she answered. "He does all the things he's always done, but I just can't bear them any more!"

"You haven't told me *why* you feel this way," Parris said quietly.

She made a frantic gesture with her hands and her voice held a note of rising excitement. "I tell you I don't know. I hate the way he wears his hair; I hate the shape of his shoes; and I hate the color of his ties; I hate his very *patience*."

"Ned is devoted to you, Mrs. Porter, and very proud—"

"Do you think I don't know that? Do you think I don't name over his good qualities every day of my life? Why, I *love* Ned. But I just can't stand the way he always talks about the *cost* of things. I've gotten so I talk about it, too."

"Isn't that rather a natural thing for him to discuss with you? Ned's a businessman, a merchant. He has to think all day about what things cost. He can't dismiss it from his mind the minute he closes his store."

"Oh, you don't understand. I feel like I've got to get away from here. I've had all I can stand."

"That's just what you need—a vacation. Don't you think Ned would—"

"That's just the trouble. I couldn't take a vacation. Why, we couldn't stand that! Oh, God! Listen to that. I've said it again!"

"Said what?"

"That thing my mother always said when I was a child. I still hear her talk about the cost of food, of clothes—of everything."

"It takes a strong person, Mrs. Porter, to rise above his childhood beginnings; and it takes a wise one to shed the inhibitions brought about by those persistent memories. But you are young and intelligent and if you will face these things—charge them frontally, and even laugh at them, you can conquer them. You'll have to do it for yourself."

"How do I start?" she asked skeptically.

"Begin by waking up to your own potentialities. Open your eyes to your own personal charm and ability, and then cultivate them."

"I wish I had the courage to make a stab at it, Doctor, but—" Her voice trailed off uncertainly.

"Mrs. Porter, your aversion to all talk about the cost of things is a symbol of—"

"Oh, I know it's a symbol, but I don't even care to know what it's a symbol of. I only know that I wait and watch constantly for Ned to bring up the subject. I'm *revolted* at my own resentment at his awkwardness of speech—and he's so *good,* Dr. Mitchell. I can't tell you how considerate he is—how patient."

"Have you told him what you are telling me just now?"

"I couldn't hurt him like that. He wouldn't understand what I meant."

"Suppose I insist on that vacation I was talking about. Dr. Waring agrees with me."

"*No.* You are saying just what Dr. Waring said—though I haven't told him how I feel about Ned. Can't you tell me how to *stop feeling that way?*" Suddenly she shot out the question that had been forming in her mind. "Do you think I am going crazy?"

"No, but I think you are nervously overwrought."

"Can you cure sick minds—really cure them?"

"Sick minds are as curable as sick bodies. But, you know something? You aren't sick—and you don't have to be, if you'll turn squarely around and face another way."

"How am I going to do that?"

"I've a double prescription. First, I want you to see what a change of scene will do for you. We all need it from time to time. The second part of my prescription is—meet new people, make some new friends."

She bit her lip with annoyance and considered not answering, but she asked finally, "Where am I to find them?"

"Mrs. Porter, you have the reputation of being a homebody, but if you would show a willingness to cultivate people, you would find them meeting you more than halfway."

"I suppose I *am* shy, Dr. Mitchell—at least I feel very ill at ease in the presence of women who have had more social experience than I. Only a few days ago Mrs. Fulmer Green called to see me and I found myself tongue-tied."

"Mrs. Green is a very remarkable woman, but with a little more self-confidence you could have as much charm."

She looked at him unbelievingly, but Parris was grateful to see that the look of strain had lessened. He felt sure she was already planning a small social campaign.

He drove immediately to the hospital and called Randy McHugh. "Randy, may I come out to see you this afternoon? I've another favor to ask. . . . At four? Good. I'll be there."

"I'm always dumping my problems on your shoulders, Randy, but this time hasn't anything to do with me personally," Parris greeted her.

"I'm glad—glad of any excuse that brings you here and gives me a chance to do something for you." Randy motioned him to a cretonne-cushioned wicker chair at the shady end of the veranda.

"Do you know Fanny Porter?" Parris came directly to the point.

"Not well. She is pretty much of a stay-at-home."

"Too much of one, Randy, and she needs the sort of help that you, not I, can give her. She's alone too much. Would you be willing to— well, to cultivate her a little?"

He could see the wheels of Randy's thought turning—speculating, wondering if Fanny Porter had become a mental case.

"Randy," he commanded, "stop thinking!"

Her laugh was gay.

"You know too much, Parris," she said. "Tell me what I can do."

"What you can to make her feel she is liked—admired, even. You might—as only you can, Randy—give her a sense of her own importance, make her feel that everyone is impressed with Ned's devotion to her. That sort of thing—an occasional compliment—might do a lot to build her morale."

"Maybe I could interest her in some sort of club work," Randy suggested. "People are always at their best when they are doing something constructive."

"That's exactly what I mean, and no one knows better how to give a person an interest in life than you do."

He was surprised and dismayed to see Randy's eyes fill with tears. "I'm sorry." She tried to smile as she reached for her handkerchief. "I didn't mean to—"

"Randy, my *dear,* you're tired. You're doing too much, and here I am, great stupid ox, putting more responsibilities on your shoulders." Suddenly he leaned forward and kissed the top of her head. The fragrance of her hair stirred him. "I have to go, Randy," he said abruptly, "but I'll see you soon."

She reached for his arm—a little uncertainly, it seemed to Parris. "Wait a minute," she said. "There is something I must ask you before you go. It's about Pick Foley. What do you know about him?"

At the mention of the name Parris pictured the rambling, dilapidated, close-shuttered house a few blocks away on Union Street where Foley lived. "All I know is that he seems to be something of a recluse. And I have heard that he lives in desperate poverty."

"Yes, that's Pick. And that's what worries me. The last time I saw him he looked half starved. I can't get him out of my mind. I'm sure he needs help."

"Hasn't he any relatives?"

"No. Since his mother died he has lived, I understand, in a couple of rooms that are closed off from the rest of the house, and the only person in Kings Row who knows anything about him is Lola Saunders, an old Negro woman who does cleaning for him on Saturdays. I tried to get some information out of her, but you know Lola! She thought I was snooping and she put me in my place—quick."

"Tell me what you find out, Randy, and if you need any help for him you know you can count on me."

"Thank you, Parris. I have always been able to count on you," Randy said. "Meantime, I'll pop in and try to cheer up Fanny Porter."

As he was cranking the balky engine of his car, he called over his shoulder to her. "Mrs. Porter seems to have a great admiration for Hazel Green. You don't suppose you could possibly persuade her to take an interest, too?"

"Why not? Hazel's a peach."

Parris had driven only two blocks when Sarah Skeffington's screen door clicked shut and Hazel Green came down the front steps. "Mrs. Green," he called, "can I give you a lift?"

"Dr. Mitchell! This is my lucky day." Her voice was warm, low-pitched. She was a really beautiful woman, Parris thought. Fulmer Green had done well.

"I'm awfully late. Mrs. Skeffington insisted I stay for a second cup of tea and I'm afraid Fulmer will get home ahead of me!"

He opened the car door for her and she settled into the seat beside him. He told her about his and Randy's plan to bring a little change into Fanny Porter's life. "Mrs. Porter," he told her, "is an ardent admirer of yours, Mrs. Green. She'd be terribly pleased if she could think of you as a friend."

"Why, I didn't even know you knew her, Dr. Mitchell," Hazel said.

"You have reason to know, my dear lady, that I rarely allow a beautiful woman to escape me."

He was surprised to see her blush, but she laughed lightly. "And what does your wife say to that?"

"I'm afraid I forgot to ask her."

"Oho!" she scoffed. "You men."

"We were speaking of women, I thought."

"Maybe the world would be better off without women."

"For me it would be a sorry place without them."

"But seriously," she said, "I am glad you suggested my going to see Fanny Porter because I honestly like her. She's a sweet and extremely intelligent young woman. I'll look her up immediately. And, my name's Hazel, incidentally."

"So it is—and a lovely word to say. I'm glad your parents thought of it, Hazel."

"Thanks, Parris."

As Parris dropped her at her gate he gave a gay little half salute.

Neither of them noticed that Martha Cotten, hurrying along the other side of the street, slowed her step and stared speculatively as Hazel went up the walk.

3

Elise found she could not practice. All morning her fingers proved obdurate and her mind wandered. It shouldn't be so difficult, she thought fretfully. Then she smiled, remembering how her father used to remind her that nothing was easy for the unwilling. That was it— she simply didn't want to practice. She wanted to luxuriate in the sun out there on that bench beside the summerhouse.

She idly fingered the scores on the piano for a moment, then abruptly turned away and went out into the sunlit garden. She sat down with a sigh of satisfaction.

Resting her arms along the back of the bench, she drifted into a wistful contemplation of the splendors spread before her by the bright summer day.

A flame of blossoms followed the curving walks. Butterflies drifted from border to border as though the flowers themselves arose from their stems and visited among their neighbors. The occasional flick of wings gave a further feeling of movement to the garden, which, for all the stillness of the fresh bright morning, was intensely alive. She expected any moment to see the whole garden arise on colored wings and whir softly across the treetops.

That sense of passing, of intense preoccupation with personal concerns—that was it! That was what made her want to reach out and seize the beauty of the moment and hold it.

She thought of her father, with the familiar pang of loneliness and longing she always experienced when she thought of him. If he were only here to enjoy this day with her! He was so good, so gentle, so absorbed in his love for the whole plant world. How was he faring in these troubled times? He was not a partisan—had never been. He knew so little of what went on in the world of politics. He must view the spectacle of war with wondering eyes. Now that we were at war with Germany, it was only a question of time, she knew, until we would have to declare war on Austria, too. Perhaps he had no work now, since the University of Vienna had been emptied of its students.

It had been so long since her father had brought her to this country that she felt no real ties with the land of her birth, but she wanted her father—desperately. If only he had stayed here everything would have been all right. He had been happy here—as she had been. Or, she wondered, *had* she ever been really happy?

The two years here at von Eln before she met Parris, newly returned from medical school in Vienna, were lonely years, in spite of the fact that she had been the almost inseparable companion of her father. She had been too consciously an alien to make friends with the young people of Kings Row, and Dr. Sandor had not realized that his young daughter was lonely. When she married Parris, she had expected to go on living at von Eln, but instead he had taken her to live among the horrors of the asylum.

Unaccountably she shivered.

She brushed her hand across her eyes as though to rid herself of an intolerable vision and looked with determined interest at the roses blooming within reach of her hand.

She reached out and almost touched the blossoms—almost, but there she held her fingers while a flicker of imagination made contact. She saw her hand poised there above the roses, isolated and clear. She noted its texture—the chiffon-like weaving of lines over it—and the patterns of veins pressing a little against the skin. Her attention was held for a moment by a hummingbird quiveringly engaged with a jasmine near by. She felt wistful, all at once—watching its tremulous absorption. She turned her eyes back to the roses. For some reason she felt the roses were important, they might explain something. It would be easy—her thoughts drifted lightly this way and that—to make symbols of them, but she could not stretch the little thread of feeling quite so far.

Just then, a disturbing memory of the sea intruded itself and a sick fear possessed her for a moment. How she hated the sea!

How she hated the memory of that day when the sea had taken her mother! Her recollection of the drowning, which she had witnessed, was less a thing of reality than a thing she remembered from later stories told her by her father. She remembered only recognizing with a secret feeling of relief that now she would have her father to herself. She would not have to share him with her mother. Now no one could interfere with her own small tyrannies over her adored father.

Later, what she supposed was her conscience had laid weighty hands upon her and she had suffered secretly and silently that sense of wickedness—and with that revulsion of feeling had come the dread of the sea which *took* people.

Here in this inland country she had not harbored such morbid thoughts, but occasionally the hated vision would touch her consciousness and at such times she became almost physically ill. Oh, it was monstrous in its indifference and its cruelty, the sea. How many centuries those tides have come in and gone out across those sands that remember nothing!

She remembered another day, long ago, another day as beautiful as this, when she and her father had been visiting in the south of France. One afternoon she had sat alone in a little pavilion watching the Mediterranean tide flow and retreat. Urgent, urgent, urgent—and then the foaming break into overlapping shell-shaped shallows in the sand, and the pathetic slip backward, retarding the onrush of the next wave, breasting it, passing beneath it back to the hidden under-tow. She had imagined the sea warning her of the life that lay ahead of her—across the Atlantic—there in that strange country where it was rumored everything was new and different. *"Patience, patience,"* it seemed to say. *"Presently the long travail of the land will be no more—no more agony of birth and death, no more expectation of spring and dread of winter, no more love and no more grief; presently there shall be only sea."*

The sharp impact of that vision left her weak and dizzy. Again as if it had been yesterday, she thought guiltily of her mother, so long dead, and experienced again the terror of her own crossing of the ocean when she had come to America. Why had the memory come to spoil this moment for her? Was it because everything here, this garden, this house, spoke only in accents of the past? She was smitten with an acute sense of time. Perhaps the pervading loneliness was responsible for her morbid fears.

She rose slowly and left the summerhouse in search of Kam. He should be having his lunch. It was heavenly good of Laurel and Paul to let their little son come so often to von Eln. Her beloved Kam. She would be lonely without him. The days were long.

A familiar stab of passionate resentment assailed her. Kam should be hers! It was not right that she should be childless. Parris wanted children and she should have had them. Surely if they had a child of their own, Parris would be more closely tied to his home. And she herself would feel more secure. That was it. She didn't feel secure as she had always felt with her father. A child—a child of their own would make Parris think less of his work and—his friends.

She would never forget the day when Dr. Waring had told her she must not have a child. Parris had held her close in his arms and reminded her that they had each other—that *she* was his child, to hold forever—but, as she pressed closer to him in her sudden need, she knew the bitterness of his regret. She did not know whether he thought of it often, now, but she was afraid.

Kam Nolan was as unlike the other Nolan children as if he were wholly unrelated to them. He was so much younger than the others that he had learned self-reliance and an extraordinary ability to entertain himself. To him, the world was shaped much like an amphitheater, with himself as its ever-changing center. He regarded it with a lively attention and invested all of its appearances with harmonizing qualities. These qualities he divided quite simply into two classes, the known and the unknown, or perhaps more primitively, good and evil.

With the immense variety of things presented to his view indoors and out—he was quite sure it would never be possible for him to complete his explorations—he had ready to his fancy all of the elements of drama. All things were conscious. The rocks that kept so still by the road, or that lay half buried in the woods, did so of choice and for reasons of their own. It was not well to question too deeply or to appear surprised when one came upon them in the morning in exactly the same place they were the day before. Best go about as though there were nothing unusual about it. Things were friendlier that way. Besides, it was polite.

It was very nice out here in the country. He liked to go to the edge of the creek and watch it hurry past. This was not encouraged, however, and he quite understood the warning. The creek was manifestly sinister despite the gay, rippling surface. One could throw pebbles and sticks to it as a sort of propitiatory offering, and the shining water would flash and wink in reply, as it swallowed the pebbles and carried the sticks away, but he was a little afraid of it.

The long avenue of cedars was rather depressing. Cedars couldn't be climbed, they resented being touched, and they were certainly the most uncommunicative of trees. When the wind blew there were no dancing leaves or hilarious gesticulations. They merely rocked and sighed like old women in rocking chairs; like the black-clad old ladies he saw at church.

The gardens were best of all, especially when, hand in hand with Lissa, he walked through them with the little dog trotting at his heels. But he was just as happy in old Nathan's company, watching him at his pruning and transplanting. The gardens were friendly, but it was always best to speak quietly to the lilac bushes as one passed. There was something *about* them.

Not everything was friendly. The dark woods that crowded along the far side of the creek seemed always ready to creep forward. Nathan, very old and very black, came and went through the woods, but Nathan was surely some sort of magician. Nathan talked to everything. Any day at all he could be heard scolding and exhorting from one end of the garden to the other, and when he went muttering at evening toward that winding pathway through the trees he doubtless spoke quite plainly to anything he encountered there.

Kam was very busy all day acquainting himself minutely with the elusive personalities of the animate and inanimate world. He would softly touch the leaves and stems, delicately finger the petals, and peer into the little tunnels where insects hurried in and out. In a sort of trance, he would rub the prickly surface of a hollyhock leaf. There was always something he was about to discover. But not often, for it only happened when no one was near. Then he would dash off at a gallop, as if to escape from the moment's dreaming, and half afraid that he might discover a secret of most surprising consequence.

Then there was something else—something different: there was the multitude of things one couldn't see. This was something over and above and through the things one could see. With all of his curiosity about it, he regarded it obliquely. He was a little fearful about it. Certainly it couldn't be spoken of to Lissa. He supposed grown-up people knew, or had known, or else they had forgotten about it. They were always busy moving things about, or reading, or writing. Nathan, maybe, but Nathan was much more like something that grew in the woods.

Nathan was, he decided, really stronger than a tree. It might be well to cultivate Nathan. For days following this resolution he hung about the old man at his work, keeping his eyes on the wrinkled black face, listening and watching, but nothing much came of it. In fact, something of the magic disappeared. The tiger lilies became— well, just tiger lilies. Apparently it was better to be alone. He wasn't at all uneasy when he was with Nathan in the shadowy wisteria arbor. That proved that something went away when Nathan came. But he felt these presences when he returned alone. One had to walk differently—be different. Perhaps it would be better not to look too closely. When he was older, maybe.

Flowers were for Kam sheer enchantment. When the apple trees bloomed in May a sort of madness seized him. He felt that he wanted to gather the whole orchard into his arms, to touch every blossom, smell each one—possess them in some way, hold them against their possible vanishment. In the brief flowering of the fruit trees he had already become acquainted with the tragedy of beauty's transience. Later, when the June blossoming of roses took place he again went through the poignant experience.

He never talked about his feeling. He was not ashamed of it, precisely, but he felt, for indefinable reasons, that it would suffer some sort of violence if it came to the matter-of-fact attention of grownups. If he was surprised in his absorbed rapture before some fresh spring revelation he would assume a casual manner and saunter away.

Every morning he roamed all over the place to see whether any changes had taken place since yesterday. Having just now satisfied himself on this point, he decided he would find Lissa. Maybe she would think it was time for lunch, and Anna would have something very, very good. He liked Anna. He brushed at his clothes. Lissa liked him to be neat. He noticed he had lost a button from his waistband and his blue linen trousers gaped away from his blouse. She wouldn't mind, maybe, and there were buttons in Anna's sewing basket, if she noticed. Maybe, he thought hopefully, maybe Uncle Parris would get home in time to tell him some more about Johnny Appleseed before he had to go back to the old hospital.

But Kam was doomed to disappointment; it was late afternoon before Parris had finished his routine visits, and when he finally arrived Kam was running about the garden with Greta, the happy, satiny-black dachshund, drawing her length along eagerly to keep up with Kam's flying feet. Elise, blond and slight, like a Dresden figure against the shadows of the giant trees in the garden, looked on, a faint smile on her lips.

There was something in her pose—a deep melancholy that seemed to pervade her that worried Parris. How thin she had grown! Even before Randy's mention of it, he believed he had been conscious of her gradual but steady loss of weight. It had not concerned him greatly, at first. It was something less tangible than this—some quality of being, something in the way she moved, too quietly, from shrub to flower. Something too passive, too gentle in the smile she turned on Kam. She seemed not only listless and wan, but consciously, willingly so, as if she had already given up the fight.

There had been something too passive, he felt—hating himself for the thought—in her response to his love-making of late. It was as if she had withdrawn into some inner fastness of her secret self and was scarcely aware of his need of her.

He remembered Dr. Waring's stated explanation of Elise's failing health. "Worry over her father, the strain—you know—the war—"

There were other strains, too, ones that Dr. Waring did not mention. There was an undercurrent of animosity growing up ever stronger in Kings Row toward Elise. Of course she felt it—that was surely the reason she had withdrawn more and more from the town's activities.

Poor, gentle darling, Parris thought as he watched her, unseen. How could anyone harbor ill will toward her! Or toward Eger, or Lenz, or Kelner. Kings Row, it seemed, had begun to boycott the German shopkeepers, and to withdraw its young music students from the guiding hands of Jacob Lenz. The three kindly old Germans had been taunted and insulted on the streets and in the square, and the little dachshunds, the litter Herman had been so proud of, were no longer seen romping about his yard.

A shout from Kam brought Parris back from his musing. The boy, with Elise's encouragement, was engaging Greta in a retrieving game.

But Parris' attention was again centered on Elise. She was like a silver tree, he thought, long invisible in silver light and then revealed by shadows of the changing hours. How different she was from Randy, with her hardy, eager grasping at life—Randy was a symbol of life itself. No, there was nothing elusive and withdrawn about

Randy. The momentary thrill he had had in his nearness to her came back to him and he put it out of his mind—almost angrily.

He called to Elise. She ran to him, suddenly gay, and caught him by both arms.

"Oh, Parris, how nice to have you home early. We have been waiting for you so ver-ry long and I have promised Kam we would drive him home. Then, afterwards, couldn't we go for a drive out the Camperville road?"

The three of them piled into the front seat. Parris, his right arm around the little boy, drove off. After turning Kam over to his mother, they drove out past Aberdeen College and turned onto the Camperville road. It was their favorite drive. They had watched the changing seasons work their magic on the gently rolling hills to the north and along the slopes that slanted sharply toward the river to the south. Parris braked the car at the top of a hill and they got out to look down at the town spread below them.

"Parris," Elise said almost timidly, "do you not think sometimes—on afternoons like this, for instance—do you not think Kings Row ver-ry beautiful? It has from this distance a sort of majesty."

Remembering the bigotry and greed of Kings Row, he wondered if he could see majesty in it. He brushed aside the resentments lurking in his mind and gave himself over to a contemplation of the pageantry he could always conjure up about this region.

Great clouds moved slowly from the west, myriad shapes, beasts and cities, armies and mountain ranges, the vast and mysterious vault above them, the warm, dreaming, earth beneath. Had the clouds looked down they would have seen, as the moving surface of the sea, the countryside sagging like a net into a knotted, twisted spot which was Kings Row.

Perhaps they were a symbol of the whole—the clouds themselves a symbol of the metamorphosing life beneath—faring from nothing, taking shape, passing beyond the horizon to dissolve again into the nothingness from which they sprang. Something of this feeling Parris tried to tell Elise. She was silent lest she disturb the flow of his thought, happy in these moments when she felt that she was being taken into his secret life, the life about which she knew so little. What she sensed instinctively was that he was living too much in the past. Only old people should do that, she thought, and surely it was not

[123]

good for a young person like Parris. He seemed happiest when he talked of his boyhood; his eyes were warm when he spoke of his grandmother. Elise wondered whether only by living in the past he was able to free his mind of his patients and their unhappy lives and hopeless futures.

But today he talked of Kings Row, the town, the men and women who had come and gone along those streets down there—the men who had fallen upon evil days—men, once important, whose successes had been talked about and applauded, but who, as years passed, had lost their youth and with it their ambition and self-confidence. Yes, there was decay and decadence in Kings Row. Youth was in danger of blight. Youth *had* to escape the kind of materialism that was there. In the past a few had escaped—those who went away to essay a larger life elsewhere. But they rarely returned, even for visits, nor did Kings Row greatly care. It was interested in its own.

He spoke of Drake McHugh, of Jamie Wakefield, of Dr. Tower, of Benny Singer, of all the varied destinies he had observed. He had the feeling that life in full career had passed blustering over the places of his knowing, laying on to right and left, elevating, exhorting, striking down, lashing, driving some out to important places, whipping others into corners, and that now a quiet almost as of death, the calm after a storm, lay over the place, wreckage on all sides, and with but a slight sense of the coming destinies of the newer young people, who seemed to be only a scattered growth instead of the mass formation of the oncoming phalanx which he felt and remembered of his own generation.

"Elise," he interrupted himself, "am I growing old?"

Elise's laugh rang out. "Oh, Parris, you are so ver-ry young! Sometimes I think you are younger than I, for all your treating me like a child. But you are ver-ry serious. I think you must have been a solemn little boy, like my Kam."

"Just now I am feeling as old as—as Kings Row."

"And there you are wrong, too. Kings Row is a young town. America is a young country. Europe is old, my Parris. That you know. But here," she spread her arms in a wide gesture—"here, everything is young—so ver-ry young!"

Suddenly it was as though a heavy burden lifted from his heart—a comforting gray mist enveloped him with a sheltering obscurity.

He took Elise into his arms. "You are a veil between me and my vision of possible failure, my darling. I could not face the future if that veil were withdrawn."

"It is only that you love me, Parris, that you think you need me."

He cupped her face in his hands and kissed her lips tenderly, lingeringly.

They drove home in silence, Elise feeling more an integral part of Parris than she had for many months.

4

Every time Parris Mitchell entered the Burton County Bank, he was conscious of a troubled concern about his old friend, Jamie Wakefield. He felt that Jamie was as complete a misfit in this place of business as any man could be, in spite of the fact that he had become First Vice-President of the largest bank in the county.

Jamie Wakefield had been such a beautiful boy, Parris thought, smiling as he recalled how uncomfortable that very beauty had made him sometimes. He used to be angry at Jamie for making him feel uneasy in his presence. Since he had come back from Vienna, he had seen very little of his old friend, who had settled down to business, hating it, Parris knew. For Jamie was a poet by inclination and by gifts.

Parris wondered how seriously Jamie's frustrated desires and his social maladjustments had affected his character. The warm, eager personality of the young boy seemed grayed and obscured in the man of business. He was affable, courteous, and charitable, but he seemed to shy away from friendly overtures. But Parris had not lost his sincere liking for Jamie and kept hoping they might come back into the old comradely relation they had had during grammar-school days.

This morning Parris paused beside Jamie's desk for a friendly exchange of greetings. Jamie, he thought, did not look the part of the successful banker. The light from the windows beside his desk fell across his thinning hair, and he had removed the tortoise-shell-rimmed glasses he usually wore. There was something sweet and appealing about the boyish face.

Jamie pushed the green shade back from his wide forehead and looked across the desk at his friend.

"How does it feel, Parris, to be doing the thing you want most in the world to do?"

"Why, Jamie, it's never possible to do exactly what you want to do. Everybody has to compromise. But—I like my work."

"I wish I could say as much. This humdrum existence isn't easy to take, Parris."

"No job is all excitement, Jamie. We have to take the monotony in our stride."

"It wouldn't be monotonous if it were what— Listen, Parris, you've always known what I wanted to do." Jamie passed his hand wearily across his brow. "I thought once that I might write a book—in verse— and so set another star against the west. Crazy idea, wasn't it?"

"Not crazy at all—"

"It's funny about this town of Kings Row. I've seen many fine-strung people—people with brains—pass here, go slack and out of tune. A few—like you—have realized themselves. But others—like myself—oh, something is wrong with Kings Row, I'm sure."

Parris realized that Jamie had spoken from a deep resentment. "You should have stood up against it, Jamie."

"I couldn't stand up against *life*. It's too big for me."

"That simply isn't so. The world needs poets even more than it needs bankers."

Jamie's voice was charged with a casual, unprotesting cynicism when he spoke again. "Utopian dreams aren't worth much, are they?"

"Not if we expect men to conform to them."

"I'm forgetting how to dream, Parris. I *hope* I'm losing the urge to write. It's made me too darned uncomfortable."

"If it means your happiness—"

"Happiness?" Jamie mocked. "Parris, I was thinking of you last night—thinking how you have attained fulfillment in your life."

"There's a big difference in fulfillment and happiness, Jamie."

"I don't see it."

Parris drew his fountain pen from his pocket and studied the design of silver filigree with apparent concentration—a sign that he was giving serious attention to the subject under discussion. "Happiness," he said slowly, "is merely a temporary condition, subject to immediate loss; fulfillment partakes of destiny and has the more lasting satisfactions."

"That sounds profound."

"Probably isn't original. I suspect that may have been a conclusion of Dr. Tower's. I don't remember—but I'm convinced of its truth."

"But what about those of us who never attain either?"

"Do you hate—all this?" Parris' gesture included the whole banking paraphernalia.

"Loathe it," Jamie said promptly. "I envy you, Parris. You went out and found what you wanted. I hadn't the courage."

"I'm still looking for something, too. I can't define it, but there's something important I have yet to find."

"I knew what I wanted and still couldn't get it."

"I guess we'll have to keep on looking, old man. Maybe it's just around the corner—the answer to our utopian dreams."

"What I can't understand is that you always seemed to me a sort of mystic, but you must have a strong practical streak or you couldn't have reached your professional goal so quickly."

"More people are mystics than you suspect. They are hunting a kind of harmony, and the plain, unromantic aspects of that mystical harmony are just simple conventions and decent behavior."

"It doesn't simplify life—that I can see." Jamie's voice carried a profound discouragement. He did not understand Parris, he thought. Parris' assertions carried a sort of compactness which seemed out of keeping with his general air of reticence. Maybe, Jamie speculated, it was the reticence of one who had attained his goal and found it disappointing.

Parris squinted his eyes reminiscently. "Jamie, I remember how I envied you when we were boys, because of your *gifted* look. I knew you were seeing things the rest of us couldn't see, and I wanted to know what it was."

"And now I see and look and talk and *feel* like everybody else in Kings Row. I try to forget that oleanders bloom in clouds along the walls in Italy. My mind has only room for the price of good wheat land, or whether Wes Cromwell will be able to meet his note next fall."

"You can recapture the dreams."

"God forbid. I've thrown them on the ash heap. I'm just trying for a little peace from now on."

The remark sounded casual enough as Jamie made it, but Parris knew an insidious peril lurked there. He looked at his watch but without noting the time. He was trying to think of the right thing to say to his friend.

"Oh, don't go, Parris. I so seldom have a chance to talk with you."

"Sure I'm not holding you up? You're a busy man."

"Not too busy, Parris. I wanted to ask you about Vera Lichinsky. I often wonder how she is getting along out there."

"I can give you a good report on Vera. She'll be sent home in a few weeks. She's the first graduate from our new Musical Therapy Department."

"You don't mean it! Why, Parris, that's wonderful. Will she play again?"

"As well as ever. She can't be separated from her violin. I'm not sure her playing has not gained in depth. She's attained emotional as well as intellectual maturity."

"Maturity?"

"Yes, just that."

"I don't think I know just what you mean."

"Oh, yes, you do. We all carry about with us some childish traits. We don't mature all of a piece. Vera's emotional life was still in the adolescent stage. She couldn't co-ordinate properly. Now I believe she is able to go on with her interrupted career. She's already sent in an application to Washington, offering her services as a concert artist to encampments and hospitals. She wants to do her part in the war effort."

"But this is the best news I've heard in a long time. I must stop by to see Amos. I've come to be really fond of Amos. He—well, he's been in the same sort of spot I'm in—not having a chance to do what he most wants to do."

"So Vera tells me. Maybe he'll be able to get at his painting now. By the way, Jamie, I hear Drew Roddy's lost his place—to Fulmer Green. How did that happen?"

"Fulmer bought it in for delinquent taxes. I don't know why Drew didn't borrow enough on the place to keep it from going."

"He probably didn't know that he could. I understand he's utterly impractical."

"Drew's difficult. He's so inordinately sensitive that you can't find out anything about him."

"I thought you knew him fairly well."

"I used to go out there occasionally—usually after I'd discovered some poem of his tucked away in one of the quality magazines. He's a real poet, Parris. His things have a shattering simplicity. But he can't be induced to talk about himself."

"Would there be any way to get back his little place for him?"

Jamie looked curiously at Parris. "Why, yes," he said. "Fulmer can't get a clear title to it for a year—two years, I believe, in this state. If Drew comes forward within that time and pays the back taxes and the costs of the sale, he can get it back."

"Then he must do it."

"Evidently he hasn't the money."

"Your bank can lend it to him."

"We would—but he didn't ask for it. And I know he'd lose it in the end because he has no way to repay the loan."

"Something's got to be done about it. I have an idea. Just keep the matter under your hat until I see what I can find out. I may have to call on you to talk to Drew when the time comes."

"Just remember, Parris, that Drew Roddy will not accept charity—you can't offer him money."

"Who said anything about offering him money? I think we can save his place for him."

"Another one of Fulmer Green's schemes going up in smoke, I hope! Good luck, Parris. You can count on me."

Parris rose reluctantly. He wanted to get Jamie to talk out his personal disappointment and bitterness, but since Jamie had deliberately changed the subject, he decided he should leave things as they stood.

"Jamie, I wish you'd come out to von Eln for dinner one evening this week. I'd like to have a good, long talk with you."

Jamie flushed slightly and fingered the blotter nervously. "Thanks, Parris. We'll talk about it later. Good of you to ask me."

Parris left the bank more troubled than ever. It was evident that Jamie was unhappy, but it was equally evident that he intended to do nothing to change conditions.

5

The day had seemed particularly long and trying to Dr. Mitchell. He felt that it had been a rather fruitless one, as well. As he drove away from the hospital he remembered what he had said only yesterday to Jamie Wakefield—that no job was all excitement, that one had to take the monotony in one's stride. That was true, but such a day's work as this did leave him in a state of depression.

There was one other thing to be done. He must talk to Randy about his impulsively formed plan for saving Drew Roddy's poor little home for him.

Lola Saunders, standing at the Pick Foley gate, watched the car speeding up Union Street and muttered: " 'Fore God, that Dr. Mitchell's goin' to kill himself if he don' mind. Wonder what's his hurry?"

Parris found Randy in the front yard examining her rose bushes. Against the bright cascade of flowering vines that covered the porch, she made an arresting picture. She looked so young and vital that Parris' spirits lifted even before she spoke.

"Hi, Parris!"

"Hi, yourself. Let's sit out here on the steps. I've been indoors long enough."

"Sure. I'm grubby—fooling around with the roses. Hope you don't mind."

He made no reply as they sat down on the steps, but he felt the warmth of her companionship settling about him as he always did in her presence.

"What's on your mind, Parris?" she asked presently.

"Drew Roddy. Did you know his place has been sold for taxes?"

"I saw it in *The Gazette*. I'm sorry. That's what happens to improvident poets. I wonder why he let it go?"

"He was evidently ignorant of the law in the matter. Drew can still recover it if he wishes."

"I know. What makes you think he *wants* to?"

"What will he do without it?"

"Parris, when you begin answering questions with other questions, I know you have something up your sleeve. Out with it!"

"It's up to us—you and me—to save the place for him."

"Didn't Fulmer buy it in?"

"What of it? Drew will be turned out of his house and he has no place to go."

"What can *we* do about it? I'd as soon think of offering money to Davis Pomeroy as to Drew Roddy."

"He has twenty-five acres. He doesn't need it all. I could buy the ten acres bordering on von Eln, or Davis Pomeroy could buy ten on his side. That would leave the house and fifteen acres of hillside. The sale of ten acres would bring enough to pay the delinquent taxes and leave Drew enough cash to live on for a long time."

"The piece bordering on your place wouldn't be worth anything. The Pomeroy end of it is a good building lot. I can see Mr. Pomeroy about it. I'd like to set Fulmer back on his heels. He's too greedy. You don't really want it, do you?"

"No, but I'd buy if necessary to save the house for Drew."

"That's what I thought. What do you want me to do?"

"Make all the necessary arrangements."

"Just like that! Will you talk to Drew? After all, we don't even know how he feels about it. Maybe he wants to let it go."

"I'm sure he would have offered the place for sale if he wanted to give it up. I know how it feels not to own the place you love."

"I doubt if many people feel the sort of attachment to a place that you do, Parris."

"Well, Drew's so impractical he probably doesn't know that he could have borrowed enough to prevent the sale. I'll get Jamie Wakefield to talk to him. Jamie is about the only friend Drew has—with the possible exception of Miles Jackson, who occasionally hounds Drew into writing something for his paper."

"Parris, you ought to do something about Jamie."

"What do you mean?"

"He's so darned unhappy. You're a wizard at talking people into better states of mind."

"Jamie's making his own adjustments, I think. He doesn't need me. Jamie's become a very useful person in Kings Row—and I think he'll be happy in time."

"He's disappointed in life—as much as Tod was about not getting to be section boss on the railroad."

"Your brother Tod, Randy, was unable to substitute any other interest when his one ambition was denied him."

"Poor Tod," Randy sighed. "It breaks my heart to remember that he died without gaining the one goal he worked toward all his life. He asked so little. It didn't matter that it was only to become section boss, it only mattered that he died grieving because he didn't *reach* his goal."

"I remember the time, Randy, when we drove out past the old railroad cut and found Tod clearing the track of weeds—long after the road had been discontinued."

"That just showed how unable he was to abandon his dream. Maybe Jamie feels like that."

"To a lesser degree. As I started to say, Jamie has substituted something else for his dream."

"Well," Randy said, "I'm sure he isn't happy. Since you refuse Jamie as a patient, how about Drew Roddy? I worry about him every time I drive out past his place. He must be very lonely. They tell me he is extraordinarily brilliant."

"Listen, Randy, you and Jamie and I ought to be able to get this Roddy business fixed up."

"Jamie and Parris and Randy—aren't we a funny trio?" she said.

"There's an old saying I've heard the Judge quote: 'Three if they unite against a town will ruin it.' Isn't it possible that the reverse might also be true—that if three unite for a cause, they might perhaps save it?"

"We can give it a try—starting on the Roddy case. You and I, at least, have been through a lot of things together. You've helped me over lots of bad spots."

"What are friends for? You've done the same for me. Sometimes I think, Randy, you are the only person left in the world who never once disappointed me—never let me down."

"You angel! I love you for saying that."

"Just love me—for any old reason, Randy. I need it."

A little silence settled on them like a cloud. Presently Parris said, almost as if he were thinking aloud, "If there were only some way to keep him from resigning himself to loneliness."

"Drew, you mean?" Randy came back with a start from her own musing.

"Yes. Withdrawal from society is such an immature solution of the problems of life."

"What do you suppose he's running away from?"

"Some disappointment. You know, Randy, one of the nicest things about you is that you face everything—in the open. I can't imagine your ever running away from anything. You are such a fearless person—and so buoyant."

"Shall I tell you the truth? I have the buoyancy of those who nurse the tender knowledge of secret sins," she pronounced with mock solemnity—and loved the quick smile Parris gave her.

"At any rate, you've lightened my mood. I was all ready to make you listen to a long jeremiad, but I've forgotten it," he said as he rose to go. "Come on out to von Eln for dinner. Elise needs a visit from you. We'll bring you home."

"Would Anna hate me?"

"Not Anna! Come on, like a good girl. Cheer us all up."

"I'll come—in the hope that Elise will play for me. Do you think she might?"

"I'm sure she will. I could do with some music, myself."

"Will I need a hat?"

"You don't need *anything*." He held out his hands to help her up and held hers tightly for an instant, and they walked quickly toward his car.

6

On the roof of the decrepit, unpainted barn a few pigeons complained, though it was plain to see they were not unhappy. Against a panel of garden paling that by some miracle still held firm, a grapevine drooped with the weight of heavy clusters of fruit, for some reason still undisturbed by marauding robins.

Drew Roddy, standing there with the weeds brushing the knees of his unpressed blue jean overalls, had the same look of unkempt dilapidation that hung about his surroundings. His shirt, clean but unironed, was not buttoned and revealed a thin, brown neck that supported a long, bony head. He was hollow-cheeked, and the great brown eyes, heavily smudged by illness and fatigue, were arresting; the sensitive mouth bespoke an impressionable nature.

He lifted a slender hand and shaded his eyes as he looked beyond the barn and the sagging fence to where a green triangle of field tilted against an uninspired hill. It was all familiar to him, yet he never tired of it. It belonged to him, or rather, it *had* belonged to him until recently. He felt ashamed because he had not had enough money to pay the taxes.

Money, he thought, had become a buzzing insistency in his mind. He wanted very few of the things that money could buy. He wanted only this bit of land and this poor old house. He'd been able to keep it all these years. If only he hadn't been too ill to work. He found that it took money to buy the food he'd always been able to raise for himself—chickens, potatoes, beans, and corn. He'd not even raised the few green vegetables he needed this summer. It was frightening to see how much those things cost when they must be bought at the stores.

And the medicines. That was worst of all. Who'd have thought drugs could be so expensive? Fortunately, Dr. Waring had never sent him a bill for his visits.

Mr. Cooper had been quite outspoken when refusing credit for the few groceries he had needed on Saturday night. He came away feeling as self-conscious as though he had tried to get the things by fraud —not intending to pay for them later. He supposed Mr. Cooper knew he was losing his place.

Of course, if he'd known how to go about it, he could have tried to sell his place. But somehow he couldn't bear to do that—even though he knew he would lose it this other way. But to try to sell deliberately—no, that would have been like the betrayal of his only friend. Still, in that way he might have gotten enough to pay the taxes and hold on a little longer until he could make some sort of plans. Oh, well, it was too late to do anything now, but he wished he had gotten up courage to ask Jamie Wakefield what to do about it. Jamie was a nice fellow, but he hadn't been around in a long time.

Drew walked slowly toward the barn but stopped after a few yards and looked unseeingly toward the hilltop. A path leading up the hill died away, smothered by dusty weeds. His eyes hesitated there where the path disappeared and his imagination went ahead, following the disused trail up and over the brow of the hill, just there between the two gray rocks—the big one shaped like the prow of a ship and the small one gently curved as the breast of a young girl. Maybe, he thought, he could find beauty somewhere else in the world—*maybe*—but to lose this!

Well, there was nothing for it now but to go downtown to ask Miles Jackson to let him write some things for *The Gazette*. He hated to walk downtown. He knew people would be saying, "There goes Drew Roddy. He's just lost his place."

Turning back toward the house, he saw Jamie Wakefield crossing the weedy yard. Too surprised to move, he stood quite still, waiting.

"Hello, Drew," Jamie called cheerfully.

"Hello, Jamie. It's been a long time since you came around."

"I know, Drew. I hope you'll overlook it. My nose is kept pretty much at the grindstone."

"And unfortunately, I don't have much business at the bank," Drew said without rancor.

Jamie flushed ever so faintly. "I've come on business, Drew."

"Business? With me?"

"Yes. I want to know if you'd be willing to sell a ten-acre strip off the north end of your place."

"I don't own the place, Jamie. I supposed you knew. Fulmer Green owns it." His voice was flat with misery.

"Not necessarily. You must know the state law. You can buy the place back any time within two years by paying the taxes and the costs of sale."

"I didn't know. I never looked into it."

"Davis Pomeroy wants to buy the ten acres adjoining his place—for orchards. He'll pay you two thousand, possibly twenty-five hundred, for the ten acres—a darned good price. It wouldn't encroach too much on your hillside. What do you think of the idea?"

Drew looked around at the barn, the grape arbor, the sagging fence, his thoughts in a turmoil.

"Two thousand dollars—are you sure it could be arranged?" he asked cautiously—afraid to believe.

"Pomeroy wants it. It's up to you. Mrs. McHugh will arrange the details of the sale as well as the retransfer of the title."

"Jamie, do you mind if we go over there and sit down? I've been bottled up for a long time. I'd like to talk for a while."

"Just what I'd like, Drew."

They walked out past the drooping sunflowers and hollyhocks and sat down on a large, flat stone in the open pasture. It was a bright, sunny day, pleasantly cool, with the first hint of approaching fall in the air.

Drew's hands nervously worried a stout blade of grass and his eyes swept the hillside as though he were seeking words for the things he wished to say.

"Jamie," he blurted out unexpectedly, "what do you see when I say *Italy*?"

Jamie seemed not surprised at the question, but his eyes were bleak when he spoke after a moment. "I see villas, snow-white above a summer sea, and cypress inked against the sky. . . . I hear laughter and I hear talk in other languages. I want to fling roses, drink bright wine, write poems in the spring of Tuscany—"

When his voice died out, Drew spoke softly. "I have here—on these few acres—all of what you see when you think of Italy."

Jamie looked about him. "Why do you love this place so much, Drew? It's not a good farm—"

"I know it's just a rocky hill. The soil is scant and thinly set with trees, but I'm contented here. I like to walk among the weeds. I don't mind that the fence is broken down and vagrant cows come in and out. They're welcome. And I like the outlook."

"Drew, why aren't you writing poetry—instead of just thinking it like this?"

"I guess all the urge went into—grubby toil right here in this unproductive spot."

"Kings Row," Jamie said resentfully.

"We stayed too long, Jamie, you and I."

"Maybe not, Drew." Jamie turned his large, overbrilliant eyes on Drew's face. "Sometimes I'm really glad I didn't go. How do you know that another turn in the road might have been better than the one we took?"

"It couldn't have been worse."

"How do you know?" Jamie insisted. "It might have led to utter chaos. Parris Mitchell said once that we couldn't leave things to chance—that man must devise his own turnings of the road."

"It's tragic to want to write poetry, isn't it?"

"Yes, I guess it is. I'm not sure."

"I'm not sure, Jamie, that the person who is fully equipped to enjoy life will *want* to write poetry."

"Why?"

"The poet is seeking something else in the pursuit of beauty than beauty itself. It's a substitute—or perhaps I should say he imagines better conditions than exist and wishes them into being."

"I still think it's tragic to wish to be an artist of any kind. Adjustments are too hard to make."

"Jamie, the artist has no business trying to adapt himself to the world at large."

"To be adaptable is to be wise. I've had to learn that the hard way." Jamie's voice was charged with an unprotesting cynicism.

"Haven't you ever fought against the encroachment of—of business?"

"I've always been at war."

"With what?"

"With life."

"I think, Jamie Wakefield, that you and I are fools—but I'd rather be a free and happy fool than be wearing bit and rein as you are doing."

Jamie laughed amiably and the mood of discontent lifted. "Haven't we been vaporing unpardonably, though? It's fun—once in a while—to talk foolishness this way. Let's get back to business. Are you willing to sell the ten acres to Pomeroy?"

"I'm only afraid he'll back out. I don't mind telling you, Jamie, that this takes a fearful burden off my mind. I love this place. I don't know what would become of me if I had to give it up."

"You know, Drew, it's a funny thing. The only other person I know who has the mystical sort of attachment to his home place that you have is Parris Mitchell."

"Dr. Mitchell was born there and his roots go deep."

"I gave up the house I was born in without a qualm."

"I think I should like to know this Parris Mitchell."

"Will you let me bring him to see you sometime?"

"If he will come. I'd like to talk with him. You think I will still own this place?"

"I know you will. Just a few dollars will redeem it and you'll have enough money to improve it and to live comfortably for a long time."

"I'll be able to write something, now that I'm relieved of worry. Couldn't you come out occasionally to criticize?"

"I'll come often—if you'll teach me some things I need to know about—just simple versification."

"Maybe, Jamie, we can help each other."

7

Winter had come early this year and Kings Row was shivering under its first heavy coating of ice and snow. Parris looked from his window and thought gratefully that this was his day off. He decided to remain indoors. There was a particularly inviting book that had just come from the publishers, and he felt quite in the mood to enjoy it. When the telephone rang, he answered reluctantly.

"Why, hello, Paul. What's the trouble?"

"Parris, there's hell to pay over at Aberdeen. I wonder if you can meet Dr. Giles at Miles Jackson's office at ten o'clock?"

Parris was mystified. What could the President of Aberdeen wish to see him about—and why at the *Gazette* office?

"Giles wants your help," Paul said. "Something very unfortunate has happened at the college. I've got to meet David Kettring and his wife at ten-forty and take them out to the campus. Their son has been badly hurt—a hazing episode. I can't be with you, but Giles asked for you specially. I think he wants you to keep Jackson off his neck."

"I'll be there at ten."

Dr. Giles was already talking with Jackson when Parris reached the office. His face, lined by years of burdening responsibility, was drawn and tense. Without preliminaries he plunged into a brief explanation. "Dr. Mitchell, I hope you can explain to Jackson and to me how group behavior works in a case like this."

"Dr. Nolan gave me no inkling of the trouble."

"Last night a gang of young gentlemen at Aberdeen went on a hazing jag. As a consequence, one of our finest students—David Kettring's son Robbie—is in the infirmary suffering from exposure and a broken leg. Two others have been treated for chill and serious bruises."

"Sorry to hear it, Dr. Giles. I thought Aberdeen was trying to keep that sort of thing down."

"Yes, we've tried, but some brigand always pops up as leader of the sophomore gang. This time it happens to be that scapegrace brother of Fulmer Green—Donny. He transferred from the university at the beginning of this term. Fulmer did the school a bad turn when he placed him at Aberdeen."

Jackson grunted. "This is as good a time as any to get rid of him. Since he's the acknowledged leader, you'd be foolish not to expel him, seems to me."

"Getting rid of one student doesn't solve anything," Parris said.

"I suppose not, but I think that is what we will do in any case."

"That'll hit Fulmer where he lives," Jackson commented.

"Dr. Giles, I hope you'll decide against that. The boy is lawless, maybe, but expulsion from school in his home town would be something he'd never live down, even if he *tried* to reform."

Miles Jackson looked curiously at Parris. Why, he wondered, should he try to save that wastrel from the humiliation he deserved?

"I don't get you, Mitchell. Aberdeen will be better off without that kid," Miles said impatiently.

"Dr. Mitchell, may I ask why you think we should keep him?" Dr. Giles asked.

"It seems just another push along a road too easy for him to follow. Expulsion from Aberdeen would probably mean the end of school for Donny, and if education is denied him, his defiance of law and order would probably become a definite trend. Aberdeen owes something to boys like that. You don't want to duck your responsibilities, do you?"

Dr. Giles smiled. "Maybe it's a question of my responsibility to the student body? Association with a boy like that is not what the patrons of the school expect for their sons."

"Maybe I'm preaching, but to me it seems that the boys at Aberdeen are there to learn how to handle contacts with society as it exists. They aren't going to be protected a few years from now when they go out to meet the world. They'd better be learning what to do about the Donny Greens they'll see on every street corner."

The lines in Dr. Giles' anxious face deepened. "I think you're right, Doctor. We'll have to see what we can do for the boy. But there's going to be the biggest scandal in the state if Robbie Kettring dies of pneumonia."

"Is he so seriously hurt?"

"He's critically ill."

"What can I do, Dr. Giles?"

"I want you to talk to Miles—and to David Kettring, when he gets here. Tell them how these boys get to be this way." Dr. Giles sounded desperate.

"Miles knows that as well as I do—maybe better, having lived more years and seen more manifestations of youthful savagery."

Jackson grunted laconically and began working on his corncob pipe. He had been moving restlessly about his desk but he spoke slowly and pointedly. "Savagery is not too strong a word for what happens in our so-called halls of learning."

A slight flush rose to Dr. Giles' cheek, but his lips twitched in a half smile. "I agree fully," he said.

Jackson heaved himself into his favorite seat on the edge of his cluttered and overloaded table, which quivered and creaked as he settled himself. "Giles," he asked in a deliberate drawl, "why don't we just come out and say plainly: We aren't very far removed from savagery, and it gives us pleasure to inflict pain on a helpless member of our organization? He can't help himself because we outnumber him. If he shows fight, as any self-respecting boy ought to do, he'll get twice as much."

"That about sums it up," Dr. Giles admitted.

"I can see," Parris said, "that Dr. Giles might be helpless in this. Any effective move toward abolishing hazing will have to come from the student body itself."

Dr. Giles shrugged. "Those lads are supposedly here for the acquisition of knowledge," he said, "but that activity is certainly treated as the least important accomplishment at college."

"You are becoming platitudinous as well as cynical, my friend. Parris, what do you do when you see the slow but sure disintegration of a formerly original and sparkling mind?"

Miles Jackson's humorous gibe did not lighten Dr. Giles' mood. He was too deeply concerned.

"We've gotten off the immediate question," Jackson said. "Will the young man die?"

"We don't know. We haven't even been able to find out how long he was in the creek before some fellow freshmen rescued him."

"How did it really happen?"

"Robbie was thrown into a hole they had broken through the ice. His leg had been broken when he was forced to run a gauntlet of club-wielders. When he fell they picked him up and threw him into the creek. He couldn't climb out and he stayed there holding on to the ice for some time before a group of freshmen heard him calling. They got him out just as he was about to let go from exhaustion. If he dies, there'll undoubtedly be a manslaughter charge—probably aimed mainly at Donny Green, as leader of that particular incident. The Lieutenant Governor will prosecute to the limit."

"Sounds like a gloomy prospect for staid old Aberdeen, but I know what I'd do if it were my son." Jackson's eyebrows bristled angrily.

Parris said, "I don't suppose any groups of hazers want to murder candidates for their sacred organizations, but it does seem to be their purpose to come as near as possible to doing so without actually inviting themselves to a seat in the electric chair."

"That this should have happened at my school—"

"It happens everywhere," Parris said. "I have a patient at the hospital right now who was removed from an important military academy after some weeks of systematic hazing."

"Sweet place, the college campus," Jackson said.

"Savagery isn't confined to the college campus, Miles. Things just as bad, and worse, happen among people who aren't in school. I know of a case right here in Kings Row that beggars your college hazings. It happened just last summer. Two men—as yet unidentified, as Miles' column would report it—raped a very young, innocent girl."

"Say, that's news!" Miles broke in. "You've been holding out on me, boy. Come clean."

"This is not for you, Miles. Publicity would destroy that child's chance at recovering her mental health. You know this town would never let her forget it."

"But, Parris, the criminals ought to be hunted down and strung up!"

"The family is perfectly right in avoiding publicity. Whether the affair will ever be avenged, I don't know. It seems unlikely the brutes could ever be found."

"I hope to God none of our young Aberdeen brigands were mixed up in it."

"They weren't, Dr. Giles. It was during vacation. Anyhow, their savagery is taken out on your freshmen."

"And we call this a civilized community!" Miles grunted with disgust.

"Kings Row is not unique, Miles," Parris said. "A slice of Kings Row will match a slice of any other town in the country, to a T. Don't fool yourself."

"I think I'll write a biography of this town someday—and I'll call on you to psychoanalyze it for me."

"That's a grotesque idea—but in its way, sublime. But in the meantime, let's hear what your editorializing is going to be like on this Aberdeen business."

"I'd like to skin those boys alive, but for the sake of some fine men on the faculty I'm going to hold off until I see how they handle it."

"That's decent of you, Jackson," Dr. Giles said, tension fading from his voice. "You know how I feel about it—but I'd like to protect the school as far as I can honestly do it."

"I know, Doctor. I'll have you in mind when I comment. I don't know what the other papers in the state will do. It depends on what happens to the youngster, I fancy."

"Yes, I feel personally responsible—and completely helpless. We've tried making rules about hazing—"

"Dr. Giles," Parris said, "there's nothing you can do about outlawing hazing. Any move, to be effective, as I said before, must come from the students themselves."

"Why do you think so?"

"Group behavior is no whit different from individual behavior—just a little more brash. That's the A.B.C. of psychology, as you know. They've got to act from inside the group."

"I wish I could make them see that."

"Let me have a try at it. I've been an Aberdeen student, myself. I might be able to talk them into seeing what they have to do."

"Do you mean, Doctor, that you'd go up and talk to the student body—try to show them what they look like to civilized society?"

"I'll make a stab at it—if you wish—and if I'm free to say exactly what I want to say. I shouldn't pull my punches."

"Atta boy!" Miles approved. "And tell 'em for me they'd do poor credit to the head-hunters of Borneo."

"I'll be eternally grateful to you, Mitchell," Dr. Giles said. They will respect you—and you can make them *think*. Tomorrow morning at chapel?"

"I'll be on hand."

"Don, were you mixed up in that hazing business?" Fulmer Green asked, a cold fury in his voice. "Well, speak up."

"All the sophomores were—were there. You know how it is—just a lot of fooling around."

"I've had about all I can stand, Don. I've tried my best to—oh, what's the use?" Fulmer turned to the window and stared out at the early morning whiteness.

Donny uneasily moved the screen and made a great to-do putting coal into the grate. After a moment Fulmer whirled about and started toward Donny, his face livid.

"Damn you, Don, why don't you tell the truth when I give you a chance?"

Donny backed toward the door, but Fulmer grasped him by the shoulders, jerked him back, and forced him into a chair. Donny's weak face stiffened with fright.

"Damn you! Damn you! I know all about it. Dr. Giles called me early this morning. Do you know you are liable to be held on a charge of manslaughter? Do *you*?"

"Robbie's not—*dead*, is he?" Stark terror filled Donny's shallow blue eyes and his voice was little more than a whisper.

"Not yet—but *it's not your fault that he isn't*. Don't you realize the mess you're in—that *we're* in? You deserve to swing for a fool thing like this. You promised you'd keep out of trouble if I agreed to let you stay here. I was a fool to think a promise meant anything to you."

"Now, Fulmer, I didn't know he'd get hurt so bad—"

"Good God A'mighty, boy, haven't you got a grain of sense? First that Jinktown affair—and now you try to kill David Kettring's son."

"I didn't try to kill him," Donny whined.

"I don't care what you call it. I'm afraid to show my face on the street. Everybody knows you led the gang."

"Who says I led it?"

"Shut up! Now you listen to me, you idiot. Dr. Giles told me Parris Mitchell's going to make a chapel talk up there at ten o'clock—on the subject of mob psychology. *You are going to hear it—*"

"Aw, Fulmer, I don't want to go to chapel. Parris Mitchell's got it in for me—"

"You fool—you double-action *fool!* God knows why he did it, but Parris Mitchell talked Giles out of the idea of expelling you."

"He did—what?"

"What I said. Dr. Giles told me an hour ago. You can't afford to stay away from chapel. You are going, and you are going to listen to what Mitchell has to say—and if you can get a chance, you are going to thank him for what he's done for you. You hear me?"

"Gosh, Fulmer, I can't do that. Why, ever since that time at his office—"

"Ever since *what?*"

Donny's confusion was pitiable. "Aw, I was just talkin' to him—"

"When—and about what?"

"Oh, some time last year." Donny tried to assume a nonchalance he did not feel.

"Tell me what you talked to Parris Mitchell about," Fulmer said menacingly.

"Oh, Hazel made me go to see him—I was nervous—and—we thought—maybe— Honest, Fulmer, I didn't go but once—"

"What did you tell him? What did he ask you?" The threat in Fulmer's voice was unmistakable.

"He didn't ask me anything. Listen, Fulmer, I'll tell you all about it."

"You'd better if you know what's good for you."

Donny decided to make an apparently clean breast of the affair, but he skirted the matter of his personal relations with his brother. Fulmer listened, controlling his anger with an effort. When Donny had finished, Fulmer was silent for so long that the boy was increasingly uneasy.

"Don, go on up to the college. It's nearly ten. Do exactly what I told you to do. I've got to think things out. Try to keep out of my sight for a while. Get out, now."

And Donny went, glad to escape from the fury in his brother's eyes.

[144]

8

The student body filed into the chapel at Aberdeen with unusual decorum. There were none of the shouting and shoving ordinarily indulged in as the boys gathered.

Through the door of the rostrum, the faculty filed in to take seats facing the auditorium. Dr. Giles, his face lined with worry and fatigue, came in with two visitors, Lieutenant Governor David Kettring and Dr. Parris Mitchell. There was a perceptible movement and murmur among the tensely watchful boys as they recognized both men.

After the usual opening of chapel exercises with a short prayer, Dr. Giles introduced the speaker.

"We have asked Dr. Mitchell to talk to the student body about the recent outrage that took place on Aberdeen Campus. I wish to say that in spite of the unspeakable behavior of some of you boys, Robbie Kettring has been pronounced out of danger. The fact that the life of this fine lad has hung in the balance for thirty-six hours is a serious blot on the scutcheon of Aberdeen College. How we shall erase that blot is your problem and mine. Gentlemen, Dr. Parris Mitchell."

There was no applause as Parris stepped forward. He stood for a moment, his sweeping glance taking in the rows of anxious faces.

"My former attendance at Aberdeen College gives me, perhaps, some right to be here," he began quietly. "Dr. Giles is placed in a difficult position by this near tragedy which resulted from what some of you thought would be great fun. Hundreds of you have left home to take up residence here because your parents have confidence in him. Presumably the object of this uprooting is the furtherance of the educational process. You are here to acquire learning, or at least the *process* of learning.

"Here, you are supposed to come in contact with some of the best minds in the country; you are to make the acquaintance of great books and great works of art; you are to acquire the technique of using great libraries; you are to hear of the great historical movements of the past. In short, you came to be educated—cultured, even— and to advance a step on the road that leads from savagery, through contemporary civilization, to some as yet unguessed but probably beneficent end.

"Presumably, some preliminary steps of education and civilization have preceded your entrance to college. There has been the church, and there has been the home. The student should not be quite a savage at the beginning of the freshman year. But, no matter what he has when he reaches these sacred precincts, he presumably has enough of his native sensibilities destroyed during the first year to join the mob the second year.

"I feel that something is seriously wrong when a boy who comes here supposedly to learn certain social processes calculated to advance the art of living shortly finds himself being beaten up and generally maltreated by those who have supposedly already advanced along that road. He meant to become gentle, urbane, kindly, maybe democratic, in theory at least—in short, *civilized*. But what happens? Indignities are visited upon him and he is turned back.

"Anyone found beating a horse or a dog into unconsciousness would be promptly dealt with by the Society for the Prevention of Cruelty to Animals, but it seems there is nothing to be done about a mob of upperclassmen who go under cover of night and beat up a freshman who will be too good a sport to complain.

"These are the same people who later become those self-appointed guardians of law and order, the Ku-Kluxers of the future, whose business it will be to drag out men and women and beat them for the 'good of the community and the glory of law and order.' The college graduate who has had three years of practice in the A.B.C. of the process will be well prepared to lead a masked mob. *And* he won't mind if the victim is rather bloody after forty lashes on the bare back. He won't mind if the victim happens to be a woman. His sensibilities won't be hurt by a few screams.

"And the leaders of such mobs are not lacking in the average student body. There's only a difference in *degree*, not in *kind*, in the impulse that moves a mob to a pogrom, or a cracker guard of a chain gang to a brutal nocturnal beating of a helpless convict, and the youthful blood-lusting impulse that sends a sophomore gang down the freshman corridor.

"I can imagine what the sophomore thinks. It goes something like this: 'In the cloistered calm of college libraries are the collected thoughts and wisdoms of the ages. All that has gone to raise the spirit of man from the level of the savage devouring raw meat, to the

Olympian heights of a Plato, an Aristotle, a Leonardo da Vinci, is in that library. It is within easy access. All of the refinements of art, the incredible miracles of science, the monuments of literature—these are all there in the libraries and in the classrooms of Dr. Matthews or Dr. Brice or Dr. Telson. But *we* are not too much impressed by these—we young moderns! *We* are not going to be made soft just because we have the advantages of an education and culture! *We* are going out tonight and beat the hell out of those freshmen!"

Parris paused and stood for a moment, looking into the embarrassed faces of the boys. Before he could say anything more, Edward Sandifer, president of the student body, rose.

"Dr. Mitchell, sir, what you have said would make me feel like throwing in the sponge and getting out of schools entirely except that I feel we can do something about this, right now. I should like to have Dr. Giles' permission to turn this into an official meeting of the student body to take action on hazing as an Aberdeen practice."

The Gazette on the following day carried the announcement that hazing had been abolished at Aberdeen College by unanimous action of the student body. Miles Jackson's editorial was less stinging than had been expected, and at Lieutenant Governor Kettring's request no details of the unfortunate affair were published.

Fulmer Green slept better that night.

9

Elise felt a genuine affection for the Nolans. Next to Randy, Laurel was the best friend she had and she was ashamed of her resentment on those rather frequent evenings when Paul drove out to spend an hour or two in talk with Parris. She knew that Paul's duties at the asylum were exacting and that he had little time for relaxation or simple friendly intercourse. She knew, too, that these visits were eagerly welcomed by Parris, who had all too little contact with stimulating and provocative minds. There was a quickened interest in Parris' general demeanor when Paul came. Perhaps, she reproved herself, she was jealous!

Ordinarily she sat quietly, listening to technical discussions which bored her. She made halfhearted efforts to follow their mental calisthenics, only to fall so far behind as to make it hopeless to try to overtake them. She turned, most often, back on herself, trying in some bewildered way to establish herself in a fixed and definite place in Parris' life. Just what that place was, she had not decided. It was all so vague, but she hoped she might eventually reach some definite conclusions.

This evening she sat by the window studying the two men, Parris and Paul, scientists both, and men of vision, she told herself. They seemed as much at home in the insecure and variable places of the universe as birds in air. At one moment she thought their talk exciting, the next she was resentful that she remained so completely outside their realm of interests. She recognized that Parris was a free soul, as untrammeled as an eagle, and as swift. Again and again she assured herself that she was willing to allow him the freedom he so blithely chose.

What a contrast there was in the bearing of the two men! Paul sat relaxed in his deep chair, his red-brown hair glinting under the lights, his blue eyes so dark that she had to remember them as they looked by daylight to know they were blue, not black. His few gestures were deliberate but his long, thin hands were amazingly expressive and eloquent. He was a restful personality, Elise thought.

Opposite sat Parris. Was it because she knew him so intimately that an aura of intense excitement seemed to surround him? The animated movements of his muscular hands and the frequent characteristic shrug of his shoulders were in keeping with his constantly changing expressions. This was the Parris she had first known—youthful, eager, purposeful. But of late he seemed to have lost something of that ardent enthusiasm that she remembered. Only on occasions like this—when Paul or Father Donovan or Miles Jackson was with him—did he seem to come to life. A small sense of guilt crept into her thinking as she realized that with *her,* he was tender and considerate, but never *glowing* as he was at this moment. How much was she to blame?

"But, Paul," she heard Parris protesting, "you have to take into consideration the many *kinds* of participation: the vast capacities and infinite functions of imagination."

"The imagination is a dangerous companion to a sensitive person.

There should be some physical means to harness it and set it to work in mundane fashion. That way the world would profit."

"Unfortunately, the imagination serves too often as a place of refuge. Witness the size of your own hospital!"

"We should learn somehow to make the retreat to the plane of the imagination not a flight *from* something, but *toward* something more important."

"Lord, how I wish such a means could be discovered!"

"You are a young man, life is ahead of you. Go ahead. Discover it."

"I wonder if—you know, Paul, sometimes when I play the piano, I seem almost to grasp something of consequence—but it slips away, just out of reach—and I don't know how to pursue the flying image."

"Music means a lot to you, Parris."

"More than I can explain even to myself. I think perhaps it is music that has revealed the vision of the unattainable, the pattern of the unachievable."

"That's nothing to be grateful for. It's better to be obsessed by a hope than overwhelmed by a discouragement."

"But great music has given me more than that. If I stay with it long enough everything falls away from it like a broken shell, leaving its heart exposed, naked and clean of association and relation. But I'm talking foolishness."

"Not foolishness at all, Parris. Just look at the good results we are having with our musical therapy at the hospital."

"I'm really excited about that, Paul. If we accomplished nothing more with it than what we've done with Vera Lichinsky, it would have made the whole effort worth while."

"She's going on tour, isn't she?"

"Yes. I hope to hear her play while I'm in the East. She's giving a concert in Baltimore about the time I expect to be there."

"A remarkable cure. And music did it?"

"Absolutely. The piano has cured *me* of many spiritual disorders, I think. Somehow it helps me to exercise my lazy moral muscles, as Father Donovan often reminds me I should. And, listening when Elise plays, I find many problems clarifying themselves."

With a happy little glow warming her heart, Elise came over and leaned against the back of Parris' chair and ran her fingers through his crisp black hair.

"Oh yes," she said, her face alight. "Father Donovan expressed it for me one day. He said something about 'exercising our spiritual muscles'—and that is what piano practice does. We have to use restraint—control—and you must admit that is what we often need. But how I sound like a music-master!" She made an apologetic little face.

"I have no knowledge of it at all, yet, strangely enough, I think I understand what you are saying."

"I shouldn't even try to talk about music, Paul. Parris says that studios are full of those who talk and talk. They have all the catchwords of art, and while it sounds well, it leads nowhere at all."

"Don't pay too much attention to Parris. He just likes to throw off on artists. Wouldn't be surprised if he doesn't have secret regrets sometimes that he didn't pursue a concert career."

"You're wrong," Parris protested. "To begin with, I'm lazy by nature and I should never have had the physical endurance to follow that career."

"Don't be absurd."

"I mean it. Playing the piano requires the 'fighting heart' as much as it is required in athletics—that extra staying power, that extra ounce of courage, that persistence over and above what you think you have which enables you to do that extra thousand repetitions—that is what counts."

"He's right, Paul, and I'm glad he's a doctor instead of a professional pianist."

"I saw a great deal of the studio product in Europe," Parris said, "and I didn't particularly like what I saw. Art is one thing—the artist is another."

Elise sat down on the arm of Parris' chair, swinging her foot and tapping her slippered toe lightly against the smoking stand beside the chair.

"Don't do that, sweet, please," Parris said. "I can't talk in rhythm."

Paul looked sharply at his friend. Presently Parris continued, "If the artist would only create and let someone else talk it might be better. But the artist himself is apt to become *soft*. The studio is to blame. There's too much talk. It's like marsh water—stagnant, going nowhere, creating a spell of beauty, but beauty that is evil—softening—

these charming people. Creating nothing permanent. Quick growths —soft, strangling, treacherous."

"I confess I'm not following you too well. Marsh water is stagnant, I admit, but it produces beauty as well as poison. And besides, it's all a simple problem of starting the water to going somewhere."

"To get it started, but how?" There was an undisguised eagerness in Elise's question.

"You have to cut a channel—cut ruthlessly, brutally," Paul said.

"Simple, but cruel."

"Not so cruel as to leave the poison."

"Oh dear," Elise complained, "I'm lost again and I don't know what you mean any more."

"We are still discussing the artist and how to cure him of his imaginary ills. Maybe he doesn't need curing at all. Perhaps it's only fey he is!"

"The artist is lonely, I think," Elise ventured.

"We doctors have yet to find a real cure for loneliness."

"I know of a remedy!" Elise assured him.

"You interest me. Could you divulge the secret without betraying the rest of your sex?"

"Women *cry* when they need to get an emotional balance such as Parris is always talking about. When we are lonely, why, we merely weep the mood away, and then we have no need to be psychoanalyzed."

Parris laughed.

"Anyhow, Paul, loneliness is not a thing to fear," she went on. "I think it is something to encourage."

"You aren't using the term accurately, darling," Parris said. "You mean solitude rather than loneliness, don't you?"

"I suppose so. On lonely days we think quietly and feel deeply. There are some things we can't think in public. We need solitude for them. Maybe that's why Drew Roddy stays up on that rocky hillside between von Eln and Pomeroy Hill. He seldom leaves the place. He must *like* loneliness."

"Drew Roddy is an exceptional case," Parris said. "He let his place go down—and he almost lost it a few months ago. But I hear he's been repairing his house and is improving it right along. Being a recluse may be getting a little monotonous."

"That could be," Elise said thoughtfully.

Parris looked at her curiously. She was unconsciously revealing the fact that she, too, was lonely.

"Speaking again of marsh water," Paul said, "I met a typical example on the street today. Pick Foley. What do you make of his anti-social behavior, Parris? Do you say he's just a recluse and leave it at that, or do you think you could do something to bring him into line with your new science?" Paul was evidently bent on changing the subject.

Flushing faintly at the fancied exclusion from the conversation, Elise went back to her chair by the open window.

"I doubt that Pick could be helped very much. He's an old man. There's a lot of flotsam about, you know. Town opinion has it he's simply lazy."

"You don't accept town opinion, do you?"

"I do not. If Pick were normal he'd be able to participate in the social life of the community and to work with others in that society. He doesn't meet that requirement."

"I wonder what happened to him?"

"He simply couldn't adapt himself to what was expected of him and he withdrew from outside contacts."

"Yes, I guess they proved too painful. Still, I wonder why he withdrew from life."

"Funny thing for you to ask, Paul. You spend your life answering just such questions. Pick hasn't withdrawn from life, only from society. He lives in a different world, that's all. The same thing is true of Drew Roddy."

"It's hard to understand the phantasmagoric world of a man like Roddy. He's not even a borderline case."

"You couldn't understand a man like Roddy if you tried. You are Irish—and too completely the extrovert."

"You are always blaming my shortcomings on my Irish blood. We are already mad and should be able to understand madness in other people. Anyhow, I'd like to understand this 'soul surgery' you psychiatrists practice."

"Analysis is not soul surgery. It's a long, slow process, as you very well know, and it requires faith and endurance. And it's not even a solution of all personal equations. Dr. Tower used to say that it was merely a method by which childish phantoms of early frights and delusions may be overcome. Science has to find *some* way to reach into those shut-off regions of disordered brains."

"I've often wondered what Dr. Tower was like. When I was a lad at Aberdeen, I used to pass his house and wish that I might know him. He was a recluse—like Pick Foley."

"Not in the least like Pick Foley. The fascination of the man was hypnotic, the glitter of his mind bewildering. The dizzy flights of his imagination, the swift analyses, the darting conclusions, the daring and fancy, the vast reach—he simply seemed to be some sort of sorcerer. Lord, what a brain!"

"You were lucky to have known him. Parris, is it too late for me to have another highball?"

"Never too late for a good thing. Let me—"

As Parris busied himself with the glasses, Elise asked almost timidly, "Paul, why are so many people in a small town like Kings Row out there—at the asylum?"

Paul took the glass from Parris and set it down carefully before formulating his precise answer. "The small town, Elise, is a haven of refuge for people who couldn't lift themselves into positions of importance. Rents are low, people are tolerant of the unsuccessful, in fact are apt to be hypercritical of those who do succeed. Naturally, you can expect a higher percentage of mental illness in the small town."

"Then why aren't the ungifted and unsuccessful happy here, and not suffering from so many 'complexes' and other dreadful things?"

"Let Parris answer that if he can."

Parris rubbed out his cigarette and gave the matter some thought. "The things that stood in the way of their development in the first place make for their lack of balance later. The average capacity of individuals can't cope with psychic knots."

"I'm afraid lots of them succumb without a fair trial," Paul said.

"You have the wrong approach, Paul."

Elise withdrew into herself. Unintentionally she had herself turned the talk into the very channel she hated—the hospital. It was too much, she felt, that the problems of the hospital must be brought to this house which was her *home*. She tried to be reasonable about it, but all this talk of mental illness brought sharply to her mind the wailing and terrified screaming of patients in the wards at the hospital. She had hoped to banish even the memory of her former distress when she came out here, but there were times when the wind whining about the house brought back too vividly the actual screams of those tormented souls—animalistic in their un-understanding of what was wrong. She never attempted to explain this to Parris. He would feel, she was sure, that she was being morbidly imaginative. But *why* wouldn't they help her to forget it? Why must Parris and Paul talk and talk and *talk* about the hospital and the patients all the time?

She forced her attention back to what Parris was saying.

"I don't consider the forms of social order a means of expression and realization and fulfillment of the individual."

"Then what are they?"

"Nothing more than a social convenience to keep the pack away from those who devise the forms. So, in the underdog thinking, revolt comes—but the forms evolved by society itself for its own liberation hold firmly."

"Underdog thinking! I could talk all night on that subject."

"Is it worth it?"

"You bet it's worth it! But I don't believe that kind of thinking can be traced to psychic sources."

"I don't agree with you there. I think at least ninety per cent of all our troubles are psychic."

"You're an extremist—and we are boring poor Elise to death with all our talk."

"Oh, no, Paul. Really. I think it is ver-ry interesting. The louder you two shout at each other, the more I enjoy it." Elise smiled at Paul's appreciative chuckle.

"I contend," Parris continued, "that our inner life can be compared to a stream with different layers flowing at different rates of speed—rushing at the surface but moving slowly deep down on its bed. These slower currents are what we call the 'unconscious.' This is not original. It's the accepted view."

"Just where do you place our appetites and desires?"

"Not too far below the surface. Under excitement of one kind or another they are apt to break through. Early influences, inborn tendencies, even atavistic memories drift along the slower current at the floor of the stream, but even these can be stirred by some violent emotion and erupt to the surface."

"And then there's the hell to pay."

"Not necessarily. Not everything submerged and suppressed is evil."

"But is it useful?"

"Of course it is. It warns us of impending dangers. Sometimes it can be tapped enough to rid us of mental worry."

"I accept your word for it, but to me some of the new stuff seems farfetched. The practice of it smacks too much of the confessional."

Parris rose and crossed to the window. Standing for a moment with his hand on Elise's shoulder, he looked out into the moonlit garden. Paul thought that for some reason he was abandoning the argument. When Parris turned again to Paul, his face was serious.

"Psychoanalysis does not call for confession, Paul. Confession is a conscious act of repentance, and a ritual. Man can only confess what he consciously knows and what makes him consciously guilty. In psychoanalysis the patient gradually reveals the unconscious sense of guilt of which he had been unaware."

Paul shrugged and got to his feet. He said, "Well, one thing is certain. I must be starting for home or Kam will find me here when he comes early in the morning. We can hardly persuade him to wait for his breakfast. Does he ever get in the way?"

"Oh no, Paul," Elise hurriedly answered. "I can hardly bear to let him go in the afternoons. I'd like to keep him all the time. I adore having him with me. He almost fell in the creek today, but Nathan was there. If anything happened to Kam I think—I *know* I should die."

"Youngsters are tough. A ducking wouldn't harm him. He has enough of Laurel's sturdiness and my Irish luck to survive. Don't you begin worrying about him. You watch out for yourself. Parris, don't you think Elise is a little too thin?"

"Paul Nolan!" Elise protested. "I'm perfectly well. You should see me eat!"

"Just think what a nuisance you'd be if you got sick on our hands."

Suddenly Elise's face whitened and she reached out and clasped her hands about Paul's arm, shrinking away from the window.

"What is it, Elise?" Parris quickly started toward her.

Through the window came a long, wavering, agonized howl that rose and fell and died away, whimpering. Elise shook under Paul's arm across her shoulders and her terrified eyes swept his face.

"Listen—that—that dog—howling like a—like a lost soul. I can't bear it."

"It's only the Pomeroy hounds, Elise—nothing to be afraid of," Paul's quiet voice assured her. He was startled at the strange look of apprehension on Parris' face. Evidently, he thought, Parris was more alarmed about Elise's nervous condition than he had supposed. But surely this was of little importance—this recoil from the "banshee" cry drifting in from Pomeroy Hill.

Parris closed the window. He seemed to have recovered his poise. "I'm not surprised, sweet, that you hate that sound. It often comes when the wind is from that direction. The dogs are harmless. You've seen them when we've driven past the Pomeroy place, and you've liked them. Please don't be afraid."

"I'm not afraid—really I'm not. It only reminds me—of—of all the *madness* in the world. I don't know why—"

Paul caught Elise's quivering chin between his thumb and forefinger and tilted her face upward until he could look straight into her eyes. "Listen, my dear," he said seriously. "You are here too much alone. You must come into town more often to be with your friends. Being too much alone is not good for the strongest of us and it can be very bad for an imaginative girl like you."

A stubborn look crossed her face and she shook her head impatiently. "No, no, Paul. I am never alone here. I have Parris and Kam and Anna. I am just ver-ry, ver-ry tired. Forgive me for being such a poor hostess—for giving you this—trouble."

"You're a sweetheart of a hostess—and we all love you. And I'm going to prove it by going home this minute and giving you a chance to go to bed."

After Paul had gone Parris said, a little edgily, "Elise, you were very frank with Paul in saying you were lonely. You might have told me you felt that way."

"I don't know why I said it to Paul, but I didn't mean to complain."

"You don't find me very good company, do you?"

"I find you ver-ry good company, Parris—when you find out I am here. But you seem most of the time to be thinking about your old hospital—or—or something you don't share with me."

"Perhaps you are right, Elise," he said. "It does seem that I can never get wholly away from the damn place. Some patient is always on my mind. I'm sorry it makes hard going for you."

"I've no right to demand more than I have, Parris. I am ver-ry conscious that I make an unsatisfactory wife for a man of your—your complexity. There are so many planes on which I can't meet you."

Parris laughed. "Good Lord, baby, how did you think that one up?"

"Maybe you should have married someone not like me at all? Or maybe you should not be married to anybody?"

"You wouldn't wish me that sort of bad luck, would you?"

"I don't wish you any bad luck, Parris. You know that. I only—I thought—oh, Parris," she sobbed, "what do you think is wrong with me?"

"Nothing's wrong with you, Elise. Look, my sweet child, whatever resentments you harbor against me should be dug up and aired, if for no other reason than to teach me to watch my step!"

"I know what you mean—you and your old psychology. I haven't been hiding anything."

"No?"

"No. Have you?"

"Not a thing. There are lots of things I don't talk to you about because to understand them or to be interested, you would need the kind of technical background Paul has."

"Parris, you are ver-ry blind. That's not what I'm talking about at all."

And nothing he could say or do seemed to bring her any comfort.

Elise took her sleeping capsule but lay awake for a long time recalling what had been said about marsh water—stagnant, treacherous, *uncreative*. That, she thought, is what I am—marsh water. Unable even to give Parris a son—perhaps even hampering him, blocking his free progress to the open sea!

It was then that the tears came, gently, unexpectedly, and she drifted into sleep.

Parris, holding very still for fear of disturbing her, lay awake wondering what he could do in the matter of Davis Pomeroy's strange compulsion. He wished he might have talked to Paul Nolan about it, but he felt that would have been a gross violation of confidence. But, he knew now, with absolute certainty, it was imperative that he do something about that puzzling case. But Elise—and her too evident need of his constant attention! What of that? To spend more time at home with her, trying to build up her self-confidence, her courage—that would mean serious neglect of his work. He had really no properly trained help in his department at the hospital. Carruthers was a blunderer and had, on more than one occasion, destroyed in some patient the confidence that Parris had built up by weeks of concentrated attention. It took only one ill-advised interview to upset the work of months.

He could not be in two places at once. Yet, he thought, Elise needed him now—and Elise was his first concern. He must in some way give her more a feeling of security.

It was almost daylight before he slept.

10

Parris slowed his small car as he neared Pomeroy Lane. He was uncertain of the advisability of this visit to the house on the hill. Still, there was his promise to Ross that he would try to get at the roots of Davis Pomeroy's strange compulsion. A promise was a promise. He turned into the big gate and drove up the incline, passing the tennis court, stark in the unshaded light.

Several friendly hounds with mournful eyes and with ears almost trailing the ground came halfway down the drive to meet him and turned back to accompany him to the porte-cochere.

Davis Pomeroy, big and gray, wearing gray tweeds, his hair and mustache graying, but with a flicker of youth about him, was beside the car as Parris stopped.

"Well, well, Doctor, I'm glad to see you here. Come in, come in."

Parris stopped to stroke the satin ears of the hounds. The dogs hunched themselves up under his touch and turned beseeching eyes toward this new friend.

"Probably I should have telephoned, Mr. Pomeroy, but remembering your invitation to come up and see your exceptional herd of cattle, I decided to accept and I simply turned in at your gate on an impulse."

"I'm glad you did. Come in, if you can get rid of the hounds. They're apt to be embarrassingly friendly. But, come in, I want you to meet my wife."

Entering the living room from the side door, Parris looked about him with quick appreciation. Not many Kings Row houses had this look of acceptance of what was comfortably modern in close conjunction with what was beautiful in the old. A delightful room, he thought, with books and magazines indicating the tastes of the occupants.

Mrs. Pomeroy was a rather imposing woman. Her black hair, smoothly coroneted on her well-shaped head, was held in place by a pair of ornamental brilliant-studded tortoise-shell pins. Parris could see how McKay had come by his dark dignity.

A little later Parris found himself really interested in the things Davis Pomeroy was explaining to him about his favorite breed of cattle, about how he had become interested in raising the big draft mules that were attracting so much attention just now. The man forgot himself entirely when he talked of the things he was doing. Parris listened carefully for some hint of an obsession that might give him a lead, but there was nothing. This was a man of business, a cattleman who was informed, enthusiastic, and capable.

"Have you always been interested in the—the evolution of a fine breed of animals?"

"No, it's a recent interest. I'm a farmer at heart. I love the land. But I wanted my children to have the advantages of growing up in a college town—of association with people of ideas. I don't want to be separated from them unnecessarily, and so I came to Kings Row, where I could indulge in both what I wanted and what I needed."

"You're a wise man, Mr. Pomeroy. Few men find such a happy compromise."

"I have done the best I knew for my boys. For myself"—he looked gravely up the wooded slope—"sometimes I've wondered."

"You came from the hills, I take it?"

"Yes, the river hills. I miss the river."

"It's so close by."

"Yes—but somehow I don't go often."

"You know, Mr. Pomeroy, there's always been a sort of romance about great rivers to me. The Rhine and the Danube are loaded with sentiment. The Ganges, the Euphrates, the Nile, are immemorial. The Amazon is mysterious with the life of the tropics and the spell of the jungle."

Pomeroy's blue eyes twinkled with amusement. "The Missouri—is just a big, wet river. That goes for the Mississippi, too. They haven't much song or story to make them anything else."

Parris was taken aback for a moment. He had the feeling that Pomeroy was making fun of him, rejecting the romantic aspects of what he had said. That, he thought, a little resentfully, was what the Middle West attitude was like ... the new country harboring a certain distaste for mellowness—the patina of age and refined custom. Still treating the outgrowths of imagination as subjects of jocular though tolerant comment.

Pomeroy spoke again. "I like this country, Dr. Mitchell. I like the very newness of it—its comfort, solidity—"

"And its utilitarianism?"

"Exactly. There's something in my temperament, I guess, that responds to it. I tried the East once—but I got homesick for the very largeness of this." He made a sweeping gesture. "Oh, I know it hasn't grandeur—the landscape's too bright—and certainly it has no intimacy. But by God, a man has elbow room!"

"A man of action needs that most of all."

"I reckon so. The boys, now—I don't know what they will think about it. McKay's the dreamer—the artist type. Maybe he won't like the commonplaceness of Kings Row. Ross is more like me, and I hope he'll stick around after this hellish war is over."

"I grew up here," Parris said, "and perhaps in some mystical way I'm attached to it. Perhaps I've been able to think into it some of the mystery and half-lights and shadows you say are lacking."

"The imagination can do wonders if you let it. I remember as a child—" Davis flushed and turned his face aside. The sentence, begun eagerly, hung unfinished.

"You were saying?" Parris tried not to sound too urgent.

"Just a foolish thing that had to do with reaching the peak of any hill I saw. My imagination told me it was—new and—and different."

"Well, wasn't it?"

"No," Pomeroy said almost angrily, and turned toward the newly planted orchards on the strip of land he had recently acquired from Drew Roddy.

Parris knew there was no use trying to get any closer to the man's past than he had done. He would have to be patient. There seemed nothing to go on yet. But he felt that the ice had been broken and that they would in time become friends.

"Doctor, the soil up here is particularly suited to certain fruit trees. Your grandmother proved that with her prosperous nurseries. Just look how the land slopes—the drainage is perfect and the southern exposure just right. Pity Roddy doesn't utilize the whole hillside for orchards."

"That's an idea. I think I'll stop by and see Roddy. As a neighbor I haven't been as attentive as I might be. I was over a few times with Jamie Wakefield during the late summer. He's an interesting man—Roddy. Do you know him?"

"Only saw him that one time when he signed the deed to this strip. Neither of us is what you might gregarious," he said with his quick, surprising smile.

They turned back toward the house.

The hounds trotted solemnly beside Parris' car until he rounded the curve in the drive at the tennis court, and then fell sadly behind. He continued, however, to think of them, and of Davis Pomeroy as he turned out of Pomeroy Lane toward von Eln.

He stopped his car at the open gate of Roddy's place. He noted that the brown weeds had been cut and stacked for burning or removal. The sagging porch had been repaired, new steps built, and a graceful railing added. The shutters had new hinges and there were lattices erected at each end of the porch for the support of vines. The painting had not been done, but a new ladder leaned against the side of the house and Parris guessed that Drew was getting ready for that job, too.

"Why, Doctor, how are you? Come in to the fire. It's a bit chilly today. Glad you came over."

Drew's words poured out with that almost breathless quality often heard from those who have lived much alone.

Parris said, "I've just been over looking at Davis Pomeroy's orchards. You know, Drew, this hillside would be an ideal soil for fruit trees and berries. My grandmother found it so. That's how she happened to develop the nurseries at von Eln. I was just wondering if you'd like to have the young trees from the ground down there that Nathan is needing for garden truck. There are pears and plums, some cherries, and any number of apples—all fine young trees. Nathan could help you transplant them here and they'd thrive—with a little attention."

Drew was silent for so long that Parris glanced quickly at him, fearing he had been offended by the offer. To his surprise Drew's lips were quivering. After a moment he spoke.

"That's awfully good of you, Doctor. I've been hoping I could manage to plant fruit trees up there adjoining Pomeroy's place. I've had an eye on the planting going on, but I wasn't sure I could manage it. There was so much the place needed in repairs. I'll be glad to get the trees—already acclimated as they are. I don't know how to thank you."

"I'm glad you can give them room. Old Nathan will be helpful about transplanting. He knows trees and loves them."

"It might be a good idea, Dr. Mitchell, if I'd go over to see Davis Pomeroy and ask his advice about how to set them out to good advantage. With his advice and Nathan's I should get a fine start."

"Good idea. By the way, Miles Jackson tells me he's trying to get you to come in with him on *The Gazette*."

"Yes, he's been to see me about it, but I don't know—" his voice trailed off doubtfully.

"It might be the saving of Miles' health. He's kept too closely confined. That paper is more than a one-man job, and Miles is not young, you know."

"I wonder if I could really do it?"

"Why not? I'd like to see you take over when Miles has to retire."

"I'd like to give it a try. Jamie Wakefield is encouraging me to make a stab at it."

"Personally, I hope you decide in favor of it. Miles is working too hard, and Miles Jackson is needed in this town. So are you. I should think you and Miles together would make a good team."

"Thank you, Doctor. Maybe you're right. I might be of some use in the *Gazette* office."

"I'm sure of it." Parris rose to go. "Well, I just stopped by to ask if you'd relieve us of those few acres of trees. It will be a load off Nathan's mind if you'll accept them. He can't bear to discard a tree while it has life in it. He doesn't really like to chop down a weed."

"I can understand that. I think I have the same feeling for trees. Come again, Doctor, and soon."

"That I will. I hope to see you at von Eln right away. I'd like to show you the plantings there."

As Parris turned into the road to von Eln, a plodding figure moving ahead of him at the edge of the road attracted his attention. As he passed he recognized Punch Rayne. Stopping his car, he waited for Punch to come up.

"Hello, Punch. Can I take you somewhere?"

"Thank you, Doctor. I was on my way to your house. I got to ask you something."

"Get right in—glad I happened along."

Punch climbed into the seat beside Parris with surprising lightness. There was something catlike in his easy movements.

"How is Dyanna?"

"That's what I want to talk about, Doctor. You reckon she ain't ever gonna get over that—that thing that happened to her that time? Seems like she's worryin' sometimes when I come on her unexpected like, and I found her cryin' several times in the night."

"It takes a long time, Punch, to get over a shock like that. You'll have to be patient and make her feel that she's wanted and needed."

"Good Lord, Doctor, I love her to death. And she loves me. Seems like she ain't happy unless I'm holdin' her tight in my arms. It's like she was scared all the time."

"I know, Punch. That's to be expected. You must be glad she isn't afraid of *you*. That could have happened, you know. Gradually she'll stop being scared, when she gets used to the idea that you are protecting her."

"Nothin' is goin' to hurt her again as long as I live." There was something grim in Punch's voice.

Parris looked quickly at the boy. "I hear you're getting to be a fine shot. Ned Porter told me he'd been hunting with you."

Punch turned his head slowly toward Parris. "I got a reason for learnin' to shoot," he confided. "Someday, Doctor, I'll find them skunks an' I aim to kill 'em same as varmints." His voice, instead of rising as his anger mounted, sank almost to a strangled whisper. His face whitened. His chin was lifted and his fury gave him a certain dignity.

Parris wondered what thoughts were stumbling down the dark, treacherous paths of this strange boy's mind. "Punch," he said quietly, "you are not likely to find those two brutes. It was dark and they were masked. Don't brood too much about it, for your own sake."

"I'll find 'em. I'd know them voices if I heard 'em in hell. I'll find 'em and I'll kill 'em."

"Listen, Punch. It would be possible for you to make a mistake. Voices often sound alike—"

"I'll know 'em when I hear 'em," he said doggedly. "I owe that much to Dyanna."

"Taking care of her every day for the rest of her life is what you can do for Dyanna. That will cure her fear and make her happy. You and Dyanna should raise a family of fine, strong children, and take your proper place in the world."

The color had come back to Punch's face and he turned his anxious eyes again to Parris. "You reckon Dyanna can have children, Doctor? She was hurt right bad that night."

"Of course she can, Punch. Just give her a little time. She's awfully young, you know. You and Dyanna have a long and happy life ahead of you."

"I don't know, Doctor. Seems like I'm just waitin' and waitin' to hear them voices—"

"Try to forget the voices, Punch. Use that time just being glad you have Dyanna."

"I'm glad I got her, but just the same, if I ever get a chance—" His voice had sunk again to that hoarse whisper.

"Here we are at von Eln, Punch. Come on in—"

"Thank you, Doctor, I just wanted to ask about Dyanna. I'll go on back now."

"I'll drop by tomorrow to see her if you'd like, Punch. I'm sure she's going to be all right. Don't worry about her."

"If you will come, Doctor, I'll be mighty thankful. I couldn't stand for nothin' to happen to her."

At this moment Nell Carruthers and Elise came out of the house.

Nell's artificially red hair and quick gestures gave her a false air of vivacity. She lifted a too-small hand in greeting to Parris and looked curiously at the boy beside him.

"Oh, Parris!" Elise called, "you're just in time. Let's drive Nell into town—oh, you have someone with you—I didn't know."

"Elise, Mrs. Carruthers—this is Punch Rayne, a friend of mine. He's going back to town. Pile in, both of you, and I'll run you in."

Elise and Nell got into the back seat and Punch sat silently beside Parris until they reached the edge of Jinktown, where he got out, lifting his hat carefully before he turned away.

"What a strange boy," Nell said, looking after him.

"He's a good, hard-working lad. I like him," Parris said.

"I always feel uncomfortable around people of that—that class."

"Why?"

Nell looked uncertainly at Parris before answering lamely, "Why, I don't know, exactly."

"Punch has certain qualities of greatness. I couldn't explain to you just what I mean—but he's the stuff martyrs are made of—or conquerors."

"Mercy! I should have made up to him."

"He had other things on his mind. He wouldn't have recognized your overtures, I assure you."

Nell laughed gaily but a little uncertainly as Parris assisted her from the car. She wondered if she had been sort of "put in her place." She wondered also how Parris Mitchell happened to be on such intimate terms with an ignorant Jinktown boy.

II

Throughout the late summer, life for Fanny Porter had stepped up its rhythm. She had found herself the object of much attention from Hazel Green and Randy McHugh. There were invitations to tea, flattering requests that she serve on this committee or that engaged in war work. At first it was stimulating, this sudden recognition of her as a person. Fanny had spent the few months in a state approaching happiness. But as the novelty wore off, her neurotic imaginings began to possess her again. She became less interested in civic affairs and in her new friends. Slowly she withdrew into the restricted round of her domestic duties.

The tattered and dripping autumn had dragged slowly for her. It seemed, she felt, not so much a different mood of nature as it was the prolonged cadence of an old one. It had been merely a weary summer, hot and dusty, and trying to nerves already taut from months of heat and glare.

Sick as she was of hot weather, Fanny was unprepared for the sudden onslaught of a particularly early and unusually severe winter. As she kept herself confined to the house, her morbid brooding deepened and a new symptom filled her with terror. So often now it was *she* who talked at length on economies and questioned, sometimes sharply, expenditures that her husband had made. A score of times lately that phrase, grisly to her in its actual horror, "We can't stand that," had sprung to utterance. She cowered before that trick of her mind.

Ten days before Christmas, Hazel Green asked her to serve on the decoration committee that was to arrange for the Sunday school Christmas tree at the First Presbyterian Church.

Ned encouraged her, and offered to be the Santa Claus for the party. Reluctantly, she accepted.

On Christmas Eve, at the church, Fanny helped him array himself in the red suit with the great pillow paunch. The tree was ready and most of the ladies had gone home. Soon the children would begin to arrive.

Ned laid aside the long beard while he climbed the stepladder and began lighting the candles at the top. Fanny lighted the lower candles as high as she could reach.

"Believe I've got 'em all now. Where's my whiskers? Don't want any of the kids catching me looking like Ned Porter," he chuckled.

"Look, Ned, there are two up there that you missed. Put the ladder back and light them—they are right in front."

"D'ye know," he said as he replaced the ladder and started up—she noticed how strange his voice sounded through the thick beard—"Ed Harper got a tree for the Methodist Church bigger'n this one for three dollars. You ought to have got him to buy your tree for you."

Suddenly everything in her brain seemed to whirl wildly. She staggered a step. Then—she never knew how it happened—did Ned lean forward toward the taper she was holding, or did some uncontrollable impulse of the strange rage that possessed her move her hand toward him? She only knew that she saw, with an abnormal clearness, the tip of his false beard catch at the little flame in her hand and crisp sharply as the crackles sped up the curling hair.

At her first scream Ned almost tumbled to the floor and she was tearing at his wig and clothes, Ned! Ned! Ned! She was quicker than the flames, but as it fell the burning fiber struck her dress and a stifling, blinding sheet of fire swept toward her face. She lurched forward into the red abyss where sharp claws tore at her eyes.

It was late in March before Fanny was able to leave the hospital. The long days of gradual emergence from opiates, awakening frenzied with pain, gave way to longer days of gray waiting. Little by little, she realized the extent of her injuries, her left hand, shriveled and helpless, her face a mass of crimson scars that puckered one cheek and her throat. The right eye had escaped, but the left, drawn sharply up at the corner, had its vision seriously impaired.

She tried to estimate what the months in the hospital with trained nurses must have cost. What inroads it must have made on their resources!

A new fear attacked her and settled in her heart like a freezing pool —suppose something happened to Ned, suppose he should fall ill, what would become of her? Day and night these fears drummed a macabre dance in her brain.

One evening Ned came in later than usual and found her sitting in the now always darkened living room.

"Good news, honey! Dr. Waring wrote to a big New York specialist who says he can fix you up all right. They can fix your face as good as ever. They've learned a lot about skin grafting."

A fear, obscure but deadly, strangled her. "Ned, we've spent too much—what'll become of us if— Oh," she wailed, "we can't stand that!"

"Don't you worry about anything," he soothed. "I've got it all arranged. We'll leave Thursday. That'll give you a week's time."

She was silent, her mind twisting and turning in an effort to escape. She lay awake and thought hour after hour, trying desperately to figure out some way to avoid what she knew would be a heavy expense. She knew she must prevent this trip and this operation. She wished passionately that she had died. She looked through the window at the moonlit world. Out there they were in bed, all of the people she knew, sleeping. *Their* faces and hands were not hideously burned—*they* were not condemned to live with twisted and scarred features! She shivered and drew the counterpane around her . . . quick! How could she do it? Where? She shuddered again and felt a little sick—would it hurt? She had had enough of pain.

Then she remembered the bottle of bichloride tablets in the bathroom—in the cabinet above the lavatory, top shelf. She rose. . . .

"What is it, honey, where are you going?"

"I'm just going to look for some aspirin—my head is hurting again. Lie still, Ned. I know where it is."

She reeled a little against the door. A short phrase sang suddenly in her brain—louder and louder. It rose to the wildness of storm. The refrain "We can't stand that—we can't stand that" became a deafening hurricane.

Going straight to the little cabinet, she placed her hand on the diamond-shaped bottle and shook some of the tablets into a glass of water. A moment later she tiptoed back to the bedroom where Ned was quietly sleeping.

Nell Carruthers entered Mrs. Fulmer Green's house out of breath. She made it a practice never to be late at a bridge appointment. It was almost a religion with her.

"Hazel, my dear, you'll have to forgive me if I'm a little late. Are Maud and Caroline here? They *are?* Well, this is the first time I've been late—the very first time—and goodness knows I have a reason. The most *dreadful* thing has happened—"

"What's the excitement about?" Caroline Thill called from the living room. "Don't you *dare* tell Hazel until Maud and I can hear! Do come on in."

Maud Laneer, thin, well groomed, and poised, sat at the bridge table, waiting. Caroline Thill, plump and brown as a robin, stood ruffling a pack of cards impatiently.

"Hello, girls. Sorry to be late. *Have* you heard the news?"

"Sit down, Nell. I've no doubt it will still be news when you are ready to tell it." Hazel Green was never hurried in manner.

"Have you heard about poor little Fanny Porter?"

Nell was pleased at the effect she produced.

"Don't tell me anything *else* has happened to that poor woman," Hazel said anxiously.

"She took bichloride tablets last night! John says there's simply *nothing* to be done. She's going to die in a few hours—or days—he says."

"Does anyone know why she took them? Surely it was by mistake."

"Mistake, my eye!" Nell said sharply. "She committed suicide. She's still alive but it's just a question of hours."

"The poor thing," Hazel commiserated. "I don't know that she can be much blamed. She was such an active person—and useful. It must have been desperately hard for her to resign herself to being a shut-in."

"Just between you and me, it could have been prevented," Nell said confidentially.

For the first time Maud leaned forward and spoke softly. "I don't understand what you mean, Nell."

Mrs. Carruthers, not quite sure of her audience, said cautiously, "I wouldn't want this to go any further, but Fanny Porter has been a patient of Dr. Mitchell, you know, and—"

"No, Nell, I didn't know. She is Dr. Waring's patient. She told me so, herself." Mrs. Green's voice was unruffled but Nell colored a little.

"Yes, I know, Hazel, but Dr. Mitchell was called in some time ago. From the time he began working on the case, Fanny got worse and worse. Instead of quieting her, he got her worked up to such a state of excitement that she just—just took poison."

Having delivered herself of this bit of malicious gossip, Nell sank back in her chair with a smug smile of satisfaction.

There was an awkward pause. Hazel's steady gaze was on Nell. "That is an absurd statement. I'm sure you wouldn't consciously repeat that kind of thing if you stopped to think. If it were true—and it isn't—it would be particularly unbecoming for the wife of a physician to breathe a criticism of her husband's colleague."

Nell had the grace to flush at the rebuke. Caroline looked uncomfortable. Maud's expression conveyed nothing.

"I suppose I'm a fool to repeat it—but I know it's a fact. I can't tell you who told me, but I'm *positive*."

"You'll do me a personal favor, Nell, if you'll stop talking about this business. You are entirely wrong about it and you could start something you'd be sorry for." Hazel spoke evenly but Nell fancied there was a veiled threat in the silken sound.

"I'm terribly sorry about it all," Caroline Thill said. "I was at the church the night she was burned. It was frightful. She saved Ned, you know. He's been awfully cut up about her accident, and they say he's heavenly good to her."

"And why shouldn't he be? He'd be a brute to be anything else," Maud interjected.

"Come on, girls, let's play." Nell judged it was high time to change the subject.

"I'm sorry," Hazel said quietly, "but I'll have to ask you to excuse me. I'm going over to the Porters' to see if there's anything I can do. I like Fanny Porter—and you will understand that I can't play bridge today."

"Why, of course, Hazel," Maud said, rising instantly. "I'd go with you but I don't know the Porters and I—"

"It isn't necessary. I'm sorry to break up the game, but—you understand. Can I drop any of you on the way?"

Mrs. Carruthers, having elected to walk home, tried to rid herself of a feeling of disquiet. Now why had Hazel Green taken up like that for Parris Mitchell? Why, she was positively unpleasant about it. And *everybody* knew that Fulmer was doing everything he could against Parris. If there was anything in the world she hated more than anything else, it was to see anybody take on that "holier than thou" attitude. Why, she had known Hazel Green since college days and she had never turned on her like this before.

Before she could find a satisfactory answer to her own question she met Martha Cotten hurrying toward her Harvey Street house.

Martha was tall and thin. She was a billow of mourning, her heavy crepe unrelieved by any grace, a mourning she had worn since her mother's death twelve years before. She literally gave off waves of black. Martha plunged into the most exciting subject of the day. *"Have* you heard about Fanny Porter?"

"Yes, I have," Nell said and waited. This was what she had stopped for. "It's too bad," Nell continued, "but not surprising. You know she's been a patient of Dr. Mitchell for some time—and you know what that means!"

"You don't say! Was she sort of—" Martha made a little circular motion with her finger at her own temple, "oh, you know—sort of crazy?"

"We-ell, I wouldn't say *that*, exactly, but when people begin to listen to Dr. Mitchell's questions and suggestions, almost anything can happen to them. He seems to get them awfully *excited*, somehow, and they just—well, they usually end up out at the asylum."

"I thought he was supposed to *cure* folks of that kind of thing."

"That's the idea, of course—but it's surprising how often the other thing happens."

"Well, I don't think Fanny Porter took that stuff because of anything Parris Mitchell said. I think she couldn't stand having her face so scarred an' all."

"I hope you are right, but it looks very strange. As long as Dr. Waring had the case she was getting along very well, but the minute Parris Mitchell was called in—pouf!" A tiny kid-gloved hand made an airy gesture suggestive of the explosion of a ripe puffball. "Poor little thing," she added unctuously.

"Oh, my goodness, Mrs. Caruthers, won't this hurt Dr. Mitchell's reputation? It don't take much to put a doctor out of business if a thing like this gets out."

"What do you mean?"

"Well, it don't seem any time since Parris Mitchell was about the most popular man around Kings Row and look at him now—everybody talkin' about how he drives folks crazy just to get them out to the asylum!"

"Oh, it's not that bad, really. We are all fond of him at the hospital. My husband admires him very much, and Elise is one of my dearest friends. She's such a sweet, helpless little thing."

"I saw Mrs. Green's car parked at the Porters' gate. I wonder what she's doing there? I didn't know they were friends."

"Oh, you know how Hazel Green is. She gets into everything in town. I don't think it's just curiosity—she really likes to help people. She gets fed up with staying at home alone, with Fulmer over at the capital so much of the time. Hazel's not too happy herself, I imagine, things being like they are."

Martha's black eyes flicked sideways at Mrs. Carruthers but she asked no questions. "Is that so?" Her voice was only politely interested. "Well, it's nice to have seen you, Mrs. Carruthers. I don't often have a chance to talk with you. Good-by."

"Hazel Green be—be *damned*," Nell murmured triumphantly as she resumed her stroll down Federal Street.

Hazel Green almost collided with Parris Mitchell as she left the Porter house. She had been crying and her face was pale.

"Oh, Parris, I'm glad to see you. I've just been trying to find out if there's anything I can do for Fanny or Ned. Dr. Waring says there's nothing anyone can do at the moment."

"I'm afraid he's right. I was just on my way to see Ned. Waring tells me Mrs. Porter had a bad heart and this added strain doesn't give her much chance to pull through."

"I'm terribly sorry about it all. In spite of myself I feel *guilty*. I feel as though I were in some way to blame."

"To blame?"

"Yes, Parris. I failed in what you asked me to do last summer. You remember you suggested that I try to make friends with her? I know what you hoped Randy and I could do—and we *tried,* Parris. Honestly, we did."

"Why, of course, I know you did. I think it was already too late."

"She tried to meet us halfway. I know she did—but she was so abnormally shy—that—oh, Parris," her voice broke pitifully, "I'm afraid I gave up too easily."

"But you can't blame yourself like this, Hazel—neither you nor Randy. This tragedy happened, really, because of the Christmas accident. A scarred face can do irreparable damage to the mental equilibrium of a sensitive woman."

"You think," Hazel faltered anxiously, "you think she was unbalanced?"

"Definitely. She had no other reason—"

"It couldn't possibly have been an accident?"

Parris was conscious of having made an unpardonable error. He had overlooked the fact that there might be doubt in the minds of some about the matter. He hesitated, then decided to be frank with Hazel.

"It was intentional, Hazel."

"I was afraid of that. If only she had allowed me to come to see her—after her terrible burns, but she refused to see *anybody*."

"I know. I haven't seen her either. I only saw her one time—the time I prescribed Hazel Green and Randy McHugh."

"And we failed to help."

"You helped. If it hadn't been for the accident at Christmas you might have won out, after all."

"I blame myself for not being more persistent."

"Don't worry, Hazel. I'm sure you did everything you could. I'm not so sure that *I* did. Maybe I shifted my own responsibility to your shoulders."

"That's nonsense. Parris, will you do something for me?"

"Anything, Hazel."

His voice was so warm that she looked up quickly, but he was not seeing her at all, she thought, with a queer, sinking feeling.

"Find out what I can do to help the Porters. I'd like to—help."

"Certainly, Hazel. I'll call you if there's anything."

Parris crossed to the curb and opened the door of Hazel's car just as Nell Carruthers passed on the opposite side of the street.

Nell did not look at them.

"I like being your friend, Parris Mitchell," Hazel said impulsively, as she held out her hand to him.

He did not release her hand at once and their eyes clung for a moment. "I like it, too," he responded, meaning it.

For some time after she had gone he stood quite still. "Now, what fool sort of exchange was that?" he asked himself sharply. Then he laughed softly. "I thought I was immune to that kind of appeal," and he shook his head reprovingly. But as he entered the house he was thinking of her overemotional face and her compelling femininity.

12

Ordinarily Fulmer Green would have hung his coat in the hall closet and placed his hat carefully on the shelf above it. But this time his coat was still on his arm as he came into the bright living room.

His wife's long gray eyes turned from her book and focused on him slowly as if she were reluctant to part with an inner vision of her own. No gesture she could have made, no word she might have spoken would have been more unsettling than this quiet ignoring of his urgency.

Fulmer Green was unaccustomed to the impact of calm at his entrance. Men were alarmed at his coming; men greeted him with hurried, nervous, mollifying words—fawning praise or explanations to disarm; they rushed to cover mistakes or conspired to put him "in a good mood." Silence, never; the added insult of boredom or reluctance to recognize him as the central figure in any room was an experience peculiar to his own home.

He waited for Hazel to speak as if, before her impassive appraisal, he feared the inadequacy of the words which rose with his anger to his lips. If she would speak, God damn it—say anything to give him an opening! But Hazel did not speak. . . .

He turned away from her, threw his coat on a chair, relit the cigar clamped between his teeth.

"So," he said, with his back turned, "what a warm, friendly greeting! Not that I'm surprised," he went on hurriedly, "after the way you seem to have been spending your time."

"I beg your pardon? It's hard to hear you with your back turned."

"You heard me!"

He faced her suddenly now.

"Spending my time?" she murmured vaguely. "Yes, I confess I've got an absorbing book here. There's nothing unusual about your coming home to dinner—"

"No, and there's nothing unusual, either, in your riding and walking, and spending God knows how many hours—or days—with that quack doctor at the asylum. Is there?"

Her face was as expressionless as if he had been speaking in Chinese. In all of his experience of cross-examination, the grueling breakdown of witnesses in which he was so expert, he had never been confronted by such open bewilderment. Was it possible—was it conceivable that he had been deliberately deceived? He could not tolerate the thought.

"Don't pretend with me, Hazel," he said. "It doesn't work."

"But I'm afraid you'll have to be more explicit. I truly don't know what you are talking about."

"I suppose you've never even heard of Dr. Parris Mitchell?"

"Oh," she said.

Fulmer Green had half rehearsed this scene in his mind. He had seen Hazel's anger, heard her faltering defense, her excuses. But he had not seen her laugh.

Now she threw back her head and the music of her mirth filled the room. It was so sudden, so wholly real, so free of any modulation of hysteria that Fulmer could not even think against it. He moved back from her, his hands feeling for the wall behind him.

"Oh, dear God in heaven," Hazel said. "How wonderful! Hazel Green and Parris Mitchell! Tell me, my dear, is all Kings Row talking about it? Why, I wonder? They have never flattered me so before! Why, this is a story any woman in town would give half her soul for. And you have brought it to *me*!"

She laughed again; then she got up and put her hands lightly on Fulmer's shoulders.

"Your compliments are rare, my dear. But in your curious way you do admire me!"

The anger moved through Fulmer's body, into his face, into his hands as they closed over Hazel's wrists. But with the sense of the cool, resistant flesh under his powerful fingers, the control came back, the restraint that had saved him in many a crisis of breaking temper. He moved her hands away and spoke deliberately, his voice rasping harshly.

"And don't think you've put anything over on me about forcing Don to go to consult that quack."

Hazel caught her breath sharply. She hadn't expected this. "Donny needed it. He was—on edge—and I thought—"

"*You thought?* By God, Hazel, if anybody had told me you could do such a fool thing as that, I'd have laughed in his face. Of all the *nerve*—sending Don to that man—giving Parris Mitchell a chance to pry into our private affairs!"

"What affairs are we trying to hide? I was trying to keep Donny out of trouble. *You* didn't seem to be able to do anything with him."

"Don's my business."

Fulmer's face was expressionless, but Hazel knew she had never seen him so angry. A thrill of momentary fear sped along her nerves, but her lifted head and steady eyes did not betray it.

"Listen to me, Hazel, I don't know whether this story about you and Parris is true or not. But when it comes to me from a client, when a client tells me Kings Row is repeating it—now, when my political future is at stake—and when it's tied to a man who has deliberately made himself my enemy, who cheated me out of that property, who hounded me and tried to set Kings Row against me for that Singer prosecution—that quack psycho-fool—by God, Hazel, I believe you are trying to lick me in my own town! You'd better be careful. That's been tried before—"

Hazel's low, commanding voice stopped him.

"Just a moment, Fulmer. Threats neither convince nor frighten me. If the time comes for our divorce—"

"What are you saying? Good God, Hazel—"

She saw the quick pallor spread again almost to his lips, clamped over the dead cigar.

"If—or when—that times comes, I promise you Dr. Mitchell will not be involved. I hardly know him. I have talked with him precisely three times. Once he drove me home from Mrs. Skeffington's. I think he asked some questions about Fanny Porter—"

Fulmer's control had come back. He took the chewed, torn cigar from his mouth and gestured with it as he spoke.

"That's another thing," he said. "That's some more meddling of this damn' so-called doctor. That time it turned out to be fatal."

"What do you mean?"

"I only know what they say. Anyone in Kings Row will tell you he scared her into killing herself."

"Fulmer, you can't believe that! You must know Dr. Mitchell is not Fanny's physician."

"You're crazy! Of course he's her doctor."

"Fanny had not seen Dr. Mitchell for months."

"How do you know?"

"From Dr. Mitchell."

"Listen to me, Hazel. I want you to stop seeing Mitchell. Do you understand? God knows there's enough conspiracy against me without your being drawn into it."

The door opened and a servant announced dinner.

"Shall we drop the subject?"

Her dignity silenced him for the moment. As they rose to go into the dining room, Fulmer remembered just in time to step aside and allow his wife to enter first. He wondered uneasily if she noticed the momentary lapse, and, already disconcerted, he was a trifle late in drawing out her chair at the table. He seemed always to have to watch out for those little things. It annoyed him that he was under that kind of tension in his own home. A fellow ought to feel free to act natural with his own family.

"So you want to drop the subject? That's an Allingham trait," he said when the maid had left them, "side-stepping an issue. There never was an Allingham yet who didn't back off from an unpleasant truth. I guess that's why they never got along any better in the world."

"My family always got along well enough," she said imperturbably. "Be reasonable, Fulmer. They managed to give us this house and its furnishings for a wedding present. And if you will remember, the money from my grandmother's estate went a long way toward establishing you in business. They've done well enough."

"I could buy out the whole kit and caboodle of them now and never miss the money," Fulmer boasted. He seemed bent on transgressing simple good manners, and Hazel winced. She was left with a kind of shyness which she hated.

But looking across the beautifully appointed table at Hazel as he spoke, the echo of Fulmer's words caught at him. The flowers, the soft light from the candles, were at sharp variance with his crude, pointless thrust—the brag of an adolescent. After all, Fulmer was proud of his home, proud to show it to his political friends, proud of the way Hazel received their guests, of her handling of the servants.

The door opened and Prentiss, their four-year-old son, ran in to say good night. Fulmer was almost fanatically devoted to the boy. His voice as he spoke to Prentiss was softer.

After the child had been sent away to bed, Fulmer knew that, for tonight at least, the argument was closed. While Hazel talked—almost as if to some visitor—of the little incidents of the day, a word kept sounding back into his consciousness. *Divorce*—she had never said it until tonight. It was a final—a devastating word. Even the *word* could carry defeat. Men against whom that whisper moved were not elected Governor—were not elected to any office; even the candidacy would be denied them. It made no difference where the guilt lay.

The question of Parris Mitchell would be wholly irrelevant if Hazel should sue. . . . He had lied, of course, in telling her that there was wide gossip. Such a thing spoken by Martha Cotten's poisonous tongue could not be taken seriously. Yet, he admitted, if the story *were* believed, then everything Fulmer might say against Mitchell in the future would be put down to a personal grudge. But, God, it was incredible. He tried to shake off the thought—to laugh with Hazel as she talked, to act as if there had been no words—never that word. He must have dreamed it. He was tired. . . . He would talk to Hazel in the morning, tell her he had been unreasonable, lost his temper.

Upon leaving the table Hazel went to her room. Fulmer moved restlessly about the lower floor for a while, made a pretense of reading the papers, finally climbed the stairs and went down the hall toward his own room. As he passed his wife's door he hesitated. No, not to-night. Tomorrow would be another day. Everything would be different by daylight.

In his own room he looked at the bed with the covers turned neatly back, the satin comforter folded conveniently across the footboard. An expression of distaste crossed his face. He dreaded the sleeplessness which in the last months had been growing on him; the hours of planning and figuring ahead to outguess opposing lawyers and politicians and . . . Parris Mitchell, who had too much of Kings Row behind him.

He sat down in front of the triple-mirrored dresser, thinking he might as well get out his shirt and tie for tomorrow. A nuisance. He was making enough money now to have a valet, but, he thought wryly, that indulgence would probably cost him votes in the next election. The country voters would consider that "putting on airs."

The mirror gave back his triplicate reflection: he—Fulmer Green, lawyer, legislator, bank director, head of the Inter-city Realty Company, the richest—well, *almost* the richest man in Kings Row, and with any luck at all, the future Governor of the state; he, Fulmer Green. Wealth, influence, power. After all, he thought, those were winning things.

They were talking about him. Here, in Kings Row—down in the stores and offices, in Camperville and Fielding—all over the state! He felt himself flow out toward those places—out like the spokes of a great wheel; he felt the flow of interest turn, flood back again toward himself, the center. He felt it, the interest, the wonder, the envy, the fear. Yes, the fear. He liked that best of all. They were afraid of him. All of them were afraid.

It strengthened him to feel it. It was a solid reality—this power, their fears. *Underlings.* How many of them there were! It fed his strength again to recall them. How many he had passed on the way. People had been exacting of him when he was an underling. Now he was on top. He could not forget. Every score had to be paid. Humiliation for humiliation, smart for smart—even to the last twitch of a nerve.

He had always aimed at this and it had come sooner than he expected. Why, he was not yet forty. Destiny had played for him. Success had come swiftly after that first big case when he had just become District Attorney—that Benny Singer murder charge. Against his eloquence then Parris Mitchell's plea had fallen on deaf ears in a courtroom where he, Fulmer Green, held the jury in his hand!

Destiny was on his side, maybe, or God. Maybe not God. That was a halfhearted thought. That was too much to believe. Strict religious training in childhood—and his mother's religion was certainly strict enough—puts a fear of God in the blood. Probably no God existed, even, but one had to say so. The church—the church was right enough in its place. It was useful. It helped him. It must be right. Dr. Cole, old ninny—Cole was afraid of him, too. A preacher ought to be sure enough about God not to be afraid of any man. Dr. Cole probably wasn't sure about God. The old man had stammered and been confused when he talked to him last week. The recollection fed him—strengthened him.

He saw himself. The mirror gave back his triplicate reflection—his; Fulmer Green's!

He stood up, forgetting about the shirt and tie, and began preparing for bed, whistling softly.

As he turned out the lights he remembered he had not raised the window. He walked gingerly across the room in the dark and made quite a clatter adjusting the shade and raising the sash. Beyond the garden he could see the courthouse dome and the spire of the Presbyterian Church. Kings Row, he thought, was a good town to grow up in, a good town to use as a starting point if you had political ambitions. As he caught sight of the chimneys of the asylum at the end of Federal Street, he made an impatient gesture with his hand as though brushing away an importunate insect. But, try as he would, he knew he would have trouble getting to sleep. This Parris Mitchell business—was it becoming an obsession? He'd be glad when something drastic was done about that. If the fellow would just do something crooked that he could lay his finger on!

13

It was only a short time before Elise began to notice the wind. She had lived in this very house for two years with her father, but she could not recall that she had ever been troubled by the sound of wind moaning around the corners. But now the sound irritated her. It was inexplicable. She tried to laugh away the feeling.

Finally, she spoke of it to Parris. "It is like something human and willful, this terrible wind." She reached down and patted the little dachshund. "Even Greta, the poor little one, runs under the sofa and hides when it blows."

"Why, Elise, this is only the usual March wind. We always have it."

"This is ver-ry strange, Parris. It is not like a wind at all. It is like—like a monstrous *tide*—and I hate the sea. If it were a storm I could understand it—and it would stop when the storm passed, but—listen how it whines about the house. *Listen!*"

"It's only that you've never been particularly conscious of it before, sweet."

"Has it always been like this?" she asked, incredulous.

"Of course. As a boy I thought it great fun to battle with it. I made games.

"Sometimes," he said, "I was the skipper of a great ship that tore through hurricanes; sometimes I was a mountain climber struggling up great peaks, watching thin clouds streaming out in currents that swept up from the other side. When I would reach the top the wind would strike me full in the face. I loved it—and I made an exciting companion of it—here, Elise, right on this hilltop."

"You never told me this before."

"We guard our daydreams and keep them secret. We share them only with someone we love and trust completely."

"And you love and trust me enough?"

"What a question! Of course I do. You don't laugh at me when I tell them to you."

"But still, Parris, I am afraid. I haven't your imagination or your courage. The wind isn't a playmate to me. It's something—hateful, something sinister. I never felt like this about it before—but now it *threatens* me."

"Would you like to go away for a while? Anna could look after things and I can get away for a little vacation."

"Oh, no, Parris. We have just come. It's only that I am nervous. Perhaps the excitement of moving has made me—uneasy. I am ver-ry happy to be here. Truly."

She opened the door leading to the terrace. A high wind still prevailed and she closed the door quickly and stood leaning against it, her face pale, the veins showing blue at her temples. Parris caught her in his arms. Looking through the glass of the French doors he could see the trees bending and laboring beneath the fierce onslaught.

He held Elise close and laid his cheek against her hair. He could feel the tormented beat of her heart. He tried to master the tide of fear that kept rising in his mind. What could be the cause of her sudden obsession?

And then, without warning, the wind veered to the south and the sun broke through the clouds.

Elise, sensing the change, stirred in his arms.

"Listen," she whispered, "listen, Parris, to the wind in the chimney. It—it *sings,* now. How ver-ry foolish of me to be afraid!"

Parris kissed the top of her head lightly, comfortingly, but he was troubled. *"Süsschen,"* he whispered softly.

"It isn't often we have a chance to sit down for a good chat, Parris. I'm glad you came in." Dr. Nolan waved Parris to a seat.

"I'm here for more than just a chat, Paul. It's a professional consultation."

"That requires a different approach, Dr. Mitchell. Cigarette?"

"Thanks." Parris took the proffered cigarette and lit it with deliberation as he watched Paul Nolan touching and moving small objects on his already neatly arranged desk. Everything in the office spoke of an orderly, fastidious occupant.

Parris smiled as his friend opened a drawer to take out a fresh note pad and a fountain pen which he laid on the blotter in front of him. There was not the slightest lost motion in anything the man did.

Paul Nolan created an air of such sanity about him that everything took on in it the seeming of its final reality. His presence was like that burst of morning light that comes when the shades are raised after a night of distorted dreams and exaggerated phantoms. If the authorities concerned had sought throughout the whole country, Parris thought, they could not have found a better man to head this great hospital.

There was something reassuring about his long and angular person, about the very look of his hands—bony, philosophic hands—with their deliberate and easy gestures. There seemed to be nothing superfluous about him. He was the embodiment of a civilized human being who had disposed of superficial emotion and wasting, roundabout ways. Everything about him was under the control of a steely intelligence. But he had emotions—that Parris knew.

"Paul, I've had a sleepless night. I need your advice—your help."

"What's the trouble?"

"I'm concerned about Elise."

"That's not surprising. She's been noticeably nervous lately. I haven't liked it, particularly considering her anemic condition."

"She's too excitable. Her sudden enthusiasms seem to verge on hysteria."

"How long has it been noticeable?"

"I first noticed it when we began to make plans for moving out to von Eln. I immediately got Anna Hauser to take over housekeeping responsibilities. Elise seemed too eager, somehow. It made me uneasy."

"She wanted to live out there, didn't she?"

"Oh, yes. She loves the place, and everything about it. But suddenly she has developed a fear of the wind."

Paul looked sharply at Parris. "That startles me a bit, Parris. Have you discussed it with her?"

"I tried to reassure her. Of course I know, as you do, that the fear is not engendered by the wind, but by something deeply hidden—something which she wouldn't recognize."

"Any theories?"

Parris looked straight into the dark, intelligent eyes of his friend and answered frankly, "I feel that it is my business to find what is at the root of this neurotic trend. I want you to help me, Paul. Elise has never noticed the wind until recently. I'm afraid in some way *I* may be at fault. I may have failed her in something."

"You're jumping at conclusions. I think it far more likely that it's a passing delusion based on nothing more than a slight physical disturbance. She looks about for something on which she can place the blame for her discomfort."

Parris shook his head. "I'd considered that possibility, but an anxiety of this kind is based on some submerged *hostility*. She would suppress any such feeling toward me."

"But not toward your work or your friends?"

"That, too, I've ruled out. My friends are hers and she loves them."

Paul rose and walked around to sit on the corner of the desk nearest Parris. He laid his hand on the younger man's shoulder with an affectionate gesture, and after a moment he asked simply, "Is Elise happy in her marital relations with you?"

Parris' eyes met Paul's frankly. "Naturally you would need to ask that. I am not sure whether there has ever been any sexual drive in Elise's make-up, or whether it is merely an outlet for psychic tension. You can understand, Paul, that the doubt in my mind tends to act as a sedative to my own urge."

"That's understandable, but that in itself can become a threat to your own stability." Paul's voice was grave.

"I've not felt it to be a threat."

"Probably not yet. We'll have to discuss that later, Parris."

"If she were not so dear to me, I should not feel so helpless. I can't bear the idea that she may have any resentments against me, unconscious though they may be. We've lived so congenially, contentedly."

"Doesn't your friend Freud contend that no neurosis can develop in a normal sexual life?"

"Yes, he does, but I don't go all the way with him, there. I think many other causatives are at work—outside of the fundamental sexual urge."

[183]

"Then let's go looking for those elements in Elise. I have a theory. Take it for what it's worth: Elise is a shy person, afraid of outside contacts. She seems to me to have a too-clinging personality. Your affection has supplied her need, not only for the tenderness she craves, but for reassurance against external threat."

Parris spoke hesitantly. "Paul, I'm sure Elise loves me as I love her."

"At the risk of offending you, I'm going to say that I think Elise has merely substituted you for her father. I'll go still further than that and say I think she's looking for a parent in all her friends—in the town—in America. Not having found a satisfactory substitute, she's homesick."

"That may be. I've known she looked to me for all the pampering affection she had from her father. But I had the feeling that I was supplying it. Perhaps my vanity had blinded me to some of the things she needs."

"Look outside of yourself, Parris. You must not feel hurt at what I'm saying to you. We are trying to get at the primal cause of Elise's distress. She is probably subjectively convinced of her deep love for you but she can still resent, subconsciously, of course, your attitude to your work."

"She's never shown the slightest sign of feeling neglected but—"

"But what?"

"She spoke once of hating the hospital and wanting to get away from it."

"Do we need to look further?"

"Still, it would be a strange substitution. Why should it be the *wind*?"

"Has she ever told you of any wind-fear in her childhood?"

"I've been trying to remember." Parris frowned, considering. Then he spoke slowly. "She told me she had had an attack of rheumatic fever when she was very young, and that—that she was not permitted to walk or play in the cold *or the wind* for a long time."

"That hardly seems enough to go on. Has she any other fears or dislikes?"

"The sea. She often speaks of hating the sea. I account for that by the fact that her mother was drowned at a bathing beach in the south of France. But she was too small to remember. She has the story as told to her later by her father."

"Strange. It doesn't add up to anything. I think it must be an anxiety caused by her feeling of insecurity—a fear that you are not always near enough to protect her."

"But my work—"

"Exactly."

Again Parris shook his head in denial. "Could her unease about her father have any bearing on the case?"

"You're being transparent, Parris. You know very well that has nothing to do with it. You've got to treat this case as you would any other. A scientist is supposed to bring cold reason into his consideration of every problem."

"Is that why you have me prescribe for Laurel or the children?"

Paul chuckled. "Just the same, my boy, you aren't going to back off from this business just because you are afraid your findings might reveal some maladjustments in your relations with Elise. You're too good a doctor for that."

Parris had begun to feel more relaxed as he talked with Paul. He felt that his sense of proportion was about to reassert itself. For hours his mind had weighed one possibility against another until he had lost perspective.

"Paul, I love Elise. If anything happened to her, I should become utterly useless here."

"You are too intelligent to allow anything to happen to her."

"I couldn't endure seeing her caught in a network of her own fears."

"I'm going to say something that may shock you. Elise's reasons for clinging to you may keep her from realizing that you are probably not the person who could fulfill her desires. Had you thought of that?"

"*But, of course!* That thought has played like sheet lightning in the back of my mind all through this worry. But I don't let myself dwell on the thought that she might have been happier with someone else. I have tried— I am still trying to find where I've failed her. She's so compliant that—"

"You've used the very word I have in mind. You have to take that very compliance into account. She probably learned early that she got what she wanted by compliance—and expected to be taken care of in return."

"Well, haven't I taken care of her?"

"You have. But you've got to face certain facts."

"I can't admit, even to myself, Paul, that Elise is a psychotic. She's very young, and she's only showing a few tendencies—and I've got to find out the trouble."

"Son, to shy at truth is a demonstration of a lack of faith—and without faith you can't hope to get anywhere—to learn *anything*."

"You're right, but my mind circles round and round my relations with Elise. With her I've made the greatest efforts to hold myself at my own highest level—poor as that may be. Sometimes it's been a tremendous task."

"It's a task we're all familiar with—but when you love someone very much, you keep on trying." Paul's mind went for a moment to his adored Laurel, grateful for the steadfast love and belief she had given him.

"Elise is intellectually and socially adult—but, Paul—I could say this only to you—she still is adolescent emotionally—excitable and unstable."

"Psychologically infantile?"

"Physiologically also, I feel. I'm sure she is still clinging to certain infantile securities—and is fearful of losing them. She doesn't want to grow up. But I'll give you another confidence. *I don't really want her to grow up.*"

"And why?"

"For one thing, she's happier this way. For another, I think I have an overdeveloped paternal instinct—and she supplies my need."

Paul did not smile. He laid his hand again on his friend's shoulder. "Listen, Parris. Here's something I've just thought of. Elise may be frightfully hurt about her childlessness. Some women react very strongly on this point. She knows that early attack of rheumatic fever makes it unsafe for her to have children. Subconsciously she may attach her persistent fears to what she remembers of that illness—that she was not allowed to *play in the wind*."

"That sounds possible, Paul. What can be done?"

"Do you think you might take the risk?"

"No!" Parris rose, his face white and determined. "No, Paul, I can't risk losing Elise. I could never look myself in the face again—"

"Sit down, Parris. You've got to get hold of yourself if you are to handle this thing sensibly."

Parris sat down again, wrenching his mind back to concentrate on what his friend was saying.

"We hoped, Laurel and I, that Kam might supply some outlet for her frustrated instincts. He adores her and is never so happy as when he is with her."

"I know. You and Laurel are generous to let her have him with her so much, and her affection for him is so intense that I have thought sometimes it seemed a little morbid."

"You're wrong. It's a perfectly normal outpouring of affection. She can't expend it all on you. You are a self-sufficient person and an independent one. You demand very little of a nature like Elise's."

"I depend on her for everything, Paul."

Paul looked at his friend curiously. "You think you do, I've no doubt. But you move entirely under your own power. In your case it is perhaps unfortunate, but there's nothing you can do about it."

"One thing I can't endure—that she should know defeat. I want to give her courage to *be herself.*"

"I know. This fear of the wind you speak of is a transparent one. Even if she could be reasoned out of it, she would merely transfer it to some other field. Don't *push* it."

"But, Paul, in some way she is in an acute dilemma without being aware of it. We are all inhabited by emotions that live their own lives, and she is more sensitive than most. I feel she is endangered by this place—this windy, stark, *unsinging* place. I should take her away—somewhere."

"Don't take her away unless she is perfectly willing," Paul warned.

Laurel noticed her husband's preoccupation at dinner, his absent-minded replies to questions aimed at him by the children, and she led him into her little sewing room for his after-dinner cigar. She felt sure he would want to talk to her about whatever was troubling him.

She sat near the light, her busy hands working with some lacy material. Paul watched her for a few moments in silence, and then, as though by invitation, said, "Laurel, what's wrong between the Mitchells?"

Laurel looked up quickly. She was not expecting this. "Several things, I believe, Paul, but it's hard to put into words."

"Just what I was thinking. Why do you suppose they ever got married, anyhow?"

This time Laurel dropped her work into the basket beside her and gave her full attention to the question. "Why, honey, you know how it happened—and all of us approved. Remember?"

"As I recall it, it seemed an eminently suitable match at the time. She was a pretty girl, engagingly foreign, a good pianist—"

"She's still all those things—and in addition she's the girl Parris chose to marry. *Love* might have had something to do with it."

"You know perfectly well what I'm talking about. Of course Parris found in her the answer to some of his nostalgic yen for the semi-foreign background his grandmother had created for him. Between you and me, I think he was more in love with that past than he ever was with Elise."

"Maybe you're right—and I think she *has* supplied what he was looking for, in a way. But that hasn't been enough."

"What's lacking?"

"Do you really want to know what I think?"

"I trust your woman's intuition."

Her blue eyes flashed a smile at him, but were instantly serious again. "Much as I love Elise, I'm convinced that she's not the wife for a vital person like Parris. She's—inadequate, somehow—too shadowy a personality."

"Don't you think they are in love with each other?"

"Don't pin me down like that. I'm trying to put into words what I feel, not what I think."

"Exactly what I want."

"Elise has not outgrown being 'Daddy's darling'—and I think she must have used her pretty little helplessness to dominate the old man. I suspect she's doing the same thing with Parris. She's not too frail to have a *will to power*."

"You may be right, but Parris hasn't found it out."

"In some ways, Parris Mitchell's blind as a bat. He feels something like protective tenderness toward her, as though she were a child—but he's not in love with her like—well, as you were with me."

"As I *am*, not were."

"Well, I don't believe Elise could ever really be in love with anybody—very much. Elise loves to be loved—and could easily confuse the feeling with love itself. She's fiercely loyal and all that, but there's something sort of—of—ethereal about her. You know what I mean."

"Sounds pretty hard on Parris, if that's so."

"Of course it's hard on him."

"He seems to be satisfied—"

"Paul, in the Irish heart of you, you think Parris Mitchell is all the man of science. But you're wrong. He's all heart—all emotion."

"You really think that?"

"Listen to me, you sweet idiot. No man with the amount of let's call it 'appeal,' that he has, can fail to be a—a furnace inside."

"Don't make me jealous."

"Don't think I haven't been conscious of his attractions! But I have my life all fixed up the way I want it. However, I've seen the light in other women's eyes when they looked at Parris Mitchell. Even Hazel Green, the proud and haughty, looks at him in a certain way that makes me glad it isn't you she's looking at."

Paul leaned back in his chair and laughed aloud.

"You may laugh all you want to, but let me tell you, women don't look like that at an iceberg."

"And you think Elise doesn't meet him on that plane?"

"She can't. Parris should have married a deeply emotional—even a passionate woman—like Randy, for instance."

"I can't imagine Parris looking elsewhere—"

"That would be unthinkable. No matter how strongly he might be attracted to someone else, he would not hurt Elise. He's too protective in his attitude toward her."

"I don't like it, Laurel. Parris is one of the chosen—one of the men of good will who must fight the battles of the underprivileged—a man of service. This—*incompleteness* in his personal relations could hamper his advancement—could stop it dead still. And he doesn't know it."

They looked up as the door opened and Kam, dressed for bed, came in, his tousled red hair glistening under the light.

"Mother, may I go to von Eln early tomorrow? Lissa said Anna would be making cookies."

Laurel assured him that he might, and as he turned away she felt newly thankful that she had at least this much to offer her friend Elise—Kam's wholehearted companionship.

14

From the open door Elise could see Kam sitting quietly on the low terrace wall, his elbows on his brown knees, his gaze fixed on the tall sycamore standing halfway down the path to the creek.

"I'll tell you what let's do, Kam," she said, coming toward him, smiling. "Let's go down and look for that old turtle who lives in the creek."

Kam considered this gravely. "He won't be there," he announced positively.

"How do you know?"

"He's only there in the mornings. I don't think he likes Greta, anyhow."

"Poor little pup! I'm sure she'd like to be friends with him."

"No," Kam corrected her patiently, "she's afraid of him, Lissa. She backs away when we meet him on the bank."

As he fell into step beside her, he caught Elise's little finger in his fist. She felt a quick throb of warmth at the endearing gesture.

"Guess what I found here on the step, Lissa?"

"What?"

"A bug with eyes on its stomach. When I turned him over, he turned right back again and went under the step. He lives there."

His interest in the bug seemingly satisfied, Kam tugged at Elise's finger and led her in the direction of the creek. "I want to show you my boat Uncle Nathan made for me."

"A real boat?"

"Yes. It's big enough for Greta to ride in but she won't get in it. She's a fraidy-cat."

"She's right, Kam darling. It's not safe for you and Greta to play here unless someone is with you—Uncle Nathan, Anna, or me."

"When can I sail my boat?"

"Someday when you are older—but not yet."

Elise showed proper appreciation of the boat, approving all the good points Kam carefully pointed out.

"When will I be older, Lissa?" he asked.

"It won't be long. Next Saturday will be your birthday and you'll be a big boy. You'll have a cake with six candles. Had you forgotten?"

"When's Saturday?" he asked wistfully.

Elise stooped to kiss the top of his head and he darted away to join the little dog who was engaged in mimic warfare with a stick.

"Don't go too far, darling," she cautioned him.

It was midafternoon of the brightest day that April had yet produced. Kam, looking desolate and bored, roamed the grounds of von Eln alone. His birthday was something of a disappointment. There had been a huge cake with candles, and a great, laughing, noisy dinner in the Mitchells' dining room. But now everyone had gone away and left him with nothing to do—everyone except his father and Uncle Parris, who were sitting on the terrace—just talking.

Kam felt neglected and very sorry for himself and decided all that was left for him to do was to take a tour of the von Eln grounds. The April wind was chilly and he buttoned his bright blue sweater all the way up to his neck. The wind made his eyes sting a little and he blinked against it.

Uncle Nathan, kneeling beside the lilac bushes, trowel in hand, squinted up at the child. "Go git yo' cap, boy," he advised gruffly. "Hit's windy out here."

"You don't have one on," he accused the old man.

"You a little boy, though. You take yo' death o' cold. Go git yo' cap like I tell you."

Kam was offended. "I'm not a little boy. I'm six years old. Today's my birthday," he added importantly. "I had six candles on a cake. A *big* cake." He held out his arms to show the size.

"Is dat right? Well, I do declare—you *is* a big boy, ain't you?"

In the face of Uncle Nathan's evident admiration, Kam was suddenly alert, and very brave. "Aunt Lissa said I'd be a big boy today—and I am! You know what I'm gonna do?"

Uncle Nathan was busy again with his trowel, loosening the dirt around the roots of the bushes. But Kam, so excited by the idea that had occurred to him, didn't care much whether Nathan listened or not.

"I'm going down to the creek and sail my boat. I'll give Greta a ride."

As fast as he could he scooted up the garden path calling to Greta, whom he found, finally, asleep in the warm kitchen. Tugging at her collar, he coaxed her outside and half led, half carried her to the creek.

"Lookit, Greta." He gave a tug at her collar. "We're going for a ride in my boat and you got to keep quiet and be a good dog."

Greta wagged her tail, yawned widely, and settled her long body on the ground for a nap. Kam had the disturbing thought that perhaps Greta was a little stupid.

Uncle Nathan straightened up painfully and knocked the earth from his trowel. There was nothing more to do to the lilac bushes. He wiped his brow with his forearm and forced himself to look up at the dying sycamore out there by the summerhouse. "It allus has been a spin'ly tree. It never was healthy like that big feller down there on the path to the creek. Still an' all, hit's a *tree*. No, suh, seems like I ain't got the heart to cut it down long's it got any life lef' in it."

He looked up at the few scant leaves on the two branches that had been able to send out buds, and then at the feathery pale green wisteria vines that seemed just ready to drop their clusters of purple blossoms down in festoons that would almost hide the dead branches.

"Can't nobody tell me them trees don't know nothin'. They seed a lot goin' on in this old garden, an' seems like they tryin' they best to tell me somethin'. Looks to me like some bad luck might happen to this garden do I cut down that tree befo' its time. Yes, *suh*! But the doctor done said. I better go git my ax."

Shaking his head mournfully, the old man turned toward the tool house, but wild yelping from Greta in the direction of the creek stopped him in his tracks. That was not Greta at play—that was Greta in trouble.

"Do Jesus, don't let it be our boy!" he said aloud as he began to run down the creek path. "Blessed Jesus," he prayed, "don't let nothin' hurt our little boy—not *him*—please, God, not Kam! I's comin', honey—Uncle Nathan's comin'. Kam, where are you—*Kam*!"

His heart stood still when he saw Greta, wet and shining, running madly back and forth on the bank, barking and whimpering. He lunged down the bank and saw the bright blue sweater in the shallow water. Kam's head was hidden by a rock that jutted out into the stream. Nathan reached the boy, who lay in water of less than knee depth. Projecting roots of a willow tree were stained red, showing how the wound on the brow had been caused.

"Do Jesus, let him live—do blessed God—let me get him there in time!" he begged as he lifted the limp little body. Without pausing in his hurried progress up the steep path, he began to call for help. Parris and Paul were running to meet him and now he could no longer see anything as tears streamed down his wrinkled cheeks.

The news that Kam Nolan had been drowned swept through' Kings Row within the hour.

Kings Row grieved. The child was known to most people, and Paul and Laurel Nolan were held in high esteem in the town. The manner in which Kam met his death was told and retold, and friends of the family hastened to offer their sympathy.

In the courthouse square the groups stood about as usual, but they spoke quietly. There was none of the customary Saturday afternoon guffawing and rough joking.

"Doc Nolan an' his wife will be sure enough broke up about this. They was crazy about that kid."

"Yeah. Pity Nathan couldn't of got to him in time."

"Wouldn't have done no good if he'd been right there. They tell me Kam's neck was broke before he hit the water. His head hit a rock or a root or something."

"Looks like there ain't no sense to things—the way they turn out. There's a man like Doc Nolan ain't done nothin' but good in this world an' then somethin' like this has got to happen. His baby boy gits drownded."

"I'm sorry for his wife. I hear her an' Miz Mitchell was both over at Mrs. Skeffington's when it happened."

"Seems the kid was in the habit of runnin' all over the place by his-self. They didn't think about his gittin' hurt."

"When's the funeral gonna be?"

"Haven't heard. I guess they'll take him down to St. Stephens to bury him. That's where the Nolans come from."

"That's right. They did come from down there. Miz Nolan is old man Sandifer's daughter. Them Sandifers are mighty clever folks. Roy Sandifer—that's her brother—is just about the best Senator we ever had in Washington. He makes 'em sit up an' take notice when he opens up."

"Ain't they kin to Dave Kettring some way?"

"Not as I know of, but Dave Kettring an' the Nolan boys growed up together somewhere around St. Stephens. That's a fine community down there."

"Yes. I reckon they'll bury Kam down there."

"They say Miz Mitchell's takin' it hard as Miz Nolan. She kep' Kam with her about as much as he stayed at home."

"Well, she's got no children of her own an' I reckon she gits pretty lonesome out there where she lives. It's like livin' in the country to be that fur out."

"Reckon so. Well, the pore little kid's gone an' it ain't no comfort to remind 'em they got five more."

"No. Can't nothin' make up for losin' a child like that."

On Sunday morning Elise went alone into the room where Kam lay under soft lights, his beautiful face alien and withdrawn in its strange framing of gathered silk, the familiar smile fixed on immobile lips. She tried with all her might to beat through that infinite distance that had fallen so suddenly between them. She reached out and touched his curls, a gesture of farewell. Turning toward the window, she stared across the wide lawn. She watched the sky and clouds bend their circles over the town that slowly, slowly came into focus, as though a glass were set to her blurred vision. Little by little, the world of roofs and chimneys painted itself on her sight.

She turned then to leave the room. Parris was standing there, his hands outheld to lead her away.

Parris was greatly disturbed by the intensity of Elise's grief. After their return from St. Stephens she spent much time with Laurel. He saw that the two seemed to cling together for support in their shared sorrow. He noticed, also, that Laurel Nolan recovered her calm more readily than Elise seemed to do. The deeps of Laurel's blue eyes were as still as a summer pool, but Elise was often weeping in her room when Parris found her alone. She was, he felt, too deeply shaken by her loss. It made him uneasy.

One afternoon Elise sat on the terrace in the sunshine. She looked about at the fresh young grass, the leaves thickening on the shrubs, and the jonquils blooming along the walks. She could remember how instant her response had been in other springs to all the piercing wonder of the heady season, but now she could not rise above her apathy.

She felt that she was only waiting for what might come—some new disaster—with neither strength of heart nor of body to combat it.

Anna, coming out on the terrace with coffee and cakes, shook her head mournfully when Elise motioned indifferently that she did not want them. Anna quietly placed the tray on a small table. There was, she thought, a sort of cloud of sorrow hanging about the slight form in the big chair.

Greta ran frantically about, getting under Anna's feet and being very demonstrative about Elise.

Remembering Parris' admonition that she was not to avoid speaking of Kam, Anna tried to make her voice sound casual. "You must not mind Greta. She has been refusing to eat. She grieves for Kam. But now that you are home, she goes crazy with joy."

"Greta, *Komm'*!" Elise invited. The small dog jumped into her lap. "Poor little one! You miss him, too, our Kam? There, there, we have each other!"

"Miss Elise," Anna said gently, "you must try not to think too much about—about Kam. I wish to heaven I could do something to help you."

"Sit down and talk to me, Anna. There seems too much time to *think*."

Anna drew a low chair nearer and sat down, taking Elise's small hand between her own sturdy, capable ones.

"Why is it, Anna, that the sun goes on shining, the flowers go on growing, the birds go on about their heartless affairs, and my—my Kam is not here?"

"Sad hearts always torment themselves with those questions and—there isn't any answer, Miss Elise. I remember when Madame passed away we—" Anna's voice broke and Elise looked quickly at her.

"You know, Anna, I keep wondering about Kam."

"Wondering?"

"Yes. He seemed always so surprised when he found something new. I wonder how he felt about the surprise of death? He couldn't have known about death. He was so pitifully young," she said, lifting a hand to her throat.

"*Liebchen,* must you talk so much about death?"

"It's this place, Anna—this garden," she said, spreading her arms in a wide gesture. "I seem to be able to think of nothing else here."

[195]

"But I thought you were happy here—you and Parris—"

"Oh, yes, I've been happy, but I've thought of death just the same. Why do you suppose I've done that, Anna? I've helped to make these flowers grow. I've given them love and care—but now—now it's as though something terrible has been waiting for me in the shadows. I don't understand it."

"Even a beautiful garden looks sad when the heart is heavy."

"That's not what I mean—exactly." She hesitated and looked about her nervously. "Anna, do you ever have premonitions?"

"Premonitions?"

"Yes. Vague forewarnings—fears you can't explain—"

"I have them sometimes. But I notice that nothing bad ever happens when I expect it, so I don't give them much heed."

"I wonder," Elise said musingly, "if the topmost leaf of a tree does not feel the first stroke of the ax laid at its root. I think that is what Uncle Nathan has tried to tell me."

"*Liebchen,* please try to throw off this heavy mood, for Parris' sake as well as your own."

"I've tried, but—oh, Anna," she sobbed hysterically, turning into Anna's waiting arms, "I'm afraid I was responsible for Kam's death."

"Miss Elise!" Anna spoke sharply. "Don't say such a foolish thing. You couldn't have been to blame. It was an accident—a terrible accident."

"He told Uncle Nathan—that day—that I had promised him he could sail his boat when he got to be a big boy—and that he was six years old now. He thought I meant he would be a big boy—big enough to sail his boat then. Oh, Anna, I can't *bear* it!"

"There, there, little one, you weren't to blame. You never brought anything to Kam but happiness."

"I want my Kam. I shouldn't have let *him* drown, too!"

Anna patted the shaking shoulders comfortingly and sighed with relief as she heard Parris' car coming up the drive.

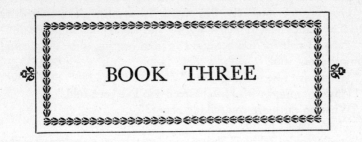

BOOK THREE

I

Sarah Skeffington, thin almost to the point of emaciation, was waiting on the east porch in her wheel chair. She was wearing a soft gray mull dress. A frilly ruffle of fine Swiss embroidery edged the collar and extended to the belt of black velvet ribbon. A cameo pin caught the ruffle at her throat.

When Parris Mitchell ran up the steps she held out both hands in greeting.

Parris placed a kiss in each slender palm and gave her hands an affectionate squeeze, noting with a pang how frail and old they seemed.

"Here I am, dear lady, right on the heels of your message."

"Is an old lady's request of so much importance to a busy man?"

"Not *any* old lady's request, but nothing could be more important to me than your wish to see me."

"A pretty speech, Parris Mitchell."

"To a pretty lady."

"Where did you learn to pay compliments to old ladies?"

For all her eight-five years, Mrs. Skeffington was beautiful. Every nuance of her exquisite old face was determined and assured by the fine structure beneath. It was the sculpture of generations of fine thinking which made that kind of physical organism.

"Yes, you are just as beautiful as I remembered you to be."

"Then why haven't you been to see me, if I am so beautiful?"

"It *has* been a long time. Elise has been so broken up by Kam's death that I've had to keep close at home."

"I know. How is Elise now?"

"Grieving too morbidly, I'm afraid. I leave her alone as little as possible. Randy is with her now. She and Laurel take turns."

"Parris, I sent for you because I've been hearing some disquieting rumors about you."

"What have I been doing now?"

"Playing around with Hazel Green—so I've been told."

"What on earth are you talking about?"

"That's what I heard."

"Surely you're joking." Parris could not believe she was serious.

"I'm only telling you what is being said."

"But that's preposterous. I remember only two occasions recently when I've exchanged half a dozen remarks with her. Both those times were accidental meetings on the street. I can't imagine—"

"It seems Hazel was seen getting into your car and riding with you all over town, and—"

"But I assure you, Mrs. Skeffington, that—"

"*Sarah!* What's the matter with you? Parris, if it had been any other woman in Kings Row, no one would have noticed, but Fulmer Green's wife! What possessed you?"

"You'll have to take my word for it, Sarah, there's not the slightest truth in the rumor."

"Well, thank God for that! She's a beautiful woman—and a superior one. Will you kindly tell me why she ever married Fulmer Green? The Allinghams are fine people."

"Fulmer had undeniable charm, Sarah, and he was making money. He had something to offer."

"Well, she's a lady. There's no doubt of that."

"And a charming one."

Sarah looked sharply at Parris, and what she saw evidently satisfied her.

"Parris, you have such an independent air—as though you cared nothing at all about what is said of you. I'm not just a meddling old fool."

"Who accused you of that?"

"I don't want you to think it, that's all."

"I wouldn't."

"Listen, my dear. I'm only concerned about a whispering campaign that might hurt your career. You are a public servant, and what touches your reputation is of concern to me and to all your friends."

"You are sweet, and more than I can say I appreciate your concern."

"Are there any of the hospital doctors after your job?"

"Not that I know of. It isn't likely."

"I just wondered."

"Now *who*, I ask you, started that absurd rumor?"

"I traced it back to Nell Carruthers."

"Oh!"

"Oh, what?"

"Nothing."

"Hazel was here to see me this morning."

"About this—this rumor?"

"Mercy, *no*! I'm sure she hasn't heard it. But"—she smiled a bit mischievously—"I found occasion to mention your name and she colored very prettily indeed."

"Then she must have heard it and was uncomfortable. What a rotten thing for her, and if there ever was an unjustified accusation—"

"Oh, it wouldn't do *her* any harm, but it might be bad for you. For a moment, when I first heard it I had the gleeful thought that you might be paying Fulmer back for some of his back-biting. But on sober reflection—as the Colonel used to say—I knew you were incapable of any such crudity."

"Of course, I don't really care what people think about *me*, but that Hazel should be annoyed is—infuriating."

"You *ought* to care what is said about you."

"It seems to be painless."

"There's an art in your blithe uncaring, young man. You remind me of a juggler who plays dangerously with swords but who seems utterly casual, utterly unconscious of danger. But the juggler knows that an instant's inattention might be fatal."

"Sarah, you are as good a friend as I have in the world, and I thought you knew me as well as I know myself, but you are talking in riddles. I've been going about my work and my personal affairs in the most humdrum manner. What is all this talk of juggling? I'm bewildered."

"There's an old saying: 'Winds howl around the highest peaks.'"

"You flatter me."

"Don't be silly. Kings Row watches your every step—and see how they interpret a harmless street encounter!"

"But I don't see, Sarah, how they can accuse Hazel Green of—"

"There's another saying, Parris: 'No woman sleeps so soundly that a twanging guitar will not bring her to the window.'"

Parris laughed. "I swear I've not been serenading under Kings Row's windows."

Sarah lifted the small fan that was dangling from a chain about her neck and shook it threateningly at Parris. "See that you don't. I don't want anybody hurt—you nor Elise nor the other woman."

"There is no woman but Elise."

"I really knew that. I only felt I must warn you about how easily gossip gets started in a town like this."

"I'll remember—but I still refuse to be rude to friends when I chance to meet them."

"You're a stormy petrel. There's always a stir going on around you."

"Not of my making."

"Probably not. I'm very fond of you, Parris."

"I don't deserve it, but I love you for it."

"If you stayed around here very much, young man, I'd become a complacent old woman, vain and assured, sleek and plump with prideful acceptance of myself. I know of only one other person of my acquaintance who leaves me feeling so warm and cozy in my nest of opinions, and that is that side partner of yours, Paul Nolan."

"Now, now, Sarah," Parris objected, "Paul and I are sincerely in love with you. We mean what we say. And so, you say you don't want to be a complacent old woman?"

"I wouldn't say that. It might be nice. If I were properly complacent, I'd be sitting very straight in my chair and my knitting needles would click with that harmonious music I have heard so often from the assured knitting needles of complacent women. They reside securely behind the entrenchments of their invincible satisfactions.

How infuriating they are! You probably don't know any women of that kind, Parris. I do, unfortunately."

"You are not consistent."

"Who cares about consistency? I'm only concerned with truth."

"Then you *don't* want to be one of them?"

"No, I don't. But I do think it must be a pleasing state. Just think of seeing others whip themselves into foam and break in futilities of spray against one's granite bastions of assurances—and certainties!"

"You sounded just like my grandmother then. She envied the smug, self-satisfied women she knew—so she *said,* but she would have fitted into their world as poorly as you would, my dear."

"I'm in a mood of self-criticism today."

"Why?"

"I was thinking, just before you came, that I have wasted the best years of my life. When I should have been thoughtfully reading great books and building a house of philosophy for refuge in my old age, I was—well, what was I doing? I don't remember." She tapped the arm of her wheel chair with her closed fan.

"Yes?" Parris urged softly. "Please go on."

"Anyway, I'm sure that's why I'm disappointed in myself now. That's why I can't sit here and enjoy great, deep, satisfactory stretches of—of—*thinking.* I'm very unhappy about my shortcomings."

"I'd like to scold you properly. None of what you say is true. You and the Colonel—"

"Ah, the Colonel! That is something else. He decorated his hours to remember with the collected fragments of a superior culture."

"You and the Colonel thought the same thoughts, lived the same experiences."

"I think I should have gone when he died. I'm old—and useless, Parris."

"No—"

"Yes. I'm lonely, too. I think maybe all the creak would go out of my legs if I just had something to do. It's rather hard to think one is not useful."

"You mean so much to me, to Elise and Randy and Laurel—to all Kings Row, in fact. We need you."

"Here I am—having lived a long life and having learned a great deal—accumulated some wisdom and common sense, and I have no one to give it to." It was as though she had not heard his protest.

She is fragile and old, but indomitable, Parris thought. All the old problems and conflicts have faded like a retreating tide. They have been fused in the great fires of life and death.

"Would you like me to go now?" Parris feared overtiring her.

"Stay awhile longer. It's nice having you with me. I sit here on this porch every afternoon and look out over Kings Row. All the shabbiness fades out from just a little distance, like this. Sometimes I think it must look wonderful to God. I like to sit here and think maybe some soul is born here today who'll be a great man in the world. So many great men come from little towns."

The unearthly peace and beauty of the early twilight which had begun to settle over them struck through Parris with an unbearable poignancy. He did not wish to move or speak.

In the friendly silence that hovered there, Parris began to sense something of the peculiar passions of later years, the concentrated gathering of the forces of life, narrowed to some still receding and elusive objective.

What, most of all, he wondered, was she remembering as she sat here in her wheel chair through these empty days? It was clear to him that she was remembering, living elsewhere rather than here.

Someday, he thought I will be old. I must not be cheated of life on the way. I must find there in that coming day something that will be for me the same solace that others so clearly possess.

Sarah Skeffington was like a gray boulder—as fixed, as still—a gray stone that seemed to be slowly settling back into the soil. Colonel Skeffington's presence had been like a gay, flowering tree beside her, casting a checker of sunlight over her, covering her with a flickering animation. Now that he was no longer there, Parris could see how gray and still she was, and yet she was not really unhappy.

Was it a kind of peace? Was it that last content—that resolution toward which the clashes and dissonances of life strive and tend so desperately? Or was it that preoccupation with memory which is the refuge and solace of old age?

He believed it was the latter. He fancied he could see this dear friend plumbing the deeps of the past with long, long recollections, bringing again to light the luminous and flashing moments of high expectations and delight—moments that glowed again, faintly, giving once again the semblance and the illusion of immediacy. He fancied her telling them over and over, repeating familiar rituals of ecstasy and grief, now become strangely alike in the afterglow of contemplation.

Parris wanted so much to know if this were true. But he could not ask. He could see how she was closing in on herself until one day, soon, she would not be at all.

Presently he heard with a sense of shock what this amazing old lady was saying. He felt that he had been jarred out of a state of infinite calm.

"Fulmer Green hasn't made serious trouble for you yet. That surprises me."

"He's probably not trying. Don't forget he's a member of our church."

She looked at him suspiciously. "More's the pity. Helps him to cover up his tracks. A few more such members and we'll become a by-word in the Presbytery."

Parris grinned wickedly, enjoying Sarah's irritation.

"Hazel must shudder at some of Fulmer's deals—if she has any knowledge of them," she said.

"Do you know, dear lady you're getting to be something of a gossip, yourself!"

"Like Martha Cotten, eh? A gossip!"

"There's nothing so endearing as a little genuine gossip. We all love it."

Mrs. Skeffington actually snorted. "If it's gossip you like, I could regale you by the hour. It's one of the compensations of age. I can sit here on my porch and learn the details of every private life in Kings Row. If one person doesn't tell me, another will. There's nothing so free as news."

"I should get you and Louis Kelner together. I shudder to think what you two could find out about us!"

"Louis is a good man. I got a tract from him once on tolerance. It amused the Colonel, although I'm afraid I was a little peppery about it. Speaking of Louis reminds me, Parris, of what I hear of the senseless persecution of the Germans in this town. Is it true?"

"I'm afraid it is. I hear rumors of a boycott."

"That's unjust. Those men are among our best citizens. The Colonel said they helped build this town."

"Of course it's unjust. I think I'd better go to see them tomorrow and find out if they need help of any kind."

"Good."

"But I want to know if you have enough amusing company these days."

"Oh yes. Dullness, at least, I don't have to bear. For a crippled old lady, I have some very good times."

Parris looked at his watch.

"Yes, run along. Elise is probably wondering why you are late to supper. Give her my love—and watch your step, young man. No philandering!"

"Can't I even *look* at a pretty girl?"

"Not even a peep."

"But you'll let me come often to see you? *You* aren't afraid of the gossips."

"The only thing I'm afraid of is that you won't come often enough. Be off with you, Parris Mitchell, and don't give me any further cause to worry about you!"

Dr. Mitchell found Louis Kelner and Jacob Lenz where he had expected to find them—sitting on the slatted bench under the big elms on the courthouse lawn. As he neared them he was conscious of the tense, unmoving attitude of both men and of a watchful look in their gentle old faces.

"*Guten Morgen,*" Parris greeted them.

"*Guten Morgen, Herr Doktor,*" they responded, and Louis Kelner added warningly, "*Sie sollten dies nicht tun.*"

"*Warum nicht?*"

Kelner hesitated a moment, then motioned Parris to a seat beside them. Leaning toward the doctor with a confidential air, he spoke almost in a whisper. "*Sie dürfen hier nicht deutsch sprechen.*"

Parris was surprised into a protest, but he answered in English. "Who forbids your speaking German?"

"All Kings Row," Jacob said bitterly.

"Yah," Louis admitted. "They threaten us—these good Americans.

They think we may be plotting against our government—our country."

"That is silly war hysteria, Louis," Parris explained. "It will pass—when the war is over. It is a disease that spreads among the unthinking. It means nothing."

"I think you are wrong, *Herr Doktor,*" Jacob said, tapping the blunt toe of his heavy shoe with his cane. "Already they have taken away our business. No pupils are left for me—as though I would harm the little children!"

"No one comes with pots to mend. And Herman, too, has no shoes to mend." Louis spoke without rancor, but with a great fatigue in his voice.

"Is it true," Parris asked, "that someone broke the windows of Herman's shop and painted ugly words on his door?"

"It is true, Doctor. Why do they think we are not good Americans? We were here before those boys were born—before their *fathers* were born—and we love our country."

"They don't *think,* Louis. They are being hysterical, as I said. You must not take it too much to heart. Where is Herman?"

"He is coming now—across the street."

They watched him come, each step labored and hesitant as though his feet feared they could not carry the burden of his slight, malformed body.

"I saw you here, *Herr Doktor,* and I wanted to speak with you."

"I'm glad to see you, Herman. How have you been?"

Herman lowered his small body to the bench and turned his large, dark eyes on Parris.

"For forty years—for forty long years I've mended shoes in my basement shop there and I did good work. No man ever complained. I saved a little money and when our government asks for the Liberty Loan, no one comes to ask *me* to buy—no one. I must go to the bank and get my bonds. Is it that they think my money is not good to help our soldiers?"

"It was the same with me, Doctor. The people I have known all these years do not even come to my shop," Louis said. "And my *Frau* —she has not been asked to sew at the Red Cross—nothing."

Parris was outraged at the blind stupidity of those who could treat these good, solid citizens of the town as enemies—but he knew there was nothing to say that would lessen their hurt.

"We have felt this animosity, too, my wife and I. We rest under the same cloud of suspicion that you do," he said.

"But you, Doctor," Jacob said, "you are important in this town and they would not dare—"

"They dare, Jacob, but we ignore it. There's work to be done and we work."

"No one wishes us to work," Louis complained. "I know the people of this town. I know them well. For years they sent their pots and pans down here for me to mend and right away I knew about that place. I knew who hated to cook and keep a house; I knew the ones that fought among themselves. They kept me interested, those pots and pans, with all their rattling gossip of the town."

"Now, Louis," Parris said, "do you think it's fair to listen to the talk of pots and pans?"

"I did more than listen to their talk; I kept a lot of tracts there on the shelf. You know those little papers from the church? Each one has got a kind of sermon on it. So when I got a stewpan from a house and saw some woman nagged her husband bad, or that some man came home drunk and hit his *Frau,* I hunted out the right tract and slipped it in the pan when it was fixed. I bet I've done a lot of good in Kings Row."

"Well, Louis, we must keep our chins up and wait. Things will turn out all right in the end. Kings Row still needs us all. And I was just about to ask Mr. Lenz if he would come to hear me play. My wife is not well enough to practice much, but I have some things on which I need help."

"But, yes, Doctor. I will come with pleasure."

"I am going to Washington for a week or two, but as soon as I get back we will get together for a long piano session."

"Thank you, Doctor. And does our President call you to help with the war?"

Parris smiled. "Not exactly. I am wanted to testify as an alienist— to decide whether some people who are making trouble for the government are—are crazy people, or are only troublemakers."

"They call the right man. You will help the poor mind-dark ones."

"I shall not be away long. I'll see all of you when I get back."

Looking after Parris Mitchell as he walked away, Herman said, in his thick Bavarian accent, "A good man Parris Mitchell surely is."

"A sad man and lonely, I'm afraid," Louis added.

"You can hear that in his voice," Jacob said. "He speaks softly, but like someone looking out of windows when he is sad."

"*Fenster Sehnsucht*. It is an old saying. It is so. I remember an old uncle of mine. Yes, it is so."

2

Instead of her father's hoped-for arrival in America, news came to Elise through the Red Cross in Switzerland that he had died of a heart attack during the late winter. No details were available—merely the bare statement that he had died.

Elise, controlling her fresh grief, made a valiant effort to be of service in all relief organizations in Kings Row. It was not easy for her to work closely with other people. But Randy McHugh and Hazel Green, leaders in all the town's war activities, did their utmost to be co-operative.

In early May Elise attended a called meeting of Red Cross workers at the local headquarters. She sat with Laurel Nolan near the front of the hall.

The meeting had been in progress for some time. Hazel Green was presiding and was appointing certain important committees. She asked Elise Mitchell to head the committee in charge of providing clothing for refugee children. Before Elise could speak, one of the members rose to say that while no one questioned the right of the chairman to appoint heads of committees, she, personally, was of the opinion that the women appointed should be real Americans whose sympathies would be beyond question.

There was a shocked silence before Hazel could protest. Then a murmur swept through the room and unfriendly eyes turned in the direction of the white, stricken face of Elise Mitchell.

Hazel's reply was drowned by the protests that sprang quickly from the lips of Randy McHugh and Laurel Nolan.

Hazel recognized Bethany Laneer, who spoke clearly and heatedly. "I came here to ask that Mrs. Mitchell should be assigned to direct the Junior Red Cross Chapter. We are making that request now,

Madam Chairman. Mrs. Mitchell is better equipped for this work than any person in Kings Row—and for that reason *only* we beg you to withdraw her name from the proposed committee work."

Elise shook her head and lowered her eyes. Laurel's hand clasped her fingers in a reassuring grip.

"The Junior Red Cross has certainly made an excellent choice," said Mrs. Green, "but when I accepted the chairmanship of this senior organization, I did so with the mental reservation that I did not wish to undertake the responsibility unless I could have my important committees headed by the women I have named today—Laurel Nolan, Randy McHugh, and Elise Mitchell. I shall of course yield to Mrs. Mitchell's decision, but I still hope she will accept the chairmanship I have suggested."

Laurel rose and spoke quietly. "Madam Chairman, there is no reason why matters of personal pique should be aired in this organization. I am shocked that it should be necessary to remind any members of this chapter that our work is a work of mercy and kindness, our purposes humanitarian. There is surely enough of dissension in international affairs without allowing carping and unfounded criticism to creep into our circle. No one can possibly doubt the loyalty and patriotism of any woman here."

Elise rose. Her face was white and strained, her eyes dark with frightened dismay.

"Mrs. Green, I am grateful for your confidence in my ability to head the committee, but I should like to suggest that you allow me to serve under Mrs. Nolan. She is much better fitted for that position than I, and I shall do better work under her direction."

Mrs. Green looked at Laurel. "Would you be willing to serve, Mrs. Nolan?"

Laurel's lips were a thin straight line of self-control, and her voice was level when she rose and said: "Only in case Mrs. Mitchell promises to work with me. I wonder if it has occurred to any of us that Mrs. Mitchell is the only woman in Kings Row who is at all acquainted with world conditions? She knows more about what is needed and what we can do about it than all the rest of us put together. Her advice means an awful lot to those of us who are just blundering along trying to help. If she agrees to help me, I'll gladly accept the chairmanship."

If there were any disapproving sniffs among the dissenters they were carefully suppressed. The meeting was shortly adjourned and Hazel Green walked from the hall with her arm linked with Elise's. She had never been so sorry for anyone in her life, and yet there was nothing she could say—nothing she could do to lessen Elise's shock. She hoped that Randy, who was so much closer to the Mitchells than she, would stay with Elise until Parris returned from the hospital.

But it was late before Parris got home, and Elise had begged so pitifully to be left alone that Randy had finally gone away. So when the door opened and Parris walked in he found a white-faced, dry-eyed, frightened child who seemed utterly unable to tell him what was wrong. She said only, "Parris, I don't want to go back to the Red Cross. I don't think they need me."

For the next few days he spent every moment he could with her, neglecting his work, but Elise remained apathetic and silent. Finally, in desperation, he went to Laurel, who was surprised to learn that Elise had told him nothing of what had happened.

After Laurel's account, Parris readily understood Elise's reluctance to continue her Red Cross work, for he knew how deep the wound had been. In spite of his burning resentment and sense of outrage, he realized there was nothing he could do—nothing. He was grateful to the friends who had so loyally stood by Elise, and felt particularly touched by Hazel Green's staunch stand.

Actually, Elise had been for a long time conscious of something inimical in the attitude of the town. Her fears had been vague, but persistent. There was malignity in the very air she breathed. In spite of this nebulous fear, she had wished passionately that she might be a part of the world about her.

But now, her reaching out lessened. Gradually a stubborn pride took its place. Gradually a contempt crept in—contempt for the stupidity and narrowness she could so plainly see wherever she looked. And there she was, turned inward as before. She thought of trying to talk to Parris about it, but she did not wish to pose any new problems that might disturb his own delicate adjustment to Kings Row.

She turned to her piano for comfort. She went humbly. The old pride in the exhilarating mental calisthenics was gone. The great work of the great masters was so dazzling that her mind went down on its knees as before a sudden revelation of divinity. It was religion; it was poetry; above all, it was a drug.

3

The shuffling figure of Pick Foley was no unusual sight along Federal Street. There had been a time when Pick could be seen almost every day trudging slowly down to the post office, though it was noted by the idlers hanging about the doors that he rarely got any mail.

After his mother's death ten or more years ago, he stopped inquiring at the general delivery window, and now, since mail was delivered from house to house, he had no reason to go in. He never needed stamps.

Pick had waked earlier than usual this morning with an uneasy sense of something hanging over him to be done. It took him some time to recall what it was. Then, he remembered. He got up and pulled on his trousers. He had not bothered to take his shirt off the night before. It was clean enough to wear down to the bank this morning.

Going to the bank had become quite an ordeal. He was compelled to pass that gang that always hung around Matt Fuller's feed store. He dreaded that. They invariably had some joking remark to make to him. He didn't know exactly why it was, but he felt vaguely that they were making fun of him and he suspected that after he had passed they were saying things about him.

He didn't care, he told himself. He didn't really care; he didn't owe them a red cent, and he wasn't asking them for anything. He'd walk past them today, and no matter what they said to him he wouldn't let it hurt his feelings. No, sir!

Pick heated a cup of water in a small stewpan and took a skimpy pinch of tea from a paper bag on the shelf. The one-burner oil stove gave off an acrid smoke that made his eyes sting, and he brushed the back of his hand across them angrily. He cut a slice of bread and leaned it against the side of the stewpan to heat. He had to watch it so it wouldn't get too hard. He had no teeth to chew toast with— never liked toast anyhow. He wished he had an egg. Maybe he'd better get a couple when he came by Cooper's grocery on the way home from the bank. He reckoned he needed an egg every once in a while. They cost a lot of money, though. Two eggs cost a nickel. Well, he'd see. He had one Saturday a week ago. Lola Saunders had brought it to him, a nice fresh one from her yard. She had been good to him, coming every week to clean up his place, and almost always she brought him something she'd cooked up.

Come to think of it, he couldn't remember anybody else ever doing the least thing for him—not since his mother died. But Lola even patched his clothes when they got torn—and she never would let him pay her anything extra for it. She was a good woman—Lola Saunders.

He was glad it was summer. Things looked better in the summer. The cracks in the walls let in too much cold in the winter. The cracks were getting too big to be stopped up with newspapers. Last winter's snows had broken through the roof of one of the front rooms. One end of the porch had fallen completely in. Maybe he'd try to get them mended before next winter.

Well, he'd better be getting on down to the bank. Jamie Wakefield was a mighty busy man and he just had to talk to Jamie about some business matters today. He hoped Matt Fuller and his gang would not be sitting around this early. He'd just as soon they didn't see him going to the bank.

But Matt was there, and Dave Brennan, Ricks Darden, and Donny Green. Pick would have crossed to the other side of the street, but they'd yell at him just the same, and that would attract the attention of a lot of other folks. He pulled his old felt hat further down over his eyes and tried to hurry past.

"Well, I be dog, if it ain't Pick Foley! You out early today, Pick. What's your hurry?"

"Want to get home before it gets so hot," he mumbled.

"Reckon you're pretty busy these days, eh?"

Pick did not answer.

"Aw, Pick, you ain't afraid of a little heat, now are you? Sunshine makes your whiskers grow. Good for you," Dave Brennan said.

Pick walked uncertainly on for a few steps, and then hesitated. They sounded sort of friendly today. Maybe they'd be glad to have him stop to talk awhile. His heart warmed a little at the thought.

"Say, Pick," Donny Green said with a wink at Matt, "there's going to be a church supper Friday night at the First Presbyterian. You ought to show up sometimes. They're pretty nice."

Pick made no answer but his look at Donny was mistrustful and wary.

At the guffaw which followed Donny's remark, Pick was blinded by a flash of fury. Why shouldn't he go to the church suppers if he wanted to? He belonged to the church—and all that good food, prepared by the best cooks in town—what did these folks know about how good it tasted to him? Why, he hadn't had any decent food since his mother died except at the church suppers and at an occasional barbecue during the political campaigns. And—he remembered gratefully—what Lola brought him sometimes.

Pick wanted desperately to get away, to leave the place where these men were *thinking* things about him. But he felt he was under attack, somehow, and a man didn't run away from a fight. He stood dumbly there, looking down at his worn brogans.

"I don't know," he said slowly. "I haven't been feeling so good, lately. I might not be able to make it."

There was another laugh and Ricks Darden said, "The ladies will be mighty disappointed if you don't show up. You're one of their best customers."

Pick wanted to say something. He felt he must uphold his—his dignity, he said to himself. But when he started to speak, he felt only a dull acquiescence. He was overwhelmed by too great a weariness for any protest or revolt.

He shuffled toward the bank at the corner.

Jamie Wakefield looked up as the shabby figure stopped beside his desk. There was the smallest fraction of a pause before he rose and laid aside the shade he had removed from his forehead.

"Oh, good morning, Pick." He spoke with a hint of impatience in his voice and was immediately ashamed. "What can I do for you?"

"I wanted to talk to you about—about some business arrangements." His voice was apologetic, but his eyes did not waver from the banker's face.

"Suppose we go back to the directors' room, Pick. It's more private there."

Pick, conscious of the eyes following him, walked behind Jamie past the tellers' windows and into a square, uncurtained room off the lobby.

"Sit down, Pick. What's on your mind?"

"I haven't been feeling very well lately, and I thought maybe I'd better be making some arrangements about my—my property," he said with something like pride in his voice.

Jamie looked at him closely. "That's a good idea. Now, let's see—"

"I want to fix it so there won't be any trouble after I'm gone."

Jamie hoped this wasn't going to take too much time. His reluctance was obvious.

Pick seemed to shrink into himself. He turned an expressionless face on the only man he felt could help him in this matter so vital to him.

Jamie looked at him for a moment and with a quick, instinctive perception he saw past the diffident manner to the frightened, lonely soul that quivered there. Jamie's sensitive face reflected his thought and Pick leaned forward confidentially and began to talk with growing assurance.

A half hour later he left the bank building with a quicker step and with his head lifted. He felt he was a man of affairs, and he walked straight up the block to Cooper's grocery. When he came out, he carried a pasteboard carton with several packages in it.

The food Pick Foley bought at Cooper's grocery that Monday morning was almost untouched on Saturday when Lola came to clean, for Pick Foley had been dead for several days.

No one had noticed that he hadn't been seen on the street all week. No one ever thought of him at all unless they happened to see the slouching, unkempt figure moving along the street.

"Malnutrition," Dr. Waring said, thinking sadly of the infinite loneliness and the infinite patience of the very poor.

The courthouse group looked uneasily at each other and unconsciously drew closer together. They didn't know why. Only Donny Green commented. "Too long between church suppers, it seems." Matt Fuller and Dave Brennan exchanged knowing looks, and after Donny sauntered away, Matt said, "He's no good—that Donny Green. No good."

Jamie Wakefield gave out information about Pick Foley's property. It seemed that when Pick's mother died, she left a small amount of money which she had saved from her husband's insurance. She had skimped painfully to do that, but the house was mortgage-free.

Mrs. Foley had adored her husband and after his death she had kept his room and his personal belongings "just as he left them," never allowing Pick, her only son, to enter the room she had occupied with her husband. It had been kept closed—a precious memorial.

Pick was a shy, inordinately sensitive boy, who adored his mother. After her death he kept the room as a memorial to her. He did not allow Lola to enter the room.

He kept the small amount of money in a safe-deposit box at the bank and used it as sparingly as possible for food and for the small pittance he paid to Lola. He lived in deadly fear of being without money in his old age and had pinched and starved through all these years in order to keep himself out of the county poorhouse.

Seemingly it had never occurred to him that he might have found work to do; he did not even work to keep his house from falling down.

But Pick Foley had been found dead in his bed. Jamie sent for Lola Saunders and told her that the Foley house and the money in the bank had been left to her in grateful appreciation.

4

Miss Hazel had gone to a committee meeting over on Willow Street, so Lola Saunders, who had been Prentiss' nursemaid for five years now, took the boy for an afternoon stroll through the shady streets of the town. It was the easiest way to amuse the child, the easiest way to keep him out of the interminable mischief he got into. It was the simplest way, also, of keeping him reasonably clean until his mother's return.

As they turned the corner into Walnut Street, Lola looked down at the boy with something like pride in her eyes. It was simply pride in his appearance, though, pride in her own handiwork. She had no real affection for the child. What pleased her was his freshly scrubbed look, the crisp white suit she had ironed shortly before, the spotless whiteness of the shoes.

His eyes were pretty, she thought idly. They were like Miss Hazel's—fine and large and set wide apart, with long curling lashes for a frame. The rest of him, though, was Green, pure Green—the slightly jutting jaw, the clumsy bull-necked set of the head on his shoulders. Lola didn't like the Green part of Prentiss. She didn't trust the Greens, any of them.

She walked slowly, leading the five-year-old boy by the hand, pausing whenever he chose to stop and stare at a passing automobile or at a child approaching on the sidewalk. It was a curious thing, she mused, that Miss Hazel Allingham had married Mr. Fulmer. It wasn't right, somehow. An Allingham should have married into quality, and had quality children, not more Greens. Yes, it was a curious thing—seemed like folks used more sense in breeding cattle than they did in breeding their own kind. Money must have had something to do with it. White people seemed to set great store by money.

Lola opened her heavy black umbrella and held it aloft as she and the boy passed through a sunny stretch of the street. She was an old woman, small and agile, a light brown Negro with high cheekbones inherited from an Indian grandmother. All her movements were brisk and quick, and the jiggling gold hoop earrings she wore added to the general impression she gave of a sparkling vivacity. This afternoon she had on a clean blue cotton dress and a starched white apron. The long skirt of the dress stood out around her stiffly, and made a rustling sound when she walked.

Most of Kings Row regarded Lola as bad-mannered in her relations with white people. "Uppity," they called her. There was something regal in her gestures, something almost defiant in the proud way she walked, back rigid, head held high. Lola was well aware of her reputation, but it had long ago ceased to bother her. She had outgrown fear. She hadn't many years left to live—what was there, after all, that anyone, white or black, could do to her?

Of all the women she had worked for, her favorite was her present employer, Miss Hazel. Miss Hazel was a kind and sensible woman. She spoke *to* and *of* colored people as if they were people, not just household machines equipped with hands to serve and feet to run errands. Yes, Lola liked Miss Hazel, yet there were times when she pitied her for the tragic ties that bound her to a hard-voiced Green for whom Lola had nothing but contempt.

A small black dog trotted past. Dr. Mitchell's dog, Lola thought.

[215]

At the corner it shied away from a group of four loitering boys who called to it. One, who chased the dog, had a limp. His right foot was bandaged with dirty rags. "Know what kind of a dog that is?" he asked his companions. "That's a German dog. They're mean," he said importantly. "All them old German dogs are mean."

"Like Huns," one of the others agreed. "Old dirty Huns."

"Ought to be a law against American people havin' Hun dogs," the third put in. "Whose is it?"

As Lola and Prentiss approached, the boys' voices grew louder, more indignant.

"Dirty old Heinie dog."

"Look at him—trotting all over people's lawns—prob'ly lookin' for a cat to chase. A pore little kitten."

"It's a her. It's a female."

"No difference. It's a Heinie dog—mean like all them Heinies."

The boy picked up a large rock from the gravel street and hurled it after the dog. As the stone struck her leg Greta ran, tail between her legs, out into the middle of the street, then turned toward the upper end of the street, where the Laneer house faced the thoroughfare.

"Catch him!" The four boys sprang into action. The dog's evident fear seemed to feed their anger. They ran in a body into the middle of the short street, scooped up rocks, and started the chase. "Catch that dirty Heinie!"

Lola forgot her charge. She dropped the boy's hand. Indignation welled up in her and poured out of her mouth in outraged shouts. "Stop that!" she yelled. "Leave that dog alone, you bad rascals!" When they paid no attention she ran after them, closing the umbrella as she ran. "I'll tell yo' daddy," she threatened. It was a threat that usually worked with the young, whether she knew their parents or not—but this time it was ignored.

"That dog ain't done nothin' to you-all," she protested. "Leave her be!"

"It's a Heinie dog," they yelled. "A dirty Heinie dog!"

The little dachshund had reached the end of the short street and was trying vainly to force its way between the iron railings of the Laneer front fence, which blocked the way. Back and forth it ran, frantically, occasionally trying another opening in the fence, finding the space too narrow each time. The boys yelled. They threw their rocks, drawing back their arms and letting go like baseball pitchers. A stone struck its mark and the dog jumped, yelped, and ran back and forth faster than before. Another stone caught her on the shoulder. She stumbled, but quickly regained her feet and started again the frantic search for escape.

Prentiss, watching from the walk, jumped up and down and clapped his hands. "Hit him," he shouted. He laughed excitedly as the dog dodged another rock.

Lola ran into the midst of the stoners. She raised her umbrella and started beating about with it, first at one boy, then another. They dodged, each seizing his opportunity to hurl another rock at the struggling dog. "Git goin', old nigger," the biggest one shouted, "or we'll give *you* a taste."

Lola whirled and, teeth clenched, she brought the umbrella down on the boy's head. He shouted, dropped the rock he had been about to throw, and ran down the street. The others hesitated. The two nearest the old woman backed away, their faces suddenly sober. "That's that old Indian nigger," one of them said. "She'd just as soon kill you as not." Cowed, they turned and followed their companion down the street.

There was only one boy left. "Scared-Eddies," he called derisively. "I ain't afraid of any old nigger."

Lola turned in time to see him run forward toward the Laneer fence, hand upraised, and hurl half a brick at the cringing dog. It struck the dachshund on the head.

The boy turned and ran down the street calling to his friends.

Horrified, speechless, Lola watched the dog struggle to rise from the sidewalk. It got to its feet but fell again, making a desperate coughing sound. Its short legs twitched spasmodically. Then, slowly, as she watched, the long black body relaxed. The legs were still.

"They done killed her," Lola said bitterly. "Them stinkin' buzzards done killed her."

The forgotten Prentiss ran up beside her, his hands full of gravel. Before Lola knew what he was doing he ran toward the dog and threw the gravel at it, first one handful then the other. "Heinie dog!" he yelled. "Hit the old Heinie dog!"

Even as she raised her hand Lola knew that she was making a mistake. A colored nursemaid did not strike a white child, no matter what the provocation. But the hand came down, hard, almost of its own volition, across the boy's face. All her pent-up rage at the hoodlums who had killed the dog was in her down-swooping hand, all her bitter contempt for the child's cruel laughter. Prentiss reeled under the blow. He howled and sprawled in the street.

There. She had done it. She would lose her job. She would have irate parents to face. Even Miss Hazel, usually so easygoing and mild, would feel outraged. But Lola didn't care. Her hands still shook with anger as she helped the squalling boy to his feet, brushed some of the road dust from his clothes. "Shet yo' big mouth," she muttered. "Shet yo' big *Green mouth*."

Dragging Prentiss along with her, she walked briskly down Capers Street.

"Bad blood," she thought, looking down at the now sniveling dirty-faced boy. Lola had known Mr. Fulmer when he was that age, too, and she remembered now the way he used to kick his pet dog in the ribs. "Bad Green blood," she said contemptuously. "Let somebody else nurse him for a while."

Mr. Fulmer fired Lola Saunders, as she had known he would do. But all in all, the interview had not been as unpleasant as she had anticipated. Miss Hazel even argued at the last that Lola should not be dismissed too hastily. "After all, Fulmer, you know how a naughty child can tax one's patience. And I'm sure," she said, smiling at Lola, "I'm sure Lola won't do such a thing again."

Mr. Fulmer would have none of it, of course, but he was more comical than terrifying in his blustering. His fat face was very red, and he spluttered. Only one remark out of all he had said had managed to prick her, to sting her—almost—into an angry retort. "Impudence!" he had choked. "That's one thing a Green won't take off any nigger living. She had the gall to slap *Prentiss*!"

As if his child was a heap better than anybody else's, Lola thought contemptuously. It wasn't so much because she had hit a child that he was furious—it was because it was *his* child.

She slowed her step as, homeward bound, she came in sight of the Foley house. She smiled. *My* house, she corrected her first thought. Every stick of it, mine.

She stared at it, stopping at the front gate to look up the long walk to the door, noticing the condition of the sagging shutters, the patched roof, the vine-tangled railings of the porch. She estimated what it might bring in a sale. Two thousand dollars? Three? A lot more, anyway, than she'd ever had before.

Feeling breathless with her own daring, Lola opened the gate and walked up to the door. It felt strange, her walking boldly up these wide front steps and across the veranda. Always before she had taken the narrow brick walk that circled the house to the rear entrance. She tried the door experimentally, but found it locked. She looked up at the many-paned fanlight above, and wondered how it would feel to live in the house. Not to sell it at all, but to move right in and *use* it.

It was a crazy idea, of course. She knew that. No Negro in Kings Row would dare. You couldn't move into Union Street alongside the Greens and the other proud white folks—not if you owned the whole damn' block. But thinking about it was fun—and exciting—while it lasted. She saw herself dressed in black silk, moving grandly from room to room through the house; eating her dinner at the round dining room table under the hanging lamp with its colored glass shade and bead fringe. She could even put in electric lights. Running water! A real bathtub in which she could soak her old, tired body whenever she pleased.

"Holy Jesus," she muttered, almost prayerfully. There was something frightening, and electrifying, in the very thought of all that splendor.

She hurried off the porch and down the walk again, peering up and down the darkening street to see if she had been observed. "Old fool nigger," she chided herself. "Daydreamin' like a fool."

But at the gate she turned back again, drawn irresistibly to a further speculation. She *could* live in it, she reminded herself firmly. The law said she could—that nobody could keep her out. Mr. Jamie Wakefield had made that clear when he explained the will to her.

She smiled maliciously and shook her head a little, making the gold earrings jiggle, as she thought how her moving into the house would upset Mr. Fulmer. What would he do, she wondered.

Nothing. He couldn't do a thing.

"Burn him up," she chuckled. "It'd run him plumb crazy!"

She toyed with the idea all the way home, feeling one moment frightened, the next moment brave.

The sight of her own cramped cottage—a shack really, she thought contemptuously—strengthened her will. She stepped inside gingerly, took one look around the cluttered shabby room, and all in a moment made up her mind.

She would move into the big house. Right away.

5

Fulmer Green's study was an extraordinary room—a contradictory room, its austerity a contrast to the appearance of Fulmer himself.

The athletic build of the man was belied by the sag of his broad shoulders, and his massive head was thrust tensely forward. His small, close-set eyes gleamed with a kind of furious intensity as he gripped a large fountain pen and drove it rapidly across the sheet of paper in front of him. He had an electric energy—a not wholly controlled power.

From time to time he pounded with his left fist on the blotter, still clutching the pen tensely in his right hand. Then he returned to his rapid writing. This speech must be finished—and memorized—before he went to bed.

The room had been added to the house quite recently and Hazel had furnished it exactly as her husband had wanted it. It was a large, square room, raised a few steps above the level of the living room, out of which it opened. A window almost filled the south wall and heavy blue silk draperies framed the square-paned glass.

Arched bookshelves were built in and filled with handsomely bound sets of standard works. Fulmer had not gone in for first editions, but here and there could be found rare volumes he had ordered on impulse. Apart from the two sections of books, the rough plastered walls were bare, except for a brilliant landscape by Kandinsky hanging over the fireplace. It was a Crimean village street, palpitating with incandescent yellows, sultry purples, and blazing reds. It seemed to quiver with its own presentment of a torrid summer day.

There were several high, carved chairs with footstools—uncomfortable, uninviting chairs. A vast table, which served as a desk, stood close to the window. It held a few books, wire baskets, index files, and two yellow jars filled with pens and pencils. It was the desk of a disorderly businessman, and utterly unrelated to the rest of the room.

The curtains were not yet drawn and the panorama of a particularly brilliant June afternoon was beginning to fade.

Suddenly, Fulmer pushed his chair back from the table and strode to the window. His frown relaxed as his eyes swept across the garden. June was his favorite month. The maples on the wide lawn were a brilliant emerald green matching the luxuriant carpet of grass spread out before him. Just beneath the window, some timid shrub had sent out a few heart-shaped leaves, yellow as gold, that pointed upward like taper flames. A clematis vine was reaching hungrily out from its trellis toward a corner of the screened porch. He liked that ambitious effort—and applauded it.

He turned back to the table and looked abstractedly at the sheet of paper he had half covered with his big, legible writing. Crumpling it, he dropped it into the leather wastebasket.

"Come in," he said in answer to a knock at the door.

Hazel stood in the doorway. "Busy?" she asked.

"Yes," he answered shortly.

She was composed as usual. But spots of color blazed in her cheeks and her eyes were unnaturally brilliant.

"Fulmer, there's something I wish very much to talk over with you."

"Let it wait. I've got things to do right now. That's why I asked for early dinner. When I get through here, I'll call you."

"Very well," she said, and went down the steps to the living room, her long rose silk dress trailing across the floor.

He closed the door behind her, turning the key.

Presently he rested his elbows on the desk and dropped his head into his upturned palms.

God, what a headache! Medicine did no good—nothing did any good. If he didn't get more sleep he didn't believe he could go on much longer.

He looked up and his eyes fell on the Kandinsky picture over the mantel opposite him. What a crazy thing—all those loud, harsh colors, those misshapen houses, those malformed figures on the street! He felt curiously uneasy when he looked at pictures anyhow. He distrusted art and artists. He knew he was superior to them because he could *buy* the product of the artist. By his ability to buy what they gave their lives to making, he proved his superiority.

His head began to pound again. A phrase he'd once heard in a sermon came into his mind—"An easy conscience makes a soft pillow." A soft pillow, that was exactly what he needed.

It was remarkable, he told himself, how much he remembered of what he had heard in sermons. So many texts, particularly the harsh ones from the Old Testament, stuck in his head. He didn't know if he should take pride in that fact or not, because he was not sure if it was a good sign or a bad one. He remembered his uncomfortable life at his mother's house—it had never been *home*. Visiting ecclesiastics were constantly descending upon the household, and the conversations were—well, frightening. Heaven was above—dazzling and forbidding—only a shade less frightful than hell, its discomforts being moral and mental rather than physical.

If he could only get more sleep! He dropped his head on his folded arms and closed his eyes. He found himself remembering a lot of unpleasant things.

He remembered Benny Singer twisting at the end of a rope down there in the jailyard. Why in hell did he have to go to the execution anyhow? He didn't really have anything against old Benny. Sure, Benny was a dope and maybe it would have been better to send him to the asylum—but, hell! His own career was more important than the life of a nitwit kid. He hadn't actually realized when he was prosecuting the case what the conclusion would be. God, it must be awful to be hanged! He remembered Parris Mitchell walking away from the scaffold before the trap was sprung. Parris Mitchell had tried to save Benny from swinging. Probably it was professional prestige that Parris was looking for, just as he had been.

And then, Peyton Graves. Peyton with his brains spattered against the wall of his office lavatory! What a way to die—in his lavatory! He backed away from the accusation that he had written a letter to Peyton which *just might* have been the cause of the suicide.

He twisted his head and pressed the back of his neck with his fingers. This damned headache was getting worse by the minute.

But of course it was that letter, what else? He twisted his head again and declared that Peyton was a thief anyhow, and that sooner or later someone would have caught up with him. But, his accusing self went on, didn't Parris Mitchell say that he and Drake McHugh were planning to fix things up for Peyton? Hell! Parris Mitchell again. Damn Parris Mitchell, God damn him!

And Drake McHugh. Drake had his legs cut off because he had to take a job down in the railroad yards. Drake used to go around looking for a job. He had turned him down. But for Christ's sake, he couldn't be blamed for that, could he? But there, clearly outlined, the old, carefree figure of Drake McHugh stood with Peyton Graves and Benny Singer. Dead, all of them.

Why in God's name couldn't he get to work and forget all this nonsense? He'd see what Hazel wanted to talk over, and then he'd take one of his sleeping pills—maybe two. He had a hard day ahead tomorrow.

He pulled the chain to light his desk lamp, and drew the curtain across the big window before he called Hazel.

She took her seat in one of the straight chairs.

"Well?" he asked. "Speak up, Hazel. I'm tired and I want to get off to bed."

She stared up at him in a calm, purposeful way that made him vaguely uncomfortable. "Then I'll get to the point at once. I meant what I said the other day about a divorce, Fulmer."

The color receded from his face, leaving it expressionless and bleak. In the hard, driving days, he had remembered that word only once; he had dismissed it as a nightmare he had dreamed. Now it was back, definite in Hazel's voice.

"But you're joking," he said, "you can't mean it, Hazel."

"I mean it."

The veins about his forehead swelled. In the silence that followed Fulmer listened to the dry buzz saw of cicadas in the garden. They streaked the silence with irritating persistence. "Those damned insects drive me crazy," he muttered. The belligerence had gone out of his voice. It was as if all emotion had burned out of him and left him almost without the will to think.

"Everything irritates you," said Hazel. "You'd better try to get hold of yourself. Even a traffic delay can throw you into a fury. And, for some reason, I seem to have been your greatest source of irritation. Something's happened to this marriage—" she paused. "I think perhaps you'll be able to get hold of yourself—after I'm gone."

"That's not true," he said quickly. "You can't go—I need you, Hazel. I tell you, I'm ill—I'm on the verge of a crack-up. That's the truth. I'll break under this God-damn' pressure."

"Then you don't need *me*," she said. "You need Parris Mitchell."

"Don't say that name to me! You keep saying it—over and over—Parris Mitchell, Parris Mitchell!"

"Do I? I didn't know I'd ever mentioned him—except once, perhaps, when you forced me to."

He got up abruptly, and leaned toward her across the table.

"Hazel! Is that it? Tell me. Is that what you want? Is that why you want a divorce?"

"I don't understand."

"Parris Mitchell."

"Sit down, Fulmer. Truly, I'm not in the least afraid of you. Try to remember that I'm neither a witness nor a defendant. Thank you. Now let us get back to Parris Mitchell. He is as thoroughly—and happily married as any man in Kings Row. If you want proof, why not call him up, now, and ask him? Only I don't altogether advise it in view of your plans."

"What do you know about my plans? And what do you care, what's more? I suppose you know that even the threat of divorce by you would kill them."

"I have considered that, Fulmer. I think I know what I'm doing. I am not in love with Parris Mitchell. I think I told you I hardly know him. Nor am I in love with anyone else, for that matter. The truth is, Fulmer, that you've never needed a woman, at all."

Fulmer's head jerked up. Did she know about—about Donny? Had she known all these years? God in heaven! No, she couldn't have known or she would have left him long ago.

"What do you mean, Hazel?"

"I mean that there's such a gap between what I expected of my marriage and what it has turned out to be that I—I see no sense in going on with it. You don't know what to do with a wife."

"Have I mistreated you?"

"We never should have been married—that's all."

"But why do you want a divorce? Have I deserted you? Have I been unfaithful to you? Don't I give you enough money, for God's sake? What in hell do you want?"

"I want to get away, and to keep my integrity. I have watched you, Fulmer, for a long time. I watched you convict Benny Singer for your own advancement—"

"Convict? How can a prosecutor convict? The jury convicts and the judge passes sentence. What do you think a public prosecutor is for? To get acquittals for murderers?"

"You forced it, Fulmer. You hypnotized the jury into believing in murder against your own knowledge. But that isn't all. You know better than I what your career has been—that you have wiped out every plea for justice, every decent impulse that has stood in your way. You have conspired against every honest person who has tried to oppose you, and you are trying at this moment to get Dr. Mitchell out of the hospital. Why? Because he defended Benny Singer, because he was on the side of justice and honor and decency, because he could not bear to see an innocent boy die for the sake of a lawyer's ambitions."

"That's not true! It's a pack of lies. Who's been telling you this nonsense? And why, after all these years, when you say you've been watching me—why wait till now to bring up these accusations, now when Singer and all the rest of it are forgotten by everyone except you; now, when everything is beginning to break right for me?"

"Yes, I know, Fulmer. I've been guilty with you. I have stayed with you, made a home for you, even helped you with my money while you were climbing up your mean, crooked ladder. I tried to tell myself it was not my business, that I did not understand what you were doing, that behind everything you had some sort of belief in your own integrity that I couldn't follow. Well, I know now and I'm not going along with it any longer. I have no trust in you, no love for you—no, not a flicker left. If I stay with you and live on your dishonest money, I shall be betraying myself. I can't do it, Fulmer."

While she spoke she saw the waves of anger come and go in his face. Twice she had raised her voice to stop his interruption. Now she saw the tightening of his jaw and knew that some sort of control was coming back to him.

"Don't you know," he said, "that you can't get a divorce on any of the grounds you have just given?"

She got up then, went to the door, and opened it.

"Maybe I can't," she said, "but I can try."

[225]

Fulmer jumped to his feet with every muscle tense.

"Hazel! Stop! Wait—let me explain! Hazel, forgive me, for God's sake!"

But the door was closed and only the long rasp of the cicadas answered.

Fulmer made no effort to see Hazel the next morning. Better give her time to cool off, he decided. But after a night of mulling over his fancied wrongs, he went to his office utterly unprepared to deal with the problems of the day. Things were in a muddle by midafternoon and he gave up the effort. A decision that had been forming all day in his mind came into the clear.

Parris Mitchell! It seemed to him he could trace every one of his troubles in some way to that man. And now, in spite of Hazel's denial, he suspected that she was—well, *interested* in Parris. Probably it had gone no further in her mind than a comparison of the two of them—to the disadvantage of her husband, he thought wryly. But he'd face the damned quack and have a showdown. Thought he could alienate his wife and his brother, did he? He'd show him!

At the thought of Donny, he remembered uncomfortably that Parris had spoken up for the boy in that Aberdeen squabble. Well, what of it? That didn't make up for all the other things he'd done.

Fulmer opened the lower drawer of his desk, lifted a revolver, weighed it experimentally in his hand for a moment, and placed it in his jacket pocket.

Parris Mitchell looked up in surprise as Fulmer entered the office without ringing.

Fulmer's lower lip was slack and moist; his eyes, which usually had avoided meeting Parris' on the few occasions when they had been face to face, stared straight at the doctor with a hard, almost feverish brightness.

Parris purposely leaned back in his desk chair in an attitude of ease and relaxation. He waved a hand carelessly and smiled.

"Hello, Fulmer! This is a surprise. Have you come to see me professionally at last?"

"What do you mean—*at last?*"

Parris shrugged. "Oh . . . you've often expressed some distrust of my particular science. I thought this visit might mean you've changed your opinion!"

Fulmer advanced toward the desk. He felt his hands shaking and he put them in his jacket pockets; his right hand closed over the revolver. It gave him a feeling of confidence, of power over Parris Mitchell.

"No, I haven't changed my opinion and I never will. You're a quack. You know it and I know it."

"Well—" Parris picked up a carved wooden cigarette box from the desk and held it out to Fulmer with a grin. "Apparently this *isn't* a professional visit, but have a smoke, sit down and tell me what's on your mind."

Fulmer refused the proffered cigarette with an angry shake of his head, and Parris lighted his own. A wasp buzzed furiously against the windowpane, attracting Fulmer's attention, but he forced his gaze back to Parris' hand holding the cigarette. It was steady, damn it. The man was inhuman. He had no *feelings!* An absurd memory of something he had heard his mother say when he was a boy flashed through his mind. "They say Parris' grandmother serves wine on the table every day. That boy's as sure to go to the dogs as anything—brought up to be a drunkard that way!"

Parris noted Fulmer's eyes fixed on his hand holding the cigarette. With deliberation, still watching the direction of Fulmer's gaze, he carried it to an ash tray on the corner of the desk. Fulmer's fixed stare followed the movement.

Parris had immediately sensed Fulmer's inner tension; now he recognized that Fulmer was in a distraught, possibly dangerous mental state.

"Come on, Fulmer, relax!" he said sharply. "I haven't got time to waste. What's up?"

The man's eyes snapped up to meet Parris'.

Damn the bastard, talking to him in that tone of voice! His fingers tightened on the revolver in his pocket.

"All right, Mitchell. First, I want to know about that visit Don made to you. I want to know what you wormed out of him."

Parris stubbed out his cigarette before he answered in a calm voice, "Don came here of his own accord. What we discussed is between him and me."

"Don't give me that sanctimonious doctor-crap."

"What are you so concerned about, Fulmer? Are you afraid of what Donny might have told me?"

"Afraid?" Fulmer drew back, momentarily shaken. "What is there to be afraid of?"

Parris shrugged. "I wouldn't know."

"Then—" A degree of confidence returned to Fulmer. "Tell me what he said."

"You might as well learn this, Fulmer; even a quack doctor respects the confidence of his patients."

"Patients, hell! He's my brother!"

"Of course. Why don't you ask *him,* then?"

"He wouldn't tell—" Fulmer broke off his speech, his lips compressed.

"No, Fulmer." Parris leaned forward and spoke with firmness. "He wouldn't tell you. You've spoiled Donny—because he was weak and willing, but you don't control him as you'd like to."

Fulmer stood motionless. Frustration and hatred showed in his working face. His hand was wet as it gripped the hard metal of the revolver.

Parris continued speaking. "I'll tell you this much—for whatever good it might do: Donny came to see me about the state of his nerves, he said. He didn't want treatment; I don't quite know what he wanted of me. He was worried, very much on edge, and irritable—I might even say *irrational.* I tell you this because perhaps *you* know what was wrong with your brother."

Alarm sent a fleeting change of expression over Fulmer's countenance. "I? No—no. Why should I?"

He took a deep breath to steady himself. How much *did* Mitchell know? There was something else he had to find out about Don's visit.

"Do you remember when he came here? The exact date?"

"Yes, it happens that I do. It was the last week of July of last year. I think I have not seen him since."

Fulmer drew a breath of relief. At least it was before that trouble with the Jinktown girl. But he still wondered if Don had hinted anything about their personal relations. He didn't know how to ask without betraying his uneasiness.

Parris stood up, suddenly impatient. "Look here, Fulmer, say what else you have to say and get it over with."

Fulmer clutched the edge of the desk. "I'll tell you, Parris Mitchell! You weren't satisfied with alienating my brother, you've managed to poison my *wife's* mind against me."

"You are lying, Fulmer, and you know it."

All the concentrated rage of years of animosity boiled up in Fulmer in an uncontrollable ferment. He forgot his fears of what this man might do, what he might *know*; forgot his usual cautious control. He was remembering in one clutching, tearing moment all the imagined insults, the fancied contempt that had been heaped upon him since childhood by Parris Mitchell. His egotistic self-protectiveness was gone and only this black impulse to kill was left. He jerked the gun out of his pocket.

Parris' eyes were trained to watchfulness by his handling of patients at the hospital. His muscular hand was as quick as Fulmer's. His fingers closed about Fulmer's wrist, and under their agonizing pressure Fulmer's helpless hand relaxed. The revolver dropped to the desk. Without releasing his hold, Parris with his free hand drew the gun out of Fulmer's reach.

Fulmer's surprise had for a moment superseded rage. But now, fear was beginning to get the upper hand. Parris had the gun. Would he use it? Even as he realized that Parris had no such intention, he was shaken anew by his old secret envy, his childish jealousies, and now, this added humiliation.

He did not know how long Parris had been talking, but his attention was snared by the mention of Prentiss, his son.

"You owe something to the boy, Fulmer. You are forgetting Prentiss. You haven't done so well with Donny—but are you going to let your son go the same way?"

Not a word about his effort to kill—only a warning about his son. Parris Mitchell was offering advice to *him*—Fulmer Green. He'd never taken advice from anyone. He would have considered that a weakness. But advice coming from this man he hated—this man who had stood in his way ever since he could remember!

Parris released Fulmer's wrist and motioned him to a seat beside the desk.

"Sit down, Fulmer, and let's talk this thing out. Let's clear the at-

[229]

mosphere. Hasn't it ever occurred to you that your distrust of people might arise from a sense of your own unworthiness of character? You can't believe good of anyone, apparently. You degrade everyone in your own mind—even those closest to you." He waited for a moment but Fulmer made no comment.

"As far as I've been able to gather, you came here to accuse me of two specific things: an improper interest in your wife, and an effort to pry into your personal affairs through Donny. Both these things are manifestly absurd. But you have built up such a case for yourself, such a buttress for your egotism, that they might as well be true. For your own sake and for the sake of your family, you've got to get rid of these obsessions—and you've got to put something in their place. And that something should be a concern for Hazel and Prentiss—and for Donny. You may even be able to do something for *him*."

"Stay out of my affairs," Fulmer blazed. "How do I know your—your interest in Don is aboveboard? Why should you bother to keep him from being expelled from Aberdeen? How do I know how—how intimate you two may be?"

A look of unbelief swept across Parris' face, but as he caught the full import of what Fulmer was saying, he rose and leaned menacingly across the desk. "Get out of here!"

Fulmer's frightened glance at the revolver caught his attention and Parris shoved it toward him. "Take your gun and get out of my office!"

After Fulmer had gone, Parris sat at his desk, sick with the reaction which always followed a fury such as he had just experienced. But when Dr. Waring came in ten minutes later, Parris was apparently calm, apparently interested in the book he was reading.

"Parris," Dr. Waring asked, "would it be convenient for you to take Elise with you on your trip east?"

"Yes, of course. I've been urging it ever since I found I had to go. Why do you ask?"

"Frankly, Parris, I don't like her listlessness—her apathy. It isn't right. Maybe a change of scene would help."

"I wish you'd say as much to her. I've done my utmost, but she seems unwilling to make the trip. Doctor, I wish you'd try to find out exactly her physical condition. She insists she is not ill, but I'm convinced there's something organically wrong. I don't want to frighten her by constant questioning, but you could insist on a thorough examination without disturbing her."

"I've been meaning to suggest that. I'm glad you spoke of it. I'll talk to her about it the next time I see her."

"Thank you, Doctor. In the meantime I'll try to persuade Elise to go with me to Washington."

6

The late sunlight has worked its miracle of gold and amber on the gardens at von Eln. In the soft spring dusk a faint fluting of frogs sounded from the pond beyond the spruce grove. There was no stir along the ground, no agitation among the lower leaves of the orchard trees, but high up, along the faces of the upper trees there was an empty swirl as though a great sail were slowly filling.

Elise sat very still in the big chair Anna had drawn out on the terrace for her. She had spent most of the afternoon sitting here thinking over the events of the past few weeks. She had been feeling resentful and hurt and sad by turns. Her mind just now was centered on Parris. In some way he had escaped the blows that had been raining on her own shoulders. Kings Row was not so unkind to him. It was because she was an alien that they would have none of her—that they persecuted her, she thought.

Perhaps they hated her because they felt she had taken Parris from them. They wanted him for their own. She knew she was not to blame for the aloofness they resented in Parris. It was not even aloofness. It was more that he seemed to rest under a cloud of gravity that they misunderstood. Parris is singularly blind, she thought fretfully—blind to the grudging envy of Kings Row, blind to the town's resentment of his seemingly easy success. Sometimes she thought she should call it to his attention, but she couldn't bring herself to do that. It would seem a petty and a spiteful thing to do—as though she were trying to strike back at Kings Row for its treatment of *her*.

She couldn't keep from wondering at Parris' strange passion for von Eln—for Kings Row. Why couldn't they go away? Why should he so flatly refuse to consider a post in the East—away from this ungracious, ungrateful town?

She remembered that she had loved von Eln, too, but now she

feared and hated it. She turned her eyes slowly and looked at the familiar landscape, at the row of Lombardy poplars that had by some miracle escaped the windy onslaughts of this tempestuous climate. They stood along the south wall of the terrace, as staunchly French as the spirit of the woman who had placed them there.

It was, she thought, a moody landscape, never given to moderation. Its rains were never gentle, but swirling; its snows and sleets were furiously driven; its suns were scorching. The whole aspect of the country forced melancholy upon her and filled her with premonitions. All the gestures of life—the wind-tormented trees particularly—represented to her in that moment the eternal onslaught of death on life. She felt too much face to face with the conflicts of the universe.

The wind was rising now, and she drew her light woolen cape closer about her throat. And, as so often happened, she felt it was not a wind at all but a *tide,* ebbing and flowing endlessly. Why couldn't she breast it? Oh, she thought, I know now! One has only to yield to the current, to be carried along with it, to be at peace. Parris—Parris had never gone with the current. There was something in his nature that made him resist that sort of pressure. He'd be easier to live with if he had a little more *give* to his nature. She looked around guiltily as though she feared she had spoken those disloyal words aloud.

Parris—who had given her all this—had wrapped her about with such security—no, Parris was not to blame that she sat here being sorry for herself.

And Anna—dear, good Anna—but after all, even Anna was a reminder that she was not capable of running her own home. Not only had she failed to give Parris a family, but someone else had to organize and manage his home. Her depression deepened.

Anna, coming out on the terrace, was for the first time frightened. Elise looked so listless, so helpless and young, and so *patient*. Perhaps, she thought, Parris should not go away and leave his wife now. The Washington trip could not be so important, surely.

"Miss Elise, won't you have your dinner now?" she asked in her slow, careful English.

"*Lassen Sie mich gehen,*" Elise said, a strange impatience in her voice.

"*Was fehlt Ihnen—Liebchen?*" Anna spoke the last word under her breath.

[232]

"*Es fehlt mir nichts.*" This time Elise's voice was unnaturally sharp. "Nothing. I want nothing."

Quick tears sprang to Anna's eyes. She hurriedly brushed them away with the corner of her white apron. What could be the matter? When Miss Elise spoke German to her something was wrong. She wished Parris would come home from the hospital.

"Is it that you grieve for—Greta?" she asked gently.

Elise shifted a little in her chair and turned her head wearily against the cushion. "Anna, does it not seem wicked that people could torture and kill a poor little frightened dog because they hated its mistress?"

"It was wicked to kill Greta, but it was not that they hated you, surely."

"I think that was the reason. Kings Row hates me—because I was born in Austria—because I—maybe, Anna, because I am married to Parris. They want to take him away from me."

"No, no, Miss Elise. You must not feel like that. You are exactly the wife he needs—and wants."

"But, Anna, can't you see how—how *hostile* this town is? Sometimes I think it is trying to—strangle me—*crush* me—it closes in on me. Only you and Parris stand with me. I'm scared, terribly scared." There was something like panic now in her voice.

"There, there, *Liebchen,* you are imagining things. Try not to worry. You will make yourself sick and Parris will not be able to go to Washington to make his speech."

"Sh-h. He's coming now, Anna. Don't tell him what I said to you."

Anna went into the house as Parris came through the French doors.

"She grieves, Parris, about Kam and her father and the little dog," Anna whispered as she passed him.

Parris stood for a moment looking down at his wife. She was like April, he thought, and wished for a moment that she might blossom into a passionate May. But he clamped his mind shut against that selfish thought. Her clear, delicate beauty brushed his eyes like a cool sweet wind.

He sat down on the low terrace wall near her and took her hands in his own, bending his head to kiss first one of her slender palms, then the other.

"Elise, honey, I'm going to take you to Washington with me. It won't be any fun at all unless you come, too."

"No, Parris. This is an important trip for you and I should only be in the way."

"I can get through the hunger-strike business in a day or two. An alienist isn't too important in a case of that kind. The visit to Johns Hopkins and to South Carolina should be pleasant for you, too. Be a good girl and come along."

"I know, Parris, that if I went you would worry about me. I'm not feeling well enough for gadding about—honestly. I think you should go alone. Please don't insist."

"I haven't any enthusiasm for the trip unless you go with me. It will be too lonely."

"And lonely for me, but I have Anna, and you won't be away long."

"Will you promise not to be afraid—of anything? Even the sound of the wind or the howling of the Pomeroy hounds?"

"I promise—and Randy will come often to stay with me. You mustn't worry about me while you are away."

And with her promise he had to be content.

Dr. Nolan was looking through a stack of unopened letters on his desk, when he came across the rather foreign-looking writing on the envelope. The name written out in full, *Doctor Paul Thaddeus Nolan,* had a stately look in Parris' meticulous script.

Dear Paul:

The enclosed clippings from Washington and Baltimore papers will give you a complete picture of what has been going on here. You will be surprised to find how our institution is being watched by these older, more established hospitals in the East. They tell me that our work is more advanced than that of ninety per cent of the hospitals in the country.

The trip has been highly profitable. On the strength of my talks with army men interested in the remarkable results just now being reported in treatment of shell-shocked soldiers at the front, Johns Hopkins asks for a series of lectures next term. Psychiatry is certainly looking up and I feel no end encouraged.

I am writing from South Carolina, where I am enjoying an amazing experience with a group of men—physicians and psychologists—who are sponsoring the movement in spectacular fashion. In the work of such men

I see more hope for the permanent establishment of this new science than in the fighting talk taking place in the journals of the medical profession. These people face the question fairly—no askance glances, such as we have accustomed ourselves to meet.

There followed several paragraphs of comment on the impressions Parris had gotten from the South, which had evidently enchanted him. Paul was pleased at the tenor of the letter and unfolded the clippings.

The first one consisted of a direct quotation from one of Dr. Mitchell's talks.

Man's motivations are the sum of all he is. In the "long memory" of his own organism, in all that ancestry and environment have made him—he, the sum at the foot of the lengthening column of figures—is the full explanation, and the *only* explanation of all that he does, and is at the same time the key to all that is possible for him to do.

The incoming impressions (stimuli, inspirations) do but awake once more that which has lived innumerable times—innumerable lives.

Very secret, very strange is the nautilus shell of men's thinking. There it is, a haunted house for the lonely wanderer that each man is.

Yet, which of us can say he never desired to enter one of the "seven towers" of Swinburne? These desires, repressed or overindulged—

Dr. Nolan leaned back in his chair and gazed thoughtfully out of the window for a few moments, then reached with a purposeful gesture for the phone.

"Get me Miles Jackson at *The Gazette* office, please. . . . Yes. Hello, Miles. Paul Nolan speaking. . . . Yes, Miles, I have just received clippings from some Eastern newspapers. It seems that Parris Mitchell's stirring up quite a little dust over there. How about giving it some space in *The Gazette*? . . . Of course. It might make a few benighted souls open their eyes to what it means to have Mitchell on this staff, but if I read aright, we may not hold him long. . . . You bet! I'll bring them down myself in half an hour."

Paul replaced the receiver, picked up the letter and the clippings, and went to his apartment to tell Laurel the news.

As Elise came slowly down the stairs and into the kitchen, Anna thought her step was almost feeble.

[235]

"Oh, cookies! I like them—but I don't seem to want food ver-ry much," Elise said, watching Anna roll out the cookie dough.

"I've been wondering how I could tempt you to eat more, Miss Elise. Can you think of anything—"

"Thank you, Anna, no. It's just that I don't seem to be able to eat."

"Couldn't you walk a little more?"

"I'm ver-ry short of breath, Anna."

"You ought to let Parris or Dr. Waring give you a good tonic. In the spring a good tonic—"

"Anna," Elise spoke nervously, "don't say anything to Parris, please. He has so much on his mind. We mustn't worry him."

It was then that Nathan brought in the afternoon mail.

There was a letter from Parris postmarked "Columbia, South Carolina. Elise took it out on the terrace and sat down to read it. She read slowly, her lips forming the words carefully.

My very dear:

I am tired, having had an exciting experience tonight. It was not a personal, active experience of my own. I've been a witness of an emotional storm that might have ended disastrously, but which it seems is going to turn out all right.

I saw McKay Pomeroy fall in love with a charming girl and get her own and her father's consent for her to marry him tomorrow. I am as exhausted as though it all might have happened to me. These lightning-swift war marriages are breath-taking. Somehow, I feel sure this one will last. They are such fine youngsters.

But now, back in my hotel room, I can see the events of the past six hours—in which all this took place—as a movie or an evening at the theater.

I come back to thoughts of you, my dear, with a warm, grateful sense of your steady, supporting sympathy. I know now that I have never told you often enough what you mean to me. You appear to me like some serene altar light, steady, untroubled, sure; a symbol of faith, a sign of refuge and tranquillity. I come to that image of you from a world racked by contrary storms and all the inner unrest of my own temperament. Brooding as you often appear, you are so secure, so correctly based. I know how good and blessed a thing for me it is that I have you.

There are so many little things that I have done for you that I miss when I am away from you—like moving your chair to the window so that you don't strain your precious eyes. I wonder if you are taking proper care of yourself. Try, for my sake.

Soon I'll be back at von Eln and shall have so many things to tell you about this enchanting place.

Never forget that I am always, your

Parris

Elise came to the end of the letter, then looked back and whispered the phrases again: *"serene altar light"* . . . *"steady, untroubled, sure"* . . . *"so correctly based."* . . . She knew that he was trying to re-assure her—to give her a little feeling of *security*.

For a long time she sat there trying to clarify in her own mind her relation to her husband. She felt that she lacked some integrating force that would have sealed their union if she had been more ade-quate in personality or soul.

She had always sensed that Parris was seeking something more than she could give him, but she did not know what it was. She had tried to anticipate his wishes; she had been proud of being his wife; but she knew that Parris would never accept more than was freely given. She wanted to give—but something was lacking.

She rose slowly and went upstairs to answer her letter—not know-ing what she could say—convinced in her own mind that Parris pitied more than he loved her.

8

It was almost time for the butchershop to close. Mr. Dyer, tired from his day's work, sighed heavily as he transferred the figures of the day's business from the little stack of sales slips to the huge ledger before him on the desk. He hoped no last-minute customers would come in to distract him from his bookkeeping. When he was tired like this interruptions annoyed him. I must be getting old, he thought wryly.

He was suddenly conscious of a minor noise that had been nagging at him for some time. He turned in his chair to watch Punch Rayne, his helper, cutting pork chops and stacking them in preparation for tomorrow morning's business. He noticed that there was a steady rhythm in the sounds the cutting made. That was why it had taken him so long to identify the source, to become really aware of it. He watched, smiling, as Punch's hand lifted a long knife from the table and made a row of neat slices into the moist pink meat. There was a second's pause while knife was exchanged for cleaver, then—chop, as the heavy blade cut through bone. Then—slap, as the small crescent of pork hit the top of the growing stack. Chop. Slap. Chop. Slap. The boy was a good meatcutter. Neat, efficient, strong. He handled the knives like an old-timer. The boy had learned a lot in two years.

It was too bad, Mr. Dyer thought, that such a good steady worker should be such a queer duck other ways. Having Punch in the shop was almost like being alone. The boy wouldn't talk, for one thing. Only time he ever opened his mouth was to answer a question put straight at him. He had funny habits, too—especially the one of turning his back on customers when they came up to the counter. The funniest thing of all was that he turned his back only on men customers, never on women. So it wasn't shyness, as Mr. Dyer had thought at first, seeing him turn his back and keep it turned, even though it meant he had to do a lot of question-answering over his shoulder.

Mr. Dyer sighed and turned back to his work. Wearily, he rubbed the back of his fat red neck. Takes all kinds of people to make a world, he was thinking.

The screen door opened and swung shut again, making a swishing sound, and Mr. Dyer looked up to see two men entering the shop. He rose reluctantly to serve them. "Evenin'," he said amiably enough. "Evenin', Mr. Green." Catching sight of the younger man, he smiled. "And how are you, Donny? Been a month o' Sundays since I saw you, boy. Watcha know?"

Donny Green grinned, his handsome face shadowed heavily from the harsh light of the lamp that hung over the meat counter. "Not much," he said easily. "Not much, these days."

Fulmer was occupied in examining the freshly cut meat behind the glass. He was silent, looking perplexed, moving his dead cigar from one side of his mouth to the other.

Mr. Dyer's sound-sensitive ears became aware of the dead silence that had fallen suddenly on the shop. Four men stood here, yet there was no sound to be heard except the faint buzzing of a fly against the screen door across the room. He realized then that the incessant chopping at the wooden table behind him had stopped, creating a sort of vacuum of sound. He turned to see Punch standing very still, the cleaver still upraised, his straight sturdy back as rigid as a statue's. As Dyer watched, the boy started to work again, but more slowly this time. Every movement of his hands was slow, deliberate, almost studied.

"Got any lamb chops?" asked Fulmer Green. "I've got to get something for Prentiss—my boy—for his supper. We're having pork roast tonight and the boy can't eat pork. Does something funny to him every time he tries it. Makes him break out in a rash."

Mr. Dyer nodded. "I can cut you a couple." He walked the few steps into the meat locker at the back and came out holding up a side of lamb.

Fulmer said, "Three thick ones will be enough."

Dyer thumped the meat down on the table beside Punch. "Mind cutting three thick chops off that for Mr. Green?"

Silently, Punch shoved the pork aside and pulled the piece of lamb into cutting position before him. Then he turned around, facing the customers squarely. "How many do you want?" he asked. He looked not at Fulmer Green but at his younger brother Donny.

Mr. Dyer thought, "He's not right in the head. That proves it. Asking 'how many' when I just told him three."

"Three," said Fulmer. "Three thick ones. And trim off most of the fat."

Punch seemed not to hear. He kept his eyes on Donny. "Hi, Donny," he said.

It was the first time Mr. Dyer had ever seen the boy attempt conversation with a customer. He stared, feeling a fresh shock of surprise, as Punch's mouth lifted at the corners—a little crookedly—to form a distorted, boyish grin. "You been out o' town a long time, ain't you?" he asked Donny Green.

Donny pulled hurriedly at his cigarette and spoke through a cloud of blue smoke. "Hi, Punch. Sure have." He blinked his eyes at the smoke, then slapped indolently at his brother's arm and turned away. "I got to be moseying along, Fulmer. See you at supper."

Punch watched him leave. Then he turned back to the table and slowly, methodically began to carve up the lamb.

Punch's hands were steady, but he was conscious of a great racking dryness in his throat. Like an echo, Donny Green's heavy, rasping voice reverberated in his ears. It was the same voice that had said, "We're guards on this place. This is state property." It was the same.

At first, on hearing it, he had felt a great surge of triumph. But now the elation was gone and a cold, dismal sense of unpleasant duty crept into him. There was no doubt, no conflict in his thoughts. There was only the passionless certainty that he had a job to do. An ugly, loathsome job. Not quick, getting it over with fast—it couldn't be done that way. It had to be a cat-and-mouse game, with death coming slowly, after torture. Any other way, the wrong wouldn't be righted. It wouldn't clear up the debt Donny Green owed Dyanna.

During the next five days Punch learned more of Donny Green's habits than he had ever known of any man's. Nightly, as soon as he had finished dinner with Dyanna and Aunt Carrie, he put on a loose-fitting coat, large enough to conceal beneath it a meat cleaver tied to his waist with a leather thong from one of his hunting boots, and made his way to the Green house. There he lurked outside, on the street, careful to stay out of the light of the corner street lamp—waiting calmly, patiently, for Donny to start out on his nightly rounds. He trailed him, silently as an Indian trailing game in the forest, through the dark streets of the town. Watching him leaning negligently against drugstore counters, flirting with girls, waiting patiently outside while Donny made his invariable evening call at Fritz Bachman's place. Learned, by watching through the big square window, what sort of pool game Donny played. Followed him by devious ways back to Jinktown, where Donny's girl-of-the-moment lived. Punch was unhurried. He even found time to take a certain wry amusement in Donny's elaborate caution to avoid being seen when he headed for Jinktown. He would stop at a corner, look up and down the street furtively, and start whistling in an elaborately carefree manner before he turned abruptly and ducked into a street that led to Myra Potter's house.

Thinks he's too good for the Potters, Punch would think contemptuously. Donny wouldn't even go up to the door and ask for the girl. He stayed outside, near the gate, and whistled to her until she came running out. All dressed up, Punch noticed, her eyes alight, smiling—pathetically eager. Proud to have been noticed at all by this handsome, worldly Donny Green.

Proud! Punch smiled his crooked smile, the first time he saw her, thinking that he would be doing Myra Potter a favor, too, when finally the chance came to get his hands on Donny.

He followed them for several nights in succession, learned that they did their furtive love-making in an abandoned, dilapidated house on the corner of Hill and Third, down close to the Negro section. Standing hidden in the shadows beneath a window of the old house, he heard the little drama enacted nightly. The drinks, first, the clink of bottle against tin cup as the corn whisky from Donny's bottle was poured. The first two nights of Punch's vigil Donny had to coax a little, to beg Myra to take the drinks. "Be a good sport, baby. Come on—do you good, sugar." Then whispered words, the frightened questions from Myra, the confident, laughing reassurance in Donny's heavy voice. Then, usually, a laughing scuffle that ended abruptly. . . .

On the floor, the bare floor, Punch thought in disgust. Like animals.

On the fifth night—Saturday—Donny took with him not just a flat bottle of whisky in his pocket, but a full gallon jug, which he hid by the fence when he called to Myra, then picked up and carried along with them to the old house. Punch, hidden and listening, heard Donny say, "We can just leave it here, see? Hide it somewhere and then we'll always have a little drink ready and waitin'."

"Oh, you can't do that, honey. Kids play all over this house all the time. They'll find it for sure." Myra laughed. "If you want that corn you sure better take it home with you."

Later, when they were ready to leave, the question of what to do with the cumbersome jug came up again. "Aw, I'll just leave it here until I take you back, anyway. I can stop by and pick it up on my way home." Donny was a little drunk tonight. His voice had thickened and he spoke slowly, painstakingly.

Punch, hearing Donny's decision, knew that the waiting was over. No excitement stirred him now. He waited calmly, crouching in the darkness, until Donny came back.

When Donny ran up the steps and through the door, Punch slipped around the corner of the house and crept in behind him.

"Who's that?" Donny whirled, jug in hand, as Punch closed the door behind him.

They were in the big front parlor of the old house. It had a musty, airless smell, faintly redolent of damp ashes and rotting wood. Enough moonlight penetrated the dusty windowpanes to give the room a hazy, smoky appearance, and through the opaque whiteness Punch could see the wide bare floorboards, the torn strips of brown wallpaper that hung out into the room, the black hollowness of the yawning fireplace on his left. He squinted carefully, watching the tall figure of Donny Green become suddenly still there in the far corner just beyond the window. Slowly, Punch moved forward, the cleaver in his hand.

"It's me," he said quietly, almost soothingly. "Punch Rayne. Remember?"

Donny gasped faintly. The jug dropped from his hand and bounced, rolling noisily on the floor. "Oh—" With an obvious attempt to regain composure Donny spoke loudly, discordantly. "Oh—Punch Rayne. Sure. You scared me there for a minute. What th' hell you doin' in here, boy?" He essayed a laugh, took a step forward.

Slowly, smiling, Punch raised the meat cleaver so that it caught the light from the window.

Donny stopped short, his eyes fastened on the glinting metal in Punch's hand. His voice faded to a whisper as he spoke. "What you got there?"

Punch kept his voice soft. This was as good as he had always thought it would be. Just as satisfying, just as easy, just as power-filling. There it was, the terror he had dreamed of putting into the man's eyes. The nervous, shaky voice. "It's a cleaver," Punch said gently. "To kill you with." He advanced slowly across the room, relishing the tight grin he felt pulling at his mouth, taking delight in Donny's every backward, unsteady step toward the corner. "Remember Dyanna Slater?" he asked.

He had planned to recall the whole incident, to remind the man of every little detail of horror, to bring it back, make it fresh in the man's mind so that he would be thinking of it when he died. But now he saw that it wasn't necessary. Just the mention of Dyanna's name had been enough. Donny Green's shocked, fear-ridden face said plainly that he remembered.

"I—I didn't do it Punch. I swear to God I didn't—" Donny was abject in his pleading, his eyes moving from the cleaver to Punch's

[242]

face and back again. "I swear—wait a minute—I swear I didn't have anything to do with it!"

A quick, vigorous impatience welled up in Punch. "Shut up," he said through clenched teeth. "You dirty son of a bitch!" He rushed forward, the cleaver upraised.

Donny shouted feebly and ducked aside. He tried to run past Punch toward the door.

Punch whirled and with one agile stoop, one fast, firm stroke, brought the cleaver down on Donny's left foot. Donny fell, screaming, and clawed at the floor. He tried to crawl, dragging the almost severed foot behind him. Looking back, he saw the trail of blood the foot was leaving, and screamed again.

Here was something Punch had not taken into account. The man's screams. Even in that split second while he hesitated, alarmed, debating what to do about stopping the dangerous noise, he wondered that he could have overlooked a thing so obvious.

Donny was lying on the floor, crawling forward, his neck stretched out toward the door through which he hoped help would come. Dispassionately, taking deliberate aim with the cleaver, Punch chopped off the screaming head.

Why, this was easy, he thought wonderingly. He was unmoved, unrepelled by the sight of the gushing blood. Murder was easy; it was no more than cutting off pork chops. He stared down at the corpse, regretting only that he had had to kill Donny in a hurry, that he had missed the ecstasy of dismembering him slowly, starting with the feet and moving upward. He had even planned, those long sleepless nights, to talk to the man as he killed him, and to wait patiently, if the man fainted, until consciousness returned.

Idly, not knowing what to do with the bloody cleaver, he threw it carelessly into a corner of the room. It clattered heavily, the noise unexpectedly loud in the deep silence of the empty house. Punch stood for a moment looking down at his bloodstained clothes, at the man lying on the floor before him. Thoughtfully, he gave the body an experimental kick, then turned and walked out of the house.

It was well past midnight, and the town was quiet. Punch walked unhurriedly through the streets homeward, feeling the soft fall night close gently about him—comfortingly enfolding him, like a blanket. Since leaving the deserted house he had become aware of a change in himself, a quickening of his senses such as he had never experienced before. For the first time in his life he looked up at the moon and saw it, truly saw it. He was conscious in a flash of the fact that the round moon looked down not only on him but on millions of others, all over half a world. He could see those millions in his mind's eye, those sleeping quietly in their beds, those up and about like himself. In houses and out of doors, thinking, moving, loving, hating, doing all the things that human beings do. The moon kept a sad, knowing silence—it was quieter than a whisper, and the light it shed was beautiful. It was strange that he had never noticed it before. As he walked, feeling the moonlight pouring down on him like some soft but tangible substance, he became conscious also of a scent that came to him faintly, delicious to breathe. He identified it as leaf-smoke from damp piles of burning leaves. He remembered now that nearly every lawn in town had been raked clean, that this was the time of year when hands pulled rakes, piled brown leaves into mounds, set them on fire.

Nearing the little house in Jinktown that was home to him, he reached out one hand, idly, and let it run along the top of a paling fence. It produced a pleasurable, throbbing sensation in his fingers, a sensation he remembered now from his childhood when this fence-feeling had been a part of him. He took a strange, sad delight in the simple act—perhaps because he felt instinctively that these things, the moon and smell of burning leaves and the running of hands along a fence, were soon to be taken from him.

Abruptly, jerking his hand off the fence, he faced the fact that he had been trying to dodge for the last ten minutes. By this time next week he would probably be dead. They would have caught him and hung him, by then.

But Dyanna would have money to live on, a lot of money. He had fixed it so the insurance was safe.

The door was unlocked. Punch let himself in quietly, thankful to learn from the silence in the house that Dyanna and Aunt Carrie were asleep in their two small bedrooms that opened out of the main room of the house. They had left the fire carefully banked so that he would have its faint warmth to undress by. Quickly he raked the ashes off the coals, tossed some kindling from the box at his side onto the fire. As the flames started up he took off his clothes—the coat, the shirt, the trousers—and threw them one at a time into the now crackling blaze. They burned slowly, smoking a great deal, sending off a pungent odor of burning wool.

He was standing in his underclothes, watching the fire, when Aunt Carrie appeared in the doorway. Her tall, spare body was encased in a flannel wrapper. "Punch—what—" She stopped, her eyes fastened on the burning garments.

"I'm burning my clothes. They had blood on them," he said simply. "I killed a man."

She said nothing for a moment, but advanced across the room slowly, her eyes on his face. "No," she protested, quietly, unbelieving. "No, Punch."

"I found out who one of them was," he said tonelessly. "Donny Green."

Aunt Carrie's shoulders drooped suddenly; she put out one hand to the back of a chair for support. She looked old. Tired. "What are you goin' to do, son?"

Punch gazed into the fire and said nothing.

She reached out to him, caught his arm. "You got to get out of town, Punch. Quick. Don't you know," she whispered, "what they'll do to you?"

He nodded. Yes, he knew—but he had always known, and it hadn't made any difference. He was sure Aunt Carrie couldn't understand, and so he made no attempt to explain. How could she know that to go on living *without* finding and killing the man was far, far worse than to die knowing that at least he had done what he had to do. Aunt Carrie believed in sin. She probably thought he had sinned in killing —how could he make her understand that not to have killed would have been a greater sin? How could he make *her* understand when at times, looking forward to this night, he had been unable to understand it himself?

But Aunt Carrie demanded no explanation. Quietly she started about her work much as she would have started about any other household job. She brought out a great armful of Punch's warmest clothes, demanding that he get into them. She brought out his rifle from its resting place in the corner, and checked it herself to see that it was loaded. Then she went to the corner of the room that served as a kitchen and ransacked the cupboard for food, which she wrapped in newspaper and placed in an empty flour sack. She added the small amount of ammunition he had for the rifle.

"Hurry, son," she pleaded when she had done all that she could. "Git as far as you can before they set out to find you." She kissed his cheek tenderly and pressed his shoulders comfortingly. "I don't think Dyanna ought to know," she whispered. "Not yet."

"Not yet," he agreed, thinking that there would be time enough for Dyanna to know after it was all over—after he either got away, made it to St. Louis, or was captured and killed. Either way, it was better than to have her held in the awful suspense that he knew the next few days would hold for him and Aunt Carrie.

Dressed and ready to leave, he tiptoed into his and Dyanna's room to lean over the bed and take a long look at her sleeping face. He was in terror lest she wake, and have to be told what was in store for them. Yet, blending in with the terror as he looked at her, there was a sort of pride, a feeling of manly worthiness that he had never achieved before. She had been wronged, and he, her husband, had avenged her. That was as it should be. This night, with all its ugliness, had made him a man. He had reached fulfillment.

Even in the face of disaster there was less of sorrow in Punch than had ever been before.

He shed no tears, although the sight of the calmly sleeping Dyanna wrenched his heart. He left the room, picked up his gun, and went out into the night. He turned back, once, to see Aunt Carrie, a lamp in her hand, staring after him through a window. Then he walked on, calmly, into the shadows.

Punch was awakened two days later by the sound of voices. He woke abruptly, sitting upright and reaching for his rifle all in one quick motion of his body. They were men's voices. The voices he had been waiting to hear, it seemed to him, for an eternity. The angry, muttering voices of a posse, which came nearer and nearer and grew more menacing even as he sat still there on the ground and listened for a moment before rising. He stood up slowly, careful to make no sound, and moved quietly behind the trunk of the biggest cedar in the grove—the one with the low-hanging limb that had knocked off his cap, frightening him, last night in the dark when he had stumbled in here to rest.

Some of the voices he recognized. There was old Sheriff Abbott's, louder than the rest, a voice he had heard—and even admired, because it was so deep and rich—all his life. There was Bud Martin's, and Peewee Egger's and Varley Craig's. It was strange to be standing here, tense, his hand gripping his rifle, in sudden leg-weakening terror of voices he had known all his life. Some of those men he had hunted with, more than once. Some he had, many years ago, called friends. Now they were enemies, out to capture or kill him, hating him as if he were some sort of monster—not understanding that he was still Punch Rayne, knowing only that he was a murderer. That's what he was to them, he knew. A murderer. Even as he moved backward, cautiously, to the edge of the grove, forcing his tired legs to seek whatever escape offered, the thought that they all hated him, now, and *feared* him, made him feel somehow sad. Sad, and bewildered.

The grove was surrounded. He discovered that, quickly, as he heard other voices, different ones, coming from behind. They must have made up their minds that he was in here. Someone, some farmer abroad in the night, or some child looking out of a bedroom window, must have seen him head this way. Punch braced himself. Now he would have to fight. He would have to kill some of these men before he could get away. He didn't want to kill them. He had nothing against any of them—they were doing what they thought was their duty. They didn't understand. They thought he was crazy, and a murderer.

Suddenly one of the voices coming from the back of the grove stood out above all the rest—a high, childish voice that snatched at Punch's attention and brought him up short. He narrowed his eyes, listening—and a great excitement surged up in him. That voice, though he didn't know its owner, was one that he recognized. It was the voice that had said, "You got no business up here at night."

Punch, hearing the voice, identifying it, was no longer bewildered. To have found the other one, too! He was exultant. Quickly, he swung up into the biggest tree, clutching his rifle, and climbed silently until he was high enough to look down on the oncoming men.

All the fear died out of him, leaving in its place a fierce, savage delight in what he was doing. He peered through the branches of the tree, carefully, turning his head slowly to avoid attracting attention from below, until he found the man with the high voice.

It was Neal. Elwee Neal! Punch remembered, now, having known Elwee in school. He had disappeared from sight and consciousness a long time ago, but here he was, still in Kings Row, a grown man now. And the possessor of what Punch had learned to call "the second voice." Elwee Neal!

Gently, smiling, his own terror forgotten, Punch raised his rifle and took careful aim. The rifle *pinged* at the pressure of his finger. Neal, stealthily advancing toward the grove between two other men, threw his hands up into the air and plunged forward to the ground. The bullet had struck him between the eyes.

The other men fell flat on the ground or ran for cover into near-by bushes. There were shouts and orders as the news spread that they had cornered the man they were after. "He killed Neal," someone yelled. "Shoot him on sight!"

"He's crazy—kill him, kill him!"

Punch, sliding haphazardly down the tree, could hear Sheriff Abbott raising his big voice above the clamor, trying to make himself heard. No one would listen. They were too intent, Punch knew bitterly, too crazily, excitedly intent on finding and killing *him*. Their voices sounded happy, as though this were rare sport.

All right, he thought in a burst of wild anger, *if it's a fight you want you'll get it!*

He was crying with rage. The fools. The blind fools.

Recklessly, not knowing or caring what he did, he ran forward to the edge of the grove and came out of it, firing the rifle at first one man and then another. Bud Martin fell, a bullet wound in his shoulder, and Varley Craig yelled as a bullet creased his cheek. Punch was taking more careful aim at another man, a man he didn't know, when Sheriff Abbott raised his pistol and shot him through the head.

9

For days Kings Row had been thrown into a ferment of excited comment and conjecture by the Punch Rayne-Donny Green tragedy. Nothing in Kings Row history had stirred so much excitement—unless it had been the Tower murder and suicide, which was brought freshly to mind by the current affair. But that had been a mystery, still unsolved, while this—why, it was clear as the nose on your face. The boy had suddenly gone crazy, that was evident. But everybody was talking about it—everybody sympathizing with the Greens, the Neals, and with Punch's little Jinktown wife.

The talk around Matt Fuller's feed store had its own tang.

"Looks to me like Fulmer Green's chickens is comin' home to roost. That was a turrible thing about Donny," Matt remarked.

"Turrible, but Punch Rayne never had nothin' against Fulmer, shorely. Reckon nobody'll ever find out how come Punch to do such a thing."

"Crazy—crazy as a loon."

"Yeah, he was crazy all right. If he hadn't of been he'd o' beat it for them river hills. They never would of got him down there."

"Bet he never once thought of that," Dave commented.

"Folks down in the river hills wouldn't turn him in. Them hills is full of outlaws, I bet my hat. He'd of been all right if he got down there 'mongst all them folks."

"You never can tell. There's plenty law-abidin' folks down along the river same as anywhere else. They wouldn't hide no crazy folks— not if they knowed it."

"Punch wasn't no more crazy than you are. He shore had sense enough to keep up his life-insurance payments."

"You don't say!"

Matt shifted the lump of tobacco from one cheek to the other. "Yep. He kep' up them two policies ever since the day he got married."

"Well, I be dog. How much his wife git?"

"Hold yore hat! *Ten thousand dollars!*"

"Good Lord! That's as much as most of them bankers carry."

"Matt, what you reckon made him think about takin' out insurance, young as he was?"

"Dunno. Old man Dyer told me that Punch asked him about takin' out insurance time he got married. Dyer sent him to see Judge Holloway about it so's nobody could put nothin' over on him."

"Good thing he did. If Judge Holloway had it fixed up for him they shore will git the money. Smartest lawyer in Kings Row."

"Dyer told me the Judge didn't charge Punch a red cent."

"What I wonder is how Punch kep' up the payments. It takes money to carry that much insurance."

Matt hitched up his galluses and spat into the coal bucket. "That little wife of his has been helpin' out right smart. She's been takin' in sewin' and they tell me she makes mighty near all the children's clothes in Kings Row."

"How do you know so much about it, Matt?"

"She tol' my wife that Mrs. McHugh give her a sewin' machine soon after her an' Punch got married and she's been sewin' for folks ever since."

"Well, now, I'm glad she's got all that money to live on."

"I jest can't figger out how he come to chop Donny up that-a-way."

Sam Winters, gravedigger and deputy sheriff and county hangman, who had just walked up to the group, heard Dave's comment.

"You know what *I* think?" Sam asked importantly.

"Naw. What do you think?"

"I think it was some sort of a personal grudge."

"What makes you think so?"

"He done too complete a job for it not to have been planned."

"What you reckon he had against Donny?"

"I don't know, but Punch was a broodin' sort of fellow and like as not he'd been cooking it up for a long time. Lord, what a sight that was! I never had a worse job on my hands. Me and that new undertaker, Morry Tiggert, got him put together purty good, though. Fulmer mighty near went crazy."

"I'll bet! It must have got his goat not to have nobody to prosecute like he done Benny Singer."

"Yep. Guess it's a good thing they got Punch when they did. I shore would have had another hangin' on my hands." Sam's tone was slightly regretful.

"Sam, you old skunk, I believe you like breakin' necks," Matt Fuller said jokingly.

"Naw, I never did like it. I ain't had it to do in a long time now. Sometimes I think I don't believe in capital punishment."

"Aw, come off, Sam. That's why you kep' the deputy's job all these years—just so you could swing 'em."

Sam turned a baleful look on Ricks and received an apologetic smile in return.

"We miss Donny an' Elwee around here. Seems funny not to have 'em hangin' about."

"Uncle Sam was gonna get 'em, anyhow."

"Not as long as Fulmer was on the job!"

There was a burst of laughter. They were relieved to get off the subject of the late gruesome tragedy.

"I see in the paper McKay Pomeroy got married down in South C'lina."

"Yep. Didn't know the kid had it in him."

"You never can tell. He ain't no more'n twenty year old, is he?"

"Jest about, I'd say. But comes a war an' they ain't no holdin' 'em."

"Well, they tell me he's a lieutenant already."

"Wouldn't surprise me none. He's a smart kid."

"Seems to me there's plenty of gals around here he could of married."

"I don't know. There's something queer about them Pomeroys. Take Ross, now. He's a captain in the army an' that pretty little Laneer girl jest a burnin' up for him an' he's skittish as a unbroke colt."

"Yeah, he acts like he's scared of gittin' hitched up. If he don't hurry up some other feller's gonna grab that girl. She's a good-looker."

"I hear her ma's a hellcat, though. Not many folks would want to get mixed up with her."

"They wouldn't be after her ma long as the gal was around."

Another wave of laughter greeted Matt's pleasantry.

"If Kings Row ain't got nothin' else," Ricks Darden said fervently, "it shore has got a lot of likely-lookin' women."

"Now you're talkin'," Dave Brennan agreed. "Looks like they get purtier and purtier as I git older and older."

There was another guffaw. Sam Winters had had enough of this lighter comment, so he grunted and departed.

"I don't see how Sam Winters sleeps at night," Dave said, looking after Sam.

"Foot! He's hard as nails. Can't nothin' faze Sam."

"I never could abide the idea of executin' folks, no matter what they done."

"Well, *somebody's* got to do it. You can't turn killers loose to keep on killin'."

"Reckon not—no, I reckon not."

When so stark a tragedy is played out it is felt in the air. There are unexpected silences in the easy talk on the street corners, little halts of rhythm, fleeting lacunae in the daily gossip.

Parris Mitchell's sensitive mind felt this as soon as he got back to Kings Row. The details of the affair had been spread across the front pages of all the newspapers. He knew at once the truth of the matter, but he had been wondering if the real cause of the killing of Donny Green had been discovered.

It was a week after the tragedy when he arrived. He had reported immediately to his chief at the hospital, made an afternoon checkup on his patients, and planned to stop for a call on Carrie Slater and Dyanna before dinnertime.

He found Dyanna ill from exhaustion. Parris tried to talk with her but she turned her face away and wept hopelessly and continuously. Carrie Slater closed the door of Dyanna's room softly behind her and spoke cautiously.

"She's been like that ever since it happened, Doctor. I been waitin' to ask you whether I better tell her that Donny Green was the one Punch had been waitin' to find."

"Does she have any idea of it?"

"No, sir. Punch ain't never mentioned it, but I knowed he was listenin' to see if he could find out who—who done that awful thing to Dyanna. Well, he found out, at last," she said grimly, "but he got killed too."

"What about Dyanna? What does she think?"

"She thinks he went crazy all of a sudden. He never let on to her."

"I think she ought to know that Punch died trying to avenge her wrong. He deserves that. She should have the satisfaction of knowing that Punch fixed it so that no one will ever hurt her again by *word or deed*."

"You think we ought to tell the truth about everything that happened? They been pesterin' me considerable, tryin' to find out whether Punch had been actin' crazy or whether he had anything against Donny Green."

"What did you tell them?"

"I told 'em they knew much as *I* did. I wasn't goin' to tell 'em nothin' unless you said I ought. Miss Randy told 'em Punch had been actin' queer for some time."

"As long as everyone is convinced that Punch was insane, you'd better leave it at that, and the talk about the whole matter will die out. Punch wasn't really in his right mind. Keeping the story quiet can't do any harm now."

"Yes, sir. I'm sure that's best. Punch had lots of insurance, Doctor. I wish you'd let us pay you for all you done for us. You never would take nothin' before."

"No, Mrs. Slater. I've been glad to do what I could. I'm glad he had the insurance for Dyanna."

"Yes, sir. He took it out when him and Dynnie got married an' they both worked hard to keep up the payments. It's a mighty good thing for Dynnie. Judge Holloway, he's tendin' to everything—him an' Miss Randy."

"Does Dyanna get enough sleep?"

"No, sir. I'm right worried about her. She just lies there an' cries an' can't sleep. I never seen anybody grieve so."

"I'm going to send you some medicine for her. It's a bromide and should quiet her and give her some rest. Let me know how she is, and if you need me, I'll come."

Parris was deeply thoughtful as he drove away from the little Jinktown house.

This tragedy, he thought, started several generations back. He imagined some power in the universe making the arrangement, slowly setting the stage, carefully building a situation until everything was ready, and then sitting back to watch the tragedy play itself out. It was a dramatic speculation, he said to himself, and one that would have pleased his old Calvinistic grandfather.

But surely there must exist in the universe a conscious and maleficent fate, his musing continued, else how could it happen that a man had ten thousand roads of fate to choose from and yet arrived at his moment of destiny punctual to a split second?

His mind reverted to the particular case at hand. He wondered how Punch had learned the truth—and if he might have made a mistake.

No one would ever know now. Fulmer must have been hard hit by this frightful thing. And Hazel. He wondered if Hazel had been fond of Donny.

10

The wind was driving up a feathery violet-black cloud from the west, and Parris thought there would be rain before the afternoon was over, but he decided he would go to see Randy. He had not seen her since his return from Washington.

"Elise, let's run over to see Randy."

"Oh, dear! I suppose I could go, but I'd planned to get this assignment done for the Red Cross."

"Any particular hurry about it?"

"Well, Anna is helping me and I'd like to get it finished today."

"You've been hard at it ever since I got home. Why not take the afternoon off?"

"I volunteered for this work." She indicated with a gesture the long table loaded with materials—heavy dark blue woolens for children's clothing. "I—I prefer it to working at headquarters."

He looked at her with concern, and she lowered her head over her work as a slow flush crept upward from her throat. Neither of them referred to the last meeting she had attended at headquarters.

"You run along to see Randy, Parris. Give her my love and explain about this work, won't you?"

"It looks threatening," he said doubtfully. "If it storms I may be late getting back. Phone me there if you want me."

Elise went to the door with him and they stood for a few moments looking down the avenue. The cedars dragged toward the east, complainingly, and the row of Lombardy poplars beyond the terrace wall bent low but whipped back furiously when released for a moment from the importunate drive of the wind.

"Sure you aren't afraid of the storm, sweet?" Parris asked, wondering if she had quite conquered her strange fear of the wind.

"This isn't going to be a storm, and Anna and I shall be too busy to notice the weather," she assured him.

As Parris left his car at Randy's gate, sudden lightning tore the sky into tatters and the wind dashed about him in mad circles. He ran up the walk and reached the porch just as the slanting rain came driving across the hills.

"You couldn't have timed a visit better, Parris," Randy greeted him. "I was feeling very sorry for myself."

"That's a luxury you seldom indulge yourself in, Randy. What's the trouble?"

"Just sad because I don't know how to comfort little Dyanna. She's inconsolable."

"I went down to see her the day I got back. She's in a pitiable state. I know you'll do all you can for her—your heart being as big as the—the universe."

"I'll bring her up to stay with me for a while, I think."

"A little later, Randy. She's too ill now. Wait a bit."

"Just as you say. I'm glad you're back to look after her."

"I believe you need looking after, yourself. Your eyes have an Irish smudge. Have you been getting enough sleep?"

"Well—" she began in an explanatory voice.

"Sit there where I can look at you. I've been missing you."

"I'm glad. And now I want to hear all about your trip. You're getting to be a very important personage, Dr. Mitchell!"

"Got plenty of time?"

"All there is."

"At Washington the newspapers were having a field day over the predicament of the police department and the administration. Some suffragettes went on a hunger strike after being arrested for 'disturbing the peace.' I was called in as an alienist and the whole business dumped in my lap. My testimony gave the police an excuse to release the prisoners. I really had a good time—especially with the reporters and columnists. It was amusing."

"Not to me," Randy said spiritedly. "Of course I can't see what they hoped to win by a hunger strike—"

"Publicity, angel, don't you see?"

"But they are right in demanding attention. The time has surely come for—well, for demonstrations, if necessary."

"Dyed-in-the-wool suffragette, aren't you?"

"Absolutely."

"I'm always amazed at your intensity, Randy."

"My Irish blood! The Irish are born politicians. Did you ever notice how many Clancys and Rileys and Murphys there are in politics?"

"Now that you mention it—"

"There's a reason for it. It's talk—and a desire to meddle in other people's affairs."

"Maybe you're right—but I must say I like your gift of gab. You're so articulate—"

"Articulate, maybe, but we aren't noted for accuracy. Fluency is more our line."

"There's a lot to be said for fluency, as far as that goes."

"Demonstrate. Tell me how you like the South."

He recounted all that he thought would interest her. A warm content wrapped them about like a cloak.

A silence fell on them, unexpectedly, and he sat looking at her in the darkening room, feeling her nearness in a way he had never been conscious of before. He rose and walked to the window and stood looking out.

Randy lighted the lamp on the table beside her. The storm was receding but she could hear the sibilant whisper of the uneasy trees and the gentle brush of rain against the windows.

Turning back to the softly lighted room, Parris looked again at Randy, so still and silent. A phrase sprang to life in his mind and he was startled to hear his own voice saying, "Dear Keeper of the Bridge."

"What did you say, Parris?"

"I was thinking aloud—a bad habit I have." His laugh had little mirth in it and she looked quickly in his direction. What she saw constricted her throat. In God's name, what was causing that bitterness?

She crossed the room to him.

"Randy," he said, and his voice was very tender, "I need your faith like a crutch."

"My faith has always been here—waiting on your need."

"Isn't this a crazy world?" he asked surprisingly."

"Surely not for you, Parris. You have things so tabulated, so arranged. Your world should be completely in order."

"It isn't. It's a patchwork, particolored—utterly without design."

"That's not like you as I know you—as all your friends know you."

[256]

"Do you think I've never known disappointment or disillusionment? No one escapes the melancholy of self-revelation."

He placed his hands on her shoulders and drew her toward him. "Randy, if I deceive *myself,* no matter how secretly, I have endangered my inner liberty. I *need* you, yes—but it would be more honest if I say I *want* you."

All she felt for Parris threatened to engulf her. Randy did not trust herself to speak.

Parris felt her desire for him even while he tried to still the demands of his own blood. Abruptly he dropped his hands from her shoulders and went to lean against the mantel. Randy slowly walked back to her chair.

Why, Parris thought resentfully, must his life always be like this? He had often seen in the lives of others the blurring and overlapping that is more common. For him there had always been this violence, this sudden and sundering change—the past going down like a stone in deep water; the future without help or guidance from anything that had gone before.

He studied her face with its soft, irregular lines, newly aware of its loveliness. He moved, shrugged off the mood of intensity, and a half-mocking quality came in its place. Randy, noting the change, felt as though a thin, sharp wind had struck across her heart. But at the sound of his voice, her doubts melted.

"I'm going, Randy—because I'm afraid to stay. I haven't said a single thing that I want to say. Do you think you might forget what I *did* say?" His voice carried a caress that was almost physical.

"I'll treasure it until the day I die—but we'll not speak of it again— ever. It's stopped raining. I'll walk down to the gate with you."

Together they went out into the early dusk. The earth seemed to press its wet face against the day as the lilac evening came on. Smoke rising from Kings Row's chimneys reached toward the thin slip of a moon which had broken through the scudding clouds.

"It looks the same," she said, surprise in her voice.

"It has changed, infinitely," he said quietly.

He closed the low gate behind him, then turned and faced her, his desire for her urgent in his eyes, his hands clenched tightly on the gate that separated them.

"Am I condemned to silence, Randy?"

"How can I say what is right for you? But for *me*, I shall say this once, that I have belonged to you for a long time. This once I want to say I love you. Perhaps, having said it, I shall not lie awake whispering it into my pillow—and *ashamed*."

"Randy—"

"Don't say anything, Parris. I don't believe I could stand it."

"Then, I *am* condemned to silence?"

"Not condemned. Committed, perhaps. No, my dear, don't touch me. Not ever again. Every woman in love is apt to overestimate her own strength."

She went swiftly toward the house without looking back.

Parris drove through the rain-drenched streets and out the Camperville road. When he reached the edge of the town he stopped his car at the top of the hill and looked back at the lights down there in Kings Row. But he could not think of the town as he had so often done from this point. He tried to force his disciplined mind into the familiar channels, but found he could not do it. He made an impatient gesture of dismissal—all those people going about strange and unimportant tasks down there!

He deliberately summoned up old memories—but they could not blot out the fresher memory of the flame in Randy's eyes, the flush in Randy's face, the warm, sensuous lips so close to his own.

He knew that something terrible had happened—as though a lightly hung sword had fallen. He looked at his fingers in a dazed sort of way, remembering they had touched Randy's shoulders a little while ago.

This love was surely something different from anything he had ever known before. Was he in love with *love,* and *sensation*—was this a purely pagan, conscienceless, amoral compulsion? Was he possessed by the very glory of the flesh, the pent-up impulses of the earth?

The blinding beauty of what he felt for Randy was terrible, oppressive like the weight of dreams. He knew that he had ceased to be reasonable because he could no longer analyze his emotions.

"Darling, darling—Randy darling," he said under his breath.

Sickeningly he realized that he had never felt for his wife what he felt for Randy. There was something else here—an emotional height he had not reached in all the years since he'd become a man. His mind circled round and round Elise. He tried to recall what he had first felt for her when he fell in love with her.

There had been, he thought now, the sweet and beautiful burgeoning of a gentle spring—perhaps no more than timid intimations of spring in an ordered and controlled garden. But it had not blossomed into the full warmth of summer. And yet, his mind turned toward her with the feeling that he was opening a door into a well-known, well-loved room. He knew deep in his soul that there was no escape from ten thousand memories. Everything was so entwined with her that to sever her from anything was to destroy all. The steady beauty of her belief had been the one perfectly sustaining thing that had upheld him through these difficult years of adjustment—years that had been particularly trying because of his own diffident nature. He would have been forlorn without her.

His thoughts of Elise opened out fanwise, thinned like lace, and a cool peace enveloped him for a few moments as his mind veered away from the emotional dilemma that had overtaken him.

A growing consciousness of smothering pain drew itself into a pinpoint of unbearable white flame—Randy!

He dropped his head to his folded arms and sat there without moving for a long time. Then he drove back to von Eln, deliberately avoiding the street where she lived.

That night he sat at his piano, playing for hours—Tchaikovsky, Chopin, Beethoven.

Randy re-entered the house which had been her home since shortly after Drake's death, a home that she had made into a cheerful, charming, hospitable place and which just now seemed unbearably lonely.

She stared blindly about at the familiar furnishings of the chintz-bright living room. She touched a table here, a lampshade there, the mantel edge where Parris had leaned and said, "I'm going—because I'm afraid to stay." Then she sat down in the big armchair that had held Parris so short a time ago. She turned her face until her cheek pressed against the cushion where his head had rested. Her eyes were hot and dry and she longed for the relief of tears. Tears? No, she had no reason for tears. Not now.

Parris loved her—and that knowledge wrapped her with a certain warmth and splendor. She thought of him as he went about his work day after day. She could see the concentrated interest he brought to bear on every individual case he considered, the absorption with which he turned to each new problem and set about solving it. She wished she might in some way have a part in his life, in his work, but she knew that could not be.

But *Parris loved her*—and her spirit expanded. No one else would ever know it, but *she* knew and she felt her life take on a unique importance. She must live up to that love.

Parris loved her—and the knowledge gave her a new dignity in her own eyes. Yet her blood stirred and protested and her nerves felt exposed. She was dismayed to find her emotions so in the fore of her thinking. She must quiet the clamor of her heart against the decrees of her head by the sharp denial of any shred of hope.

Parris loved her—yet all they could have was that look that had passed between them—a transfiguring, transcendent understanding.

But what of her love for him? That she could not think clearly about—not yet. She turned fiercely away from the knowledge that she had already met defeat. She could not muster a single defense against her desperate need of him. This terrifying onslaught of elemental forces had crashed through with a weight and urgency that found her unguarded and helpless.

She stirred restlessly in her chair and the tears came. Even as she turned out the lights and went slowly up the stairs, she made no effort to check them.

II

Parris had been reminded by McKay Pomeroy that the boys had not given up their hope of solving their father's strange compulsion. He was expecting the call from Ross when it came.

Ross, newly made *Captain* Pomeroy, called from Camp Pike to ask if Parris could be free to go with him at once to visit Miss Dixie, the old aunt down in the river hills. Captain Pomeroy had been granted a leave of two weeks before reporting to the Eastern seaboard and would reach Kings Row on Sunday night.

Parris readily agreed to go. He tried to think if there were any new angle from which to approach the question. Suddenly he leaned forward and picked up the desk calendar. Yes, the moon would be full on

Monday—and it was on Monday they were to go. Perhaps the timing of the visit was a stroke of luck. It was just a chance—but it might happen to work.

Early as it was when they left Kings Row, it promised to be one of those rare summer days following a storm, when the air is cool and wine-sweet. Driving through a rich, prosperous farming section of the state, it seemed incredible that the country could be at war.

Kings Row itself seemed strangely denuded, so much of its life had centered around its young men. They were no longer there.

Parris noted the fine, fresh coloring of the face of the young captain at his side, the strong, determined set of his jaw, the imposing breadth of his muscular shoulders, and thought: With troops made up of raw young recruits like Ross and McKay, we are breaking the heart and morale of the seasoned, arrogant Germans. Americans waken slowly, but their tenacity and ingenuity once aroused and set free are astonishing the world.

"Ross, look at all this." Parris made a sweeping gesturing. "Don't you think it surprising to see things so untouched by war? We read every day of the destruction of cities and forests and—men, and just look at this country!"

"The Middle West is prospering, Doctor. We are getting rich out here. The world has suddenly found out it needs *mules,* and we raise bigger and better mules than any other section of the United States. It's a fine thing for us that we can provide the army with something of real importance."

"We're supplying a good many fine young soldiers—like yourself."

"Thanks—but I'm not much of a fighter. I'm just an engineer. But I'm going across right away. That's why I feel I have to get this business about Dad cleared up, Dr. Mitchell. I won't be a very good soldier until I have a little more peace of mind about Bethany."

"Why don't you go ahead and marry her, Ross? I assure you you've nothing to fear. McKay believed me."

Ross' jaw took on a grimmer line and the car shot forward as he smashed down on the accelerator.

"Hey, there, are you trying to commit suicide?" Parris was really alarmed.

"Sorry, Doctor. I'm in a hurry to get down to the crossing."

"I understand that, Ross, but an hour's difference isn't worth taking

[261]

too much risk on these roads. When the war is over there'll be lots of work for you young engineers in this part of the world. Improving these roads; building railroads; flood control. Do you plan to stay here, Ross?"

"I'm not sure. Sometimes when I think of the Middle West bulging with opportunity, I think it's the only place in the world I'd want to live. And then I think of the ignorance and the prejudice and the dull misery that you can find over nearly all of it, and I change my mind. It destroys my—my provincial loyalty."

"Not provincial, Ross. *Regional* is the word. And let me tell you that to be regional in one's point of view is admirable in a way."

"Somehow, Parris—excuse me, that slipped out. Do you mind if I call you that?"

"Not a bit. I like it. What were you about to say?"

"Only that I hardly expected to hear that kind of talk from Kings Row's one cosmopolite. You never seemed, somehow, to be quite regional in your own point of view."

Parris laughed. "But you see, Ross, *I* think regionalism can be downright virtuous."

"My complaint is that we seek too little contact with the outside. We are so damned smug and self-satisfied. The East will pick itself up and walk away from us."

"You're wrong there. We are a part of the ongoing movement whether we will it or not. We can't help ourselves."

"Maybe we measure up pretty well when it comes to business enterprise, but it's discouraging when we think of the cultural end of things. I've been wondering about McKay. What will become of him out here? He hopes to become a writer one of these days, but what help will he get in Kings Row?"

"It's too bad that literary criticism has outgrown the creative energy of this new country. It's as though a cold, stinging wind came out of the East and brought with it a covering of frost, impalpable but devastating. But the West is tough. It will survive."

"But will McKay survive?"

"McKay will in all probability come out of this war with a larger outlook, and certainly with a clearer idea of what he wants to do and be. He has a wife to help him make up his mind—and from what I saw of her, she'll know what he wants."

"Is she much in love with him?"

"Deeply in love."

"Glad to hear it. He's always been a strange sort of kid. He said something to me not long before he went away that I'll never forget. Does this bore you?" Ross looked quickly at Parris.

"Not for a minute. I'd like to know more about McKay."

"Well, McKay is the closest observer of things and of people I ever knew. I've seen him sit and stare for a long time at some object—a rock or a flower—as though he were hynotized." Ross hesitated.

"Yes, Ross, I quite understand that. I've done the same thing myself."

"Well, one day when he was looking in that concentrated way at a tiger lily, I asked him what he was thinking."

"What did he say?"

"The darnedest, most unexpected thing! He said—I can't quote him exactly, but it was something like this: 'I want to reproduce it in some other medium—not just the way it looks, but the way it makes me *feel,* the way it must be a symbol of something of enormous importance. I want to give it some kind of immortality, preferably in the elusive medium of words!'"

"Good Lord! The boy's a poet. I don't think you need to worry about McKay. He's learning to isolate each thing he sees and to *say* it in the 'dear and intangible sound' of words."

"You are talking poetry yourself."

"No. I'm talking about what an artist, a creative artist, must feel. It's a heartbreaking thing the artist is up against. He knows he cannot do all he is sure *may* be done, and against that knowledge he hurls himself in despair. Life signifies nothing unless he may write his partial failure in stone or music or words."

"But would he be able to do it in Kings Row?"

"That's for him to decide when the time comes. Personally, I'd say a writer should not get too far away from the sources from which he draws his material."

"And that brings us back again to the Middle West. Look at those beautiful farms out there, Parris. I tell you they are not the results of healthy toil, but of monotonous, backbreaking, heartbreaking, stultifying *drudgery.*"

"Maybe, but that doesn't necessarily preclude—"

"Oh, *doesn't* it? Believe me, it precludes in the majority of cases any chance of the development of tolerance, pity, and other such qualities."

"I hadn't thought of that, Ross. You are probably right about tolerance and pity. Those qualities grow out of meditation, and there's not much room for that in the Middle Western scheme."

"The thing that drives me wild, Parris, is the sort of 'shamefacedness' we exhibit before the manifestations of elegant living, refined manners, and distinction in dress. Even you and I fall under the frost of disapproval—you, because of your 'foreign ways,' I, because of my 'Harvard manners.' "

Parris leaned back and laughed at Ross' outraged and resentful tone. "They are only showing disapproval of the thing that is different —whether in clothes or manners or habits. The accent here is placed on the bucolic, the folksy, and—God help us—the *uniform*."

"Yes, our writers reflect that attitude, come to think of it. And the life they depict is really dull, vicious, small, gossipy and backbiting. Why aren't we doing something about getting to know the rest of the world?"

"We are—plenty! But you can't shirk your own responsibility. You can take no active interest and get no positive gratification out of a town to which you give nothing—no constructive ideas, no—"

"Hold on, Parris Mitchell! It's not that I don't want to build up Kings Row. My Dad's been working at it for twenty years—and— *meaning* it. Why, he loves Kings Row—and I guess I do, when it comes right down to honest facts. I'm just not the booster type."

"Thank the Lord for that. But did you ever think what has gone into the making of Kings Row? Or the whole country, for that matter? This country had to be *built,* and the architects developed a booster spirit, an ongoing temper. They were inclined to disparage the past—a purely Western characteristic."

"They call it 'democracy.' That's what they think they are developing."

"It's what you are fighting for. That's what your uniform means."

"I wonder! Here—and here—my country has helped me and now I have a chance to help my country. Am I fighting for democracy? Perhaps."

"Carry that idea a little further, Ross."

Ross threw his head back and laughed. "Oh," he said, "I see what you're getting at. You think that after I come out of the army, if I'm that lucky, I should fight for Kings Row and the Middle West?"

"Roughly, that's the way I see it. The Middle West is going to need you boys—badly. McKay and his kind as much as you and yours. This is a good place to be. A man may live in the Middle West without loss of stature, and that is important."

"When you say 'without loss of stature' do you refer to the flat, unrelieved stretch of the land itself?"

"In a way. Its largeness without grandeur, the homely accent of its vegetation—"

"Come to think of it, it has a certain beauty of its own, hasn't it?"

"Of course. No grass country is ever ungracious—and the Middle West is a grass country throughout its bounds. Grass tells of a sweet and amiable soil beneath. The simple presence of grass softens and blurs all outlines and clothes any landscape with a certain tenderness and invitation."

"Parris, I think I'll report you to the Chamber of Commerce. They should have you making booster speeches all over the country! And do you know, I've often wondered why you stay here."

"Perhaps I've drunk 'lonesome water.' "

"What's that?"

"Don't you know the legend? Mountain people believe that there are certain hidden springs in the mountain coves from which lonesome water flows, and any man who drinks from them is chained to the hills and can never get away."

"A rather terrifying idea, isn't it? We seem to be coming into Warren's Crossing and we'll soon be in the hills ourselves. I hope you aren't going to mind the hour's horseback ride to Aunt Dixie's."

"No, I'll enjoy it. I love the hills."

"I pray to God we can get something out of her this time. I'm sure you can make her talk, Parris."

"I hope she'll *want* to talk."

"Parris, if we get anything to work on, I'm sure I can get Dad to co-operate."

"That would be necessary. I can't help an unwilling patient."

"I can talk to him now. This army business has somehow put us on a sort of man-to-man basis. I can get him to come to you. Aunt Dixie's got to talk, Parris. Dad's got to have help."

Parris had forgotten how very beautiful the river hill country was. He had once spent a week in this region when he had come with Drake McHugh on a camping trip.

Now he and Ross fell silent as they rode along the roads which grew narrower and rougher as they proceeded. They could tell that wagons rarely came that way. The sprouts were waist-high between the ruts. Before long they reached a trail too narrow for a wagon, and they rode in single file, Ross leading.

Parris gave himself over completely to an enjoyment of the day and the season. The pungent smell of wet earth and leaves excited him. Blackjack and white oak trees were in full leaf, and he glimpsed from time to time blue patches of wild pansies and violets on the shaggy slopes of scrub oak. He caught his breath as he passed a clump of wild plum trees. They made him think of Renée, and for an instant he recaptured the throbbing delight that was like pain—and then it had passed. A fleeting thought of Randy was as quickly banished.

Once Ross turned and pointed to an opening in the trees, and for a moment they glimpsed the brown river, then once more they were hedged in by the sun-swept silent hills.

The road wound down the hillside, across a narrow valley, and climbed the rise ahead of them. A creek rustled out and laughed at them and scurried back to cover. Parris knew that the personalizing of elemental things was but a trick of fancy, the play of his own imagination over the changeless mask of reality that confronted him, but on a day like this he took an almost childish delight in seeing the whole world wake up and take part in the pulsing activity of his universe.

The reeds growing tall and straight down by the hidden creek were watching him boldly as he passed, and his eyes looked back at them as at old friends. At the top of a flinty slope a squirrel darted up the trunk of a giant walnut tree where little nuts were already forming among the tufts. Flowering Judas trees made a purple haze in the brushwood-fringed hollows.

They came suddenly upon a gray cabin half hidden on the slope. Ross called out to a little brown wisp of a man and asked him to take charge of the horses until they called for them. They were to walk on from here by a path Ross knew. The old man came down to the trail and looked with frank curiosity at Ross' visitor. He was followed by two lazy hounds who didn't bother to pay any attention to them.

Ross and Parris climbed slowly over a knobby hill and went down a slope on the other side. Fallen logs obstructed their passage and leafy branches held them back. Over their heads buzzards prowled the sky.

They crossed a rocky little stream by a narrow wooden bridge with handholds on either side. The water was noisy underneath, and a crow with full-throated cry made them pause and look up as it wheeled above them. A milky smoke hung over the creek downstream, where a ravine opened to receive the troubled water.

And then they came into a small clearing and there, with smoke curling from the chimney, was the cabin of Miss Dixie Pomeroy.

Parris had known what to expect. He had seen these river hill cabins before. There were two log-built rooms and a boarded-up lean-to. The chimney was of rough stone and tilted a bit. Ferns and grasses and buckberry bushes grew right up to the stone slab steps. Three or four lean, rangy hounds yapped from the side yard.

Miss Dixie, incredibly thin and raw-boned but straight in spite of her ninety years, squinted beneath a sheltering hand and recognized Ross before they reached the yard. She quieted the uneasy hounds and greeted him affectionately.

Ross patted her wrinkled cheeks and accused her of painting them with possum-berry juice so she'd fascinate the young doctor he had brought down to see her.

At the word "doctor" she looked shrewdly at Parris before inviting them into the house.

"You ain't brung him 'cause you think I'm crazy?"

"Of course not, Aunt Dixie. He's my best friend and he wanted to come down to see my best sweetheart."

"Jest lissen at that young un an' his sweet-talk! Come in, Doctor, an' set. You two give me the all-over fidges jest standin' there. I ain't usen to town ways."

"I'm mighty thankful to Ross for letting me come along. He's a captain now, you know."

"Is that so? Wal, the Pomeroys has allus been able to shoot straight, an' like as not he's as good as the next un."

"I'm sure he is. I hope you are feeling well."

"Wal, I been dauncy for a right smart time, but I ain't afeared. I'll likely be grabblin' goobers this time next year. I've lived glad an' I ain't beholden to nobody."

Ross laughed and called Parris' attention to the strings of popcorn and red peppers hanging from the rafters of the lean-to. "Did you ever see anything prettier, Parris?"

"I never did," Parris said, and meant it, looking at the colorful loops against the powdery white walls.

"You mean them burny-peppers? Wal, I reckon they are as purty as any I ever strung up." Aunt Dixie peered in the direction Ross had indicated. "I'm plum fergittin' my manners. Can't I fetch you a gourd of water?"

"I'd like a drink but I hope you'll let me get it for myself."

"You'll find the bucket right there in the window. I jest brung it up from the spring."

She continued to watch this young doctor closely. She had discovered in the first visit from Ross and McKay that they wanted to find out something but she couldn't make out what it was. But they kept coming back and asking her questions about things she couldn't remember. And now Ross came bringing a doctor down here. Hell, she didn't need a doctor. Something told her they were trying to dig up some family secrets.

Family secrets. Of course every family had secrets. But no use digging them up after they were dead and buried. They might stink. Everything was hunky-dory now and she'd be dog if she'd let on that she knew about any secrets. *She* knew how to keep her mouth buttoned up, doctor-man or no doctor-man. She wished they'd stop pestering her.

Parris knew he was facing a wary adversary. He felt that to come out bluntly and tell her what they wanted to know would shut her up completely. She would resent direct questions. Independent, proud, remarkably clear-headed, salty and sharp, she would talk only of what she considered proper that an outsider should know.

It was evident that she was fond of Ross. She asked after McKay as though she loved him. She wanted to know how they liked being in the army. She spoke with pride of Davy's achievements, but of nothing that might have brought about the strange compulsion of Davis Pomeroy that was the object of their search.

The late afternoon faded quickly into a bright starlit evening. Ross produced the sandwiches they had brought and helped Aunt Dixie make coffee and prepare a bowl of gruel for herself.

From some place in calling distance a neighbor boy had come to feed the stock and milk the cow. He went silently about his chores and looked with unconcealed interest not unmixed with distrust at these intruders from town. He departed as silently as he had come.

"Where'd that young un git to?" Aunt Dixie asked querulously. "He's snuck off slick as a whistle. I never seen him dust out o' here in sich a blame hurry."

"Maybe he doesn't like strangers," Parris said.

Miss Dixie indulged in a dry cackle. "Likely Cal 'lowed you was jest two hatefuls from town."

"Very likely," Parris agreed amiably.

She looked closely at him as he sat on the doorstep just at her knee, and she warmed to the quiet young doctor. He wasn't trying to worm anything out of her, she decided. He just sat there looking out toward the great hump of hill that faced them. She sat in a low splint-bottom chair that her pa had made before she was born. The two men sat on the flat stone slabs of the steps.

The little cabin was smothered by trees on three sides and the hills pressed down on it. But at the front, the clearing allowed them a full view across the little tobacco patch to the high peak of Old Bald Top, the highest hill around here.

The scent of pawpaws and damp leaves and logs drifted toward them and—yes, Parris recognized again the almost unbearable fragrance of plum blossoms. His mind struck savagely at the nostalgic thrust aimed at him.

The stillness of the country night fell about them. The hours of talk had yielded nothing on which he could build any theory as to the thing that troubled the mind of Davis Pomeroy. He felt tired and baffled. For some reason a thin shiver of fear passed through him.

The silence was complete when suddenly a great moon broke across Old Bald Top and the valley became a place of magic.

Aunt Dixie broke the silence. "Are you uns worrit some about Davy?" she asked suddenly.

"What do you mean, Aunt Dixie?" Ross was startled out of a deep reverie.

"Hit jest come over me maybe Davy might be out o' kilter. I seen many a one go out o' these hills an' die afore his time when like as not he'd a still been kickin' eff'n he'd stayed here where it's healthy. I 'lowed maybe he was gittin' dauncy."

"He's not really *sick,* Aunt Dixie."

"I'm proud to hear ye say that. Reckon this here doctor-man could kyore him eff'n he was to need it," she said with a chuckle.

"Aunt Dixie, do you think Dad ought to have stayed down here in the river hills?"

"Naw, son, I reckon yore pa did the best thing for him. It'd fret me right smart eff'n I'd had to go myself, but yore pa was a peart young un an' he done all right to git out."

Just then a hound came into view above them on the hillside and set up a clamorous howl. Ross started from his seat and then sat down again with his head in his hands. Parris watched the old lady closely. She peered out at him from under her overhanging white eyebrows.

"That's old Belle up there howlin', ain't it?"

"Yes," Parris said, "I think so."

"I can hear her. My hearin's good as it ever was." She squirmed in her chair and looked curiously at Ross.

The unearthly clamor continued. The other hounds lying by the step lifted their heads from their paws and made deep complaints in their throats. They, too, seemed uneasy. The valley echoed with the savage cadences.

The old woman spoke sharply. "What's the matter with you, boy? just a hound dawg howlin' at the moon, ain't it?"

Ross stood up. "I can't stand it. I've got to stop it."

"Wait a minute, boy. What you so upsot about? What is it? Tell me. What's all this about? What y'all ferever comin' down here pesterin' me fer?"

The two men were silent.

"Y'all can hear, can't you? Why don't you answer me?" She turned suddenly on Parris. "You, Doctor whatever your name is, what you doin' down here? Listen to me now, sharp. Got anything to do with that dawg howlin' up there by the barn? Has it? Eh? Why don't you answer me? Got anything to do with that an'—an' Davy?"

"Yes, Miss Dixie, that's it."

"Davy in trouble, somehow?"

"Yes, Miss Dixie. And the boys—they don't understand. They're troubled."

"Why didn't you tell me? In the Lord's name, why didn't you tell me two years ago? Eff'n I'd a been thoughted enough I'd a knowed what you was after. It jest goes to show you don't know what's a-goin' on in other folks's heads."

"Well—"

"Davy in trouble—wal, now, I'll tell you what you want to know. Set down, Ross, set down. Don't give me the fidges."

Miss Dixie began talking slowly as though it were hard for her to reach back so far. She spoke of her father, old Andrew Pomeroy, who was Davis' great-grandfather. He had married Myrtle Sanderson from over the other side of the river.

"They was good people, but strict—too religious. They was Hard-Shells. They had seven chillun. The boys, they lit out soon's ever they got knee-high to a duck, but Newt—that was Davy's gran'pa, he come back after he married Emmie. The gals married an' went as fer away as they could—all 'cep'n me."

"Why didn't you get married, Miss Dixie?"

"Wal, there was a good reason. Men was sort o' skase in them days an' I never could got away from home. I jest missed out, seems like. I was the oldes' one an' I had to work purty hard to make a livin' fer the young uns, bein's Pa was allus off to some holyin' or other."

"What happened to Newt, Aunt Dixie? He was my great-grand-father, wasn't he?" Ross asked the question cautiously.

"Hol' your 'taters. I'm fixin' to tell you, ain't I?"

"Go ahead, Miss Dixie," Parris urged.

"Wal, like I said, Newt he come back after he married Emmie. They never had but one young un—Dana. She shore was a purty little thing.

"Newt was a mighty religious man—taken after Pa that way. An' Emmie was mighty nigh as bad. When Dana was jest about husband-high, long about fifteen, she fell in love, head over heels, with a young whippersnapper from over back of Bolton's store. Awful backwoodsy place. Them folks over there was nuthin' but trash any way you look at it. Nobody with any gumption ort to of looked at him twicet.

"Anyhow, this feller, name was Hoby Johnson—this feller Hoby kep' pesterin' Dana to run off with him.

"Newt jest up an' had a fit when he heerd about Dana an' Hoby. Newt was a mighty pop'lar preacher at the holyin's. He knowed he'd be ruint eff'n Dana got to frolickin' around with any of them stark-sinful hill boys, so he kep' an eye on her.

"Emmie was in cahoots with Newt, an' they wouldn't let Dana go to ary one of the frolics down the creek. An' it wa'n't nobody had a chancet to sweetheart her. No, sir! She was purty as a pictur', too, an' nigh 'bout all the boys in the country was a lookin' at her whenever she went with her pa to the meetin's.

"She had to be mighty keerful not to contrary her pa an' ma, but she slipped off one time an' went frolickin' down to Crown Holler. When Newt missed her he took off like the devil was a chasin' him. He 'lowed he'd fetch her back in a hurry. He found her an' brung her home an' whaled her good an' proper. I heard tell he rocked her clean home.

"She don't git no chancet to even speak to Hoby an' he's skairt to go up aroun' Newt's house. He knowed Newt was a layin' fer him, an' when Newt's rifle-gun speaks he gits his squirrel ever' time.

" 'You lissen to me, you Dana,' he'd tell her ever' day, 'eff'n I hear of you meetin' that Hoby Johnson again, I'll whup you till you cain't set down! You hear me?'

"But, Lawd a mercy, he might as well been talkin' to the hick'ry tree in the calf lot. She usen to lissen till she heered a certain kind o' bird call an' off she'd go, night or day. Then oncet she slipped off an' didn't come back. Newt taken his rifle-gun an' lit out. He found her after 'bout a week an' brung her back, but he didn't find Hoby. That feller was a slick un.

"When the baby come, Newt nigh 'bout *killed* Dana, he give her such a whuppin'. They was after her all the time, a readin' the Scripters an' talkin' 'bout hell till she was nigh 'bout crazy, an' one day they found her in the creek drownded.

"They let out that she fell in an' broke her neck, but more'n likely she couldn't stand no more of their jowerin', an' she jest put a stop to it herself.

"After that, Newt an' Emmie didn't know what to do with little

Davy—an' they do say never was a purtier little woods colt bawn than Davy was—so them two Hard-Shells jest kep' that po' baby in the shed where the dawgs slep' an' the young un never had nobody to teach him to talk nor to eat nor nuthin'. He usen to run aroun' on his all-fours like the dawgs. He et with the dawgs, an' slep' with 'em. His gran'ma an' his gran'pa never let on he was there.

"But one time Newt fell out uv a bee-tree an' broke his laigs—both of 'em. Emmie knowed she'd hafter git Doc Crawford to come, an' she sont little Davy off with Cousin Tama that lived over in Neshoba County, an' that was the last anybody aroun' here ever seen of Davy till he was growed.

"He usen to come back down here then an' ask questions, but most of the old folks was dead by that time an' them as was left didn't know nothin' to tell him."

"Why didn't *you* tell him, Aunt Dixie?" Ross' voice was bitterly accusing.

"I didn't see no use to tell him what would jest hurt him. I tol' him his pa an' ma died when he was a baby an' that's all he could find out."

"But what a dreadful—what a *horrible* thing for him to live through."

"Wal, all I knew was what Cousin Tama told me. It all happened when I was livin' with old Aunt Nance over to Rocky Creek. But she *did* tell me the po' little feller was awful skairt of folks an' when he got in a hurry he usen to run on his all-fours.

"But he was a smart young un, she tol' me, an' he larnt fast. Purty soon he was like any other young un. But he was allus a set-along chile from time he was big enough to know which from t'other.

"It wasn't till two years after Cousin Tama took him that she heard Davy one night goin' on jest like one of the pack, runnin' back an' forth in the moonlight an' howlin' like all git out. Cousin Tama was skairt, but she jest natchelly 'lowed it was the jedgment of the Lawd on Newt an' Emmie for their wickedness. From time to time I heerd somethin' from Tama 'bout this moonlight goin' on, but I taken it that it stopped after a while.

"It never come into my head that that was what was wrong up at Kings Row."

Miss Dixie had told the story sadly, with an old, old woman's deep pity for the tragedy of blind human affairs. When she had finished, Parris laid his arm about Ross' shaking shoulders. It was a pitiful thing to see a man cry like that.

"Thank you, Miss Dixie. This is a fine thing and a good thing you have done tonight. We are grateful—and we think we can help Davis Pomeroy now." He could think of nothing more to say.

"Wal, you-all can stay up longer if you've a mind to. I'm tired now. Hit looks like hit might be clabberin' up to rain t'morrer."

12

For days following Parris' return with Captain Pomeroy, Kings Row had been sweltering under one of the hottest spells in its history. A burning wind sweeping across the prairies rattled a macabre accompaniment to the sharp, importunate phrases of the cicadas. The ferocity of the July sun mercilessly destroyed the flowers.

The gray-green mullein stalks remained upright, it is true, but one expected those candles of St. Martin to melt and fall sideways in the dejected and oily curves taken by their brother candles on the drawing room mantel. Everything seemed to have become of the nature of sun, and to give off, each one, a separate and individual heat. The lilac bushes radiated a dark warmth; the verbenas, flat in the sandy flower beds, a flaky, spicy heat; the poppies, their spirals of insidious discomfort; the pods of hollyhock, a furry, fuzzy, prickly heat that once it touched the fingers spread over the skin on little spiny feet. The sand and rocks sent up a grainy texture into the air. The suffocating chickens walked about slowly and disconsolately, staring at the world with outrage and question in their flat, angry eyes.

Parris recognized his unreasoning irritability for what it was, and made no effort to rationalize it. He couldn't bear to look at the suffering garden and sought escape from the heat by following the creek to where it swung like a scythe blade about the hill. On Sunday afternoon he decided to climb to the rocky ledge overlooking the pond. There he felt that it might be easier to air and settle the problems that threatened to engulf him.

His white shirt, open at the neck, clung damply to his shoulders. At the foot of the bridge he knelt and thrust his hands into the clear stream. He scooped up the water and wet his crisp black hair. Shaking off the drops that ran from his brow, he looked up to see Davis Pomeroy on the bridge above him.

"Hello, there! Where did you come from?" Parris hailed him.

"I hope I'm not inconveniencing you by coming without an appointment." There was a confident ring to Pomeroy's voice that Parris had not heard before.

"Shall we go up to the house or would you rather cool off up on my favorite rock—in the shade of that big maple?"

As they strolled slowly along the path beside the creek, Davis commented on the beauty of the setting of von Eln and its willow-bordered pond. On the outcropping ledge at the top of the rise they rested, and Pomeroy plunged at once into an explanation of his visit.

"My son Ross tells me, Dr. Mitchell, that you have been good enough to help him in his effort—"

"Yes, Mr. Pomeroy, Ross came to see me some time ago, deeply concerned about your condition."

"Doctor, I want to talk to you about this strange streak of in—"

"If you are about to use the word 'insanity,' sir, you are being inaccurate."

"Then, for God's sake, what is it?"

"A simple compulsion growing out of an unfortunate childhood environment."

"Ross tells me he is sure you can help me."

"I think I can show you how to help yourself, and I think, too, that I can promise a cure."

"Do you really mean 'cure,' Dr. Mitchell? I've been in the grip of this—"

"Compulsion," Parris supplied the word casually.

"Of this compulsion—all my life. I have lived in mortal terror of the madhouse. You and Ross give me hope that—"

"That you can get rid of it? I hope we can convince you."

"I'm afraid to believe, but I'm anxious to try anything that will help to free me. Even talking it over with my son has made a difference. All these years it's been haunting me."

"I know, but if I read the signs aright, Mr. Pomeroy, you are not in serious need of an analyst, and if you will report to me—say once a week—for a few months, I'm confident you will rid yourself of your anxiety."

"What is my part in this cure?"

"Do you remember anything of your early childhood—before your aunt took you to live with her?"

"Nothing. I was only three—or maybe four, but I remember nothing that far back."

"That isn't surprising, since you knew no words. You had no memory apparatus. But you *do* accept Miss Dixie's version of your circumstances?"

"Absolutely. She would know."

"Then you have taken your biggest hurdle. The rest should be easy."

"But will knowing the *why* of the compulsion help to control it?"

"It's difficult to explain in untechnical terms about this, sir, but I can outline your part in your treatment—if you wish to call it that."

"Please do."

"First of all you must learn to speak frankly to me of all that occurs to you—no matter where it leads."

"Yes—but to what purpose?"

"So that I may know how your mind works. *What* you say to me has no bearing on the case."

"What then?"

"Learn to change those attitudes that disturb your relationships with the outside world."

"That sounds too *general*. I want *specific* directions."

"Those will evolve in time."

"Could you explain my—trouble?"

"We have a name for it—repetition compulsion, which means merely a compulsion to repeat former experiences even though they may have been painful."

"I can't see for the life of me why I should want to do what tears the heart out of my body and tears my throat to shreds." Davis had begun pacing nervously back and forth.

"Mr. Pomeroy, children learn by imitation. You learned to do what you witnessed—the behavior of the hounds you were surrounded by."

"God, what a beginning!"

"But see where you are today! The elements of character that enabled you to survive that unfortunate experience will help you to take the necessary further steps to free yourself of the burden. You have an enviable place in the business world, a fine wife, fine children. There is no reason why you should not live the normal life you deserve—free of anxiety.

"Doctor, Ross tells me you assure him there is no taint of congenital insanity about this."

"That is true. This is purely a temporary compulsion, and your recognition of it will help you to act accordingly."

"Has the—the full moon anything to do with this strange act of mine?"

"Any change of weather conditions is likely to be an exciting agent—and weather changes are apt to occur at changes of the moon. The 'full moon' theory is a popular but false one."

"What am I to do when I feel—that urge?"

"Simply substitute some other action. Go for a long walk with your wife or a friend; rake the leaves in your yard; get in your car and drive to Camperville—anything other than what you have been doing. And, above all, don't hesitate to speak of the matter to members of the family. I suspect that will help most of all."

Pomeroy stopped his restless pacing and sat down again. "All this past week, Doctor, I've been fearful of a seizure, but somehow, just talking with my son has kept me from yielding. Then, there's been so much happy excitement on Pomeroy Hill over Ross' marriage to Bethany, and over a wire from McKay that he's coming home on leave next week. He's bringing his bride along. We are being mighty happy about it all."

"That's as it should be, Mr. Pomeroy. You have a family to be proud of."

"Doctor, you'd be surprised to know how different the world looks to me today. Why, it looks really *friendly*."

"A greater friendliness will come automatically as you rid yourself of anxiety. Don't try too hard to control life. Don't be too watchful lest you be caught off guard. Don't try to ward off intrusion. And there endeth the *don'ts*. *Be* friendly."

"I feel friendly toward the world. I hope this outlook stays with me."

"It will."

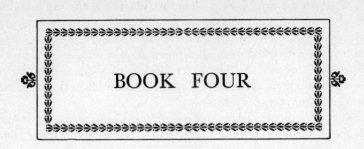

BOOK FOUR

For days Randy McHugh lived in a storm that drove her first one way and then another. She did not have one clear-thinking moment. What had been a steady assurance of awakened love rose now to a clamor of protest. One moment she felt she could become ruthless, sinister; the next, there rose to the surface thoughts of Elise's tender devotion, her undemanding friendliness.

Yet Randy could not blind herself to the fact that Parris had reached the place where he needed more than Elise could give him. It seemed more than she could bear to know that she was prevented from supplying Parris with the courage and initiative he so badly needed now.

This afternoon she was trying to busy herself with small tasks about the house. She was determined to put the disquieting thoughts out of her mind. But time after time she whispered the name of Parris, seeing nothing but his challenging eyes, hearing nothing but the cadence of his voice.

Her mind began its restless circling about the question. As long as she could keep Parris at a distance, she could give the whole matter a detached consideration, but he had a way of taking possession of her as though he were actually standing here talking to her, touching her.

Her hours of alternating rebellion and renunciation confused her. Neither her deep love for Parris nor her sense of tender obligation to Elise would let her mind alone. But she knew she could not depend on her emotions. She must bring cold reason to bear on her problem.

Abruptly she turned away from the desk where she had been absently arranging some papers, and saw Elise Mitchell hurrying up the walk, her small, white-clad figure seeming almost to float in the luminous afternoon light. Randy's heart missed a beat at the sight of Elise's face, clear and delicate. She looks like a bird about to take flight, Randy thought irrelevantly—a sort of expectant lift in the tilt of her head and in her eager eyes.

Randy's smile was warm and welcoming when she met her friend at the door, but somewhere inside her she had a hateful feeling that she was greeting some gentle stranger. She rejected the thought in its inception and held out her hands.

"I'm so glad to see you, Elise. You must have known I was needing company. Are you a mind-reader?"

"No, indeed. I came because I had a longing for some talk—and I have a new piece to play for you. Sibelius. Just wait until you hear it. You'll love it as Parris and I do."

"I'm sure I shall. Let me have your things."

"I'll run upstairs and leave them. I want to phone Parris to come by and pick me up when he's through at the hospital."

Randy's heart constricted at the thought of seeing Parris, but she resolutely thrust aside any consideration of it. She would meet that when the time came, somehow.

Elise's playing had been for years one of Randy's keenest delights. She sat intently listening to the music and a soft serenity took the place of the unrest in her heart. Music, she felt, was coming to have a deep emotional significance to her. Elise had given her this much understanding of it. Now it seemed that it held a sort of self-contained glory as though it existed on some other plane, for its own special pleasure. She felt her heart grow lax under its spell.

By the time Parris arrived Randy felt she had won through to something that might sustain her in her resolve to stand alone against whatever emotional onslaughts assailed her.

Nevertheless she was suffocatingly conscious of the sudden rush of joy she always felt when he came into the room. She met his eyes frankly but looked quickly away as she read there a vigilant preoccupation that dismayed her. The words she had so carefully rehearsed for this inevitable meeting retreated like the hopeless, untidy march of defeated soldiers drearily trudging toward an alien prison.

Just being here with Randy filled Parris with a passionate contentment, and he knew that he wanted more than anything in the world to stay. He spoke of his day's activities, of Paul and Laurel and of Ross and Bethany. He hated the fluency of his talk—this talk about everything in the world except the one thing that possessed him. He saw that Randy was playing up to him, laughing a little too often at remarks that were not really amusing. Parris was suddenly embarrassed, as though he and Randy were deliberately engaged in a conversational conspiracy.

A ray of sunlight suddenly altered the room and he started to his feet.

"Elise, don't you think we should be going home?"

"I'm sure we should. I've been here all the afternoon, making poor Randy listen while I played almost my entire repertoire."

"But, Elise, I can't tell you how I loved it. It means a lot to me—your music."

"Still, sweet, we must run along. Don't move. I'll go up and get my things. I want to get a recipe from Aunt Tempy, too. I promised Anna."

Parris and Randy were sharply conscious of Elise's light footstep on the stair. The room was very still and the warm, gold afternoon seemed to tremble with uneasy ghosts. Suddenly Randy uttered a little hysterical, sobbing sound, took a quick breath and her hand went to her throat.

She rose abruptly. She turned uncertainly toward the great west window and stood with her hands resting against the glass, her eyes looking unseeingly out at the sunlit lawn.

Parris, following, reached past her and took her hand in his. It was icy cold.

She turned back as if she were under a spell. It was like those helpless moments when a rushing catastrophe holds every motion in the grip of a relentless paralysis. She watched with cold fascination the precipitate rush toward the vortex.

The next moment she was in his arms and his lips were on hers; she had no time to think; she couldn't want to think. But she pushed

[281]

him away at arm's length to look at him. His eyes were stormy but his smile was confident. A sudden despair swept over her.

He laughed softly and her despair vanished. She laughed, too, hysterically, and dropped her head against his heart.

"Listen, darling," he whispered, "and you'll hear the stir of it. It's yours, darling—darlingest—all of it."

"Parris—what are we doing? What of Elise?" The last word was only a form on her lips.

"I love you, Randy. That is all I can think of now. Love me, Randy —only love me—"

"I do—Parris—I do love you."

"Enough?" His voice was harsh.

"In every way that even you could wish, darling."

"There must be two of me, Randy—but the demanding one belongs to you. The other—that must wait."

"No—Parris. We've got to *think*."

"I am thinking. I know I must have you. Neither you nor I could endure halfway measures."

"But, darling, neither you nor I could endure carrying on an undercover relation."

"Then what's going to become of us?"

Her troubled eyes searched his face. She stirred in his arms, but he only held her close and his lips swept her eyes, her cheeks, and came at last to her answering mouth.

Elise, halfway down the stairs, caught her breath when she saw them standing there, forgetful of everything but each other. She turned back and went softly up the stairs, her mind in a turmoil. She moved and thought as one does in that dumbly mechanical moment after great physical catastrophe before the ensuing tidal wave of pain transforms the ordered processes of the brain into a ghastly confusion. She seemed to wait, in full knowledge of the disaster, for the hideous clamor of outraged nerves.

The moment passed and from somewhere deep in her own nature an instinctive control rose like a tide. Presently her laugh, a little gayer than usual, rang out and she ran lightly down the stair, calling a bantering farewell to old black Tempy.

"Ready, Parris?" she asked from the doorway.

"Ready," he answered, "and reluctant."

"I know." She blew a kiss to Randy. "I always feel like that when I leave Randy. But it's never for long. There's tomorrow, you know."

In the car on the way to von Eln, Parris tried to steady his mind. His thoughts were like quicksilver—flying into pieces at a touch. He felt that he must somehow get hold of a coherent point of view.

Against his silence Elise flung her inconsequential chatter, carefully avoiding any comment that would demand an answer. She wanted passionately to help him set up his pitiful defenses—knowing that he did not even suspect how flimsy and ineffectual they might be. She was not thinking of the effect of this revelation on her own life. There would be time for that later. Now she must help Parris.

Elise wanted time to think about her discovery—to relate it to her own place in Parris' life. She found she was too restless to lie in bed, so she went to sit in a low chair beside the window overlooking the orchard. It was not yet dark and a luminous sky was bending down to touch the terraced hills. The poplars leaned to a gentle wind that was rising, and it was easy to forget the oppressive heat of the day just past, heat that had added threads of brown to the jade and emerald tapestry of the hills. She thought of this and of other aspects of the landscape, knowing that she was only postponing the moment when she would have to think of Parris and of herself and—of Randy.

Now, she thought, *this night,* there is something I must decide. What can I do about arranging my—my life? How am I to adjust myself to this unwelcome knowledge?

She was dismayed when she remembered that this was something she would have to work out for herself. She couldn't ask Parris for help. For the first time since she had known him he moved out of reach—out of call. She had forgotten how to make decisions for herself—or had she *ever* been able to do so? The very sense of aloneness threw her into a panic. Her thoughts circled on themselves—refused to stay in line. They darted about like a flock of frightened birds.

How did she really feel about—about Randy? She must decide that first. Somehow there was a gentle, flowering sympathy growing in her heart. Randy—dear, generous Randy, who gave so much of herself to her friends, to Kings Row. Randy should have everything she wanted out of life—she deserved it. But now—she wanted Parris!

How did Randy think of her? Was she, too, hating her as Kings

Row hated her? No, she thought generously, Randy would never harbor resentments against her.

Did Randy need Parris? Oh, surely not so much as she herself needed him. "What could I do," she whispered wildly, "without Parris?"

And Parris, what of him? Did he need Randy? Her answer to that was honest. Yes, he needs her terribly. Maybe that is what he has always been seeking—only to find it too late. But was it too late? If *she* were not here—

She closed her mind to the thought. She knew this new experience had found her unprepared. She could not face the thought of giving Parris up. Where could she go? What could she do?

Strangely enough, she felt a sense of security growing up deep within her when she thought of Parris. He would never blame her for his dilemma. He was too good—too kind—oh, no, Parris would protect her from—yes, even from himself and his own desperate need of Randy.

Sitting there as the dark came on, she heard Parris crossing the terrace. He had been walking about the gardens, she supposed. She noted his step as he came up the walk. It sounded like a man who goes too often upon a well-known way, assured of no new turning or surprise. This, she thought with wide-eyed wonder, is surely the way death begins!

But she must not think that word. She must think of what she owed to Parris. Love owes no debt to anything but love, she thought. How could she pay? In what coin could she settle her enormous debt to Parris who had given her—everything?

She tried to summon up a feeling of resentment—to think of this thing as a betrayal—but she could not do it. She was hurt, but she felt that the pain arose from her sense of her own inadequacy. She had given all she had to Parris, but she had always known it was not enough. Their relation had been too shadowy. They had seen *each other* as shadows—and dear as those shadows had been, they had not been able to reach each other through the obscurity. This she had always known. But she was nonetheless forlorn.

She could see the glow of Parris' cigarette below her on the terrace. A rush of tenderness rose in her like a tide. What was he thinking—

what was he suffering down there alone? Thinking of Randy, she felt sure, but not being angry with *her*.

Please, Parris, she begged silently, what can I do? Will I wrong you more by staying or by going? Oh, my dear, my ver-ry dear!

For some reason Randy did not slip away from her as Parris seemed to do. She stood there as always in Elise's confused mind, a sturdy, upright figure—dependable, unshakable. If I could only be like Randy, she thought, I should know what to do. A flicker of envy was gone before she recognized it for what it was. She would try to emulate Randy's own strength.

Gradually the ache in her heart eased and she lifted her head, a growing purpose filling her mind. She *could* stand alone among crumbling supports. However much she might fail and fall, she thought, the few moments or hours or days of *standing upright* would be the full payment—the full reward of being. Parris would be ashamed of her if she failed to measure up to that standard. She remembered he had once said, "Standing upright is the aristocratic stamp."

Like a storm-confused bird that had finally found its direction, her mind settled softly down. A few minutes later she was back in bed listening drowsily to the sound of the piano. Parris was still playing when she slipped into sleep.

Parris, walking restlessly about the grounds, was trying to bring some order into his turbulent thoughts. His eyes registered details of the landscape with unusual clarity. He noted how the light slid over the burnished trees and stabbed at the rocky creek-bed. He stopped and looked down at the water with its lacy edge adorning the shallow banks. His hands grasped the railing of the bridge tensely until his forearms began to ache. Lifting his hands, he looked at them curiously a moment, thrust them into his coat pockets, and walked back toward the house.

The shattering personal revelation that the world inside his mind clashed completely with the outside world appalled him. This conflict of primitive desire and the trends of social order presented a highly destructive element—a power to transform the natural and beautiful into the ugly and hateful. He was glad to remember that nothing in his past relation with Randy had been associated with anything cheap or sordid—anything distasteful. He could not visualize Randy in any situation from which her own good taste would recoil. He was not sure how far the clamor in his own blood might drive him, but he knew that she was right when she said, "We cannot carry on an undercover relation."

As a biologist he recognized the artificiality of the marriage convention, but as a fastidious human being he could understand its rigidities. But his heart protested. She was there in her house—Randy, the heart of his world, the woman his whole being cried out for—and she would not turn him away if he came. One of him—a feverish, demanding one—would go gladly, unrepentantly; but there was another Parris Mitchell who stayed in the hope that it might mean something to Elise.

A smothering commiseration overwhelmed him at the thought of Elise. The tendrils of her love had wound so closely into his being that he could not face the thought of losing her. Here on the thin edge of twilight her presence was so real that he felt he had only to reach out his hand to touch her. But with the major memory of Randy possessing him, he could not establish himself—quite—as Elise's husband.

Suddenly the moon rose beyond the hill, seeming to walk along the treetops. Under its spell he tried to recall some of the fervor of his early love for Elise, but it was like music passing down the street; he had to strain to hear it.

He turned into the house and went directly to the piano.

2

"Parris, the Board of Managers has formally demanded your resignation."

The tone of Dr. Nolan's voice struck through the kaleidoscopic confusion of Parris Mitchell's thought. He realized that Nolan was not joking—that the words made sense. There was no mistaking the bitter resentment in his friend's voice.

"On what grounds?" Parris heard his own voice asking calmly.

"On the grounds that your department is an unnecessary one and a waste of the taxpayers' money!"

"That is to laugh!"

"It's an imbecile idea to advance, but they've been coached politically. Parris, we know this has been instigated by Fulmer Green. He's been working toward it for a long time. Dave Kettring was unable to stop it. Green has succeeded in ousting us."

"*Us?*" Parris asked. "What do you mean?"

"You know, of course, that if your resignation is forced I should not dream of staying in this institution?"

"But, Paul, you can't resign. The hospital would go to hell without you. You are indispensable. You *can't* leave."

"I'm leaving if you do."

Parris had the odd sense of something outside of himself acting for him. It was as though invisible shifters of scenery had suddenly placed about him an entirely new setting. Here was the familiar violence of change that had marked every transition of his life. Everything that had gone before was instantly without meaning and without power.

"Paul, this thing has left me unable to think clearly. In spite of the rumors that I've heard I hadn't really expected this. But I do know that your duty is to this hospital."

"Damn the hospital! I'll not be dictated to by a gang of cutthroat politicians who are ignorant of—"

"Listen, Paul," Parris broke in, "this asylum was almost medieval in its methods when you took charge. You've built it up to be one of the finest in the country."

"With your help. Don't forget that."

"Nonsense! If ever an institution was built on the personality of one man, this is the one. You can't just step out."

"Why can't I?"

"Because the whole business would collapse. The place would become chaos again—or, worse still, a hellhole."

"Parris, you're a puzzle to me. How under heaven can you still interest yourself in a place where you have been so abominably treated?"

"I've given nearly ten years of my life, and certainly all my best efforts, to the hospital. Naturally, I have its interests at heart."

"I'll be damned if I'd feel that way in your place."

"It wouldn't be so bad if some good man were following me. But to have my work thrown out as useless!"

"That Board of Managers is ignorant of the whole business!"

"Well, they've acted, and I've been thrown out. I came back from the East on fire with purpose and plans. Now," he shrugged, "I don't know what to think."

"This is not aimed at you, Parris, any more than it is at the rest of the staff—including myself."

"Don't be an ass, Paul. It's been dictated by personal venom. But it's bad that it has to affect the institution."

Dr. Nolan narrowed his eyes, and his voice carried threat. "I uncovered the man on the staff who has been in on this—and there's only one."

"Could you tell me?"

"John Carruthers."

Parris was silent.

"But his double-crossing backfired. Instead of getting the promotion he hoped for—your job—the Board abolishes the whole department."

"That's irony for you!" Parris said.

"But wait for the pay-off. Before I quit I'm going to have the unholy satisfaction of firing Carruthers."

"He's an able man in his field. Better think twice about that. Paul, don't let this business get you. I'll work out something."

"Of course you are too well established in your field for this to have any real effect on your future."

"I wonder."

"We must make plans as soon as we can. This isn't the only hospital in the country. Other and better positions will be open to you—and I hope to me."

"Please don't resign, Paul. I appreciate the loyalty that prompts you to fling that defiance in their faces, but I'd be terribly distressed if you did that. At least wait until we can think this through."

"It's outrageous that Swenson put so many of Green's men on the Board. The stupid act of a stupid executive!"

Parris rose to go. "Never mind, Paul. My resignation will be in your hands tomorrow morning."

Paul laid both hands on his friend's shoulders. "We'll weather this *together*, Parris."

Three hours later, Parris sat at the desk in the living room at von

Eln, formulating a letter of resignation. He found it hard to concentrate. He kept thinking of Elise's stricken face and her pitiful effort to comfort him when he told her. "Now," she had said, "you will have time to write the books you want to write—and to play the piano—and to take the long rest you need!" Poor little Elise, frightened by this new evidence of hostility.

He dropped the pen, rose, and walked to the window. Leaning his forehead against the cool glass, he peered at the trees bending in the wind, presaging storm. He drummed on the windowpane with his fingers. The clock on the mantel tinkled. Eight o'clock. He must finish his letter. Paul should have it early tomorrow.

He turned from the window, rubbed the cool spot on his forehead, and glanced toward the telephone. No, that would not do. It would be grotesquely impossible now for him to tell Randy of his—failure, for that was what he should have to call it.

"Randy, my dear," he whispered as his head dropped on his folded arms, "you can't even come when I need you so."

When he lifted his head he saw that the rain had come.

3

There was little outward evidence of the dismay that Parris Mitchell felt at his dismissal from the hospital staff.

Elise watched him with astonishment. She knew that to a hypersensitive person like Parris, this was a blow all out of proportion to its actual importance. But only in a few instances had she detected a cynicism in his manner at some chance reference to the asylum. He made no accusations, voiced no regrets.

She was with him most of the time, and she made frantic efforts to overtake his agile and penetrating thinking. She tried to see and think as he saw and thought, only to realize in the end the hopelessness of the effort. At last she recognized that she did not know what was in his mind at all.

With this knowledge there grew up in her own mind a fear that she was in some way the cause of his dismissal. Kings Row hated her. Of this she was becoming increasingly aware—and now they had turned on *him*—on Parris, who had been so absorbed in his work that he had not dreamed it might be snatched from him. The injustice sent her mind racing this way and that, turning on itself and retracing its frantic steps in her effort to find some way to help Parris. And then, watching him at the piano or reading on the terrace, apparently contented and unperturbed, she wondered if he had actually been hurt at all.

Parris on his part had determined that Elise should not be disturbed as he was. He carefully controlled his consternation when Elise was present, but when alone he gave way to deep depression. He was trying to relate himself to the new conditions that had been thrust upon him, but each effort seemed to bring on a deeper depression. His depressions, in turn, were followed by a sort of fury at his own spirit-sickness that drew down upon him an inertia which was maddening. He felt that, if he but knew how, he could relate these periods of indecision and inertia in some way to his adjustment to a new life—but he could not get them into their proper places. He had seen other people behave like this and had circumvented their losing contact with reality. Why could he not do as much for himself?

"Damn it," he said one morning, "I've got to stop prowling around myself this way. I've got to find work to do. Without work a man has no dignity of soul." Then his sudden resolution withered and collapsed as he remembered that he had no work, that it had been taken away from him.

It was not the loss of the job that mattered—there were better positions open to him. It was the shock of feeling that his work had been considered unimportant, a thing to be dispensed with at a moment's notice. He began to doubt himself—his motivation, his ability to react normally to stimuli.

So many times in his life he had found himself facing a wholly changed world, and had been compelled to take stock of it and review it. But now, without recognizing the increasingly recessive tendency of his own nature, he accepted his defeat and retreated still further into himself.

He would go out to walk about the place, drawing from its dear familiarities something of the security he had lost. A worshiper of the eternal great processions of stars and clouds and trampling seasons, his clear eyes caught something of chance light on sumac berries, and the incredible marvel of world-under-world in the quiet reflections on the grass-edged pond. The serenity of von Eln enveloped him for hours at a time, but there always intruded itself that bitter, tormenting question, *How had he failed?*

He was confused, and his state of mind manifested itself in an accentuated preoccupation. He was engaged in a hunt for mistakes he must have made before this thing had come about. He reviewed in detail his work at the hospital, his personal behavior. He knew that some reviews were merely sentimental—regretful looks backward and therefore useless unless there was a counterbalancing and comparative look forward. But his mind balked at any thoughts of the future. He deliberately turned back on himself.

Often he was tormented by thoughts of Randy during those dark days, but he tried resolutely to set his mind against them, knowing the hopelessness of the situation. He recognized the conflict but was unable to renounce one of the contradictory issues. He could clearly renunciate neither his love for Randy nor his protective tenderness and sense of obligation toward Elise. He could not assume the responsibility of deciding either way. It was an inner moral conflict that rendered him helpless—paralyzed him. He cursed his weakness.

Disturbed at times by Elise's anxious scrutiny, he wondered if her sensitive mind had fathomed his secret, and he drove himself in his efforts to make up for his defection. Torn by the conflicting emotions, he found it an actual relief to turn to problems dealing directly with his dismissal.

Why, he wondered, was he so determined not to leave von Eln? Kings Row had turned its back on him, had effectually blocked his further progress, his future usefulness. He could not understand his willful clinging to the place of his birth. And yet he flung a furious rejection against any slightest thought of going away.

Could it be, he wondered, that he was rejecting any idea of retreating when he was under attack? Was he determined to stay here until he had routed Fulmer Green? He fought down a violent resentment of Fulmer, who had engineered his humiliation. He felt a profound contempt for the pettiness of the gesture. His knowledge of human motivations and resultant human behavior gave him a clear picture of the man, and he found himself harboring a sort of pity for the leanness of soul so sharply depicted.

How had the old feud begun in the first place? In school Fulmer had been the little gang leader. Parris remembered the day Colonel

Skeffington had said to Madame von Eln that Fulmer really belonged in a reform school. But the little hoodlum gang leader had become an important citizen of Kings Row—District Attorney and now a legislator—as powerful a leader of politicians as he had been of the young ruffians who had followed his bullying progress through grammar school.

Since those early days Parris had arrayed himself against Fulmer and his activities. But those were childish things and not on any account a basis for such bitter animosity as Fulmer's attitude so plainly attested. Surely a youthful grudge could not force a man to destroy another—as Fulmer had sent Benny Singer to the gallows; as he had driven Peyton Graves to suicide; as he had refused a job to Drake McHugh when it meant life or death.

Thinking of Drake and his tragic death, Parris' mind went like a homing bird to Randy—her bravery and her fortitude. At thought of her an eagerness lay on his mouth, and his heart quickened. But what had he to offer Randy? He had never brought into her life anything hurtful; he would not do that now.

All his life, he thought bitterly, he had brought trouble to those most dear to him—to Renée, to Cassandra, yes, even to Elise in some unintentional way. Randy he would spare. He swore it under his breath, and was immediately assailed by the unendurable prospect of life without her.

4

Dr. Waring finished the tedious examination and pushed aside the last of his instruments with an odd gesture, the finality of which Elise recognized. She felt the probing scrutiny of his cold, scientist's eyes. But this time he was not appraising the physical machine; he was measuring her soul.

"How much courage have you, Elise?"

"Enough, I think," she said. And then, "When?"

"Any time. No one can say. Next week, next year—or tomorrow. But with care—"

She gestured impatiently. "Which is more likely—next week or next year?"

"I don't know, Elise, I—"

"I've known this for a long time, Doctor."

"Do you mean—"

"Perhaps I'm psychic," she said with a wan little smile. "I know my heart has been acting crazily—but I've grown accustomed to its erratic behavior."

"But, Elise, why haven't you told me—or Parris?"

She motioned him to stop. "Will you insist on telling Parris?"

"The decision rests with you, but I'd prefer—"

"I'll tell him myself, at the proper time." And Dr. Waring knew that to press the point further at this time would be futile.

"And now, my dear, you must listen to these instructions as to the proper way to care for yourself—"

"I'll do what you say."

After he had gone, she went out on the terrace. She found there a world completely strange. All the mists of existence lifted and cleared in one instant of time, and all the material aspects of the garden froze into crystal clearness. In that one stroke of vision she saw everything as for the first time.

She was not frightened, but the new sense of precarious minutes sliding through the strokes of the clock's pendulum made her heart drive hard against her side—the very thing she must guard against.

And Parris—she must somehow protect him from this new threat. It was fortunate that she would not have to face him just now, before she had had time to adjust to the new situation. For three days more he would be in St. Louis, where he had gone with Paul Nolan to hear some lectures on hospital management.

She wondered, with a curious indifference, just what it would be like. Would it be a sudden, sundering knife-thrust, or just an onrush of blackness? Would she know? Would there be, maybe, a hateful, caved-in feeling that would crush the breath out of her? Or would it be, some night, that she would go with slowing breath deeper and deeper into sleep?

When Parris returned, he brought Elise some fine new recordings for a birthday present. She had forgotten all about her birthday, but Parris and Anna had planned a festive day for her. It was hard for her to think of birthdays. Something else was in her mind, darting about her and through her, making itself felt again in a tension that sharpened every sense and set a sort of magnifying glass in her brain. Looking through that glass, everything leaped into relief—isolated and clear.

She felt her way cautiously, persuading her mind to walk on honest ground as Parris had taught her to do. And she could say to herself that she was not afraid, and she said it with certainty—with her hand in Parris' firm clasp on her birthday.

She felt she must achieve a few hours of clarity. That last glimpse, if she was to come upon it, might be her eternity.

Suddenly she found, somewhere in her searching, that the great disturbances of love and passion had gone like the storms that passed over this landscape on their way east. Had her pitiful little pride been wounded? She couldn't remember now. Had she felt resentful at fancied wrongs? That, too, she had forgotten. Old loyalties, the memory of her father, home and friends, and the land of her birth became brittle as a mummy cloth. They retained a form but were without power to bind.

And the dear figures of Parris, Randy, Laurel! Hovering above and below them, surrounding them, now discovering and now hiding them, and finally bearing her away from them into a savage loneliness, moved all the forces of life. She wanted passionately to be *just*. She wanted to understand fully all those dear relationships. A new pattern was imposed upon her heart and mind—a deepening, widening pattern that enriched and, instead of complicating, clarified. The warring contradictions were gone. Sometimes—for a whole minute at a time—she even forgot that she was going to die.

It was only at night that the loneliness and fear crept back, a fear that had nothing to do with her relations with Parris. She recognized, without thought of blame, that there had always been a distance between them—impalpable, unexplainable, but a *distance*. When morning came, Parris' dear presence dispelled the cloud and she felt again almost at peace. She even felt an edge of thrill along her nerves as she sometimes sat still, counting her heartbeats, wondering if they could continue for a hundred more, a thousand, or maybe only ten. Sometimes she felt there were no sharp divisions of time, there was nothing but time, aeons of it, infinities of it. The periods of morning, of afternoon, of evening, seemed to divide and subdivide again and again into repeated mornings and afternoons and evenings of almost endless duration. The minutes seemed often to be without end. A sense of waiting pervaded them, stretched them out, and peopled them with multiplied repetitions. Surely there was a premonition of eternity in that!

In those moments she became clairvoyant. She was one with time and space, mystically united with the movement of leaves, of clouds. She almost forgot what she was waiting for. The very waiting became a kind of participation, and she lost identity.

But this thing Elise felt she had accomplished: she had resolved her life into an attitude; she had placed each residue of hope and pain and passion in relation one to the other. Some mystic relationship between bone and flesh and the earth itself spoke in accents so hushed and faint that there was no recoil, no shock. She could think calmly of the slow compassion of the earth which was to receive her. Life and death became so interlaced and merged that they appeared to be one inseparable whole.

Life and death wore the same face.

Parris was at once aware of an increasing remoteness in Elise's manner. Her steps lagged, and too often she drooped against him. One day as they walked on the terrace in the bright sunshine he held her at arm's length. "Elise," he said, "what is wrong? Tell me. You must trust me more."

She turned into his arms, sobbing and speechless.

An hour later Dr. Waring had made a full report to Parris, had insisted that Elise should be kept in bed and given constant attention. Anna had been offended at the suggestion of a nurse from St. Louis. She had cared for Madame and she would care for Miss Elise! So she was established as nurse, and the housekeeping was taken over by old Nathan's daughter.

As the days passed Elise was increasingly unwilling to let Parris leave her sight, and yet she talked little, appearing scarcely aware of her surroundings. Sometimes, as Parris sat beside her and talked quietly, she thought of her painfully garnered bits of knowledge, most of them acquired from Parris. Could she resign herself to their cessation? But, she thought, she was not *afraid*. She recognized fear as the mirage that Parris had told her it was. She was not fearful, either, of what might happen to Parris after she was gone. She felt she had contributed to the disasters that were overtaking him. Without her, Kings Row would take him back. And there was Randy.

One morning Elise waked from an unhappy dream and a strange impatience possessed her. She could not define it, but neither could she rid herself of the feeling that she must hurry to get something important done—there was some decision to be made. Then it came to her: there were things she must say to Parris before she went. She must keep her mind clear until that was done.

That afternoon Dr. Waring came out on his daily visit. Elise's hands and arms were giving her considerable pain, and her breathing was heavy. She was propped up very high on her pillows. Her nitroglycerin tablets were always at hand, but Dr. Waring gave her a sedative and didn't leave her until she had slipped into a heavy sleep, when he insisted that Parris should get a little rest. Parris went to his room and lay down on the bed, where he fell asleep instantly.

He waked suddenly with a feeling that someone had come into the room. The shades had been drawn and the room was dark. His eyes hunted through the shadows until they found her just inside the door, holding to the casing.

"Elise, *darling*! What are you doing out of bed? Why didn't you call me? Anna—"

"Sh-h," she whispered. "Don't wake Anna. The poor thing is so tired. I want to talk—to you, Parris—just—to you."

Parris lifted her in his arms, crossed the hall and laid her back among her pillows.

Anna, startled from sleep, was protesting that Elise had not called her.

"That's all right, Anna. You get some sleep now. Run along. I'm going to stay with her for a while."

"But, Parris—"

"Do as I say, please, Anna. I'll call you later."

After Anna had reluctantly left the room, Elise spoke.

"Parris, I want you to listen. I have so many things I want to say— so many things. Parris, my dear, you have been so good to me—so heavenly good, that for that alone I could regret to die—but for you, my dear, my dear—"

He slipped an arm under her pillow and spoke softly, as one speaks to a child. "Don't talk if it's hard for you. There can be nothing—"

"Oh, yes, there is something, but—it—it's about you. You will be hurt, I'm afraid, but I must say it for your own good, my dearest. I must set you, somehow, free from yourself."

"Elise—"

"Please. Please. Let me talk. What does it matter? By tomorrow—" Tears blinded her. "Parris, this is what you did not know. You have never loved me—"

"Elise!"

"No, no, Parris! Let me finish. You have thought you loved me, but you never have."

"Yes, Elise, yes, with all my heart."

She turned her head away. "You thought so, you dear, you poor dear. But you have loved someone else—maybe little Renée, maybe Cassie, maybe someone who never was, but you have not loved me."

"Elise, darling, I—"

"Wait. You have been an angel to me, and all that was good *for* me—but I tell you this to set you free—"

"Free?"

"I mean this. Soon I shall not be here. You know that. I see it in your eyes. I saw it in Dr. Waring's eyes too."

"Darling, I am holding to you so tight—"

"You must not be enslaved by another memory, Parris. Renée—Cassie—they together were a part—maybe a part of something you seek in the world. You have not found it. Maybe I, too, am a part of that which your heart asks of the world, of life. I should be ver-ry glad if I could know that I *was* a part, even so small a part as might be, but I think not. I think I have always been a—a phantom—just something you dreamed, Parris."

"You have been—you *are* all I ask, Elise."

"God bless you, my dearest. To me you have been all that the earth could give."

He tried to speak but could not.

"Don't look like that, Parris. I must go out of this life remembering something else than—than pain—or disappointment—"

"Then I have failed you—oh, my sweet—"

"Oh *no,* Parris, you do not understand. Please try to understand that I make a possible future for you because I am giving you back a past. Don't be afraid, Parris. There's nothing back there that can harm you. Relive it—once—and destroy its power to hurt you. You can't find your happiness in the past, either, darling. Happiness lies ahead of you. Randy will help you find what you want."

Parris' heart stood still. Then she knew! She had known all this time! Anger at his own stupid, blundering behavior crowded out for a moment the poignant grief of this hour. He had believed he was protecting her from hurt—from *fear*. She had endured this knowledge without complaint. Elise, who was afraid of so many things, had met this—this *betrayal*—without flinching.

He dropped his head against her frail hands. She felt his warm tears.

"Parris, my ver-ry dear, you must cure yourself as you have cured others. Look at me, dear—"

"Darling, *darlingest*—I can't understand. I've not meant to withhold anything—"

"You have not withheld anything from me—not *anything*. It's only that you are always fearful of—of remembering—fearful of hurting yourself, or me. Don't be afraid—ever again."

For a moment there was silence between them, his hand stroking the soft hair back from her brow. The whole movement of time, which had seemed always to creep under the incalculable weight of its own eternities, sped forward in a vertiginous whirl. She caught both his hands in hers and held tightly to them as though she might by that gesture arrest the flight. She thought, if I could hold myself still in the perilous insecurity of time for a little while, that I might divide and subdivide the minutes and pour into them the measure of this moment, I would be content to go.

She touched his face tenderly.

"Parris, you wrote me a letter that made me ver-ry happy. You said I had been like an altar light to you. I hope, in some way, that light may go on shining—but you must not be troubled by it—only comforted."

"My sweet, perhaps that light may help me to find my way. I think I shall never again dream of anything but peace."

"Oh, Parris, my dear—dream greater than peace—dream *service*!"

Parris pressed his cheek against hers and when he lifted his face she was quietly sleeping.

He tiptoed out of the room and summoned Anna, who moved

about quietly arranging the lights and drawing the curtains for the night.

Parris fell into a sleep of exhaustion.

At three o'clock Anna came to call him. She was weeping.

"She went away in her sleep, our *Liebchen*," she said brokenly.

Parris yielded to the gentle pressure of Dr. Waring's hand and slowly left the room. His face was whiter than that of Elise resting on the pillow, the hair still damp on her brow. The sounds of approaching day were drifting in, drifting like blown leaves on a little wind. A tattered cloud swept across the moon, darkening the garden beds that had been drenched with light but a moment before.

As Parris turned away from the old South Cemetery, another great wave of personal isolation went over him. The first had been when Renée had been taken away, then his grandmother—Cassie—Drake. Now Elise. Who, what was there left?

Paul Nolan put his arm around Parris' shoulders. "Will you come home with me for a few days? We want you there."

"No, Paul, I want to be at von Eln."

"Let me be with you then for a day or two."

"No, I must tackle this thing myself. God knows what the answer is, or what may be the cost to me, professionally or—or spiritually, of my adjustment. At this moment the only thing I can see or feel is the utter finality with which the white flame that was Elise went into darkness, a darkness that to me is impenetrable."

"The man of service is always lonely, Parris, but he must cling to his idealism, to his faith in ultimate good. He must never forget that first and last he *is* the man of service."

"Strange that you should speak of service today." Parris made a supreme effort to control his voice. "The last thing that Elise said was, 'Dream greater than peace—dream service!'"

"What a wonderful thing to remember!" Paul said.

After a few days Parris began to feel that he had attained to some degree of equanimity, but the house seemed empty and cold. The light had gone out of it. Yet, he had to establish himself *in this place*. Von Eln had always been the one place where he could see all values clearly. Here, life and its relationships resolved themselves simply into their relative values. Whatever curse might hang about the familiar walks, whatever thing of evil might brood perpetually over the hills, yet it was here alone that he could hope to estimate his own value as a human being.

A sort of twilight settled upon him, a twilight that settled upon the whole outside world—the world he had known and loved. He was bewildered by the conflicts in his own mind, and bitterly remorseful that he had not known and helped with those in the mind of Elise.

Isolation! The intolerable weight of it! He was assailed from every side. A sense of smothering unrest settled over him like a heavy cloud. He was unable to concentrate on his books, and he turned away from the piano with sick distaste. He began patiently and methodically to review his four years of marriage. How had he failed Elise?

She had been cheated of something in their earliest relations. She had been forced by the lack of unity to become one of those self-absorbed and lonely exiles whose place is "far in the unapparent." How much of the blame, he agonized, was his?

Parris was fully aware of the significance of that last talk. It was clear to him that Elise had destroyed even the illusion of her own happiness in order to set him free. Free? Free from what? To be forever lonely? To set his soul on some quest? She had been partially mistaken, but not altogether. She had been only a part—but a part of what? Renée, Cassie, Elise—they—what were they?

Time after time he went into her empty room and looked about as though he expected the walls to answer the question that pounded in his mind. Time after time he looked up at her photograph for understanding of the moment's mood, the moment's grief or pain. The awakening in the morning to her absence was his worst hour.

During the weeks that followed he reached the lowest ebb of courage he had ever known. Loneliness settled upon him like a pall. It was useless for him to say, "I've only to walk away from here—to step into my old place in the lives of my friends. Paul and Laurel, Father Donovan and"—his mind stumbled before he added—"Randy." He could not allow himself to think of his old relationship of easy friendliness with them. He closed his mind deliberately to any consideration of Randy. What had seemed at one time an almost insoluble problem was a problem no longer. It was as though he existed in a vacuum where nothing reached him.

Parris deliberately avoided his friends because of a fear that they would try to draw him out of his seclusion, and the thought of leaving von Eln to take up life again would bring searing flashes like the sudden burning of old scars. He found solace only in the seclusion of this place—these few acres—that had become holy ground through his deeply mystical attachment to it. His determination to stay here burned with an intensity high and clear.

Everything he viewed here seemed a touchstone to some experience clearly remembered. The recollections of a consolidated and unified past hung in the great bell of memory and time like a motionless clapper. One might tap with feeble fingers on the rim of the bell and awake faint echoes, but the full-throated burst of sound had vanished into an illimitable universe.

5

Parris stood one afternoon on the terrace looking out across the slopes along the creek. In the summer the slopes were steeped in a yellow shine, but as Parris watched the amethyst mist rising he felt a sense of growing panic as he remembered that it was late September. How was he to endure the long winter that was coming? Yesterday the shade under the maples had been thick and luscious. In the night some slight shrinkage had taken place, and now the shadow was lean. The greater trees had a withdrawn and introspective look as though they had finished with their pageantal manner for the year and were now intent on matters important to trees, making conscious preparations for change. There was a sense of departure on the hills, the feeling that hangs about docks and piers of great seaports where the sweeping prows of titanic liners wear a high look of transience.

Yes, there was a sense of journeying upon the air ... that stillness, a single instant of poise, before the long, slow motion of setting out.

As Parris turned back to the house, Laurel Nolan and Randy McHugh came up the path.

"Are we intruding?" Laurel asked.

"Of course not! I'm glad to see you two. I've just discovered that winter is not far away and I don't like the prospect at all."

"It's getting cold already," Randy said with a little shiver.

"Come in by the fire and Anna will give us coffee."

"We really can't stay, Parris," Laurel said. "Paul and I are going to St. Stephens for the week-end, and we hoped you'd go with us. Won't you come?"

"I'm afraid not, Laurel, but come in for a few minutes anyhow."

They talked quietly for half an hour. "Parris, we miss you—all of us. When are you coming back to us?" Laurel asked.

Randy caught her breath and gripped the arms of her chair as she waited for Parris' answer.

"I'm not fit company for anyone now, Laurel. I'm sorry."

"But, Parris, with all the new and exciting fields opening up, it seems to me there's never been such opportunity for men in your work."

"You are right, Laurel, but what incentive is there? A man might set himself on what he thought the right road, only to find himself effectually blocked by obstacles set up by the very people he was prepared to help."

"Parris," Randy said, "that is the first bitter remark I ever heard you make."

"I'm whining, am I not? Never mind, Randy, no mood lasts forever. It just happens I'm at my all-time low today."

"Would you play for us before we leave?" Laurel asked.

For a long time Parris played. A Bach chorale was followed by a movement from the Beethoven *Appassionata*. Then followed a ballade by Chopin and the profoundly moving *Doumka* of Tchaikovsky. When he rose from the piano, he seemed, to Randy, to have grown in stature somehow. It was as if he had drawn from the music something that renewed his strength.

Randy drew a breath of relief and rose to go. The uneasy sense of strain had lessened, but, she thought with a quick stab of pain, he has forgotten me. He doesn't remember.

Gradually Parris' friends, realizing the recessive nature of his behavior, stopped coming to von Eln. Only Paul Nolan and Father Donovan felt sure of a welcome and came often.

It was in the midst of a discussion with Paul of philosophy and religion that Parris spoke of the "houses of the spirit" that live on after

[302]

the body has fled. "Elise," he confided, "is closer to me now in many ways than she was when I could put out my hand and touch her. *We live not in a world of the living but in a world dominated by the dead, good and bad.* So we have not only the good and bad of the living, but the powerful good and bad of the dead—a world of increasing weight, an intolerable burden on the spirit, which is seldom free, and seldom knows how to free itself."

"The trouble about playing around with that belief, Parris," Paul said, "is that you do not take into consideration those great and fundamental passions that swim in the blood of Earth's sons and daughters."

"I know how insistent those can be, Paul, but with the spirit so bound down, the body cannot respond to the old urgencies that once seemed so vital."

"Parris, that is fallacious reasoning. If you follow the lines you speak of you are in danger of becoming like your friend, Dr. Tower."

Parris was startled. Dr. Tower! *He* had thought it wise to live in the impregnable places of the mind—but had it been wise?

"Paul, I want to be honest with myself—with life. I feel that I must set my own mind in order. To do that I have to review my findings, evaluate them, and relate them to each other."

"But your preoccupation with self denies the life around you."

"I do seem to be prowling continually around myself, don't I?" Parris smiled deprecatingly.

"You are being both mystical and impractical. That is not consistent with your training in science. Of what use is it to blast a thousand details and sequences from the stubborn fabric of forgetfulness?"

"I have the usual reward of the explorer—discovery."

"But you find only fossil bones of a life that is no longer articulated and that can never again have any power of motion or any sound of speech of its own. What remains is only a residue, in solution, so to speak, in your own being, *an eternally present past.*"

"I don't see anything too disturbing about that."

"Much better to be looking for the eternally present future."

"Still, I contend that the past is more important than the present—or the future."

"What you are doing is reviewing and regretting past alternatives, and that is paralyzing."

[303]

"That's not what I'm doing. I'm sure it isn't."

Paul narrowed his eyes and considered. "You've got to learn to *play,* Parris. You always carried the burden of your work with you. That sort of thing saps your psychic energies and keeps you from getting any joy out of living."

"I can never learn to be a good party person."

"You've got to be a good party person for the sake of the genial humanity developed that way—and for the pure joy of knowing pleasant people. Parris, people want warmth—and they simply can't get at the flame in your heart. Just a few of us get close enough to you to feel the glow. You surround yourself with an atmosphere of—shall I say the *frost of a Puritan conscience?*"

"In my field of work—"

"Don't be absurd. I'm not talking about your field of work. I'm talking about human relationships. You've never been really happy in your life, Parris. And you aren't going to find happiness or fulfillment sulking here in your tent."

"I'd be an utterly useless member of society in my present frame of mind. It isn't just the loss of Elise, it's the loss of faith in myself, in my work. It's been thrown out as a silly piece of embroidery on the fabric of healing."

"You've got too much sense to accept the verdict of a half-dozen moronic politicians on the worth of your work. You, Parris, are one of the *appointed* of the world."

"Appointed? Don't make me laugh."

"You are a young man, Parris, much younger than I, and you are hiding out from life. I'm not going to see your spirit wither—not if I can shake you out of your lethargy. You've got to listen to me, Parris. I've got to make you understand that man is too lacking in self-sufficiency to live in isolation. You'll stop growing. Together men complement each other, enrich each other. Your own thoughts need to be cross-fertilized with the thoughts of others if they are to grow and improve. I'd like to pull you out of this morass."

"How would you suggest that I go about the resurrection?" Parris asked.

"You've got to explore with your sensitive fingers until you find the pulse of the world before you can identify yourself with its rhythm."

"I didn't begin early enough, Paul. I think my fingers have been at my own wrist all these years."

"Don't be a damned fool. You've dreamed all your life of *service*. You don't toss those dreams aside at the first setback. Get out of here and open your eyes. Look around until you find fulfillment—*physical and spiritual*. You are wasting yourself on a past that's dead as Hector."

6

To Parris Mitchell, coming up the walk, Sarah Skeffington still had an air of worldly competence and consequence. Her face retained its granite strength and endurance.

From her wheel chair on the porch, the old lady returned Parris' greeting with a reproach. "It's been a long time, Parris Mitchell, since I've seen you. You are a bad boy to neglect an old woman so long."

"Don't scold me, Sarah. I've thought often enough of you to deserve a warmer welcome."

"I don't believe a word of it. Do you find it chilly out here? We can go inside if you'd like."

"Oh, no, please. It's been almost like an Indian summer day, and it's lovely out here. Are you properly tucked in?"

"I'm just right. You know, Parris, I've come to like this monstrosity," Sarah tapped the arm of her chair. "It enables me to carry on a rather active existence."

"Glad to hear it, Sarah. The last time I came you were glaring at its angles and protuberances as though you'd take delight in demolishing it."

Sarah laughed. "I've grown used to it, now."

"You're a remarkable woman, Sarah."

Sarah leaned forward in her chair and asked abruptly, "When are you coming out of hiding, Parris?"

"Would you love me more if I would?" he asked evasively.

"It's a mistake to cut yourself off from human contacts as you've been doing."

"I have no courage."

"I never thought I'd live to hear the grandson of Marie von Eln say such a thing. Aren't you ashamed?"

"I am, but I don't seem to be able to start making a new life that will make up for the old."

"Forget the old—and look around you."

Sarah was thinking of Randy and wondering why Parris had never been conscious of the profound harmony that existed between Randy and himself—as though every fiber of their flesh responded identically to all that came in from the outside world.

"Parris," she said gently, "some men go starving all their lives for what you have had—and for what is waiting for you—of love and sympathetic understanding."

"I've had more than I deserved. But I seem to bring only trouble to the people I love."

"For a smart boy, you talk an awful lot of nonsense. Can't you look for a little joy in living?"

"I get an occasional glimpse through my music."

"Bosh! What you get from your music is entertainment—that's not enough."

"What *do* I need?"

"People—and *love*."

"You didn't promise to love me more if I would come out of my seclusion."

"You're no good at evasion. Are you ever going to grow up?"

"Now, Sarah, what's wrong with youth? It's got a questing sense—an incurable spirit of adventure. That's what makes the world move on."

"That sounds unpardonably smug, coming from a youngster."

"You surely don't class me in that category, do you?"

"I do. I'm talking about age and experience. Furthermore, Parris Mitchell, your youthful certainties annoy me at times."

"Certainties? Those are what I lack, exactly, Sarah."

"Well, maybe I'm just a testy old woman."

"You talk too much about being old, Sarah. You have a remarkably youthful viewpoint. I don't know anybody who has more faith in on-coming generations—or who is more tolerant of youthful manners."

"Just because manners are changing it doesn't necessarily mean that they are *worse*. Sometimes they are, but sometimes they are better. On the whole, looking back over some hundreds of years, it rather looks as though the generations haven't done so badly for themselves."

"I agree with you. I'd begun to think that the youth of the nation lacked a sense of adventurous daring, but see what they are doing in this war! If ever a spirit of chivalry was rampant it is in nineteen-eighteen."

"Yes, we old ones are having trouble trying to match their hardihood with our quiet faith."

"We need a few steady voices, Sarah, to quiet this hysterical age. Young people are apt, during the youthful, tender years—"

"Stop right there, Parris Mitchell! That's the most ridiculous misapprehension in the world. The tender years of youth! Youth is *tough*. The tender years are those of old age—the years when your joints creak and your bunions hurt. Youth is resilient."

"It's just like you to hoot at traditional phrases that must have grown out of experience, else they wouldn't have lived so long."

"Nonsense. People find it simpler to repeat what someone else has said than to think up something original to spice their conversation."

"Again you speak with the Colonel's own words."

Sarah sighed. "Parris, my dear, maybe if the Colonel had lived he would have helped you make some improvements in Kings Row."

"But, Sarah, you don't picture me as a reformer, do you?"

"Heaven forbid! The world could do without reformers. So many things take care of themselves if we let them alone."

"But you spoke of Kings Row—"

"Parris, some people—and I include myself—will tell you they don't like this town. They tell stories of accident and human ill as though they thought the land itself were set against its living brood, and filled with threat. That's wrong—it simply isn't so. The good outweighs the bad."

"You are a very charitable lady."

"No. I sit here on my porch and think about Kings Row every day," Sarah said dispassionately. "I remember how often the Colonel and I talked about it. He used to say he liked to watch the life and work of Kings Row weave back and forth and make an endless chain that no one saw, although the links bit deep. He'd say that men walked here and there making a sort of pattern, bringing things to pass, and every step was just another link."

"He said the same thing to me once," Parris said. "I've never forgotten it, though I was too young then to understand what he meant.

I remember that he said he watched to see men bind themselves still tighter with the chain, and that the last link was fastened to a stone in the old South Cemetery."

"That sounds exactly like him, Parris. He saw things clearly—and still he was as near a saint as we are likely to see."

Parris patted the wrinkled hand gripping the arm of the wheel chair. "Sarah, he had a dream for Kings Row—and I have dreamed, too, but now—do you really think I owe anything to this town?"

Sarah held Parris' hand tightly between her own while she studied his face for a full minute.

"Parris, my dear, this you could do for Kings Row, and make a finer and better place of it." She hesitated. "You could beget sons, rear them properly, teach them to go on building and loving the place. Through your sons' sons you could give to Kings Row something of what you have dreamed in your heart for this place of your birth."

Parris took her face between his hands and kissed her forehead. "I promise to think over what you have said, my dear. You are very wise—and very, very sweet."

"If you want a full life, Parris, *reach out and take it*. It's there—waiting for you. Don't shut yourself away from your friends. You'll rust. Rust attaches itself to the most brilliant metal if it lies long enough."

"Thanks for everything, Sarah, my dear. I'll be in to see you again—very soon."

He's wretched, she thought as she watched Parris drive away. It shows in the defiance in his eyes; in the bitter tang in his short laugh; in the challenging lift of his chin. I don't like it—and I love him as though he were my own son.

7

It struck gently at first, stealthily.

When the influenza pandemic broke out at Camp Funston, physicians of Kings Row had expected its appearance at any time, for the plague rode the winds. But as the summer passed without any outbreak in the town, people ceased to think or speak of it, though by the end of August the death toll from the disease had trebled the battlefield toll.

Paul Nolan, alone, had done all he could to prepare for the on-slaught. He had trained his nurses and orderlies at the great hospital in the ways of preventing the spread of the disease and in the care of patients.

By mid-October Kings Row was in desperate straits. Epidemic proportions were reached with incredible speed. The public schools were closed; public meetings were prohibited; Aberdeen College and the College for Women became little more than poorly equipped hospitals.

Early cases, lacking proper care, developed pneumonia and died; there were many cases of encephalitis lethargica, terrifying and dis-couraging.

Sheer panic walked the streets. Desperately ill people had to wait for hours, sometimes for days, before hard-pressed doctors could reach them. Coffins were stacked on the sidewalks outside the undertakers' for lack of room inside. Sam Winters had to get unskilled labor from the country to help with the grave digging.

For some inexplicable reason, the disease seemed to spare elderly people, and aged men and women could be seen on the streets, hurry-ing to the aid of younger friends and relatives who were less fortunate.

In the lower part of town, the clay-pit workers and Negroes and other unfortunates were in the worst straits of all, for they could not get medical help. The few civilian doctors left in the town were work-ing night and day, with so little sleep that they themselves were scarcely able to move.

Parris Mitchell, secluded at von Eln, did not know that conditions were so serious. Paul Nolan, working night and day at the hospital, thought of calling him but felt he had no right to ask that Parris come into the institution from which he had been so unjustly ousted. So he waited.

But one stormy morning a haggard, dripping worker from Jink-town trudged wearily up the avenue at von Eln and stood nervously twisting his hat in his hands when Anna opened the door to his timid knock.

"The Doctor—is he here?"

"He is here, but—"

"Please, ma'am, I want to talk to him."

"Come in to the fire. Sit down. I will see—"

When Parris came in, the man, still standing just inside the door, seemed uneasy.

"Good morning. You wanted to see me? Sit down, won't you?"

"Doctor, they need you so—"

"Who needs me?"

"All of us—us poor folks—Doctor, we are dying down there. Nobody comes—the doctors are all too busy. I got four sick in my own house and they'll die if you don't come."

At the desperation in the man's voice Parris' throat constricted.

"I am not practicing—" he began uncertainly.

"But they are dying," the man repeated tonelessly.

Parris made a halfhearted gesture of refusal and stared down into the open fire. He was remembering something. Once he had urged Herr Berdorff to forsake his pulpit and take the chair of German at Aberdeen College. He recalled vividly the old minister's stern indignation. "Parris, I am a preacher!"

And then he remembered that Kings Row had turned its back on him, Parris Mitchell, when he was ready and anxious to heal and to help. What did he owe to this ungracious, ungrateful town? He shook his head in denial but was instantly assailed by thoughts of the admonitions of his grandmother, of Dr. Tower, of Paul Nolan, of Sarah Skeffington. This town, he reminded himself bitterly, had turned on Elise—poor, helpless, frightened Elise! And then he heard clearly Elise's voice, *"Dream greater than peace—dream service!"*

The man's heavy breathing rasped in the silence of the room, but he gave a gulp of relief as Parris stepped into the hall and put on his overcoat. They went out into the storm together.

From the first outbreak among the poorer people about Jinktown, Father Donovan and Randy McHugh had devoted their time and energies to those in distress. They were both almost at the point of exhaustion, but their spirits soared when they saw Parris' car turn into the narrow street. Randy reached a shaking hand to clasp Father Donovan's arm, and he said simply, "Thank God, Parris is here."

For three weeks Dr. Mitchell worked day and night in the lower end of town and in the near-by countryside where the miners lived. Father Donovan and Randy were unable to keep up with him, for he worked like a man possessed. Paul Nolan sent him two orderlies from the hospital who took over the cases after the crises had passed.

Parris was amazed at the fortitude of these poor families. They had very little but they rarely complained—and they did what they could to help others who were in worse state than their own. He felt that he must match their stoicism. He would not take time to rest.

"My son," Father Donovan, himself gray with fatigue, protested, "rest is as necessary to the body as prayer is to the soul."

"There will be time for rest when the emergency is ended," Parris invariably replied.

The Armistice came, but Kings Row heeded not at all. People had little heart or little time for rejoicing. Too many were dying before their eyes.

The clay-pit worker's house was hardly more than a cabin with its two small square rooms and its shed kitchen. The two kerosene lamps, one in each of the sickrooms, gave a feeble light that was hard to work by. But the lack of proper light was nothing, in terms of discomfort, to the lack of ventilation. Four influenza victims lay on cots in these two rooms, and the stale air was heavy with antiseptics and too-warm human breath. Parris straightened up suddenly from an examination of one of the patients and looked about the room in a dazed fashion. He ran one tired hand involuntarily across his wet forehead. The movement loosened one of the ties of his white mask, causing it to slip.

Randy, who stood at his elbow waiting further instructions, reached up and adjusted it. "Are you all right?" she asked quickly, as she had been asking at intervals all night. "Parris—it's nearly daylight. You've simply got to go home and get some sleep."

He was too tired to answer. He turned to the next patient, who lay not six feet away from the first and whose labored breathing told Parris that he would witness death again before noon.

What noon? he wondered irrelevantly. He spoke to Randy as she thrust the tray of medicines, gauze, and instruments before him. "What day is this, Randy?"

"Tuesday," she said, her voice muffled through the mask she wore, and turned quickly to the patient awaiting attention. The boy, Peter Irak, was groaning in his delirium.

[311]

Parris tried to adjust himself to the fact that this was Tuesday, that he had been steadily working without sleep since Saturday night, and for a moment he forgot where he was and what he was doing.

The patient! he reminded himself sharply, and reached for a hypodermic needle. Noting the unsteadiness of his hand, he tried deliberately to control it. If Randy saw the shaking she would start again about going home.

When the sun came up, bleak and wintry and pale through the dusty windowpanes, Parris knew that he had done all he could for these four. "Where next?" he asked, turning vaguely to Randy, and finding not Randy, but Father Donovan, at his side. That was strange —he hadn't known of Randy's leaving or of Father Donovan's entry into the house. Everything seemed strange, as if he were moving through a dream. His eyes searched the room and found Randy, at last, in the doorway. She was putting on her coat.

"I'll drive you home, Parris. Come on."

Although he was not aware of the movement of his lips he heard himself protesting that he couldn't go home. Not yet. That he must go on to the next house. Patiently, he explained to Randy and to Father Donovan, who was tugging persistently at his elbow, that influenza couldn't wait, that time was an important factor in treatment. Or was he actually saying it? Perhaps he was just thinking it, or dreaming it. Perhaps he was too tired to get the words out of his mouth and was imagining them instead.

Father Donovan was talking. But he mumbled; it was impossible to make out what he said. Parris leaned forward, listening carefully, until his face nearly touched the black-robed shoulder. His vision blurred.

The last thing he saw was Randy running forward. The last thing he heard was her frightened scream. *Parris!*

Parris was taken to the infirmary at Aberdeen College. During the weeks following. Dr. Nolan and Dr. Maughs from the hospital cared for him. "The blade has worn out the sheath," Paul Nolan said in bitter discouragement when it seemed they could not save his life.

When he finally emerged from his delirium, he was incredibly white and weak—but he would live.

It started in the lower end of town, the quiet tide of grateful talk, but it rose with such speed and spread so widely that all of Kings Row was soon engulfed. While his life was still hanging in the balance, Parris Mitchell's name was heard everywhere. The broadsides that Miles Jackson, Judge Holloway, and Sarah Skeffington were ready to fire were not needed. No one could be found who did not have a good word to say for Dr. Mitchell and his self-sacrificing devotion to the poor and unfortunate during the epidemic. If there were enemies of the young doctor, they had taken to cover.

Matt Fuller hitched his chair a little farther away from the stove that glowed like a red-cheeked farm girl.

"I always told you Doc Mitchell was a good man," he said, looking straight at Ricks Darden, who was tilted against the wall in a splint-bottom chair.

"Well, I got nothin' against him," Ricks said grudgingly. "Seems to me *all* the doctors done their share durin' the flu siege."

"Doc Mitchell done more'n his share. He nigh about killed hisself."

"No more'n he oughta done," Ricks said stubbornly.

"What's put your nose out o' joint, Ricks?" Dave Brennan asked, shielding his face from the heat of the stove as he adjusted the damper. "What you tryin' to do, Matt, smoke us out? Hottest stove I ever seen."

"It'll burn out toreckly," Matt said indifferently. "I put too much coal in it while ago."

"Bet this business shuts up Fulmer Green for a while."

"Yeah. He's liable to git in Dutch if he goes shootin' off his mouth around Kings Row about Doc Mitchell now. Folks don't forgit things like this epidemic soon."

"I don't see how come Mitchell done it. He didn't owe this town a damned thing."

"That's the truth, Matt," Dave said.

Ricks scratched his head under the uplifted brim of his soft felt hat. "Well, take Fulmer Green now—"

"You take him, Ricks, if you want him. He's washed up, I'd say."

"He shore has piped down about Mitchell lately. Haven't heard much from him since Donny got killed. Reckon that knocked the fight out o' Fulmer."

"Fulmer's a funny feller anyhow. He flies off the handle at nothin' these days. Hear about how mad he got at Albert Hyde last week about the horseshoe?"

"What horseshoe?"

"Aw, it was just a joke. You know how Albert is—always joshin'. Well, Albert says he seen Fulmer stop in the middle of the street to pick up a horseshoe. He asked Fulmer if he was superstitious about 'em. Fulmer said he shore was, an' Albert told him that they was a sign of—you know what. An' what you reckon Fulmer said? He got red in the face an' said Albert must of got that from Parris Mitchell— that Mitchell was allus full of dirty talk like that."

"Well, I be dog. He's got to haul in his grudge ever' time he opens his mouth. He's gittin' too big for his britches."

"You said it."

"Wonder if Fulmer signed that petition Davis Pomeroy an' Judge Holloway was circulatin' askin' Governor Swenson to give Mitchell back his hospital job?"

"Reckon he wasn't even invited to sign. They got no use for Fulmer."

"Say, I was in Herman Eger's place this mornin' to git my shoes, an' he said he's gonna have another litter of them funny little dachs-hund puppies soon."

"I'm glad of that," Matt said, taking an apple from his pocket and biting into it. "Shame the way them hoodlums killed all that last litter."

"Yeah—makin' out they was bein' patriotic."

"Well, seems to me we ain't got room to talk. None of us paternized them old Germans the whole endurin' time the war lasted. We acted like they was poison."

"Got another apple, Matt?"

"Naw."

"They was treated pretty bad. Fer as I know nobody even went to their shops but Doc Mitchell."

"Well, after all, we was fightin' the Germans an' they was killin' off our boys over there—"

"You're crazy. Them old Heinies here wasn't doin' nothin'. They bought more Liberty bonds than any of us, too. I feel bad when I think how they was treated."

"Me, too," Matt agreed. "But folks already forgot about it. Seems like they got all the work they can do, now."

"Funny how a war can git the whole country turned topsy-turvy. Lookit the way Parris Mitchell's got the town eatin' out o' his hand now, an' not long ago he was kicked out o' his job."

"An' while you lookin', jest take a look at the man that did the kickin'! Fulmer Green's walkin' around like he's afraid to put his feet down—like a man does when he seen a snake there yesterday."

This brought a guffaw from the crowd and finished up the gossip for the day.

<h2 style="text-align:center">9</h2>

One bitterly cold morning in late December three men sat in conference in the small private office of Lieutenant Governor David Kettring. In the air of easy friendliness that prevailed, Kettring relaxed. He was pleased to have this visit from his close friend, Dr. Paul Nolan, and Judge James Holloway of Kings Row.

"Yes, Dave," Paul was saying, "the Swenson administration has been a good one, so far."

The Judge nodded his agreement, then sat forward to lean his ivory-headed cane against Kettring's desk. "Yes," he said gruffly, "barring a few mistaken moves such as the one that brought us to the Capitol today." He opened the worn leather briefcase on his lap with that air of deliberate and lordly condescension with which all his movements were invested, and drew forth a thick sheaf of papers. "Petition," he grunted, and set the papers on the desk with a little confident slap of finality that drew a quick smile from Paul Nolan.

"Those are signatures," the Judge stated, "of good solid citizens— *and voters*—in Kings Row, who know that Parris Mitchell belongs in the State Hospital and want him put back there. In spite of the Eleemosynary Board's decision," he added, drawling the last three words heavily, to indicate his contempt for the Board's members. He cleared his throat. "My name heads the list," he pointed out, waving a hand toward the large, flourishing signature at the top of the first page.

"Well, Judge Holloway—" Kettring hesitated, his eyes on the papers. "The Board of Managers—I agree with you perfectly, of course, but I don't know whether I can be of any help in the matter."

The Judge chuckled. "Young man, are you Lieutenant Governor of this state or aren't you?" he demanded. He leaned closer to the desk and shook an admonitory finger at Kettring. "You work on Swenson —get him to call another meeting of that da—that Asylum Board— make 'em reverse that ridiculous decision. Don't know what got into that bunch of loons, anyhow!"

Kettring nodded, fingering the papers abstractedly. "You know I'll try, Judge—"

The Judge snorted. "Try, nothing. *Make* him do it. Tell him, for one thing, that Miles Jackson is getting ready to launch the damnedest newspaper campaign this state ever saw—against the administration —if Parris Mitchell is left out in the cold another week! It's the truth, young man—tell Swenson that. *He* knows the political power of Jackson's *Gazette* and the smaller papers that follow Miles' lead." The Judge paused, but only for the space of a deep breath. "And tell him this, if he doesn't know it—public sympathy in our part of the state has swung around—toward Parris Mitchell and away from Fulmer Green, and it'll swing away from the whole Swenson outfit if he doesn't get busy on this Mitchell thing."

"He's right, Dave," Paul said.

Kettring's eyes twinkled. "You can rest assured I'll 'tell him,' Judge —but if I wangle this meeting—and I think I can do it—I'd like Paul to appear and point out to these men that the hospital suffered a crippling blow when it lost Mitchell."

"I'm ready to do that at any time, Dave," Paul said.

"Too bad about the Green-Mitchell feud. I knew it existed but I don't know too much about it."

"I'll summarize it for you," Judge Holloway said, "unless Nolan—"

"Go ahead," Paul urged.

"Those two were born on opposite sides of the fence. If ever there was a case of right against wrong, it has existed in the relationship of those two men. Mitchell has always stood for decency against vulgarity, intelligence against stupidity, compassion against intolerance, democracy against snobbery—oh, why not sum it up as general good

[316]

against evil? And that's where he came up against Fulmer Green, who has stood for all the things on the wrong side of the fence."

"Any specific cases you want to mention?"

"I'd only splutter if I tried. I get burned up when I think of the petty, mean, wire-pulling maneuvers of Fulmer Green in his campaign against Parris Mitchell."

"Dr. Mitchell strikes me as a sort of latter-day pioneer."

"Exactly. He's a *cutter of dead wood*. But you know what I think? I think men like Fulmer Green are in mortal fear of the sort of pioneering Mitchell does. They're afraid the town will wake up and take a good look at them and see them as they are."

"I suppose," Dr. Nolan said, "that in a small town like Kings Row we have a clearer view of the spiritual clash between the visionary and the industrial protagonists for control of the place. It makes us tremble when we see the visionaries begin to topple."

"Then it's time to rise up and fight," Kettring said.

"Oh, we do rise up," the Judge protested. "I'd rather perish fighting than never to have known an honest scrap. That skunk has been trying to get the reins into his hands so he can run the town, and he's come pretty darned close to doing it. If it hadn't been for a few men like Mitchell and Pomeroy and staunch old Miles Jackson, Fulmer would be holding the whip hand over us this minute."

"Miles Jackson can turn back a regiment with that vitriolic pen of his if he takes a notion," Kettring commented, grinning reminiscently. "Jackson's an iconoclast, I take it. I like his paper."

"He's not an iconoclast, really, Dave," Dr. Nolan said, "for all his hooting at tradition. He's really an idealist, hiding behind mockery and harsh attacks on society."

"Maybe you're right, at that."

"Miles is all right," Paul asserted. "He seems almost wistful in his hope that people may surprise him by proving finer or nobler than he expected."

"It takes a certain amount of detachment to preserve that attitude in the world today," Kettring said a little sadly. "We've been thrown badly off balance by this war, Paul. It's going to take men like Mitchell to restore our equilibrium. It's deplorable that even one such man should be forced into retirement. In this case I'm glad I can be of help in righting an injustice."

"I knew you'd react like this, Dave, and we are confident you will handle the matter deftly. You are the one person who can make Swenson see the light."

"Oh, Swenson has brains. He knows better than to buck public opinion this early in his career. He will see the advisability of asking the Board to reverse its decision in the Mitchell case. If they should prove recalcitrant he would immediately appoint a new Board. He could, you know."

"There will be a load off my mind when this thing is settled."

"You'll be safe in reappointing Mitchell at once. I can promise you that much. We'll act within the week."

"Thanks, Dave. We need a greatly augmented department of psychiatry out there, and I want Parris to head the department—and I want him to be free of interference. I can get the appropriation next month from the legislature. I have enough support for that."

Governor Swenson bowed his massive blond head gravely to the six men who had risen as he entered his office.

"Be seated, gentlemen," he said in his deep, suave voice.

"You sent for us, Governor," the Chairman of the Board said.

"Yes. I wish to express my thanks for your gracious compliance with my request."

The formality of his manner and his speech made them uneasy. They felt a trifle abashed as they watched him arranging some papers on his desk. The sweeping line of jaw, the cold blue eyes, the restrained mouth, impressed them with the rugged power of the man. His fine, high-arched nose gave a keen, almost predatory look to his face. They felt the grave beauty of his restraint.

"Gentlemen, we have had, recently, in this state an example of the thing General Robert E. Lee once recommended. 'Human courage,' the General said, 'should rise to the height of human calamity.' The example to which I refer is that of Dr. Parris Mitchell, a former member of our State Hospital staff, but latterly removed from that position by this Board of Managers. Each of you has been apprised of Dr. Mitchell's self-sacrificing devotion throughout the recent emergency. You will say, 'It is the duty of every physician to meet such calls,' but you must realize that you—that *we*," he corrected, "had deprived Dr. Mitchell of his practice by our act of dismissal. In spite of that, he offered his life, and all but lost it, in an effort to save the lives of the poor and unfortunate. It is my wish to offer you the privilege of reversing your decision in the matter of the dismissal of Dr. Mitchell."

Governor Swenson paused for a moment, then resumed, choosing his words with care. "The hospital must have intellectual freedom. It cannot be controlled by the traditions and prejudices of a few individuals. The right to think implies the right to disagree.

"I well understand that the uncertain tenure of office makes sustained policies impossible. But when a definite mistake has been made, it is the duty of this office to correct it. Such a mistake has been made in the case of Dr. Parris Mitchell.

"Gentlemen, intelligence is the purest gift of the gods. It is an odd thing that there are few proverbs in the world concerning intelligence, while there are thousands about wisdom. Wisdom is the fruit of experience and reflection, but *intelligence is wisdom beforehand.*

"This Board of Managers has an opportunity to rectify a great wrong—an unintentional wrong, I insist—but with a little exercise of *wisdom,* you can undo an *unintelligent mistake.*

"The challenge of life itself, the call of destiny inherent in the character of Dr. Parris Mitchell, struggle to prevent his retreat from life. It is your business to force him again to move to his predestined place in the advance lines of service.

"Gentlemen, what is your wish in the matter?"

The men nodded uneasily at each other and the Chairman of the Board arose.

"Governor, we don't mind admitting we made a mistake. I'm not trying to justify the action of the Board, but I will say that we were misinformed. We are ready to agree to any suggestion you wish to offer."

"Thank you. It is my wish, and the wish of Dr. Nolan, that Dr. Mitchell be named as head of a greatly enlarged department of psychiatry at the State Hospital. Thank you again for being so co-operative."

10

The late winter was bitterly cold. The snow and ice stayed later than usual. As Parris gained strength he braved Dr. Nolan's wrath and went out when the house seemed too haunted with poignant memories. He went into the supernal hush of the woods, where every ghostly branch seemed to hang rapt with the consummation of some great miracle.

He felt at these times that he was resting on the edge of the world, and he wondered when time would stop to change. And there, amid the fantasies of frost, the crowded agonies of his life again reviewed themselves. The white days flowed through a mighty arc in which there were no hours—only a vastness filled with the infinity of light. The deep past, spectral and primitive, became one with the insistent present.

During the past year he had come to identify himself more with this country through his very isolation—through the perspective gained by retiring from it to a place where he could see it clearly. He knew that his findings had been retarded by his periods of unrestful introspection and self-appraisal. But he realized that his own transition from youth had occurred simultaneously with the transition of Kings Row to a new era. With the war, wider horizons had opened out for the town as well as for the individual. He had become, with the town, a product of the twentieth century.

He felt, too, that he had touched the pulse of the whole vast country, and it was fevered, unsteady. Where was the alchemy that would allay, cure the disorder? He must search until he found it. In this cure, much must be done in his own field of work. If psychiatry was to come into its own, he could not afford to stand idly by and wait for other pioneers to blaze the path. A sense of guilt settled heavily on his conscience. Paul and Mrs. Skeffington had been right.

Parris had always been able to invest Kings Row with much more than the outward seeming of a small town. He saw it with the wide sky over it and the great earth beneath it, with the changing weather and the pageantry of seasons. The result was a mighty stage—a great sector of the world, in which and through which a tense drama was always playing.

But now he saw his own life playing itself out on that stage, and felt that he was able to witness the mistakes in his planned and purposeful behavior. He knew what a waste of time it had been to strive to break life into "panels of action" so that its general architecture could be perceived. The finished edifice was enough.

Dreaming is an adventure—yes; but life has to be lived on its own terms, not on ours, he thought. His constant measuring of the accidence of circumstance by a dream synthesis—the spring lights through the trees, the silvery laughter of an Elise, the sultry passion of a Cassandra, the shy, frail music of Renée's small voice—all of this was useless and wrong. They had left their mark—but life was to be lived and work was to be done.

Work! The word pealed through his brain like a mighty bell that calls to action, the penetrating sound struck through with mystery and terror and crushing beauty, but with insistent command.

This, he determined, was the last time he would allow himself to review and regret what had gone. He must set about finding a cure for his bewilderment, and he asked himself what he would do for any patient who was troubled in the same way. Suddenly something suggested itself to him. He returned to the house and went straight to his piano.

For weeks he spent most of his waking time in the familiar room. He played more than he had since he had been a student with the fear-inspiring Herr Professor Doktor Berdorff.

He began to feel the whole range of life at his finger tips. He had the lofty, spiritual contemplation of Bach; the harmonious and balanced beauty of Mozart; the heroic struggles of Beethoven; the casual and immortal singing of Schubert; the theatrical sensualism of the lazy voluptuary, Rossini; the lusty footings of the peasant, Dvořák; the cries of Tchaikovsky "speaking for the outraged and the insulted"; the pathological sighs and screams of Scriabin; the sane music-building of the prophylactic Brahms; the magnificent heroes and blazing passions of Wagner; the Catholic mysticism of the Flemish introvert, César Franck; the impressionistic pastels of Debussy; and the gorgeous pageantry of Richard Strauss. The diversity of mankind was here, and the infinite variations of human experience.

Parris was half mystified by his reactions. He knew the nature of music, its strength and certainty, precision and mystery. He knew that at some moments it could threaten and terrify. But he knew that he had found the therapy that was right for his own mental disarray —had found it through the medium of music. It had wakened in him an interest in his return to work. Now he had to get his physical strength back as rapidly as possible.

He felt that the whole world was coming into focus after a long period of distortion and senseless motion. His thoughts began to settle like a flight of birds which had been scattered by a sudden fright and had discovered they were in no danger.

His spirit was finding serenity. He could think of Elise without the agonizing fear that he had failed her. She had become that "altar light" she had wanted to become—steady and clear.

As opposing themes in a symphony strive together and finally subside in peace, so had he learned to put contradictory things together and to see them in their transcendent harmony. He reached out to capture once more his dream of what Kings Row might become.

One morning Parris turned from the piano to see Father Donovan standing at the door.

"My son," the familiar voice came to him like a blessing, "it is a beautiful day and the wind is dying down. Do you feel equal to a little walk down the creek?"

"Nothing could please me more, Father. I'm glad you are here."

The unaccustomed lilt in Parris' voice caught at the old man's attention. "My son," he said, "something wonderful must have happened to you."

"Something has happened," Parris said. "I can't talk about it—not yet. Today has seen a sudden sweeping away of all that I had built against myself, and I see the way clear ahead of me—a wide and sunlit road."

"And time it is that you should take that road."

"I'm afraid I've been too self-centered of late to think of the future at all."

"It is understandable, Parris, that you should have gone through this period of grief and introspection, but the world has more need of men like you than ever before."

"The war we've been through, you mean?" Parris asked as they walked across the terrace and started toward the bridge.

"Yes. It's been a pretty bad slip-back."

"Maybe it's only a dip in the graph?"

"You can help in the up-curve. The world must keep on inching along."

Parris answered the old man's smile with a confident nod. "For the first time I'm sure I can go forward."

"This town needs builders."

"But there have always been those who built. Colonel Skeffington, and Miles Jackson, and my old German music teacher, and there was my grandmother."

"There are those, too, my son, who busy themselves in tearing down. Sometimes it seems that the destructive elements are in the ascendancy. The forces of greed and avarice and stupidity are loosed too often. The Kings Row that is grim and secret, dark and retentive, must be brought out into the light. You must do your part."

"I want to do that, Father. I'm awake—completely. It's as though I had come back from—from death itself. Everything seems to stand out in sharp relief—even the town of Kings Row. I see how it was built."

"Just what do you mean?" Father Donovan slowed his steps and turned to look curiously at Parris.

"It's this: the cities men build have a shape that is the shape of their lives—the minute agglutinated remains of the forms of many lives—a coral reef."

"You are right there. You, yourself, will leave this town the richer if you and all other men of good will endeavor to make each day as good as possible. That's the only way to leave an imprint that will add to the up-curve of the graph."

"Mrs. Skeffington said one day that she was sure the good outweighs the bad in this town."

"She was right. I've lived in Kings Row a long, long time. I've seen the evil things that move forever in men's shadow—seen them pass and be forgotten while the good lived on."

"It looks as though we are participants in some long plan."

"We are, Parris," the old man said, his eyes following the crescent flight of a blue pigeon across the slope. "It's a plan with maybe a bit of 'give' to it—not too much. May I give you a homely illustration of what I mean?"

"Please do."

"You've seen a wagon on a sandy road with wheels worn till they had a little play from side to side. They slant this way and that, and as they turn they make a crooked track. It seems there are a lot of folks like that—good wheels with just a bit too much of play; but still, they roll. The wagon gets to town, and that's the point. The wobble doesn't count."

"That's a sermon I needed to hear, Father."

"Then I may take myself off with a good conscience, my son. It has done me good to find you in your present mood."

Parris walked back to the house and called Paul Nolan. He wanted to get back to the hospital and to his work at once.

II

Randy stood leaning against the long window frame and looked out at the maples just beginning to put out timid points of yellowish green. She was glad to see the first new patches of color on the thrift beds. Spring was particularly tardy this year, she thought with exasperation. All at once she did not see how she could bear the gray, reluctant season another minute.

She sat down in the big chair that faced the window and waited for the lavender dusk. Somehow it seemed to bring a soft healing to her tormented heart. All the day's distresses dimmed, and dreams rose like a soft wind and swept her mind clear of resentments and fear.

This afternoon she had visited Sarah Skeffington. She didn't understand old people. Age seemed to wall them off from experience or from thought common to youth. She imagined them all as level and still inside, beyond turmoil and desire, with, maybe, gentle regrets that they were no longer young.

Young? Was that a desirable thing to be? The desperate longing in her own heart was tearing her to pieces. She turned her face sideways against the back of the chair and pressed the fingers of both hands against her quivering lips. She wished she could know just what Parris was thinking at this moment. She missed the old comradeship while she longed for something more. She wanted keenly to be a close-woven part of the world she glimpsed through the bright colors of his mind. Her intuition could always follow his thoughts and their intricate processes where her intelligence could not take her. And her love—her love filled every crevice of her heart and soul.

Slow tears escaped from her closed eyes. Oh, Parris, my dear, I've been waiting for you, wanting you. Why don't you come?

[324]

Slowly, opening her eyes, she *willed* him to come. It was a habit that had become dear and familiar to her during the past months of loneliness. Tonight it did not fail her. In her fantasy he stood before her, proud and tall and laughing, the Parris she had known a year ago. He looked at her—and in that look the obscuring mists of the past year thinned and vanished.

"Randy," he said softly.

"Parris." It was as though a strong silken thread were drawing them together.

The fantasy dissolved, but slowly, gently; she parted with it reluctantly. Reality brought, as it always did, bewilderment. Had he forgotten? *Could* he have forgotten that night in May when his tormented eyes had told her he loved her? Didn't he know that lovers had passed through darker doors than death and found a radiance on the other side? Would he never learn how much greater a shared love could be than one's own?

Her thoughts were circling around her in a mad dance, but one thought held still in a frozen gesture of threat—what if he never came!

Restless, she rose from her chair and moved aimlessly about the room. He *had* meant it. He *did* love her. She reassured herself time and again, but through the reassurances crept the persistent question she could not shut out. *Why didn't he come?*

She touched the edge of the mantel where Parris had leaned that evening in May. "Parris," she whispered, "oh, Parris."

12

For the mental unrest of other men, Fulmer Green had never had any patience. He knew what he wanted. Money he must have—and power. He had attained both, and he should have been a happy man. But lately he'd been compelled to fight his way through too many obstacles. Ordinarily he didn't mind a fight. It whetted his brain, excited him. But since Donny's death he had little heart for combat. He was simply in a more or less chronic state of irritation.

For several months he had been working at the ridiculous problem of getting Lola Saunders out of her house on Union Street. He had found no loopholes in the will of Pick Foley. Jamie Wakefield stubbornly refused to give an inch in his determination to see that the terms of the will be upheld. Lola was spiteful and refused to budge. Finally, Fulmer had been forced to ask Randy McHugh's aid.

"Randy," he asked, "can't you get Lola to sell that place? She won't sell to me."

"That's not surprising, Fulmer. Lola likes to see you squirm."

Fulmer's wry smile was his only comment.

"I think I'll make a try, Fulmer. That place is an eyesore. I'd like to see it improved—a new house built there."

"Can you get her to sell?"

"I think so. Davis Pomeroy has asked me to find a nice place for Ross and Bethany. They could build a lovely house on that lot. The Pomeroys would pay what it's worth, too."

"Randy, I see why we men are having such stiff competition from women these days."

"Don't be silly. Women are born to co-operate, not compete. I'm proving it right now. This is co-operation, isn't it?"

"Of the first water, Randy. I'm afraid I'm losing my grip. Can't swing things the way I used to do."

"Nonsense! Your hands are tied in this deal, that's all. It will suit everyone concerned—and Lola will profit by the sale."

That had happened a week ago. Randy had put the sale through, seemingly with no trouble. What a woman! Fulmer thought with grudging admiration.

And now something more devastating than the Lola Saunders affair assailed him. He tried to convince himself that Hazel was not serious when she told him definitely last night that she was leaving him—and taking Prentiss with her. But he was no fool. She had meant it, and had locked her door against him to end the argument. He had gone at last into the room where Prentiss was sleeping. As he stood looking at the child his heart warmed, then seemed to freeze with fright. Suppose Hazel never allowed him to see his son again! First, Donny—now, Prentiss.

His sense of outrage was tempered by a kind of incredulity. Maybe they would come back. In the meantime the whole thing must be kept from public knowledge. Why, if it were known that his wife had left him, his political prospects would collapse. Fulmer realized the extent of the disaster.

Thinking of that, he forgot for a moment his personal outrage. He even convinced himself that if he could keep Hazel's defection secret, he could manage to get himself elected Governor. Hazel would be glad enough to come back to him then. He couldn't get rid of a nagging suspicion that Parris Mitchell might have something to do with Hazel's decision. She's denied it and—oh, hell—he couldn't make any inquiries about it. He had to keep this thing quiet, somehow.

Fulmer glanced apprehensively into the mirror as he started out for the office. Yes, he was growing visibly older. Worry and loss of sleep, he thought. He wondered how true it was—that thing he heard once about insomnia meaning certain insanity? If he just had the nerve to ask Parris Mitchell he could find out. Probably it was just something to scare folks.

He paused on the step and looked about him. A shadow blue as a dove's breast lay under the trees, but he didn't see it; he was annoyed that the lawn had not been cleared of fallen leaves. He shivered in the sharp wind that searched him out as he started down the walk. His small blue eyes, red-rimmed from sleeplessness, squinted a bit against the light, but he walked briskly toward the square.

Against his will, thoughts of Donny hurled themselves against his consciousness. If Donny just hadn't gotten into that scrape with Elwee—but then boys were always into something like that. Why, when he was that age—oh well, no use to think about it now. The thing was done, and Donny—Donny was gone. If it hadn't been done in that horrible way—if he'd been shot and killed instantly, like Elwee, it wouldn't have been so terrible. He simply couldn't rid himself of the persistent memory. He'd tried in every possible way to see some sort of purpose in the dreadful thing. He couldn't see that his search for comfort in religion had been any help. What was the church for, anyway, if it couldn't help you to understand?

His efforts at justification of his past life were failing him, too. Even when he admitted to himself that some of the things he had done were—well, inexcusable, he got no relief from the heavy burden of grief. He had loved Donny with all his heart, and had such high hopes of seeing him become an important man.

[327]

And now again he remembered that there was still the chance that the whole nasty business might leak out. He thought with sickening dismay that Parris Mitchell might have information that was dangerous.

As he reached the courthouse square he saw Parris emerging from the Burton County Bank. With sudden decision he quickened his steps and overtook him.

"Parris, there's something I've got to talk over with you. Got time to drop into my office?"

Parris gave a quick glance at the courthouse clock. "I've a few minutes before I'm due at the hospital."

At mention of the hospital Fulmer visibly winced. His face reddened a little as he turned with Parris to cross the street to his office.

"Cigarette?" Fulmer asked, motioning Parris to a seat.

"Thanks, I have one here."

Fulmer reached across the desk to offer a light but Parris was already bending to the match his hands were sheltering.

"Parris"—Fulmer's voice was gruff—"I want to ask you something —and I want the truth."

"Go ahead."

"Do you know the real reason Punch killed Donny?"

Parris looked quickly at the man facing him, noting the feverish gleam in his eyes, the unnaturally enlarged pupils. He hesitated a moment.

"Yes, I know the facts."

Fulmer leaned forward suddenly. "Then, why in hell haven't you told it?" he demanded, pounding the desk with his fists. "Why haven't you told?" He was almost shouting now.

Parris blew the smoke from his cigarette straight as a lance before him. "I had my reasons," he said with maddening deliberation.

Fulmer's eyes narrowed to slits and his thick fingers clutched tensely at the edge of his desk. "Did you—were you protecting Hazel?" he asked with an effort.

"Hazel?" Parris asked with obvious astonishment. "Why, no. I did it to protect Dyanna."

"Dyanna?" Fulmer stared, unbelieving. "Christ, man, didn't you know that if that got out it would ruin me?" He was leaning across the desk again, his face incredulous. "Tell me, didn't you know it?"

"I hadn't considered it from your viewpoint—only from that of my patient. I wanted to save her mental health."

"Parris, you're a bigger fool than I thought you were. You had a chance—you've still got it—to get back at me for everything I ever did against you. I don't get you."

"You wouldn't."

"What in hell are you waiting for? Why don't you tell it and get it over with?"

"Is that what you would do in my place?"

"Wouldn't that be the natural thing to do?"

"Listen, Fulmer, you aren't a mirror of humanity."

"Well, you've always fought me—"

"Try to get it into your head, Fulmer, that I've never been fighting *you.*" Parris was angry now. "I've fought some of the things you stood for—"

"Same thing."

"No! I fight for the sake of my own principles."

"We all act according to our lights."

"Yes, we see what we want to see. You worship power, Fulmer, and you've used it rottenly, too. Power to send a man to the gallows; power to drive another weak man to suicide; power to take a job from an unimportant doctor—just in order to show your little world what you could do!"

As he talked Parris observed Fulmer closely. At this moment Fulmer was confused, uncertain, and scared. But Parris could also see that the fissures in the heart, mind, and character were already there. The disintegrating character of the man stood out with frightful emphasis. It was like a smothering fire; through the murk flares of his old despotism and headlong fury would certainly break sooner or later.

Parris rose to leave.

Fulmer's gaze, following Parris as he left the office, had the lucidity of a cat's stare, blank but malevolent. He was seething with resentment that he should be placed under any sort of obligation to this man he hated. Whether Parris told what he knew or kept silent, Fulmer knew he could never again be free to fight Parris Mitchell openly.

[329]

13

A light wind had blown the fragments of white cloud into a feathery foam against the cobalt sky, but Hazel Green was not seeing the billowy flight as she stood looking up toward it. Her gloved hand rested hesitantly on the latch of the gate. She was almost regretting that she had come to see Mrs. Skeffington.

Hazel felt exhausted from the strain of the past few days. She had been torn by conflicting emotions, had made decisions and backed away from them. This morning she knew definitely what she must do and she had come to tell Mrs. Skeffington her decision.

From the wheel chair drawn up near the open fire, Sarah looked up and exclaimed in delighted surprise at this early visit. She was genuinely fond of Hazel.

"Why, my dear, how nice of you—"

"I've come to say good-by."

"Good-by? Where are you going?"

"I'm leaving Fulmer, and I'm taking Prentiss with me."

Mrs. Skeffington's face expressed no surprise, only regret. "My child, is it as bad as that?"

"It's impossible. I've tried—you've no idea how I've tried to make a go of my marriage, but—I don't know—it's just that Fulmer and I have never belonged together."

"I've always known that, Hazel. But there's Prentiss—"

"It's for my child's sake as much as for my own that I've made this decision. I can see that he's already learning the—the wrong values. I'm determined to bring him up to respect other things than money—and *power*."

"But, my dear, he belongs to his father, too. Fulmer has a right to—"

"No!" Hazel spoke sharply. "Fulmer has forfeited his right to Prentiss. I refuse to bring up my child in a house that is filled with bickering and—and drunkenness. It's not too late for me to make a decent life for Prentiss—and for myself."

Sarah, looking at the lovely face of her young friend, said a small prayer that she might be able to make such a life for herself. There were pride and dignity in Hazel's face, in her firm chin.

"Have you tried, Hazel, conscientiously, to make all this clear to Fulmer?"

"Of course, but it's no use. I tried to think he was simply ill—irresponsible. But I know that is not true. His suspicions of me—his accusations are unendurable."

"Accusations can't harm you, Hazel. What does he accuse you of?"

Hazel's face slowly crimsoned, but her gaze did not falter. "He accuses me of being in love with Parris Mitchell."

"And are you?" Sarah asked gently.

"Well, suppose I am? I know and Fulmer *should* know that nothing could ever come of it. Parris is hardly aware of my existence."

"Since you aren't emotionally involved with Fulmer, can't you work out some sort of compromise existence—in the same house with him? It's been done countless times by countless unhappy women."

"I've been trying—honestly, I have. But he wants to dominate everybody he comes in contact with—and me most of all. I can't stand it any longer. I'm taking Prentiss with me to my people—and we are *not* coming back."

"You realize that Fulmer's political career will suffer if you leave him, don't you? You know how Kings Row behaves. The only things lacking are the ducking stool and the pillory."

Hazel smiled wanly but answered with spirit, "I don't care in the least what happens to his career. It's been dishonestly built from the beginning and I want no part of it. I'm tired of feeling so degraded. I'm going to be able to lift my head again."

"My dear, dear child, I wish there were something I could do for you."

Hazel suddenly rose and said, a tight little smile touching her lips, "There is. You can explain to Parris why I am leaving. I should like him to know I'm not just being a piker. I tried to stand up to my marriage contract—but it wouldn't work. I don't want Parris to think badly of me."

Before Sarah could answer, Hazel kissed her cheek and hurried from the room.

14

Spring came with a mighty, surging wind that swept away the last harsh vestiges of winter. Following the deathlike sleep of nature, Parris could not believe in the coming of spring. But today he felt the stir in the earth which marked the beginning of the new season. He went to the hilltop and the wind fought with him like a bitter enemy, but he exulted that it could not beat him down.

The wonder and the glory of feeling again the pulse of spring's awakening! The blithe young green—so tender it was more gold than green—ran like a dance of light through the woods. Points of scarlet showed above the gray as though the same flame which had died down in the fall sprang up again in the changing winds. Dogwood blossoms lay on the still leafless twigs like a hovering of butterflies. Jonquils stormed through the gardens. This morning he had come upon a scarlet tulip flaming vividly among dull weeds. He tramped across the fields and along the slopes with the old feeling that he was witnessing a miracle. From the bridge he looked down to the green and yellow and pink rocks lying so still under the rippling water. A pagan music seemed to beat through the soft whispering to shake his heart.

He detected a changed note in the air—a lyric note sounded briefly but with clear intonation. The breath of April was like a fragrant scarf wind-blown in the soft spring day. He wanted to reach out and hold it as it swept wraithlike across his uplifted face. He yielded to the transparent, shimmering beauty of the day—a beauty that was breath-taking. He was untroubled by any slightest unanchored fragment of memory.

He felt that the last reef in him was broken up, shattered and laid level. No more of the halfhearted acceptance with which he had resumed his place in the work at the hospital, but a new and burning intent that urged him to immediate action.

It was at this moment that the flame revived—the flame which, like a smoldering forest fire, had been creeping unsuspected under heavy blankets of dead leaves. And in the sudden light of this flame something that had been lustrous in the past went suddenly dim.

Parris walked down the soft decline of the green slope to the edge of the water. He had been there so often that he knew every step of the way with his eyes closed, but now, curiously, the familiar scene had changed. The vision of Renée that had always come to him here was absent, and with all his effort he could not evoke it. In its place something new, incredible—vibrant, provocative, the echo of Randy's warm voice saying, "This once I shall say I love you."

Abruptly he sat down on the grassy bank and yielded himself to flooding memories of something deeper than reason, something that could so easily become a passion of the flesh. It spiraled into an urgency as compelling, as uncontrollable as that forest fire he had once seen in the West, or the spring floods that swept through the river country. He tried to recall certain elements of the past that he knew had shackled him, had held him back from free movement. But he was unable to recover any sense of that past. He had a wonderful feeling of being untethered. It was as though a singing flood poured over him. It was not just spring or summer or desire that went out on this particular tide—it was, indeed, himself.

Restraint vanished in one searing flash of light. He saw no longer those dim shadows that had clouded his vision, heard no longer the attenuated voices of the past. He saw only Randy walking radiantly about this place he loved, heard only the clarion call of the future—a future he visualized with an ever present Randy. Randy—the fulfillment he craved.

And he had now something to offer her. He could match her winged vitality with his own ardent, buoyant will to live. There was no humility in his thoughts of her—only an elation that surged through him and brought him to his feet.

Anna saw him run across the terrace and into the house to the telephone. She listened anxiously.

"Randy—Randy darling, may I come—now? Yes . . . I'm in a desperate hurry. I love you so—darling—*darlingest*!"

Anna smiled happily and said under her breath, *"Er stirbt noch nicht."* Aloud she said, "Dinner, Parris?"

"Dinner? What is that?" Catching Anna in his arms he planted a resounding kiss on her cheek. "Anna, she's coming to live with us—my Randy!"

"*Ach,* Parris, how happy I am! I'll hold Madame's great-grandchildren in my arms yet."

Still smiling, she watched the car speeding down the avenue toward Kings Row.